something like **lightning**

D1738623

Jay Bell Books
www.jaybellbooks.com

Did you buy this book? If so, thank you for putting food on our table! Making money as an independent artist isn't easy, so your support is greatly appreciated. Come give me a hug!

Did you pirate this book? If so, there are a couple of ways you can still help out. If you like the story, please take the time to leave a nice review somewhere, such as an online retail store (my preference), or on any blog or forum. Word of mouth is important for every book, so if you can recommend this book to friends with more cash to spare, that would be awesome too!

ISBN-13: 978-1500831950

Cover art by Andreas Bell: www.andreasbell.com

Something Like Lightning

by Jay Bell

Acknowledgements

It bears repeating that writing a book is *not* a solo job. You only see the author's name on the cover, which might create the illusion that I sat down one rainy afternoon and hammered this story out. The words might be mine, but the hammering is done by editors and proofreaders such as Linda Anderson, Katherine Coolon, Claire King, Zate Lockard, and Kira Miles. And my mom, who made me, and by extension is the person most responsible for these books existing. Let's not forget my husband, Andreas Bell, who not only helps with proofreading but also creates the cover art. So if you enjoy this story, please pause for a moment afterwards and send a quick telepathic "Thank you!" to each of these fine people.

To my sister Shannon, who taught me that love is always worth chasing after, even if that means sneaking out a midnight window.

Part One:
Austin, 2007

Chapter One

I am untouchable. When I'm like this—just a shadow, just a ghost, just a whisper on the breeze—nothing can get close enough to drag me down. I feel invincible, which is why I find myself returning to this high over and over again. Feet tapping pavement, each a brief reconnection with the earth before I continue to fly. Even the wind can't keep up as my arms pump, as the sweat abandons my brow, as I find perfect stillness in the midst of so much motion. Somehow, while running, I manage to stop time. Silence. Solitude. Nothing can touch me here, and yet… lately I find myself wanting to be touched.

Kelly Phillips blinked and turned his head slightly. Part of him did so unwillingly because this meant breaking the spell. Then again, the figure he saw out of the corner of his eye summoned up another sort of magic. Jared was running beside him—or more accurately, somewhat behind him. The thick jaw that normally jutted to the side when he smiled was now clenched in concentration. Jared's fists were balled, his muscles tense as he tried to catch up, to overcome and pass before they reached the white finish line. Kelly almost laughed, but not mockingly. Even with his face screwed up, his blue eyes bulging, and his brown hair in disarray, Jared was handsome.

But he would never win. Not like that, all tensed up and stomping the pavement. Why was Jared trying so hard? Running was akin to gliding across water, sliding between blades of air, letting the world fall behind and disappear. Kelly sighed. Time to come back down to earth. Keeping an eye on his friend, he slowed his pace, hating how heavy his legs felt as gravity took hold once more. Jared noticed the advantage and gave an extra burst of effort, but even then Kelly had to restrain himself lest he win the race.

Jared reached the white line first, leapt over it and spun around with an expression of exhilaration. "Yes!" he shouted, pumping a fist in the air. Then he bent over and placed hands on his knees, panting to catch his breath.

Kelly came to a much more controlled stop next to him, smiling as he too worked on refilling his lungs. "Not bad," he said.

"Not bad?" Jared looked up in disbelief. "I beat your sorry ass, didn't I?"

"This time," Kelly said. "Care for a rematch?"

Jared panicked. "No! Ha! No way. We've trained enough, don't you think?"

Kelly shrugged and glanced around at the empty track. Classes were over for the day, most students having wandered off to begin the weekend. The normally chaotic high school campus was now serene. With the oppressive heat of summer finally at an end, Kelly was happy to get his body sweating in a more enjoyable fashion.

"We're done here," Jared said. "I've got it nailed anyway. Right?"

Kelly eyed him. "You need to loosen up. Let your arms and legs do what comes naturally instead of trying to control them."

"What comes naturally to *you*," Jared said. After a pause, he added, "You let me win."

Kelly fought down a smile. "You would have pulverized anyone else on this track. That's what counts."

"Then I'm glad we're not competing." Jared grabbed the front of his shirt and started agitating the fabric back and forth to cool his chest.

This sent a whiff of sweaty air to Kelly's nose, one that must have been filled with pheromones, because it made him heady. "You're going to own this triathlon," he breathed. "There's no competition."

Jared raised an eyebrow. "Only because you opted out. Not that I'm complaining."

"I'm not much of a swimmer," Kelly said dismissively.

"Neither am I. I've got biking down. You're right that no one is faster than us, but I'm still worried about the swimming part."

Kelly scoffed. "How many times did you drag me to the pool this summer? I don't remember any lifeguards coming to your rescue. Despite your best efforts."

"You mean when I pretended to drown?"

"When you treaded water while shouting 'help' a few times. Very convincing."

Jared grinned. "Seemed smooth to me. It's not my fault she didn't take the bait."

Kelly didn't smile in return. The lifeguard had been a forty-something blonde woman with ridiculously big breasts. A poor man's Pamela Anderson. He was pretty sure Jared hadn't found her attractive and was only trying to be funny, but even the idea that he could be straight had made Kelly jealous. Still did. Of course Jared probably did like women. He certainly talked about them enough. Kelly knew his own fantasies were hopeless but that didn't dispel the increasing hunger inside of him.

"Wanna hit the showers?" he asked.

"Okay." Jared led the way back to the main school building. As he walked, he seemed lost in thought. They were entering the locker room before he spoke again. "There's this guy..."

This guy I like. Who I really really *like. My best friend, actually.* Kelly fantasized Jared saying these words. He kept quiet, just in case he'd turned psychic.

"He's on the swim team," Jared said instead. "Supposed to be good. William something-or-other."

"That's an unusual last name," Kelly replied.

Jared snapped his fingers. "Townson. William Townson. You know who I mean?"

Kelly checked his memory, coming up with a foggy image of a scrawny guy with a mop of blond hair. "I think I had a class with him in seventh grade."

"Oh," Jared said. "Well anyway, people keep saying he's going to win the triathlon."

"Because he can dog paddle?" Kelly rolled his eyes. "All the distance, all the speed, happens during the cycling and track segments. Splashing around in water doesn't count for much."

"But that's how the race starts," Jared said. "What if he gets a big enough lead? They want us to do twelve laps."

"Twelve?" Kelly asked as he opened his locker. "Wow."

Jared nodded, leaning against the locker next to his. "Exactly. That's why I asked for your help. I'll need to make up for lost time in the final stretch."

"You'll overtake him on your bike." Kelly allowed his eyes to dart downward. "You've got strong legs."

"Thanks, but get this: During lunch, someone told me he bikes to school every single day."

Kelly stopped digging around in his locker and turned to face him. "William?"

"Yeah." Jared's face was surprisingly vulnerable, like a kid convinced he wasn't getting the toy he wanted for Christmas.

"Maybe William is fast in the water," Kelly said, "and maybe he likes riding his bike, but you *know* how hard running is. Remember when we first started out? How winded we'd get even over the shortest distance? Make it through the first segment of the triathlon and William will be a fish out of water. You'll breeze by him while he's floundering on the pavement."

Jared grinned. "I want that trophy so fucking bad!"

Kelly smiled back. "It's already yours."

Jared studied him a moment longer, slammed his fist against a locker, and nodded. "It's already mine!"

Kelly kept smiling, shaking his head as he slowly got undressed and Jared went to do the same. His happy expression soon faded as he listened to what took place behind him. The rustle of fabric as a shirt was pulled up. Shoes thunking on the floor as each was kicked off. The gentle plop of shorts hitting the ground. The sound of bare feet padding toward the showers.

Kelly followed a moment later but waited just long enough that the shower water was already running. He wouldn't look. Kelly never looked. Not even a peek. Just the thought of Jared naked—water streaming over the curves of his body—was enough to make the blood rush to Kelly's cock. So he didn't glance over at Jared or even let himself think. Kelly willed his mind to go numb and went about showering, not even acknowledging how his own hands felt when soaping up his body or rinsing out his short-cropped hair.

Kelly finished first and got dressed slowly, facing his locker and not responding to whatever joke Jared made when he returned from the showers. Only when he heard the metallic grind of jeans zipping up did he allow his shoulders to relax. Then he turned around.

"You all right?" Jared asked, pulling on a T-shirt. "You always seem so tense after a run. Maybe you need to jack off or something."

Kelly raised an eyebrow.

Jared leaned toward him, put an open palm next to his mouth, and stage-whispered, "Everybody does it!"

"Now I know why you take so long in the shower."

"Hey, I only do it in the safety of my bedroom. I even wait until my parents are asleep."

Kelly smirked. "How very considerate of you."

"I think so." Jared pulled on a fresh pair of socks. "So what's going on this weekend?"

There was no doubt they would spend it together. They had done so ever since Jared moved into town last year. Only recently had things become complicated. Now being with Jared was something he needed instead of wanted.

"It's family night," Kelly said. "Tomorrow... I don't know. Just hang out, maybe make a night of it. Want to crash at my place?"

Jared nodded curtly. "Cool."

"Cool," Kelly echoed, even though what he felt was closer to warmth. "Just promise me you don't 'relieve tension' once I've fallen asleep. If I roll over into a sticky puddle, you're sleeping on the floor from now on."

Jared laughed shamelessly and shook his head. If only he knew the truth: For the past month, Kelly had lain in bed with open eyes, staring into the dark and waiting for Jared to fall asleep first. His intentions were more innocent, or so he tried to convince himself. Kelly wasn't horny and seeking release. Maybe his infatuation had started with such thoughts, but now what he wanted from Jared was more than just physical. Although some emotions were best expressed that way. Kelly knew he was playing with fire. Getting caught could change everything. But if the stirring in his heart was anything to go by, tomorrow night he would risk it all again.

On Saturday afternoon, Kelly yawned his way through math homework. His parents sat to either side of him at the kitchen table, his mother flipping through a magazine, his father playing *Mario Party* on a Nintendo DS. All these diversions were infinitely more appealing than typing numbers into his cell phone's calculator, but Kelly was nearly finished. Then he'd be free to meet Jared and really start his weekend.

That was the deal with his parents. Get good grades and he was free to do whatever he wished. No curfews, no tedious rules—just one responsibility that he was expected to uphold. The same work ethic was shared by his parents.

Doug the plumber and Laisha the bankruptcy lawyer. An odd combination, but his parents shared one thing in common: Both worked their asses off. They did so with the weekend in mind. Every Friday evening, their cell phones were turned off and remained that way until Monday morning, regardless of emergencies. His mother had an assistant to deal with such occurrences, and his father usually had a reliable apprentice or two. The focus of the weekend was spending time together.

This began with a night out on Fridays. Kelly and his younger brother Royal weren't obligated to join in, but with their parents in high spirits and feeling generous, neither liked to miss out. Last night had been okay. They went to the cinema and watched Captain Jack Sparrow swagger around the screen, but all Kelly could think about was how much Jared gushed about the movie when he had seen it during the summer. He had gone with a neighbor girl, referring to her as a date before they actually went. Afterwards Jared had only talked about the movie, never mentioning the girl. Kelly had felt relieved by that. Encouraged even.

"Your aunt called," Laisha said. "She wants to know what you want for your birthday."

"Money," Kelly answered immediately, not taking his eyes off his homework.

"You haven't given us many ideas either," his mother continued. "I miss those lists you'd make when you were little. Always in alphabetical order."

"I can still do that," Kelly replied. He thought a moment and glanced up. "Cash. Followed by gold, money, stocks, and wealth."

"Why do you need so much money?" his father asked.

"I plan on blowing most of it on horse races. The rest will go to booze and rent boys."

Doug paused his game and raised an eyebrow. "Rent boys?"

"Male prostitutes," Laisha said, "and before you panic, he's kidding."

"I sure hope so," Doug replied. "Gay or not, our boy is too handsome to pay for it."

Kelly shook his head. "Awkward. Thank you, but seriously… Awkward."

"Then tell us what you want," his mother said.

"I'm saving up for a new camera lens. I need to buy it myself, since there are complicated technical details and compatibility issues to keep in mind."

"Then maybe we'll take you shopping for one," Laisha said.

"Or how about a nice disposable camera?" his father suggested. "You use them once and drop them off at the drugstore. No fuss, no muss."

Kelly ignored him and addressed his mother. "Telephoto lenses are expensive, but maybe we could combine my birthday and Christmas presents into one."

"You won't be sad, having nothing to open on one of those holidays?"

"Absolutely not," Kelly said. "This lens is all I need. Seriously!"

Laisha nodded to his homework. "You just keep working hard and we'll see."

Kelly grinned at her and returned his attention to the task at hand. He felt doubly motivated now. An awesome birthday to look forward to at the end of the month, and—after a few more equations—a weekend spent with Jared. The second he was finished, he slammed the book shut, grabbed his phone, and sent a quick text message to his friend. He sat waiting for a response, watching his father lose himself in the latest *Super Mario* game.

"I don't get it," Kelly said. "You work as a plumber all week. Why do you want to play one on the weekend?"

"Mario isn't just a plumber," his father said, continuing to hammer buttons. "He's practically the patron saint of this family."

"Speaking of false religions," Kelly said, "I'm going to 'church' tomorrow. Jared is spending the night, so play along, okay?"

Laisha shook her head disapprovingly. "He's your best friend. You should tell him the truth."

"That I'm gay? You have no idea how wrong that could go."

"And yet you came out to us," his mother continued. "We could have kicked you out or taken you to some quack of a doctor. So much could have gone wrong, but you were brave and did the right thing anyway."

Kelly sighed. "Because I know you guys love me. The worst that happened is Dad couldn't stop laughing."

"I kept picturing when you were eight years old and dressed in drag for Halloween," Doug said. "I thought there would be more of that."

"It wasn't drag," Laisha said. "He wanted to be a nurse!"

"In a wig," Kelly admitted sheepishly. "I could have been a male nurse, but no. I insisted on wearing nail polish too."

"And lipstick." His father fought down a smile. "So many people that night complimented me on my pretty daughter. I felt oddly proud. In fact, I haven't felt as proud of you since. Maybe

Nurse Kelly should make a comeback." When his wife glared at him, he quickly returned his attention to his game.

"Anyway," Kelly said, "I knew you guys would have my back. Jared doesn't share that obligation, and school is miserable enough without broadcasting my personal life."

"Eventually he's going to notice," Laisha said. "Or someone else will when they see you together. Lately it's hard to miss."

Before he could respond, the phone chimed. Kelly grabbed it and read the text message.

what are we doing

Kelly searched for a good idea but came up empty, so he went with the default. *The mall?*

on my way

Kelly pocketed the phone. As he stood, he saw his mother's worried expression. "There's nothing to tell. We're just friends."

Laisha considered him. "When I was in college, your father kept saying the same thing. He'd show up at my dorm room day after day with a bouquet of flowers, and he'd always say—"

"Flowers for my best friend," Doug said. "You looked terrified each time. Somehow it worked though."

"Yes, but all you needed to do was tell me the truth. Instead of flowers, I wanted to hear how you really felt about me."

His father appeared puzzled. "But you liked the flowers, didn't you?"

"Not as much as I liked you showing up. And I wasn't terrified. I was excited. And nervous."

Kelly watched his mother's eyes shine at the memory. A little persistence and a bunch of flowers. If only it could be that easy for him, strolling up to Jared and thrusting out a bouquet of roses that communicated everything he felt. Or better yet, forget the flowers. Kelly would rather speak those three magical words. What a way to come out! No careful explanations, no awkward questions afterwards. Just the truth, spoken aloud, carrying countless implications in so few syllables.

I love you.

Jared was easily entertained. Kelly couldn't remember ever seeing him yawn, even near bedtime. Thank goodness, because this was their third trip to the mall this month and November was still young. They strolled through stores long-familiar to them both, eyes scanning inventory that hadn't changed since their last visit. Neither was looking to buy, so they mostly just talked.

"I can't believe you brought that thing along," Jared said.

"Why?" Kelly asked, reaching for the camera that hung around his neck.

"It's so nerdy."

"The camera is awesome." Kelly lifted it to his face and clicked the shutter. On the display screen flashed an image of Jared looking annoyed. He'd add it to the collection. Kelly lowered the camera slightly and glanced around for inspiration. "Grab that dress and hold it up."

Jared appeared puzzled before taking a dress off the rack. He held it away from him, looking like a bullfighter wielding a black flag covered in sequins.

"Hold it *against* you," Kelly said.

"You're crazy!" Jared guffawed, but did what he was told. "You're not going to take a photo, are you?"

Contrary to his words, Jared was clearly amused by the idea. He even flipped the hanger over so it couldn't be seen, holding the dress fabric right up to his neck. Like Kelly, he had a runner's build, meaning he was lithe enough that the dress might actually fit him.

"Looking good," Kelly said as he snapped a few photos. "I think we might have found this season's top model!"

Jared jutted out his hip to appear more feminine. After a couple more photos, he reached for the camera. "Your turn."

"Not a chance," Kelly said, taking a step back. "My drag days are firmly behind me."

Jared snorted. "Just as well. You know you can't compete."

"You're probably right."

One of the salesclerks gave them the evil eye, so they put the dress back, left the store, and headed out to the mall corridor. Kelly flipped through preview images on the camera as they walked. One was a close-up of Jared's face, and for once he didn't look annoyed. Damn that smile was gorgeous!

"Stop messing with that thing," Jared hissed.

Kelly glanced up at him, then followed his gaze to a group of girls coming toward them. Not wanting to embarrass his friend, he slung the camera around to his side where it stood out less. Jared started strutting just as the girls were passing, his head turning to follow them. Then he pretended an invisible force was dragging him backward, like a hooked fish. After hopping on one foot a couple of times, he winked and resumed walking normally.

The girls giggled. Kelly turned away from them with a grimace. Nothing confused him more than the fairer sex. Did their giggles mean they thought Jared was stupid? Were they mocking him? Or, like Kelly, perhaps they found his antics more adorable than embarrassing.

"You've got to work on your moves," Kelly said once the girls were out of earshot.

"They liked me," Jared said, oozing confidence. "Besides, I didn't see you trying."

"I let the ladies come to me." Kelly instantly hated himself for pretending. He should be brave like his mother kept insisting he was. Besides, what did he have to gain by playing straight? If Jared was interested in him, this little charade would send the wrong signal. Coming out would be more strategic. That way Jared could do the same and they could finally admit the truth to each other.

Yeah, right. Kelly sighed. He already knew the truth. Jared was straight. There wasn't a chance in hell they could be together, but in the meantime, at least he could pretend. As long as he never gave Jared an opportunity to shoot him down, Kelly could keep dancing with his own delusions.

"Sorry, man," Jared said, mistaking the reason for his exasperation. "I was only kidding. Besides, who am I to talk? When's the last time I got any action?"

Kelly grinned. "When your cousin tried to kiss you."

Jared winced. "Don't remind me."

They both laughed, but as they kept walking, Kelly glanced over at Jared and wondered why his friend was always single. Sure he had sort of a big nose and his forehead was often a battleground for acne, but past these imperfections, he was downright fine. If the ladies couldn't see that, it was their loss.

"Hey, we never go in there," Jared said, bumping against Kelly and forcing him to enter a store.

A moment later Kelly found himself surrounded by princesses, pirates, and animals wearing human expressions. Disneyland had come to Texas, or at least its gift shop had. He followed Jared, who picked up various items and made snarky comments. Kelly barely heard his words, amazed by the sheer amount of corporate propaganda stuffed into such a small space. He lifted his camera and took a few photos, feeling like a tourist at the actual theme park. When they circled back around to the entrance, a pile of stuffed animals caught his eye.

Eeyore—the eternally depressed donkey from the Winnie-the-Pooh books. As a child, Kelly had always liked him best. Unlike the other maniacally grinning characters in children's stories, Eeyore seemed much more honest. With his big fat back turned away from the world, he seemed to say, "Prepare yourself, kid. Life sure can suck sometimes." Here the message was loud and clear. Eeyore the stuffed animal wasn't even allowed his individuality anymore, set among countless plush clones of himself. Adding insult to injury was the sign above him advertising seventy percent off the normal price.

"We don't want him anymore," Kelly said, peering through the camera's viewfinder. "Take the miserable ass home with you." He snapped a couple photos and was steadying himself to take another when a concerned face filled the lens.

An older man stood between them and the display, an open palm raised as if he were a celebrity trying to fend off paparazzi. "I'm sorry, but we don't allow photos."

Kelly lowered the camera. "Why not?"

"Company policy," the man said, hand still poised in the air.

"It's just a bunch of stuffed animals," Jared replied.

"No," the man corrected, "it's company property."

"What if I bought one?" Kelly asked. "Then it would be *my* property and I could take photos of it all I wanted."

The man hesitated. "That's correct."

"So then why does it matter?" Kelly pressed. "If people can take photos of them at home, it's not like there's some big secret worth protecting. You can probably find hundreds of photos of these things on eBay right now."

The man dropped his hand and glanced around helplessly. Then another idea must have occurred to him, because he stood up straight and sniffed. "You can't take photos of the store," he said. "Company policy."

Kelly snorted. "Trying to stop your competitors from stealing your amazing marketing secrets?"

"Like putting sale items by the entrance," Jared said. "To lure in customers."

"Or how the cartoons playing at the back of the store get kids in the rest of the way, dragging their parents along with them."

"Or the impulse items near the cash register," Jared said.

Kelly nudged him playfully. "Gosh, no one has ever thought of that before!"

The man glanced between them, his face turning red. Finally he sputtered, "Do I need to call security?"

"Don't bother," Kelly said. "We were just leaving."

Before they went, he took one more photo, this time of the man's blood-flushed face.

"I had no idea how much fun that camera could be," Jared said as they continued walking down the mall corridor. "It's annoying when you point it at me, but I never realized it would piss other people off. Let me try!"

"No way," Kelly said. "It's expensive. Besides, that guy was a big enough asshole to actually call security. Let's go before they show up and make me delete my photos."

They arrived safely at the car without incident, which was almost disappointing. Then they grabbed some fast food from a drive-through and cruised around Austin as the sun set, not having a destination in mind and not caring. Being free was enough. No parents, no school. No rules except for traffic laws, and Kelly broke most of those at one point or another. As long as the car was in motion, they were free. Jared was DJ, choosing songs from the MP3 player connected to the car stereo. Occasionally, when some random thought occurred to him, he would turn it down and they would talk.

In other words, the perfect night. On Monday when he was back at school, other people would no doubt brag about a big weekend party or whatever. Kelly would simply say that he and Jared drove around, but that didn't communicate just how amazing a time this was. Hanging out together felt good. Simple as that. From the frequent grins Jared flashed him, he felt the same way.

So maybe there was no chance of them getting physical, but surely this was the reason Jared was single. No girl could offer him companionship like Kelly could. Aside from sexual frustration, Jared probably didn't feel he was missing much of anything. Kelly sure didn't. Sex together would be awesome, but they already had everything else.

The contents of the gas tank dwindled to fumes as the night

wore on. Neither of them had cash for a refill, so they drove back to Kelly's house. Hopefully one of his parents would take the car out on an errand in the morning and fill it up again. Otherwise he'd be pushing it anywhere he wanted to go.

Once upstairs in Kelly's room, they watched TV, the queen-sized bed doubling as a couch. After catching the second half of an instantly forgettable action movie, they shut it off. Jared flopped onto his back and stared up at the ceiling. Kelly sat cross-legged and watched him, resisting the urge to grab his camera. The sole illumination came from the off-white Christmas lights he'd hung in one corner. The shadows cast across Jared's face made him appear much more introspective than usual, but when he spoke, his words didn't suit the moody scene.

"I wish I was the fastest man alive."

Kelly chuckled. "Why?"

"Because I need to win that race."

"The triathlon?" Kelly shook his head. "Why are you so obsessed with it?"

Jared rolled over to face him. "Because winning a bunch of ribbons and medals isn't enough."

Kelly glanced over at his underwear drawer, where he'd carelessly stashed his own awards—all of them first place except for the events he'd allowed Jared to win. Both he and Jared were competitive, a trait that drew them together. Kelly worried it could also tear them apart. Lately Jared's enthusiasm had begun to fade. The one time Kelly asked why, Jared simply shook his head. All that changed once the triathlon had been announced and Jared found his competitive fire once again. But only after making sure Kelly wouldn't be entering.

"Do you resent me?" Kelly asked. "I know I win a lot of events, but I didn't want—"

"It's got nothing to do with that," Jared said. "Yeah, I wish I was as fast as you, but even if I'd placed first in every event last year, it still wouldn't have made a difference."

Kelly's brow came together. "Made a difference how?"

"To my dad. I thought he'd be impressed, but when I tossed those medals on the table, he just nodded and said 'good job'. Then he started talking about Steven again."

"Your brother." Kelly nodded his understanding. Steven was two years older, currently at the University of Texas on a football scholarship and playing for the Longhorns as a wide receiver.

"I'm so sick of living in his shadow," Jared said. "I'm not strong enough for football, and my hand-eye coordination sucks, but I can haul ass. I could leave my brother in the dust, not that it matters to my dad. It's all Steven and his stupid pigskin. Especially now, with big-league scouts chasing after him."

Kelly's eyes went wide. "Seriously?"

Jared nodded. "Yup. Two more years and he'll probably be in the fucking NFL. But before that happens, just once, I'd like to get my dad's attention. Have you seen the trophy?"

Kelly had, because three weeks ago, Jared had dragged him to the front of the school to bear witness. There, in one of the glass cases, was the trophy. Coach Watson was campaigning to get the school behind an official triathlon club, even pushing the sport as a potential elective. Desperate to get as many students signed up for the race as possible, he'd chosen a trophy that was an ornate disaster. Three pillars rose up from a bronze plate, forming a pedestal, and on this sat some ungodly version of the Holy Grail—a golden cup complete with looping handles and three fake rubies.

"Exactly," Jared said, misinterpreting Kelly's look of abhorrence as one of awe. "Just imagine me slapping that thing down on the dinner table. It'll blow Dad's mind."

Few trophies, if any, could compare with getting headhunted by an NFL scout, but Kelly didn't have the heart to tell Jared that. "I'm sure your dad is proud of you already," he said. "He'd be crazy not to be."

"Maybe," Jared said, rolling onto his back again. "He'll be way more proud if I bring home that trophy."

"And you will," Kelly promised him. "On Monday, it's back to training."

They mapped out a rough plan of areas to strengthen. By the time they were too tired to discuss it anymore, Jared was smiling again. After taking turns in the bathroom, they stripped down to their underwear, just as they always did. Once under the sheets and the room was dark, they went to sleep. One of them did, anyway. Kelly remained awake, listening to the sound of Jared's breathing. When enough time had passed—more than an hour according to the red digits on the nightstand—and when he felt certain that Jared was deep asleep, Kelly shifted in bed.

To an outsider, he hoped this sudden movement appeared careless and impulsive, maybe a reaction to a dream, resulting in his arm pressing along Jared's side and one knee nestling against Jared's leg. Kelly remained rigid, terrified as always that the body contact would wake his friend. When it didn't, he allowed himself to exhale and relax, basking in how warm their skin became where it touched. Unable to resist any longer, he moved once more, resting an open hand on Jared's back. This was all Kelly ever allowed himself, and frankly, it already seemed too much. But he liked it. Only in sleep could Jared be his unknowing lover, providing him with comfort impossible in the waking world.

Chapter Two

When Kelly awoke the next morning, Jared's side of the bed was empty. This caused a jolt of fear, accompanied by nightmare images of their bodies getting tangled up during the night, Jared waking to find Kelly's arms around him. Then he heard the drone of television, the volume turned down low. Nothing had happened last night. For better or worse, everything was still the same.

Jared sat on the edge of the bed, watching the original *Terminator* movie. At the moment, a waitress with heavy-metal hair was locked in combat with an evil Arnold Schwarzenegger. Jared, having put on his jeans, watched all of this while chuckling under his breath.

"Laugh all you want," Kelly said, yawning and stretching. "It's a true story. I'm actually from the future. I was sent back to protect you because one day you'll save the human race. To do so, first you must win the triathlon."

Jared glanced back at him. "You seriously need to get a Blu-ray player up here. Nothing sucks worse than Sunday morning television."

"Feel free to buy me one for my birthday." Kelly sat up and watched the screen, waiting for his morning wood to go down. Once it had, he slipped on his jeans and went to use the restroom. When he returned, the television was off and Jared was putting on his shoes. "Leaving already?"

Jared nodded. "You've got church, don't you?"

"Yeah, but there's still time for a bowl of cereal."

"No thanks."

Kelly blinked. Maybe something *had* gone wrong in the night. "You sure? We've got Count Chocula. Or Boo-Berry. Lady's choice."

"Definitely not. I've been drinking protein shakes in the morning. Part of my training." Jared finished tying his laces and glanced up. "We still on for tomorrow? After school?"

"Totally," Kelly said, relaxing a little. He walked Jared to the door, then strolled into the kitchen to gather his breakfast. He ate while sitting on the couch, watching his little brother play video games. Royal challenged him to a round of *Mortal Kombat* afterwards, which turned into a multi-hour marathon lasting through lunch. Kelly wasn't pulling any punches, leaving his little brother sulking.

After one particularly bad beatdown, Royal paused the game and glowered at Kelly. "Aren't you supposed to be at your gay-ass club?"

Kelly noticed the time, tossed the controller aside, and gently smacked his brother upside the head. "Don't get lippy or the fighting will move from the screen to this floor."

"I'm shaking," Royal said sarcastically, smiling when Kelly failed to make him flinch with a faux punch.

His little brother wasn't so little anymore. Not only was he growing at an alarming rate, but he'd be starting high school next year. During Kelly's final two semesters, they would be passing each other in the hall. That was a sobering thought.

"Have fun playing with yourself," Kelly said, hopping to his feet and heading upstairs.

After a thorough shower and half an hour in front of the mirror, Kelly felt as close to perfection as he ever did. Not that it would matter. There were guys he found attractive at most meetings, but for the last few months, Kelly had been practicing celibacy. Sacrificing the needs of his body added credence to the claims of his heart. Jared might not ever know it, but Kelly was proving his dedication to him, no matter how impossible the odds. How noble! How romantic!

How nauseating. Laughing at his reflection in the mirror, Kelly flicked off the light and headed downstairs. After saying goodbye to his father and kissing his mother on the cheek, he hopped in the car and started driving.

He really was going to church. That much wasn't a lie. There just wouldn't be a service when he got there. Kelly had first made the trek across town three years ago when he was thirteen. He had gone by foot, a grueling two-hour hike that concluded with him standing on the opposite side of the church parking lot, too scared to go inside. At the end of the meeting when everyone came outside, Kelly saw his first gay people in the wild, stunned by how normal they all looked. Even the two guys holding hands—a vision that made his heart flutter and confirmed what he already suspected: He was gay, and this was the life for him.

Two weeks later he returned, this time by bicycle. Working up the courage to enter hadn't been easy, but Kelly had done so. His reward was disappointment. The group leader, Phil, felt Kelly was too young. Apparently the "youth" part of a gay youth meeting didn't start until age fourteen. Kelly had waited outside in the parking lot, this time by the door, one of the older guys stopping to talk to him briefly. That had been thrilling, and was enough for Kelly to keep coming back sporadically, slowly getting to know the regulars and tagging along for coffee a few times, even if he was the only one who drank soda instead.

Then his fourteenth birthday came and went, and Kelly brought along his birth certificate, just in case Phil tried booting him out again. But he didn't, and it made all the difference. Being gay started to feel normal. Guys loved guys, girls loved girls. Kelly had a chance to see that every week, and to experience relationships, dating, and all the complications and delights that came with them. Being gay was no longer abstract or lonely, which made Kelly happy. Mostly. Having a boyfriend again would be nice. One that lasted more than a few weeks anyway.

Kelly made a slight detour on his way to the church, pulling into a nearby neighborhood and parking on the side of the street. He glanced over at the one-story house, tapped his horn when he saw that no one was standing behind the glass door, and started fiddling with his MP3 player. A few minutes later the passenger-side door opened, and a slight figure climbed inside, a whiff of men's cologne accompanying her.

Kelly inhaled. "Someone smells good today!"

Bonnie crinkled her nose at him. "Do you like it?"

"I do, but it's such a manly smell that I'm getting confused. I sort of feel like kissing you right now."

Bonnie raised a seductive eyebrow. "Maybe I'll let you!" She leaned over, but instead of going for his lips, she gave him a harmless peck on the cheek. She was laughing and about to pull away when she noticed the dashboard. "Is that supposed to be lit up?"

Kelly followed her gaze and swore. The gas light was on. So much for his parents paying for a fill-up. He dug out his wallet and found a limp and lonely five dollar bill. He held it up and shrugged helplessly, causing Bonnie to moan. "Why can't we be rich?" she cried. Lifting her rump, she yanked on the thick metal chain hanging off her jeans, bringing her own wallet into view. She managed to triple their income with ten bucks.

"I'll pay you back," Kelly promised.

"Don't worry about it," Bonnie said. "You've been giving me rides for how long now?"

Kelly whistled under his breath as they cruised out into the street. "We must be getting close to our one-year anniversary."

"Really?" Bonnie flipped down the visor and glanced in the mirror, brushing at the short-cropped hair she had dyed cranberry red a few weeks back. Already her dark roots were showing, but it looked cool. "We should do something special. Maybe a candlelight dinner followed by matching tattoos."

"I've been thinking about getting my lip pierced," Kelly said.

Bonnie brightened up. "Even better!"

"Of course such things require cash. Bank robbery?"

"Hmmm. You willing to change your name to Clyde?"

It took him a moment to get the joke, but he laughed once he did. "We could get jobs together somewhere."

"Or maybe a rich girl will be at group today. Someone who wants to shower me with gifts. And affection."

"You never know," Kelly said, pulling into a gas station.

As he stood at the pump, he considered how the most exciting part of each meeting was the time leading up to it. By now he knew all the regulars. Any guy he found attractive—and who liked him in return—had already been his boyfriend, or in a few rare examples, a casual hookup. The biggest problem so far was finding someone he had anything in common with. Being gay was only enough bond to get a relationship through the first few weeks. That's why Kelly looked forward to each meeting, hoping someone new would turn his life upside down.

By the time he and Bonnie arrived, the meeting had already started. Everyone was seated in chairs lining the walls of the basement classroom, which made scanning for a new face easy. Zip. Nada. No new love this week.

"Mr. Phillips, Ms. Rivers, please take a seat," Phil said with a country twang, which suited his appearance well, since he looked fresh from the county fair. The plaid shirt, the thick mustache, the brown hair with feathered bangs... He had an impressive physique too, leading to inevitable crushes among the group, but Kelly had never quite seen eye-to-eye with him. Not since that first meeting when he'd turned Kelly away. "We were just starting a discussion on unrequited love."

Once they sat down, Bonnie leaned over and whispered, "What's 'unrequited' mean?"

Kelly jogged his memory, unhappy when the answer came to him. He turned a miserable expression on Bonnie, enough for her to understand. "Oh," she said. "Straight people."

"That's a good example," Phil said, overhearing her, "and one of the most likely scenarios. Every day we are surrounded by heterosexual friends, coworkers, and peers. It's only natural to develop feelings for someone you find attractive. But what happens when that person is straight?"

"Then you're shit out of luck!" lisped Layne, a younger guy who was always playing for laughs.

"Language," Phil said warningly, "but you're right. A heterosexual person can't reciprocate those feelings. No matter how much you love them, he or she can't feel the same way in return. That's what 'unrequited' means."

"Are you sure?" Lisa asked. She was small and quiet, her voice barely a squeak. Bonnie once had a fleeting crush on her, until their first date together. Afterwards she said something about needing more fire. "Emotions aren't sexual."

"Mine are!" Layne declared.

"Lisa is right," Phil said. "Loving someone doesn't require being sexually attracted to them. But there is a difference between platonic love—which is what you have for your family and friends—and romantic love, which almost always involves sex. Unless you've been together as long as my husband and I have. Ha ha." No one else in the room laughed, so Phil cleared his throat and continued. "How many of you have loved someone who didn't reciprocate your feelings?"

Most of the hands in the room went up.

"I definitely did," said a chubby guy named Scott. "My best friend. I didn't know I was gay until I fell in love with him."

That got Kelly's attention. "What happened?"

Scott blinked. "What do you mean?"

"Did you tell him?" Bonnie asked, realizing the significance.

"Yup!" Scott's face lit up. "All at once. I told him I was gay and got down on one knee. I know! But it just felt right. Then I told him that I was in love. With him."

Kelly swallowed. "And then?"

Scott fanned himself dramatically. "He helped me to my feet

and hugged me. I cried. It was totally embarrassing."

Kelly's jaw was already hanging open, so he used it to speak. "Are you guys together now?"

"Yes!" Scott said happily. "Oh! But not like that. He's straight, but he's been wonderfully supportive. He never lets anyone say anything bad about me. He's a good friend. I couldn't ask for more."

Yes he could! Kelly slumped back in his seat, imagining the same scenario playing out with Jared and wondering if he could feel satisfied with friendship and nothing more.

"So anyway," Phil said, taking control of the meeting again, "many of you have already experienced unrequited love, and I'm certain not all of you have had such a sympathetic response. Loving the wrong person can hurt, which is why you should avoid it at all costs. When you notice yourself becoming attracted to someone who isn't gay, stop yourself before things go too far. Don't feed into any sort of fantasy or false hope. You're better off directing your attention and energy elsewhere."

"If it were that easy," Kelly said, "none of us would be here right now."

Phil turned to him. "I beg your pardon?"

Kelly crossed his arms over his chest. "If we could choose who we love, none of us would be here. We'd all be chasing after the prom queen or whatever."

This was met by an awkward silence, which Layne eventually broke, but for once he wasn't kidding around. "I'm proud of who I am. I like being gay!"

"Me too, but wouldn't you rather be able to date half the population? Aren't you sick of your options being limited to this room?" Kelly glanced around in exasperation, seeing expressions both offended and—perhaps worse—assenting. "Whatever. I need some fresh air."

He stood and kept his eyes down as he left the room. He heard someone following behind, which made him tense. As he stepped into daylight and turned around, he discovered it was Bonnie.

"You okay?" she asked. "That didn't sound like you at all. Well, the attitude maybe, but do you really want a girlfriend?"

"No," Kelly said, leaning against the church and looking skyward. "I like being gay. I can't imagine myself any other way.

But I want to walk into a mall or a grocery store, look at every guy there, and know that I could have any one of them."

"Someone's full of himself," Bonnie teased, "but I know what you mean. Some of my straight gal pals have a new crush every week. All those different guys they can choose from, and no matter how hopeless their chances, at least they're compatible at the most basic level. My female friends like guys, and most guys like girls. Simple as that. At least for them. Must be nice."

"Exactly," Kelly said. "I don't wish I was straight, but I do wish all guys were gay. Forget propagating the species. Could you imagine if everyone at your high school was a homo?"

"Absolutely," Bonnie said with a wistful sigh.

"Me too. I've thought about it a lot."

"And out of all those guys, who would you choose?"

Bonnie already knew the answer, but Kelly humored her. "Jared. I'd run right up to him and just... everything."

"Tell him!" Bonnie pleaded. "You've been talking about this for months, but you haven't done anything about it. Stop running in circles and find out, one way or the other."

"Yeah, I know," Kelly said.

"Did you see how happy Scott is?"

"I know," Kelly repeated. "God, that would be awesome! And sad. Ugh!"

"It'll be bittersweet," Bonnie said. "If you love Jared, he must be a nice guy, so I don't think he's going to freak. But you're also hot as hell, and if Jared was gay, he would have made a move by now."

Kelly looked her square in the eye. "You're just trying to cheer me up."

"Is it working?"

He thought about it and nodded. "Yes."

"Good. Now let's go back inside and make peace. You're not getting me kicked out of the one place where I—where both of us—actually have a chance of meeting someone."

Kelly sighed. "Show me a gay pride parade and I'll be right up front, waving a rainbow flag and twirling a glittering baton."

Bonnie slapped him on the ass on the way in. "Attaboy!"

Chasing after Jared. Kelly had been doing so for months, except now the situation had become literal. Ahead of him on the track, Jared sprinted, limbs stiff like a Barbie doll. Despite this, he was still fast. Kelly needed to exert little effort to keep up with him, but he was certain Jared had untapped potential.

"You need to relax," he shouted.

"I'm running!" Jared shouted back. "Who the hell relaxes when they run?"

Kelly would have shrugged if he hadn't been in motion. The runner's high felt pretty good to him. Afterwards, all tension purged from his body, he always felt relaxed. Jared, on the other hand, seemed to get more knotted up the longer he ran. Time for a new strategy.

"None of this matters," Kelly panted, catching up with him. "Right now we're just practicing, right? So let it go."

"Let it go?"

"Unclench your hands."

Jared did so, making him at least appear less rigid.

"Good, now take a deep breath."

Jared glanced over and laughed. They were already huffing and puffing, but he forced himself to breathe deeply, at least once. His limbs became somewhat more fluid.

"Now pretend you've already won," Kelly coached. "The triathlon was yesterday. You totally nailed it. The trophy is at home, sitting in the middle of the dining room table, and it's all your dad can talk about."

Jared smiled.

"Right now you're just running for fun," Kelly continued. "And you feel so damn good about winning that you're faster than ever. You're unstoppable. Everyone knows it. Even me."

Jared's smile became a wild grin. Then he shot forward, not just in a short burst of speed, but in a long stride, his feet flinging behind him one after the other. Kelly stared in shock for a moment before he raced to catch up. And he struggled to do so. The finish line was just ten yards away, and Kelly wasn't holding back anymore, but he was still behind. He gave his absolute best, and only managed to get shoulder to shoulder with Jared as the lap came to an end.

"Holy shit!" Kelly panted as they jogged to a stop.

"Holy fucking shit!" Jared amended. "Did you let me win that time?"

He shook his head, letting the surprise remain on his face.

Jared chuckled. "Looks like you've finally got some competition."

"Good," Kelly said, and meant it, because he knew he would push himself even harder—maybe become even faster—now that there was someone to outrun. "If you can do that next Friday, you'll be done with all three events while everyone else is still climbing out of the pool."

Jared appeared cocky before growing somber again. "I saw William today."

Kelly shook his head in confusion. "Who?"

"The swimmer guy. People keep telling me he's hot shit, so I had someone point him out. I figured I could intimidate him a little, so I went up to the guy and told him he was going to lose."

"You said that?"

"Yeah. I got all up in his face. Said he didn't have a chance, that it was hopeless."

"Wow." Kelly raised his eyebrows. "You've been watching too much fake wrestling on TV."

"Maybe."

"So what happened?"

"That's the worst part," Jared huffed. "The guy just smiled at me. It wasn't even a sneer or whatever. He just smiled like I'd said 'good morning' or something friendly. The dude wasn't shaken. Not at all. It's like I didn't even matter to him."

Kelly clenched his jaw. "Where did you find him?"

"After lunch outside Biology. Why?"

"Because I want to see what we're dealing with."

Jared exhaled. "He's big. Lots of muscle."

"Which will only make him slower."

"Or give him more power when he swims. Or bikes."

"Maybe," Kelly said. "Don't worry about it. You keep running like you did just now, and you'll have the advantage. He'll never catch up with you."

"You think so?" Jared asked.

He looked so vulnerable that it made Kelly's heart melt.

"I promise."

Kelly wandered down a hall stuffed with students, occasionally stopping to stretch up on his toes to get a better view. He was beginning to suspect he was wasting his time. The school had a lot of science classrooms, and tons of people were coming and going. He barely remembered what William looked like, and what Jared had described didn't mesh with the scrawny beanpole Kelly had once known. He made one more trip down the hall and was about to give up when he did a double-take.

Leaning against the wall next to a classroom door was a figure with strong arms and a meaty chest. The primary-green polo shirt detracted from the sex appeal, as did the khaki pants. He was dressed more like a teacher than a student. His face eventually lured Kelly's attention away from the impressive physique. Like a detective searching for a missing person, Kelly aged the image in his mind. Melt away some baby fat from the cheeks, add definition to the jaw and easy smile, thicken the eyebrows above the amused eyes, and make the nose just a little wider... Yup, this was their man. Their enemy.

Kelly reassessed the scene and felt somewhat disappointed. William had his back to the wall more than he was leaning against it. He held a book clutched over his stomach, like he needed to protect himself, but the only person interacting with him was a skinny girl with long red hair. William was nodding along with whatever she was saying and appeared to be slowly inching his way toward the classroom door.

Really? This was their competition? An overgrown boy who still got nervous when talking to girls? Kelly snorted and pushed past a few students to reach him. "William." Kelly said the name loud enough to make the girl turn to see who had spoken. Kelly swiftly took her place, nudging her aside to stand directly in front of his prey. He stared hard into those green eyes... and didn't see any fight there. Just confusion, and perhaps a little concern.

"Uh," William said.

"Do you know who I am?" Kelly asked, arching one eyebrow.

"Kelly... Right?" William searched his face, brow furrowing. "Yeah. Kelly Phillips."

Okay. The question was meant to be rhetorical, which threw Kelly off, but he found a way of squeezing in his next line anyway. "Wrong. I'm the fastest guy in school. No one can outrun me. No one's ever come close."

William glanced around. Students were gathering, feeling the building pressure. Already the word "fight" was being hissed excitedly. Now the green eyes filled with worry. "Are you saying you want to race?"

"I'm saying there's no point," Kelly snapped. "You'd never

keep up with me. I thought no one could, but yesterday, Jared Holt beat me."

"Jared Holt," William repeated. Then recognition dawned. "The guy from yesterday?"

"That's right. So when he came up to you and said you'd never win, you should have listened. Don't even bother showing up next week, because—"

Someone shoved Kelly from behind, probably hoping to trigger a fight. Kelly spun around, but there were too many leering faces to see who. When he turned back around, William was also eyeing the crowd uneasily, which was surprising because he really had a lot of muscle beneath that dopey polo. He could imagine William taking on the whole mob and coming out victorious. No wonder Jared was so intimidated!

"You might be good at swimming," Kelly said, "but most of this race is on foot."

William frowned. "I'll keep that in mind. See you at the finish line."

"I won't be there," Kelly said, "but Jared will. He'll be waiting for you." Glaring again for good measure, Kelly turned and pushed his way out of the crowd. He glanced back once more when he reached the end of the hall. Most of the crowd was still swirling around William as he tried to explain what had happened. One thing was clear: William was upset. He'd be stewing over this encounter in the coming days, letting it eat away at his confidence. Hopefully, this would give Jared the advantage he needed.

"Fuck."

One word, and hardly elegant, but it summed up the situation nicely. Kelly sat on the metal bleachers near the school's track. Jared was next to him, but he wouldn't sit. He stood, using the metal steps to give him extra height so he could see better. For the last twenty minutes, they had remained silent while watching William run. Circle after circle, lap after lap, William was running. The pace was controlled, the movements graceful. Like a swimmer. A lot could be done to improve his form, but two things were abundantly clear: William had endurance, and William had determination.

Kelly swallowed and tasted guilt. William wouldn't be here

right now if not for the confrontation earlier. Jared wouldn't be freaking out either. Yesterday had been so positive. Now they were back to square one, and Kelly couldn't bring himself to tell Jared that this was all his fault.

"Fuck," Jared repeated.

"Would you stop saying that?" Kelly stood. "Staying here isn't going to help. Let's get out there and show him how it's really done!"

Jared didn't move. Instead his eyes followed William as he made another loop. He came to a stop just in front of the bleachers, grabbing a towel and a bottle of water. As William took a swig, his eyes briefly moved to where they were, then flicked away. After slinging the towel over one shoulder, he turned and walked away.

"Fuck," Jared whispered.

"Come on," Kelly said. "Enough freaking out. Show me what you did last time."

Jared was tense, but after some coaching from Kelly, he loosened up and hit his stride. Kelly caught up, matching his pace, surprised when he saw the scowl plastered on Jared's face. Anger seemed to be his motivation now. That was good. Kelly was the same way. Why sit around feeling miserable? Get up and actually do something! Burning in anger's inferno was always better than drowning in sorrow's dark sea. Jared pushed himself harder than ever, and once they were headed back toward the locker rooms, Kelly was no longer worried about William's performance on the track.

Despite all of this, Jared's mood hadn't improved. He resisted any attempt at small talk and was still fuming as he got undressed, slamming the locker door shut as he stomped off to shower. Was this how he'd behave for the next week? They were getting dressed again when Jared finally spoke.

"You just had to open your big mouth, didn't you?"

Kelly's shoulders tensed. "What do you mean?"

"You think I don't know? Everyone is talking about it. Some even said there would be a fight after school."

Kelly stared into the shadow of his locker. "Obviously there wasn't."

"What the hell is wrong with you? Seriously!"

Kelly put on his shirt and shook his head. "I was doing the

same thing you did. I thought we could psyche him out."

"Fine, but I don't need you fighting my battles for me. It's fucking embarrassing! You think you're my big brother or something?"

Kelly spun around, ready to retort, but Jared was wearing only his jeans. His chest was heaving, his wet hair plastered to one side of his forehead. Kelly lowered his eyes, but even the bare feet made him feel stupid things inside. "I was trying to help."

"Well, it was creepy. You don't wanna know some of the stuff people are saying about us now."

"Screw them!" Kelly said, raising his head. "Let them say whatever they want! I don't care. We'll be the ones laughing when you win next week."

Jared studied him a moment before the strained expression faded. "You're crazy, you know that?"

"Yup," Kelly said. "I'm proud of it too."

Jared chuckled as he put on his shirt, a smile on his face when it popped through the neck hole. Okay. Crisis averted. Kelly felt so buoyed by this, so certain that they could overcome anything together, that it seemed like the right time. He didn't let himself overthink it. He simply let the words come unhindered.

"What if it was true?"

Jared sat down on a bench to pull on his socks. "What?"

"The things people are saying about us now. If it was true, would that really be so bad?"

Jared laughed. "You're sick."

"I'm serious," Kelly responded.

Jared's brow furrowed as he yanked on a shoe and tied the laces. Then he reached for the other, repeating the process. All of it seemed to take an eternity. Kelly's mouth had gone dry. He couldn't think of anything else to say. The truth was out. All he could do was wait for a response.

Once both shoes were tied, Jared stood and looked right at Kelly, his expression reassuring. "You're not gay. Don't worry about it."

Kelly didn't hide his puzzlement. "I'm not worried that I might be. I *know*."

"No," Jared said as if it were his decision to make. "Come on, man. It's bad enough that you're black."

Kelly's jaw dropped, his head feeling light. "That I'm black?"

He raised his arm, looked at his flesh as if seeing himself for the first time. Of course he was black! His skin tone was so dark that it left no room for doubt. But what the hell did that have to do with anything?

"I don't mean it like that," Jared backpedaled. "I just figured that's why you never have a girlfriend. Most people around here are white, and you'd be surprised how many of them are racist. Just because a lot of girls won't give you a chance, doesn't mean you need to turn gay."

"That's what you think I'm doing?" Kelly asked incredulously. "You think I'm so desperate for a date that I decided—out of the blue—to start sucking dick? I don't see you going on a lot of dates, and you're not black. If your luck doesn't improve, do you honestly see yourself turning gay?"

"No!"

"Then why do you think it works that way for me?"

Jared chewed his lip. "I don't know. I don't understand any of this."

"Well you got one thing right," Kelly said, grabbing his backpack. "It is surprising who turns out to be racist. Especially when it's your best friend."

"Hey, wait!"

Kelly ignored him as he rushed out of the locker room. Once he was in his car, he slammed his fist against the steering wheel and screamed. How could he have been so naive? Why didn't he keep his mouth shut? Kelly gritted his teeth, started the car, and began the drive home, wishing he could tear his stupid heart from his chest and throw it out the window.

A person who is racist is invariably ignorant, but a person who is ignorant is not always racist. Kelly's grandmother had first told him this when he was little. She had served as an ambassador in three different countries and believed strongly in the value of peace. As Kelly got older—and angrier—she often reminded him that not all people were beyond redemption. Change was possible, but it took patience and understanding.

Kelly had very little of either. He always feared Jared would reject him for being gay, but what hurt most was that one twisted little sentence. *It's bad enough that you're black.*

As the night wore on and Kelly's rage began to weaken,

he tried to disarm the phrase, clip a few wires to make it less explosive. *Isn't it hard enough being black?* Or maybe: *Don't you already face enough prejudice as a black man?* But those were questions, requests for information as to how Kelly felt about who he was. Ignorance rather than racism. Jared had uttered a statement. A judgment. *It's bad enough that you're black.*

What little sleep Kelly found that night was fraught with nightmares. In each he faced a new conflict. Fist-fighting William in the hall, being chased around the track by the leering faces from his high school, Jared yelling at him—his words complete gibberish but the emotions behind them unmistakable. When the alarm clock buzzed, Kelly welcomed it for once, despite still feeling exhausted.

He spent longer in the shower than usual, trying to decide what to do. Play sick? Skip school? He sighed and pressed his forehead against the tile. He needed to hear what Jared had to say. They were best friends, after all. Or had been. Maybe they could get through this. At the kitchen table, Royal begged him for a ride so he wouldn't have to take the bus. Normally Kelly teased him and said no, but today he wished he could bring his little brother to school and cling to him like a teddy bear. For so long, seeing Jared had been the highlight of every day. Now that prospect filled him with dread.

Once he'd dropped Royal off, Kelly drove to school and parked in one of the spots farthest from the building, just like he and Jared always had. This allowed them to get the same spots almost every day, or at the very least, park next to each other. Kelly stayed in the car, tensing up when from the corner of his eye he saw a vehicle pull up next to his. He kept his attention forward until he heard a tapping on the glass.

He glanced over, Jared's face apologetic. That was a start. Kelly's heart shoved anger aside so love could take the lead. Sighing, he opened the door and got out of the car.

"I'm not racist," Jared said. "I totally fucked up what I was trying to say."

Kelly crossed his arms over his chest. "Then try again."

Jared looked wide-eyed to the horizon for a moment. "I honestly thought girls weren't giving you a chance because of the color of your skin. I don't care that you're black. Wait, African-American."

"Black is fine," Kelly said. "It's not like I call you a whatever-the-hell-you-are American."

"Half-Polish, half-German. Oh, plus a little French and Irish."

"Right," Kelly said. "I've got Spanish blood on my great-grandfather's side, so I'm more than just African, and I'm more than just the color of my skin."

"I know," Jared said. "If it mattered to me, I wouldn't be your friend."

"Just because you're friends with a black person, doesn't mean you can't be racist."

"I don't care what color you are!" Jared insisted. "I was trying to say that other people do, and that sucks. I'm sorry."

Kelly considered him for a moment. "Okay."

"Okay?" Jared looked relieved. "Good."

Now they could walk together into the school. They'd take the main hall to their lockers, which were side by side. They had talked a freshman into trading lockers at the beginning of the year, just so they could have a few more minutes together between classes. They would meet for lunch like they always did and no doubt laugh about the whole dumb misunderstanding. After school, they would focus on the triathlon again. Everything would be perfect, just as long as Kelly didn't push his luck.

The silence in the air was thick. Neither of them had moved, both sensing that the next move was Kelly's. All he need do was keep quiet. Just this once... and any other time his heart started feeling funny. Like now.

Kelly took a deep breath. "What about the other thing?"

Jared looked pained. "Just drop it, okay?"

"No," Kelly said, keeping his tone neutral. "I know that there can't be an *us*. Not like that. But I need you to be okay with it."

Jared looked away.

"I'm gay," Kelly said. "You're straight, I get it. That's cool. I'll respect that, but I need you to respect me."

Now Jared was glancing around, as if worried they would be overheard. When he saw they were alone, he looked to Kelly again. "Are you going to tell everyone?"

Kelly shrugged. "I'm not going to keep it a secret."

"Yeah, but people are already saying things about us."

"So what? Tell them that they're wrong. I'll tell them too."

Jared licked his lips. "But they're not wrong about you."

"No, they aren't." Kelly was apprehensive about where the conversation was heading. He struggled to find some reassuring words, but his mind was filling with a very specific fear, one that Jared verbalized.

"Maybe we should keep our distance. You know, just until the rumors blow over. I don't want anyone getting the wrong idea about me."

"What about the triathlon?" Kelly said. "Our training plans?"

"I think I've got what I need." Jared took a couple steps backward. "I'll be okay without you."

Kelly watched him turn and walk away. Under his breath, in a voice so weak he barely recognized it as his own, he said, "I wish I could say the same."

Chapter Three

Everything was different now, and not in a way that Kelly had ever imagined. Jared didn't meet him at their lockers between classes. During lunch he didn't sit at their usual table. When their track teammates asked if he was sick, all Kelly could do was shrug. Maybe Jared had gone home just to avoid him. Maybe he would enroll in another school rather than let anyone think he was gay. Of course Kelly had imagined all of this going wrong before, but he'd always assumed that he'd be the one left on the outside, the one eating lunch in some lonely hallway to escape ridicule. Somehow this was worse. That Jared would willingly abandon their mutual friends just to avoid being near him...

The thought left Kelly thoroughly depressed until the end of sixth period. When the bell rang, he felt one more pang of hope. Nothing mattered more to Jared than winning the triathlon, and while he might have said this morning that he didn't need Kelly's help, his confidence rarely lasted. Half the task of coaching him had been keeping his ego upright and stumbling along. So Kelly felt nearly certain that Jared would be waiting for him at the track.

When Kelly arrived there, the empty arena matched the feeling in his chest. It was over. No more hope. No chance of reconciliation. His best friend was a homophobic coward. Jared could have let him down gently and taken Kelly's unwanted affection as a compliment. Instead he turned his back completely, all because someone loved him who he couldn't love back. Was that so wrong? Even if the feelings couldn't be reciprocated, didn't it feel good knowing someone out there cared?

Clenching his jaw, Kelly headed toward the track. He hadn't changed clothes, still wearing tight jeans and a light hoodie. Regardless, as soon as his feet crossed the white line and touched the rubbery track surface, he broke into a run. His shoes were heavy and his clothes restricting, but Kelly ran anyway. No more holding back. No more coaching. Just him and the wind, moving too fast for all those ugly events to keep up. Kelly ran until his clothes stuck to his skin, until sorrow released its hold and tumbled away into the distance. As he jogged to a stop, only one emotion remained.

Anger.

Fuck Jared! Damn right he wasn't going to be a part of Kelly's life anymore! This was a divorce, and Kelly was keeping the house and kids and car. He snorted at the thought and turned back toward the school. That's when he noticed a figure approaching. For one second, all the anger and determination caught in his throat. But it wasn't Jared. Of course it wasn't. William was back for more practice. Kelly's anger rose up again, eager for a target.

And yet, everything was different now. His friend had become his enemy, and his original enemy was nothing at all. What point was there in hating William? If anything, Kelly should be cheering him on instead. Not that he stood a chance. Or did he?

Giving in to curiosity, Kelly made a u-turn and headed back to the bleachers. By the time he sat, William had reached the track and begun practicing. Eventually he picked up the pace, gaining a respectable speed, but he still looked like a man out for a brisk jog. This continued for the next twenty minutes. Those impressive arms and legs were pumping with the patient rhythm of a swimmer, but William was more like a speeding bus than a Porsche. Too bad, because seeing Jared lose would have been revenge served piping hot with an extra portion of suffering.

"Any pointers?"

Kelly glanced up to find William standing in front of him. His chest was heaving, his normally blond hair closer to brown now that it was drenched in sweat. He wasn't glaring. Nor was he smiling. The question didn't seem to be rhetorical, so Kelly decided to answer it. "Go home and watch YouTube."

"Funny," William said, shaking his head and starting to turn away.

"I mean it," Kelly said. "Search for videos of sprinters running in slow motion. They look like they're leaping over and over again. It's practically ballet. Do the same with distance runners. Notice how they move their arms and hold their bodies. Running isn't just practice. It's form."

William, hands on his hips, considered the words and nodded. "Okay. Thanks."

"No problem." Of course, a lot would have to change if William hoped to keep up with Jared. Even if Kelly decided to coach him, skills like these weren't learned overnight. William's only hope was to get a large lead during the swimming portion. "Shouldn't you be focusing on your strength? You don't want to fall behind."

"Swimming?" William asked. "I do that every morning. I'm not going to forget how."

Snarky! Kelly liked that. "Where do you practice? The school doesn't have a pool. Do you fill up one of those plastic kiddie pools to flail around in?"

"Something like that," William said, appearing amused. "There's a public pool down the road. They set aside certain hours for the school. Not in the morning though, which is when I like to swim, but the YMCA not far from here opens nice and early. Thanks for the pointers. I gotta get to work now."

"Wow," Kelly said. "When do you find time to sleep?"

"That's what class is for." William winked. "See you around."

He turned and strolled back toward the school. Kelly watched him and shook his head. Nice guy, not that it would matter. He remained convinced that Jared had the advantage. Maybe not in the water, but he'd be lighter on the bike and thus faster. And when it came to running, there was only one person in school faster than Jared.

Oh.

He considered the idea. Why not? Just entering the triathlon would unnerve Jared enough to cause his defeat. Unless anger spurred him on like it had last time. Regardless, Kelly stood a very good chance. At least when it came to the running segment of the event. He hadn't ridden a bike since he'd gotten his driver's license, and when at a pool, he played around instead of doing laps. He'd have to start practicing right away. Or early tomorrow. Kelly watched the quickly receding figure in the distance and smiled.

The morning remained dark in all but the easternmost sky, where an orange glow hinted of the day to come. Kelly stood outside the YMCA and shivered. Arriving here so early had seemed humorous, since it meant he might run into William. Fitting revenge for him encroaching on Kelly's territory. Now, glancing around the parking lot, Kelly realized he had no idea what William's car looked like, or if this was even the right

YMCA, since Austin had more than one. With only forty minutes remaining until class started, he adjusted the backpack slung over one shoulder and went inside.

"Good morning!" said the woman behind the reception desk.

Kelly winced at her enthusiasm. How could anyone feel so cheerful this early in the morning? "Hi," he managed to respond.

The woman scrunched up her nose and smiled. "What can I do you for, hon?"

Ugh. "I want to swim."

"Great! Are you a member? No? Well, the good news is that your first time here is free. After that, the daily rate is eight dollars, so the membership pays for itself very quickly. If you enjoy yourself, I highly recommend it, but today we invite you to go exploring and see everything the YMCA has to offer."

So. Many. Words. Kelly took the pass the woman slid across the desk and considered asking if anyone else was at the pool today. Fearing this question would trigger more chipper conversation, instead he nodded cordially and headed deeper into the building. The signs made finding the locker room easy. Kelly changed into his swim trunks, his feet cold on the tile floor as he hurried across it toward the connecting pool. Maybe he'd hit the hot tub instead. Assuming the YMCA had one.

He stumbled into the swimming area and paused, impressed by its size. Sky lights above allowed sun to filter in, or would have if it had fully risen. Fluorescent lights lining the walls compensated, illuminating the large pool. One half was open, a diving board off to one side. The other half was divided into lanes. Only two other people were in the water. An old lady— complete with bathing cap—waded around in the open side of the pool, while in the dedicated lanes, a body was churning through the water like the paddlewheel of a steamboat. He couldn't be sure if it was William or not, but the pale arms plunging in great arcs looked about right.

Kelly walked over to the lanes, abandoned his towel, and dived right in. He did his best to focus on getting his body moving and warm. Last night he'd taken his own advice and watched YouTube videos, studying swimming techniques. The front crawl seemed to be the best stroke for speed, so Kelly went with that one. Swimming lessons taken when he was a kid had taught him the basics, but he was seriously out of practice. He managed fairly well considering, except for when he reached the end of the lane. Professional swimmers turned around by flipping underwater and pushing off the wall. Or something like that. Kelly couldn't figure it out, so each time he felt his hand touch the wall, he would stop and turn around.

He found this frustrating, since he was used to picking up speed and not stopping until the race was won or he was exhausted. Here he was forced to stop just as he was getting started. After about ten laps down the lane and back, Kelly noticed a figure standing at the edge of the pool, watching him and drying off. William's baffled expression was priceless.

"Got any tips?" Kelly asked as he pulled himself out of the water.

William stared a second longer, then looked him up and down. "Lose the swim trunks."

"Skinny dipping?" Kelly glanced over to where the old lady was still wading around. "Think she'll mind?"

William snorted and shook his head. "I mean you should get a pair of these." He tugged at the waistband of the skimpy blue briefs he wore and let the elastic fabric slap against his skin. "Those trunks you're wearing are like a parachute behind you, dragging you back. Did you feel the water pulling on them when you climbed out?"

Kelly nodded. "So I need to buy some underwear from the little boys department instead."

William held up his hands. "Joke all you want. My scuba panties will give me the edge in the triathlon. If your friend shares your fashion sense, he'll never keep up with me in the water."

Kelly was torn between smiling at William's wit and frowning at the mention of Jared. He opted to do neither and instead fetched his towel to dry off. When he turned around, William had his own towel wrapped around his waist, which still left his impressive upper body exposed.

Kelly allowed himself to openly consider his physique as he dried off. "Maybe I should do some heavy lifting too. Is that how you move through the water so fast?"

William shook his head. "You have a better build for swimming than I do. Once I hit puberty, the weight started piling on. Because of that, I'm not so fast. Normally I don't care. Endurance is more important to me."

Kelly didn't hide his puzzlement. "Not big on racing?"

"Not usually. I'm training to be in the Coast Guard."

"You know they've got boats these days, right?" Kelly said. "You don't have to swim everywhere."

William smiled. "We'd better get going. School starts in fifteen minutes."

Kelly followed him back into the changing room, glad their lockers were in different aisles since the dynamic was starting to remind him of Jared. Despite being two rows over, William continued their conversation.

"How come you're here instead of your friend? I got the impression you weren't entering the triathlon."

Kelly hesitated while pulling on his jeans. "I changed my mind."

"Oh."

"Does that scare you?" Kelly asked. "Is that the sound of your knees knocking together?"

"After what I saw today," William said, "I've got nothing to worry about."

"Harsh!" Kelly said, grinning to himself. "But probably true."

"Of course I haven't seen you running yet. I've heard there's no one faster. Then again, you were the one who told me that, so…"

"I'll be on the track this afternoon. After school. Come and see."

Kelly heard the sound of a locker slamming shut and a few footsteps, which paused briefly. "Yeah, okay. See you there." Then the footsteps resumed. A door squeaked open and closed again before the room went silent.

Kelly felt unsettled as he finished getting dressed. William seemed like a nice guy, but getting chummy with him neared treachery, even if he and Jared weren't speaking anymore. William was also back to being the competition. Maybe treating him as an enemy was too extreme, but Kelly didn't plan on being friends with him. Regardless, at least the end of the school day now promised more than just a lonely ride home.

Of all the organs in the human body, the heart is by far the most treacherous. For centuries poets have claimed that love originates in the heart, radiating forth from this most special of places. But like most factories, the heart pumps out more than one product. Desire and desperation are two of its most popular exports, but most notorious of all—and perhaps the most damaging—is false hope.

Jared was back, and Kelly couldn't help but feel optimistic. Surely his friend had missed him during their day apart and had used the time to reconsider his actions. A new morning, a fresh start. Jared stood at his locker, twirling the combination lock to reset it. When he turned and saw Kelly staring, he gave a quick upward nod before heading to class.

Okay. Not exactly an apology. But he hadn't avoided Kelly outright like before. Kelly waited impatiently through his first two classes, watching the clock intently like the final day before summer break. He and Jared always met between second and third period. Would they do so again? When the bell rang, Kelly practically sprinted down the hall to reach his locker first. Then he waited. Sure enough, Jared showed up just like he always did. He made eye contact with Kelly and even offered a greeting.

"Hey, how's it going?"

"Good," Kelly said. He struggled to find words, grasping for something to say as Jared opened his locker and began swapping books. Eventually he settled for the most recent gossip. "Did you hear that Felicia Sanders might be pregnant? Keep in mind how she's always fawning over that teacher's assistant. You know, the one with the big Elvis sideburns?"

Jared shut his locker door, gave a half-hearted smile, and walked away. Kelly stared after him a moment before sighing in resignation. Of course. Why would anything have changed overnight? Why bother hoping for a little compassion and understanding? Stupid treacherous heart.

Kelly spent the next class period wishing it would never end, because afterwards he would be heading to lunch. That meant half an hour sitting at the same table as Jared. He already knew what would happen. Jared would engage their friends in conversation, steadily ignoring Kelly or responding with the bare minimum. Kelly *could* sit elsewhere, but eating alone would be pathetic. He wouldn't let Jared win so easily, but he did take his sweet time walking to the cafeteria. After buying his food and sitting down with his tray, Kelly prepared himself for the worst... and had greatly underestimated what that would be.

Jared was already deep in conversation with one of their teammates from track. Just as Kelly had imagined. What he hadn't expected were the guarded expressions—how every person seated there seemed to reevaluate him. They still greeted him, still responded to conversation he made, but somehow everyone felt distant.

Had Jared told them? Did they know now that Kelly was gay? Surely not, because that would implicate Jared. The one reason they were no longer friends was because Jared didn't want to be gay by association. Outing Kelly to the school would only spread more rumors about their relationship. Jared understood that, didn't he?

"—my girlfriend—"

Kelly only heard a snippet of the conversation, but these two words were enough to make his head whip up as Jared continued speaking.

"—matching rings. We've been together for one whole day. Isn't that a little fast?"

"Maybe she moves fast in other ways too," joked one of the guys.

"Who?" Kelly said. His voice came out terse and faint, but he was heard anyway. A number of heads turned in his direction, one of the guys snorting. They knew, all right.

"Martha Huffman," Jared answered smugly.

"*Martha*?" Kelly repeated disbelievingly.

He wasn't totally surprised. Martha had left a note in Jared's locker at the beginning of the year. Jared had been interested, but also concerned about his reputation, since Martha wasn't exactly cool. She sported bright pink glasses, giggled when she was nervous—which was most of the time—and always wore a scarf, even in warm seasons. Despite being weird, she was cute in her own way. Regardless, Kelly had encouraged Jared to keep looking, hoping he would notice the person already at his side.

"She's got a nice body," said the guy across from him. "Not that you would have noticed."

"Oh, I've noticed," Kelly said. "I just didn't think she was desperate enough to date Jared."

The expressions at the table turned to surprise as they looked to Jared for a response. "Whatever," he said with a shrug. "You're just jealous."

Now all eyes returned to Kelly, but he didn't have a snappy comeback because it was true. He was jealous on so many levels that it made his head spin. He wanted to trade places with a nerdy girl in pink glasses. He wanted someone to leave a note in his locker declaring secret love for him. He wanted to be with Jared, or be with another guy, or be anything but single and the only gay person sitting at the table right now. Expressing any of this was impossible, so he just looked away. He tried his best to ignore the sniggering, or that the fried fat in his food was congealing as it turned cold. He tried to forget the entire world around him until the bell rang. Then he was on his feet, eager to flee.

Despair made a pass at him, but Kelly clenched his jaw, crossed his arms over his chest, and refused. The triathlon. Being the first across the finish line. Jared's miserable face when he realized he had lost. These thoughts kept Kelly afloat throughout the remainder of the day. He would have his revenge.

When the sixth period bell rang, Kelly yearned to hit the track and start running, but his teacher kept the class behind to dole out an assignment. Kelly seethed during the delay and was first out the door when they were finally granted permission to leave. He headed straight to the locker room, got dressed, and walked outside. Halfway to the track, he stopped.

Jared was there. Kelly had been prepared for this possibility and had decided that it wouldn't hold him back. But he hadn't expected to see a girl with pink glasses in the bleachers, one who clapped happily when Jared sprinted past her. Kelly watched for a moment, noticing how well Jared was doing, but mostly taking in the smile plastered on Martha's face. Did she have any idea how lucky she was? Probably, since Jared had steadfastly ignored her after getting her note. Now, all these months later, her wish had finally come true. That must be nice.

Sighing, Kelly turned and headed back to the locker room. Then he changed into his normal clothes. He was leaving when William appeared in the doorway.

"Hey! Sorry I'm late. Why do girls like to talk so much?"

Kelly just glanced at him, not wanting to hear about another happy heterosexual couple. Instead he moved forward, forcing William to step out of his way. This didn't dissuade him from following Kelly down the hall.

"Aren't you training today?" William asked. "Wait, don't tell me you're done already! You're not *that* fast, are you?"

Kelly shook his head. "Not quite."

"Then where are you going?"

Kelly considered his options. "I'm going to get in my car, find a really tall bridge, and drive off of it."

"Awesome," William said. "Mind if I tag along?"

Kelly glanced over at him. "You have a death wish?"

"Not really, but I was hoping you could give me a ride home on your way. I've been biking to school every day, and honestly, my legs are still sore from the run yesterday and everything else."

"You need to take a break," Kelly said. "Give your muscles time to heal and build up." He glanced over at William. "Not that you need to get any bigger. You really want a ride?"

William adjusted the pack hanging off one shoulder. "If you don't mind. There aren't any bridges on the way to my house, so we should be okay."

"I thought you had an after-school job."

"I started a lawn mowing business when I was twelve. Most of my clients have moved away or now have kids old enough to do it themselves, but some still depend on me. I'm not busy every day, leaving my afternoons free to beg strangers for rides."

Kelly allowed himself to feel amused. Was William always so chipper? If so, being around him could be nice. Kelly had promised himself not to get too friendly, but then again, he needed a new best friend. He had Bonnie, but she went to a different school. As they reached the car, he considered William over the top of it and felt less certain. Preferably his new friend would be someone impossible for him to develop a crush on. Like a girl. He wasn't eager to experience another Jared. A cool breeze blew across the parking lot, so he pulled the light jacket he wore closer to his body.

William, still waiting by the passenger door, raised his eyebrows. "You all right?"

"Yeah," Kelly said, shaking his head. "I thought I forgot something, that's all."

He pushed the button on the keychain to unlock the car, and once buckled up, asked where William lived. He knew the area, and needed little prompting to get headed in the right direction. As they pulled into the neighborhood, lone drops of water splattered against the windshield, followed by a steady patter of rain.

William leaned forward in his seat to consider the sky. "Now I'm glad we bailed on training. Looks like a bad storm blowing in."

Kelly felt smug. "Anyone still out on the track is going to get soaked."

"For sure," William said. "I actually swung by there looking for you. Saw your friend Jared running like a mad man."

"He's not my friend," Kelly said. "Not anymore."

"Oh."

The car interior was silent until William pointed out his house. Kelly pulled into the driveway so William wouldn't have to get too wet. Maybe he was waiting for the rain to stop entirely, because after unbuckling his seatbelt, he didn't move. Eventually he shifted in his seat to face Kelly.

"I don't get it," he said.

"Get what?" Kelly asked.

"You and Jared. At the beginning of the week, you're ambushing me in the hall, trying to get me to drop out of the race. Then you show up at the pool this morning, acting friendly. I figured maybe you were doing a little reconnaissance for Jared, but then it turns out that you're also in the triathlon and you guys aren't even friends any more. Is that why? Did he get pissed because you entered too?"

"I don't think he knows yet. But when he does find out, he's going to freak. And when I win..." Kelly made an evil face.

William shook his head. "You guys are intense. It's just a race. You know that, right?"

"Then why did you enter?"

"For fun!" William said in exasperation. "Now I feel like I'm caught up in some sort of sports mafia or something."

"I just really wanted him to win."

"And now?"

Kelly exhaled. "He doesn't like who I am. And I like him a little too much."

"Oh."

"Yeah."

"Do you want to come inside?"

Kelly glanced over. William's cheeks were red. Was he

trying to be nice? Or prove that he wasn't like Jared? Surely he understood what Kelly had meant. Right?

"It's okay," Kelly said. "I should probably—"

"Really," William insisted. "We can hang out. It'll be fun."

Kelly wasn't sure of that, but it beat going home and moping around the house. He killed the engine, feeling apprehensive as he followed William up the walkway. He didn't know much about the guy, but he did seem nice. Kelly's aunt always said that God didn't take a dump without opening a window. Or something like that. Now he was entering the home of a person who had been his mortal enemy just last week. And it smelled like cookies.

Kelly wasn't particularly proud of his own house, since he had very little say in its appearance, and not a single dime of his went into its purchase. Regardless, he couldn't help but compare it to any other home he entered for the first time. His own had high ceilings, large open spaces, and an abundance of natural light. This house was smaller, the rooms stuffed with furniture and shelves filled with knickknacks. Curtains made of thin fabric covered each window, which would probably be cozy when holding back the glare of summer sun. On a rainy day like today, it made the house too dark for Kelly's liking. Despite being a little cluttered, the home had a mellow vibe, much like William himself. And not at all like his mother.

"Willy! I didn't expect you home so soon." Mrs. Townson was tall and lanky, the same beanpole build that Kelly remembered William having when he was younger. Her hair was blonde, her smile bright as she rubbed her hands together self-consciously. Or maybe she had just applied lotion. Either way, the same nose as William's sat above a broad smile. "And who's this?"

"Kelly," William said. "He's a new friend of mine."

"Oh, nice to meet you!" Mrs. Townson walked over and offered her hand, which was indeed soft and moist. Kelly could smell the fragrance from the lotion after they had shaken. Afterwards she hugged her son, who groaned like he was embarrassed but smiled over her shoulder. "Cookies and milk?" she asked.

"I would," William replied, "but we're going to hang out upstairs."

"You're a big boy now," Mrs. Townson said, sending a wink

in Kelly's direction. "I think you can handle eating in your room. I'll bring some up. Just try not to get crumbs all over the place."

"No promises," William said, gesturing with his head that Kelly should follow.

He did so, climbing the stairs and glancing at the family photos hanging on the wall. He saw a couple of older guys who looked like doppelgangers of William with slight variations. One had black hair instead of blond and wore the uniform of a Marine. Another shared William's blond hair but sported a goatee, a woman standing at his side who bore no family resemblance. Finally he saw a full-blown family portrait, this one old enough that all three brothers were still little boys. In the photo, Mrs. Townson's hair was shoulder-length instead of short, the man next to her sharing William's build and the dark hair of the oldest boy.

"Coming?" William asked.

"Yeah, sorry," Kelly said, hurrying to catch up.

William's room was a couple of doors down a hallway filled with plants and bookshelves. Unlike the rest of the house, things were more orderly here. A twin bed was pushed against one wall, above it a large vintage poster advertising the Coast Guard. In it a sailor seemed to be jerking a thumb at himself while wearing a shit-eating grin; above him in the sky, italic letters asked, *Going my way?*

Kelly glanced with little interest at a small entertainment center and a flat-screen television. The other walls were taken up by shelves and a dresser. The bed was made and everything seemed to have its rightful place, prompting Kelly to wonder if William kept things so tidy or if his mother took care of it while he was at school. As an experiment, Kelly removed his jacket and tossed it carelessly on the bed before continuing to survey the room. On top of the dresser were a number of medals and ribbons, all of them relating to swimming.

"Now I see why you invited me up here," Kelly teased. "You're trying to intimidate me."

"You're not far off," William replied. "Those are usually in a drawer, but when you came up to me last week..."

Kelly spun around, amused to see that William had picked up his jacket and was carefully folding it over the bed frame. "Seriously? I actually got to you?"

William shrugged. "A little. I put those out to remind me that you don't have a chance."

"We'll see." Kelly turned back around, noticing how many ribbons were for first place. "Would you say you're the best on your team?"

"Sometimes I win, sometimes I lose. I don't worry about it much. What about you?"

"I worry about it all the time," Kelly admitted. "I have a very competitive nature."

"I hadn't noticed."

There was a knock at the door. Kelly was closest, so he opened it. Mrs. Townson entered, smiling her appreciation as she carried in a tray. On it was a plateful of cookies and two glasses of milk.

"You're not lactose intolerant, are you?" she asked.

"No," Kelly said.

"Most people are to some extent," she said. "I read an article about it once and switched the family over to soy milk. You wouldn't believe the gas it gave us all!"

"Thanks, Mom," William said, his face turning red. "I'll bring the dishes down when we're done. No need to come back up here."

Mrs. Townson rolled her eyes and smiled at Kelly.

He smiled back, laughing after she'd shut the door. "My mom's the same way. If you ever come over to my place, it'll take her two minutes to show you a photo— Well, you'll have to see for yourself, but my point is that it's embarrassing. Moms love to humiliate their kids, I swear."

"I'm glad I'm not the only one," William said, walking over to take a cookie. "Help yourself."

Kelly nodded, more interested in further exploring William's room. He checked the bookshelf, which only held a few volumes, most of them common choices; the complete Harry Potter series, a dictionary that looked like it had never been opened, and some collected editions of Calvin and Hobbes. A selection of DVDs filled out this row and kept the books from toppling over.

The rest of the shelves were filled with the little souvenirs of life. And a large number of plastic animals. A rhino hung out with a gorilla, a rat, and a cheetah. This was a fairly normal gathering compared to the next shelf up, where a tyrannosaurus kept company with a giant spider, an even larger scorpion, and a surprisingly small pterodactyl. The models weren't at all realistic or in scale. In fact, they appeared to be nothing more than toys. Kelly grabbed a falcon and held it up, turning to William for an explanation.

"Oh," he said, as if embarrassed. "I've had those since forever. They're actually robots."

Kelly blinked. "You mean like Transformers?"

"Yeah," William said, joining him at the shelf. "But not like the crazy movie that came out earlier this year. These are from when we were little. Do you remember *Beast Wars*?"

Kelly shook his head. "I was into *Power Rangers*."

William grimaced as if this was distasteful. "I could never get into that show. *Beast Wars* was so much better. It was all CGI, which was rare at the time, and the plots were amazing."

Kelly took in how excited William was getting and smiled. "Wait, do you collect these?"

William made a face, like he was trying to be cool. "Nah, they're just sort of around. I've had them since I was a kid. Don't know what to do with them now."

Kelly glanced back at the display. The carefully arranged figures were dust free. And they were numerous. More than most parents would buy their children of any one toy line. "You know," he said, "my kid brother is still young enough to appreciate these. I'd be happy to take them off your hands for you."

William's eyes went wide in panic. Then he realized he'd been caught and his shoulders slumped. "Don't tell anyone," he said. "It's my deepest darkest secret."

"I can only imagine the scandal this would cause at school," Kelly teased. "So show me how this one transforms."

William took it from him and happily demonstrated. "The falcon is actually female. I know what you're thinking, how can robots be male or female? I don't know either, but I think it's cool. In the show she's actually dating the white tiger over there. It's sort of romantic, especially what happens to them in season two."

Kelly raised an eyebrow and tried not to laugh. He failed.

"Don't judge," William said. "At least not blindly. We could check out some episodes together. It's not like there's anything else to do."

Kelly glanced over at the cookies and milk, at the toys, then at William himself, who sort of had that big-kid vibe. He found himself matching William's smile and nodded in agreement. Soon they were sitting side by side on the bed, watching computer-generated animals have serious conversations or do battle. The show wasn't bad. Some poor writer had surely been hired by a toy company to come up with a reason why a bunch of robots would need to disguise themselves as animals, many of which were already extinct. And somehow the end result was compelling. Maybe a little campy at times, but he soon found himself concerned for the welfare of the characters.

"I can tell you like it," William said after the third episode. "Go on, admit it!"

"My expectations were low," Kelly said. "It's not exactly a Pixar movie."

"The animation was groundbreaking at the time," William insisted. "You at least liked the story, right?"

"Yeah," Kelly said. "I did."

William beamed. "If you want, we could watch a few together now and again. It doesn't take long to get through the series. And just wait until you get to a certain episode in the next season! You'll cry. Not that I did or anything. Um."

Kelly glanced over at him. Of course he wanted to do this again. William was easy to be around. And kind of cute, which was enough to make Kelly's smile fade. He wouldn't put himself through this. Kelly didn't want to start a new friendship because more likely than not, it would lead to unreciprocated feelings, and that hadn't been the worst of it. What hurt most was Jared rejecting Kelly as a person. Even if they couldn't be together, they could have at least remained friends. Maybe William wouldn't react the same way. Maybe he would. Either way, Kelly needed to know now, before things went too far.

"Did you get what I said earlier?" he blurted out. "When I said that I like Jared too much, did you get what I meant?"

The carefree light left William's eyes. "What did you mean?"

"I'm gay," Kelly said.

William searched his face, as if gauging how serious he was. Then he looked away. Maybe that's how straight guys dealt with what they didn't approve of. They simply turned their backs. So be it. He and William barely knew each other. The rejection still hurt, but not as bad as it would have months or even years from now.

Kelly stood, grabbed his coat, and headed for the door.

"Wait!" William stood and put a hand on his shoulder. "You don't have to go."

Kelly spun around. "Don't I?"

"Uh." William glanced past him at the bedroom door. Then, in a quieter voice, he said, "It's okay. What you said. I'm okay with it."

"That I'm gay?" Kelly asked.

William winced at the volume of his voice, responding in a whisper. "Yes."

"Then why are you—" Kelly lowered his voice. "Are your parents homophobic or something?"

"I don't know," William replied. His green eyes seemed to be pleading with Kelly, like he wanted him to fill in the blanks.

Kelly immediately jumped to one conclusion, but he didn't have much faith in it, because he'd been so wrong when it came to Jared. "Look," he said. "There's one more thing I'd like to get out of the way, because it'll make things easier on me. And don't get all offended, because this doesn't mean I'm hoping that you are, or that I'm even interested. But I've told you what I am. So now it's your turn."

William glanced at the bedroom door again. Then he moved his mouth without saying anything. Finally, he managed one short sentence. "I don't know."

Kelly stared at him. "You don't know?"

William swallowed, eyes darting to the door. "This probably isn't the best time."

"Okay," Kelly said quickly. "I get it. I think. Do you want to go for a drive?"

William shook his head. "Dinner will be ready soon."

"Yeah, it is getting late," Kelly said, unsure if he was being sent away. His head was spinning. Instinct told him he needed to retreat, that any more pressure now would be detrimental to... well, whatever. "Maybe we can get together tomorrow?"

William nodded. When he spoke again, he no longer sounded like he was choking on his own words. "When do I get to see you run? I'm starting to think you're all talk."

"I'll prove I'm not. After school. Tomorrow." He thought briefly of a happy face behind pink glasses. "Let's go somewhere else. I'm sick of the track. I know a good park with jogging paths. Meet me by my car?"

"Yeah," William said. "Okay."

They eyed each other for an awkward moment. Then William insisted on seeing him out. They were on the front walkway, struggling to find parting words, when a cherry-red sports car roared into the driveway, music blaring. The windows were up, so Kelly couldn't make out what song it was, but the beat sounded contemporary. The man who stepped out of the car wasn't quite so fresh. Kelly recognized him from the family portrait, except now his hair was thinning, his features lined. He had a nice build though, and a friendly smile when he pumped Kelly's hand.

William seemed a little embarrassed. "Dad, this is Kelly. Kelly, this is my dad."

"Hey man, how's it going?" Mr. Townson said. "What do you think of the car?"

"Very sexy," Kelly said. "Is it new?"

"Just got it last week," Mr. Townson grinned. "Not sure what the point is, because now I'm working overtime every night."

"Then you should let me have it," William said.

Mr. Townson feinted like he was boxing with his son and laughed. "Not a chance. You staying for dinner, Kelly?"

"No, I better get home."

"Maybe next time." Mr. Townson threw an arm around William's shoulders and dragged him toward the house, in his wake a whiff of cologne that smelled more fruity than musky.

Kelly watched them go for a second before he got in his car. William's parents seemed really nice. Not at all starchy or conservative. If William was gay, why would he worry about his parents not accepting him? Or maybe that's not what he was trying to tell Kelly at all. Either way, he wouldn't find out until after school tomorrow.

"He's gay," Bonnie said firmly.

When she noticed that Kelly still had his doubts, she crossed her arms and leaned against his car, despite it still being slick from the recent rain. After leaving William's house, he had driven straight over to her place, sending only a quick text that simply read *CALAMITY*, their code word for a dramatic emergency. She had met him in the driveway so they could have privacy, because when it came to Bonnie's sister, not only did the walls have ears, but the ceilings and floors did too.

"He could just be questioning," Kelly said.

Bonnie smirked. "He needs to be answering, because it's obvious. It reminds me of all those closeted celebrities who, when asked about their sexuality, respond with 'I want to keep my personal life private.' Straight people *never* say things like that. Or at least they have no problem admitting they like the opposite sex, even if they don't want the world to know who they're dating. So when someone gets all coy about their sexuality, it's a total giveaway."

Kelly studied his shoes and nodded. "Yeah, probably. Unless he felt sorry for me and was trying to make me feel less alienated."

"No," Bonnie said.

"He *is* really nice. Ridiculously so."

"Maybe, but no. You said you felt like he wanted to talk about it. If he was pretending, what would there be to say?"

Kelly raised his head, considered all the evidence once more, and finally gave in. "Okay. You're right. He's gay."

Bonnie peered at him. "Then why don't you sound happier? From what you described, he sounds hot. I'd love to date some sexy swimmer chick."

"Finding a pretty face has never been the issue," Kelly said. "If that's all I wanted, I would have shacked up with someone in group by now. I need a guy I can connect with on a deeper level."

"Like Jared," Bonnie said, her tones sympathetic.

"Yes," Kelly said. "Someone like that. Except reciprocated."

"I'm sorry. I shouldn't have pushed you to—"

"No, you were right. The guy is a dick. It's good I found out now instead of later. I just wish I could erase him from my mind because he's in there way too deep." Kelly pressed his back against the car, feeling water slowly soak into his shirt and chill his skin. "You're right that I should be excited. William is hot. He's sweet. He's motivated. All things that I look for in a guy."

"Plus he's got an awesome Transformers collection," Bonnie said.

Kelly snorted. "Right. I just feel like the timing is off. If I had met him before I really started falling for Jared. Or maybe a year from now when I'll finally be over him—"

"It won't take that long," Bonnie said. "Trust me. You just

need to keep your distance from Jared and let William get closer. Mother Nature will take care of the rest. She knows how to make you gay boys dance."

"Maybe you're right," Kelly said. "But I'm not done with Jared. Not yet."

"Your plan for revenge. How could I forget?" Bonnie shook her head. "Let it go."

"Nope," Kelly said. "I hurt him back first. *Then* I move on."

Chapter Four

Jared seemed in high spirits. He wore a constant grin when Kelly spotted him at his locker between classes. During lunch he could barely stay seated, his voice loud. Jared always behaved that way when exceptionally happy. These good vibrations didn't extend to Kelly, who he steadfastly ignored. Trying to do the same, Kelly kept his focus on his cell phone screen while he ate, willing the world around him to disappear. He failed, of course, his fork jabbing the lunch tray harder when Jared mentioned how Martha planned to switch lunch periods just to be with him. Kelly already knew he wouldn't be able to handle that. Either he needed to find a different table, or he needed to change lunch periods. Hell, maybe he and Martha could go to the office together and offer to swap.

When he was finished eating, Kelly left the cafeteria early and headed to his locker. There he fetched the books he needed for the rest of the day so he wouldn't have to return between classes and see Jared again. This made his backpack tediously heavy, but he told himself it counted as weight training.

Once the school day ended, he waited by his car. When William showed up, Kelly tried viewing him without bias. No Jared, no bruised-and-battered heart, just him and another guy meeting for the first time. A plain white T-shirt hung off William's impressive chest, the fabric loose around the narrow waist. He wore shorts today, showing off muscles rounded and soft, unlike the tight and ropey legs of a runner. The pale skin and blond hair couldn't have been a starker contrast to Kelly's own, but they shared the same slightly troubled expression. Kelly realized this first, forcing himself to smile. William soon did the same, his green eyes lighting up a moment before uncertainty returned. No doubt about it. The big talk would happen today.

After a standard greeting, they got in the car and headed to the park. Conversation floundered along the way. William mentioned how he'd skipped swimming to save his strength, and how he had even slept later than usual. Kelly's responses were polite but minimal, since he wanted to give William the chance to broach a more important subject. Or maybe Kelly was expected to raise the issue, since by the time they reached the park, the car interior had gone silent. Kelly parked, shut off the engine, and waited.

"Nice," William said, nodding through the windshield. In front of them, a paved path wound and disappeared into a thick forest. Away from human bustle, the birds here were confident, their song more robust. A pair of squirrels chased each other up a tree, and in the patches of unmaintained lawn, butterflies flitted around tufts of wildflowers. "Very nice."

"It is," Kelly said, unbuckling his seatbelt. "Secluded too. It's just you and me out here."

William's head whipped around to face him, the concern transparent.

"Easy now," Kelly said. "That wasn't a pickup line. I only mean we have privacy to talk."

William laughed. That was progress. Then he seemed to consider everything he needed to say and shook his head. "I knew you were all talk. About being so fast, I mean."

Kelly smirked. "Okay. If that's how it's going to be, let's go."

Once out of the car, his body tingled in anticipation. He needed this. To run again, not just physically but emotionally—to escape all the drama at school, all the knowing glances, or worse, the one person who now refused to look at him. Kelly knew he should be responsible and show William the right warm-up exercises, but screw it. The sun was peeking from between the clouds, a light breeze tickling their skin, and a long empty path stretched out ahead.

"So how do you want to do this?" William asked. "Should we race or take turns or—"

"Just run," Kelly said, hesitating no more.

He took off toward the path, forcing himself to start with a slow, controlled pace. William was at his side, having no trouble keeping up, even when Kelly picked up speed. The trees blew past them, the birdsong lost to the rhythmic sound of feet hitting the pavement and breath puffing from their lungs. Warmth filled every inch of Kelly's body, a light sweat breaking out on his skin. Soon endorphins rushed through his blood. It felt so damn good. Like sex. Occasionally the path would grow narrow, or they would round a tight curve and William's shoulder would nudge his. Usually, Kelly remained lost in his own little world while running, but these fleeting moments of contact reminded him he wasn't alone. He was in motion, but this time someone else was there and keeping pace. So far.

"Ready to start running?" Kelly asked.

"I thought we were already," William huffed.

"Ha!" Kelly replied. "See the light ahead? That's a clearing. I'll race you there. Give it everything you've got. Ready?"

William nodded. "Ready."

"Go for it!" Kelly let William launch ahead a few paces. He wanted to measure just how fast William could go and was surprised by how well he carried his weight. The boy had determination. That was for sure. But he was no sprinter. Halfway to the clearing, Kelly finally followed his own rules and gave it his all. Within seconds he had passed William and left him behind. When he reached the clearing, he had enough time to turn and hop up on a picnic table, sitting there casually when William finally appeared from the trees. To his credit, he kept running all the way up to the table, even though the race had long since been lost.

"Holy shit," William panted, splaying hands on the table's surface to support himself. "You're like the Flash!"

"And you're like Aquaman," Kelly said. "Out of your element."

William raised his head and grinned. "Tomorrow. You and me at the YMCA. Then we'll see who's out of his element."

"It's a deal," Kelly said. "Although not in the morning. I hate getting up early. After school?"

William thought about it and nodded. "After school. Every day. We'll keep switching back and forth, teaching each other our tricks. You show me yours, I'll show you mine. That way we're on even footing for the triathlon."

Kelly nodded. "Agreed. Frankly, I don't care who wins as long as it isn't Jared."

"Still pissed at him?"

"Yeah," Kelly huffed, but not because he was out of breath. "Want to know why?"

William nodded.

"He said it was bad enough that I'm black without being gay too."

"He said that?" William's brow knotted up, the green eyes hardening. "What an asshole!"

"I know. As if I have a choice. I can't change my skin color *or* who I love."

"I wanted to talk to you about that."

Kelly raised an eyebrow. "You want to be a black man?"

William laughed. "No, but for the record, I think it's cool. That you're black, I mean." He looked worried. "Wait, is that racist?"

"Probably, but I'm flattered and willing to forgive you." Kelly considered him. "So it's the other thing you're worried about?"

"Yeah," William said, breaking eye contact.

Kelly brushed leaves off the table, clearing a spot. "Come tell me about it."

William took a deep breath and hopped up next to him. With his feet on the bench, he rested his forearms on his legs, hunching over and staring at the grass below. "So you're gay."

"Yup," Kelly said, even though it wasn't a question.

"How did you know?"

Kelly thought about it. "Around the time other guys were noticing girls, I starting noticing them noticing girls." He chuckled to himself, then cleared his throat when he saw William frown. "It's all down to attraction. Put me in a room full of supermodels with guys on one side and girls on the other, and I know which direction I'll be looking."

"But have you ever looked at girls too?" William asked.

"Sure. I've done more than just look, because all of this is confusing. If you like vanilla ice cream but everyone else eats chocolate, eventually you're going to give chocolate a try. So, uh, which flavor do you like?"

"Strawberry," William said. He sat upright and turned to Kelly with an expression of hope. "So if you've looked at girls before, do you think it's normal that guys sometimes check out other guys?"

"Absolutely. Even if it's just to compare size in the locker room, or figure out how they stack up in other ways. But that's not the same as attraction."

"But it's normal," William pressed.

Kelly wasn't sure what he meant exactly, but he felt confident about his answer. "All of this is normal. Yes."

"Good." William exhaled. "I scope out a lot of guys in the hall. I don't during swim practice because that would be creepy, but I'm always looking around. I make myself look at girls too, and I know everything works in that regard."

"Wait, what?"

"You know." William glanced around the clearing to make sure they were alone. "Have you ever jacked off?"

"Once or twice," Kelly answered carefully before snorting. "Are you kidding me? I'm a pro! I'm probably nearing a world record by now."

"Oh. Well, I can jack off while looking at nude women. Everything works down there, if you know what I mean."

"A demonstration might help," Kelly said before nudging William to show he was teasing. "And for the record, the gay youth group I go to has plenty of guys who lost their virginity to a girl but still identify as gay."

William's worry deepened. "But how can they sleep with a girl if they're really gay? How can they even get it up?"

Kelly shrugged. "Hormones are hormones. Tell anyone this and I'll kill you, but I once jacked off to Aladdin."

"The cartoon?" William asked.

"Yeah. I was thirteen and clueless, okay? Besides, Aladdin is kind of hot. But that doesn't mean I'm Disneysexual or whatever."

William laughed. "Yeah, but at least Aladdin is a guy."

"He's a two-dimensional drawing of a guy wearing parachute pants, a dopey vest, and a fez. My point is that when we're horny, all sorts of crazy things can turn us on."

William frowned and went back to contemplating the grass.

"Returning to my original scenario," Kelly said. "Say you're in a room with the hottest guy in the world on your left, and the hottest woman in the world on your right. Which direction are you going to be looking?"

"Is anyone watching me?" William asked.

"No. Better yet, you're invisible. No one can see you no matter what, and the guy and girl are both slowly getting undressed. Which one do you want to see get naked?"

William was silent for a moment. Then, under his breath, he swore.

He sounded miserable, like it was the worst news possible. Kelly remembered feeling overwhelmed when figuring out the truth, but also sort of excited, like an entire new world had opened up to him. Maybe William just needed to say it, to finally get it out in the open.

"Which one?" Kelly pressed.

"The guy," William snapped. "I'd want to watch the guy."

"Is that so bad?"

William glanced over at him, his glare intense, but as Kelly held his gaze, his features softened somewhat. "I want to join the Coast Guard," he mumbled.

"So? It's not like the idea of a gay sailor is anything new."

"That's the Navy. I'd be a coastie, and it's the idea of an openly gay sailor, coastie, soldier, or anything else that's the problem."

"Oh." Kelly leaned back. "Right. What about Don't Ask, Don't Tell? Doesn't that protect you?"

"Yeah, but only if I live a lie." William hopped off the table and started pacing back and forth. "If I fall in love with some guy, or if someone catches us kissing, or if I even talk about it, I could get kicked out. I can't exactly go four years without dating anyone. That would raise suspicion too, so I'll have to get a girlfriend. That's why I've tried a couple times to… You know. I need to figure out if I can do that, if my body will go along with me."

"Or you could not enlist."

William spun around. "What about you? What if gay people weren't allowed in the Olympics?"

Kelly bit his lip and nodded. "Okay, that would suck. But I'm in a similar situation. How many openly gay athletes can you name? There aren't a lot, and I worry about not finding a coach or a sponsor just because of who I am."

"So what are you going to do?" William asked.

Kelly thought about it. "Fall in love with the most wonderful guy possible. If I'm going to risk my entire athletic career, he better be worth it."

"Seriously," William pressed.

"I am serious. I refuse to change who I am to please people who are bigoted and small minded. Why let them win? I've had to put up with this crap my entire life. I wish I could make you black, even just for one day, because that's not something you can hide. I can't mosey down the street and pretend to be white— everyone can see that I'm not. In fact, it's the first thing most people notice. So I'm used to it. All I can do is wait for the world to get over it and start noticing the rest of me."

William was standing perfectly still, an expression of awe on his face. "Would it be cheesy if I started applauding?"

"Normally," Kelly said, "but considering that we're alone out here, go for it."

William grinned and clapped a few times. Kelly batted his eyelashes and pretended to fan himself, as if all the flattery was causing him to overheat.

"So let's hear you say it," Kelly said. "The big scary 'G' word. You're still tiptoeing around it."

"Okay," William said. "I'm gangsta!"

"No," Kelly responded. "You're definitely not. Come on. For real this time."

William glanced around, stopping when he noticed the path that had brought them here. "Okay," he said, "but only if you can beat me in another race. First one to the car!"

He was already running, shamelessly stealing a head start. Kelly didn't let this worry him. He remained seated, inspected his nails, and counted to ten under his breath. Then he hopped to his feet and took to the wind. He passed William at the halfway point. By the time he reached the car, the path behind him was empty. Kelly caught his breath and waited patiently. When William did appear, he was stumbling, the front of his shirt soaked in sweat.

"Well?" Kelly said as soon as he was near.

"I'm gay," William moaned. "And I'm fucking exhausted."

Kelly smiled. "I have that effect on a lot of people."

"Most of my friends are girls," William was saying. "I used to think it would keep anyone from getting suspicious. That's not the only reason I'm friends with them, of course, but I figured people would think I was—"

"—a pimp?" Kelly interjected, signaling before turning left into William's neighborhood. After their run, they had driven around aimlessly, talking about whatever came to mind, although William didn't seem too eager to discuss his sexuality. Until now, that is.

"Yeah, maybe. Totally backfired since two of my friends have crushes on me, and even my mom is hounding me to choose."

"So what are you going to do?" Kelly asked.

"Stop bathing," William said. "I figure if I'm constantly surrounded by a cloud of stink, all my dating troubles will be over."

Kelly nodded his approval. "Good plan. Is it this turn or the next?"

"This one," William said.

The sun had set during their drive, and as much as they were enjoying themselves, their stomachs rumbled with hunger. Kelly struggled to remember which house was the correct one until he spotted the cherry-red sports car in the driveway. It definitely stood out in this neighborhood. William didn't live in a shack, but most of the houses in his subdivision were a little worn down. Money wasn't tossed around carelessly here. Not usually.

"What's your dad do for a living?"

"Roofing," William said.

"Does that pay well?" Kelly asked, eyes still on the sports car as he parked.

"He does okay, but not well enough to afford that car. He and Mom have been arguing nonstop about it. That's why he's been working late, but of course that only causes them to bicker more. At least he's home before dinner tonight. That'll help."

Kelly tried to imagine a roofer working after the sun had gone down. Maybe he wore one of those helmets with a light on them, like miners do. "So, swimming tomorrow? In the afternoon. No way am I getting up early on a Saturday."

William nodded. "Around three? I'll pick you up, since you've wasted enough gas on me. Text me your address and keep your eyes peeled for that beat-up piece of junk."

Farther along, parked parallel to the street, was a blue Ford Taurus. The car wasn't a piece of junk by any means, but it did have signs of heavy wear. "That's what I'll look for tomorrow," Kelly said.

"Cool. You know, you could probably come in for dinner. I'm sure Mom made enough."

Kelly laughed. "I'm so hungry that I'd probably eat everything on the table. Besides, my mom promised me meatloaf."

"Oh, okay." William's hand was on the door handle, but he didn't open it. "Thanks for talking to me about everything. I feel… I don't know."

"Less lonely?"

William brightened. "Yeah. That's it exactly."

"As odd as it might sound," Kelly said, "so do I."

Martha. At the lunch table. Surrounded by guys like a geeky princess attended by loyal subjects. Of course it didn't hurt that she was the only girl present. With no one to compete with, she seemed to be basking in the attention. Kelly had to admit he was impressed. Last week she'd been nothing more than a distant memory. Now she was Jared's girlfriend, and in a way, Kelly's replacement. So much accomplished in so little time. She certainly was cheerful. And talkative. Kelly had forgotten her hokey accent. Where was she from? Minnesota? Wisconsin? Regardless, like the rest of her, he found it sort of cute.

The more she talked, the more he realized she was nervous. Martha babbled non-stop, but not about topics anyone on the track team cared about. They were happy to stare at her, but everything she said was met with silence she seemed driven to fill. She started to flounder halfway through the meal, Jared incapable of bailing her out. So with a heavy sigh, Kelly started talking to her. Her relief was transparent, as was Jared's discomfort. This only encouraged Kelly. By the end of the meal, he and Martha were practically old friends. "Kill them with kindness" wasn't his usual strategy, but it brought him some pleasure now. Regardless, he headed straight to the office afterwards to talk about switching lunch periods.

The secretary insisted it wasn't possible, which annoyed him because clearly it was. Just not for him. Maybe it was the color of his skin. Or maybe Martha had friends in high places, or had told a convincing sob story. Kelly decided he had enough to be angry about without adding this to the list. He would be able to switch next semester, which wasn't so far away. Until then, he'd continue to pal around with Martha, just to watch Jared squirm.

His mood improved considerably when he met William after school. Every training session brought him one step closer to winning the triathlon—to hurting Jared back. Kelly enjoyed William's company too. Everything was easy with him—no unwelcome complications or ill-timed crush. Kelly's heart was still too busy sulking, and William wasn't dropping any hints that he wanted more. At least, not until just a few days before the triathlon.

They were at the YMCA, sitting on the edge of the pool after a successful swim. Kelly practically felt high because he'd finally gotten the hang of flip turns, the maneuver swimmers used to change directions at the end of a pool lane. This saved a tremendous amount of time and would provide him an advantage in speed.

"Tomorrow's the last day to train," William said. He had his feet in the water and was leaning back on his elbows, stretching out his torso. This made him appear leaner than usual, although plenty of muscle remained on display.

Kelly averted his eyes, sitting cross-legged and draping a towel over his shoulders like a cape. "We should take tomorrow off. Make sure we're well-rested for Saturday."

William didn't look convinced. "I'm still nowhere near as fast as you. In fact, I'm pretty sure you've learned more from me than I have from you."

Kelly shrugged. "Blame the student, not the teacher. One more day won't make much difference. Save your strength and load up on carbs."

"Wow, free time after school. What will I do with myself?" After a pause, he added, "Maybe we should celebrate."

"We haven't won yet."

"No, but we've been working hard. I figure we deserve some fun." William looked away, eyes on the water. "You know how to play pool?"

"You mean the non-swimming variety? No."

"Me neither. We'd be on equal standing for once. Maybe afterwards we can get some of those carbs you mentioned."

Kelly nodded. "Yeah, okay."

He didn't give it much thought after that, not until the next day after school. Instead of meeting at their cars like they usually did, William had suggested they meet directly at the pool hall. He'd texted Kelly with directions earlier in the day, along with the time. Six in the evening. That had taken him aback. Why not head there immediately after class and start playing? What point was there in going home for a few hours first? Kelly remained clueless until his mother raised the question he should have been considering.

"Is this a date?"

Kelly was in the kitchen, gnawing on a raw carrot when she asked. He froze, one cheek still bulging with carrot pulp.

Royal, who was sitting at the breakfast bar doing his homework, started laughing. "He's terrified!"

"I'm not," Kelly said after chewing a few more times and swallowing. "I just don't want William to get the wrong idea."

"Oh no!" Royal said. "He might think you're gay!" Then he started laughing harder.

"Hush," Laisha said, glaring him into silence. Then his mother turned a much more pleasant expression on Kelly. "You said William came to terms with himself, right?"

Kelly shrugged. "He doesn't talk about it much."

"Nevertheless, going out with another boy on a Friday night, one who just happens to be gay himself, is probably significant to him."

"You think so?" Kelly chomped the carrot again and chewed thoughtfully. "Should I cancel?"

Laisha looked down her nose at him. "I'm sure it took a lot of courage for William to ask you out. Find something nice to wear and show him a good time, even if you aren't interested."

"That means you've gotta kiss him," Royal said. He grabbed his homework and fled the room when their mother gave him the evil eye.

As soon as he was gone, Kelly turned to her. "*Do* I have to kiss him?"

"I didn't mean anything physical. You aren't a gigolo. But I do expect you to be a gentleman. Take his feelings into consideration while being true to yourself."

"All I've got to do is hang out with him and play pool?"

His mother smiled. "That's all."

"That's what I was going to do anyway."

"Yes, but now you won't make that 'I just pooed my pants' face when realizing you're on a date. Go get changed. Your shirt, I mean. Unless you really did have an accident."

"Ha ha," Kelly said.

He loitered around the kitchen and finished his carrot, just to prove she wasn't completely in charge of him. Then he went and did what she suggested. Once upstairs and buttoning up a purple dress shirt, he allowed himself to feel nervous. What if William was standing outside the pool hall, holding a bouquet of roses or something equally humiliating? As Kelly brushed his teeth, he considered an even worse scenario. What if he showed up and William was wearing a T-shirt and those ripped jeans that revealed his pale skin, or in a few places, tantalizing hints of what sort of underwear he had on. Hot, but not formal enough for a date. Then Kelly would be the one looking hopeful.

He drove to the pool hall wishing his mother hadn't opened her big mouth. Kelly probably would have gotten through the evening without suspecting a thing. Unless William tried to kiss him. Then Kelly would have to… what? He tried picturing it for a moment, surprised he hadn't done so already. Ever since Jared, he'd been clamping down on his feelings, even the sexual ones. Heart and hormones lead to hurt. That's what Kelly wanted to avoid, including tonight.

When he arrived at the pool hall, he knew his mother was right. William was waiting outside wearing a baby-blue dress shirt. His hair was gelled stylishly to one side, and he fidgeted while standing in place. The bouquet of roses was absent, thank goodness.

Kelly parked and got out of the car, greeting him like he always did. No hugs. No looking him over and praising his appearance—even though he did look good. None of that. Just the briefest of smiles and a quick hello before Kelly led the way inside. Or would have, if William hadn't lunged for the door to open it for him. What did he intend to do next? Carry him over the threshold? Kelly thanked him anyway, noticing a hint of sandalwood when passing by him, a cologne he was sure William didn't normally wear.

"So," William said once they were both inside. "Where do we grab some balls?"

"I'm more interested in the poles," Kelly replied, hoping this banter wasn't supposed to be flirtation.

William strutted up to a counter, speaking to the man there while Kelly glanced around. The pool hall was just about what he'd pictured. Half a dozen pool tables on either side of the room, clusters of stools set against the wall, and an old jukebox in one corner. A bar filled the space toward the back, a wide chalkboard on the wall advertising drinks and food. Only the heavy clouds of cigarette smoke were absent, but Kelly was happy for them to remain in his imagination.

"This is our table over here," William said, carrying a tray of billiard balls to the front. "We're right by the window."

"Where everyone outside can see how bad we suck," Kelly said.

William chuckled. "Then let's hope we don't draw a crowd. Can I buy you a drink?"

Oh boy. "Sure. How about a glass of champagne?"

"No problem," William said, hurrying away.

Kelly watched him go, eyes travelling over his body. Normally he didn't allow himself this freedom, which was surprising. Had they been strangers passing each other at the mall, Kelly would have mentally counted to three and turned around, just for one more peek. Of course he checked out a lot of guys. Yes, William was attractive, but that didn't count for much. The smile that accompanied William on his return… that gave Kelly pause. He tore his eyes away, noticing the two champagne glasses he was holding.

"Don't get too excited," William said. "Ginger ale, but it's got bubbles and is just about the right color."

"Close enough." Kelly smiled in appreciation as he took one. The glass was halfway to his lips when William stopped him with words.

"We need to say a toast!"

"Oh. Right." Kelly braced himself for something romantic. To the first day of the rest of our lives, or something nauseating like that.

"May the best man win," William said with a gleam in his eye.

"You mean me, right?"

William shook his head. "Not necessarily."

Kelly nodded appreciatively, feeling more at ease. "Challenge accepted."

They clinked glasses, then sipped their ginger ale as if it were delicate and rare.

"Nice vintage," William said.

Kelly swayed a little. "I feel tipsy already!"

They set their glasses on a nearby table and tried to figure out how to play pool. They didn't even know how to properly arrange the balls in the triangle, so they scoped out other tables. When this didn't help, Kelly insisted on putting them in rainbow order.

"Gay billiards!" he declared a little too loudly.

He expected William to flinch self-consciously. Instead he just grinned and grabbed a pool cue. Not familiar with the rules, they took turns trying to shoot balls into pockets, which was challenging enough. A few rounds later, William was clearly getting the hang of it while Kelly still struggled. After watching William pocket three balls in a row, he glanced around, searching for anything to rescue him.

"Hey, they have a dart board over there," he said. "My brother has one in his room. We should try playing that instead. It'll be less humiliating."

"But I'm having so much fun!" William said, leaning over the table to take another shot. This time the cue ball didn't connect with anything. "Or not. How old is your brother?"

"Royal? He's thirteen."

"Lucky," William said, looking wistful. "I've always wanted a little brother."

"And I've always wanted to be an only child. So, darts?"

William shook his head. "I'm hungry. Aren't you?"

"Now that you mention it. Let me use the restroom and we'll go. Champagne always runs right through me."

William laughed, plopping down on one of the stools and looking happy. As Kelly returned, William's expression couldn't have been more different. He was staring at the pool table unseeing, his features troubled. Just as they had been when Kelly pulled into the parking lot. Did he still struggle with his sexuality? Kelly stopped and watched him for a moment. The crinkles on William's brow deepened. He even shook his head slightly.

"You okay?" Kelly asked when he was close again.

"Yeah!" William said, his face lighting up. If their little date was the problem, he sure didn't show it when they were together. "How about a nice steak dinner to go along with that champagne?"

"Burger King?" Kelly suggested.

"Sounds perfect."

And not at all romantic. Once they were seated on plastic benches, a deep fat fryer beeping in the background, Kelly felt even more relaxed. A fast-food joint was the kind of place you went to with a friend. So far William hadn't tried holding his hand, or found any excuse for them to touch. Maybe his mother was wrong. Maybe this wasn't a date after all.

"I still think we should have gotten extra fries," William said, nearly finished with inhaling his meal. "You said we needed to stock up on carbs."

"Yeah, but if we eat anymore grease, our hearts will be too clogged to run."

"All that fat will make us float better," William tried. "That'll help in the pool."

Kelly shook his head. "I keep telling you, the swimming portion of the race doesn't matter. The run at the end will determine who wins."

William leaned back. "Then why did you spend so much time with me at the pool?"

"Because—" The answer caught in Kelly's throat. Sure it was good to learn how to flip turn and to refresh his swimming skills, but hanging out with William was fun too. Kelly liked that they were both driven, William pushing himself just as hard in the water as Kelly did on land. Most of all, he simply enjoyed spending time with the guy sitting across from him.

"Go on," William said, as if he could read his mind. "Say it."

"Say what?"

"Swimming is important too. The *most* important."

Kelly's muscles unclenched. "Yeah yeah. Okay. Just go easy on me tomorrow."

"Nope." William grabbed his drink and sucked on the straw, eyes twinkling as he watched Kelly make a face.

"So what happens once it's all over?" Kelly asked. "Are you going to keep running with me every other day?"

William grimaced. "I'd rather go back to swimming in the mornings. I have the most energy then. Unless you want to keep practicing. Then I guess I could wait until the afternoon."

"No," Kelly said. "The Olympics aren't looking for swimmers. Well, they are, but that's not how I'm hoping to get there. So I guess we're done training together."

"Everything ends eventually," William said in lofty enough tones, but then that troubled expression returned.

"Of course, there are plenty more episodes of *Battle Beasts* for you to show me."

"*Beast Wars*," William said distractedly. Then he looked up. "I still want to hang out with you. A lot. Every day."

Kelly considered him a moment. "Is something wrong?"

William sighed. "Sorry. I promised myself I wouldn't let it ruin our night."

"It won't," Kelly said, not knowing if that was true. "Tell me."

"My mom," William said. "After school she sat me down at the kitchen table. She said she needed to talk, but then she just started crying."

"What? Why?"

William clenched his jaw a few times. "She's been arguing with my dad a lot. I don't know why. They always bickered, but lately it's gotten really bad. Bad enough that she's thinking of leaving him."

"She said that?"

"Kind of. She said they might take a break. Then she asked who I'd want to live with." William's face became strained. "I couldn't answer. How am I supposed to? I love both of them."

Kelly didn't know what to say. He tried to imagine his parents asking him the same question and knew he wouldn't be able to choose. Maybe he would go with one of his parents, and Royal with the other. That would be the only fair solution, but William's brothers were older and already out on their own, so that wasn't a possibility for his family.

"They just need a break from everything else," William said, "not each other. I told them to take a trip together. I don't remember the last time we had a family vacation, and now I'm old enough to stay home. They just need to reconnect."

"Probably," Kelly said. "All couples argue."

"Exactly." William scowled. "I'm having a talk with my dad this weekend. No stupid car is worth ruining a marriage over."

Kelly suspected there was more to it than that. He thought again of a roofer working late, in the dark, and how unlikely that was. Or of the cologne that had smelled more like perfume. Maybe Mr. Townson had paperwork to finish in the evenings, or a client he needed to meet with. But most likely, another sort of rendezvous was taking place, and Mrs. Townson probably knew that.

William sighed again. "I should get home. To be honest with you, I feel a little guilty having fun when I know my mom is so upset."

"Okay," Kelly said. "I understand completely."

He drove them back to the pool hall, where William's car was still parked. He pulled up beside it, turned off the engine, and got out of the car. William was quiet—had been during the entire drive. Maybe a goodbye kiss would cheer him up, especially since it would be his first. Then again, what sort of memory would that be? With the possibility of his parents' divorce looming on the horizon, surely this wasn't the best time for a blossoming romance. The timing wasn't right. For either of them.

"You'll be okay," Kelly said, walking around to the front of the car to meet William. "No matter what happens, your parents love you. That won't change. Even if they split up—and they might not—you'll still be the bridge that connects them. You'll still be a family."

William stared a moment before throwing arms around him. Kelly stumbled under his weight, having to hug him back just to keep himself upright. Then William eased up a little, his nose and mouth pressing against Kelly's neck, but not in a kiss.

And it felt good. He was warm and strong and anything but reserved. Their bodies were touching in so many places, and for a brief second, William pulled Kelly even closer before letting go and stepping back.

"Thanks," he said. "For everything."

"Yeah," was all Kelly managed to say in response.

"Okay." William bit his lip and nodded once. "See you at the race tomorrow."

"See you there," Kelly said. He turned as William walked past him, watching him get into his car. Just before his head disappeared inside, William glanced over at him and flashed a vulnerable smile. Then Kelly got into his own car and sat there thinking, long after William had driven away.

Chapter Five

The triathlon began at the same public pool that partnered with the high school swim team. When Jared first signed up, Kelly had imagined him and thirty other guys diving into a lake, eventually reaching the other side and hopping onto bikes to continue their journey. While he'd gotten the number of participants about right, he'd failed to consider countless other details. Would the rest of the race be run in a swim suit? If not, when and how were they supposed to change clothes? Would they all have equally tuned bikes, or would some be better than others?

Most of this was probably covered in the information packet given to each participant, but Kelly had only browsed through his, mostly focusing on the maps for the biking and running portions. Now that the moment was finally here, Kelly wished he'd paid more attention. At least he could rely on William. He'd know what was going on. In fact, he was already there when Kelly arrived.

"Hey," William said, beaming at him.

"Hi," Kelly responded, not feeling quite as relaxed.

William glanced around. "Where's your family? I'm looking forward to meeting them."

"Out by the finish line. I told them to wait there instead of hurrying from event to event."

"I told my parents the same thing," William said, stripping off his shirt. He was already wearing nothing but running shoes and Speedos. That, and a goofy silicone swimming cap.

Kelly had opted not to wear one since his hair was so short. And because he didn't want to look dorky, no matter how great the advantage. He pulled off his shirt and shoved it in his backpack, eager for the sun to warm his skin. "So what now?"

"We have to swim a quick lap to qualify for our starting positions. Then we set up our transition station."

"Right," Kelly said, only vaguely understanding what that meant. He didn't have much time to dwell on it either, since he noticed Jared coming through the pool gate, Martha in tow. This made Kelly nervous. Originally he had planned on strutting up to Jared, revealing his presence with villainous flair. But now he found he didn't want to be seen. Kelly moved on the opposite side of William, hiding behind his bulk.

Before long it was time to begin. Or at least get the preliminary tasks out of the way. Coach Watson blew his whistle to get their attention, asking the spectators to return to a cordoned-off area. The remaining participants gathered around the pool.

"Thank you all for joining me for what I hope is the first of many triathlons. With the school's backing, maybe a future race will begin with a swim across Lake Travis. For this event, I was asked to keep all activities on school property as much as possible. That created a challenge when it came to the pool, but I think I've come up with a fair solution. In a moment, you will each be swimming a timed lap. Your performance determines your starting position. The fastest swimmer will get to go first, the second fastest will enter the pool five seconds later, and so on."

Kelly did some quick mental calculations. If he achieved an average placement, he'd be behind the first swimmer by a minute or so. That was a huge disadvantage. He understood the coach's reasoning, since if they all started at the same time from a lake shore, the fastest swimmers would pull ahead anyway. Regardless, he still found this news unnerving.

"As you can see," Coach Watson continued, "the pool is divided into twelve lanes of twenty-five meters each. You'll swim to the end of one lane, touch the wall, and cross under the buoy rope to the next lane. You'll repeat this process until you've worked your way through the entire pool. But first, you'll each swim your qualifying laps. Okay, let's start with Anderson."

Kelly turned to William, showing his concern.

"You'll be fine," William said. "Even if we're forced to go last, we're still allowed to pass other people. Just swim nice and steady like I showed you."

This did little to allay his fears. He wished they had practiced switching lanes. Would his turn flips still be useful? Probably not if he had to visibly touch the wall at the end of each lane. And, if he was successful enough, how would passing work?

"Phillips, you're up!"

He walked toward the coach, passing a familiar face on his way.

"Kelly?" Jared's eyes were wide, his mouth hanging open.

Rather than reply, Kelly kept his expression calm and

continued on his way, anger gobbling up his nervousness. *Too black. Too gay. Too fucking fast to lose this race!* Kelly was going to own this. He stepped up to the edge of the pool, put on his goggles, and nodded when the coach asked if he was ready. The shrill twirl of a whistle sent Kelly plunging into the water. Nice and steady might be what William had taught him, but this test was the equivalent of a sprint. He needed an extreme burst of speed. All he could muster. Despite his best effort, Kelly didn't feel that fast. Not like he did when on dry land. After switching lanes, he did manage to push off against the wall, which helped. Or so he hoped.

As he climbed out of the water, the coach was already calling the next name, giving no indication of how he'd done.

"What do you think?" he asked William

"Hard to say. Looked good to me."

He waited impatiently for the others to take their turns, only paying attention when Jared and William were qualifying. Jared did better than Kelly cared to admit. William was a torpedo, which was no surprise. When he climbed out of the water, he was smiling, like all of this was a load of fun. Kelly wished he could feel so carefree.

"When I call your name, proceed to the transition station and set yourself up, left to right. Don't choose a bike just because you think it looks prettier. Take whichever bike is farthest to the left and unclaimed. Okay, in the number one position... Anna Herbert."

Kelly looked over at William, not hiding his surprise.

William shrugged. "I never said I was the fastest."

"Is she on the swim team or something?"

"Nope."

"Number two..." Coach Watson continued. "William Townson."

William nodded humbly and walked toward the lined-up bikes. Kelly stood there and listened to another name being called out. Then another. He had already accepted not being anywhere near the front when the impossible happened.

"Number five, Kelly Phillips."

He jumped up and down in excitement, which was embarrassing afterwards, but so what? Out of thirty or so people competing, he managed to be in the top five. Not bad!

He grabbed his backpack and hurried over to his bike. It

looked okay. A ten-speed, just like Coach Watson had asked people to lend for the race. Kelly no longer owned one, but he'd biked enough that he wasn't worried about this stretch. What he was currently supposed to be busying himself with was of more concern.

"Congratulations," William said, placing a hand on his shoulder.

"Thanks," Kelly said. "So what exactly am I doing here? Should I douse the bike in holy water or something? Can I get a priest to bless it for me?"

William chuckled. "Just make sure your stuff is ready to go. I put my shoes next to the rear wheel, since I'll need them first. I'm not bothering with socks, are you? I'm also leaving my pack open, so I can pull on my bike shorts. The girl next to me is swimming in hers. That's either clever or stupid. I can't decide."

"I wouldn't bother at all if no one was around," Kelly said, "but I don't want people to see me running around in scuba panties."

William smirked. "The pros use special suits for the entire race. Anyway, be sure to check your bike helmet too. Mine had the strap buckled, which would have slowed me down."

They worked together on getting him set up. Kelly had decided to drape his shirt and running shorts over the seat, happy to fret over the details since it distracted him from the pre-race jitters.

"What are you doing here?"

At the sound of Jared's voice, his muscles tensed up. Kelly made sure he was wearing a cool expression before he turned around. "I took another look at that trophy and decided it would look good in my room. You didn't have any plans for it, did you?"

Jared's face flushed as he stared hard at Kelly. "You're not going to ruin this for me. Either of you." He spared William a glance before he stormed away.

As usual when Jared was around, Kelly's heart thudded in his chest. But with anger this time, not affection. He stared after his former best friend, shaking his head.

"Geez, you must really like him," William said.

"Seriously?" Kelly said through gritted teeth. "That's the vibe you're getting?"

William shrugged and frowned. "If you didn't care about him, you wouldn't get so upset. It signifies an emotional investment or whatever."

"'Whatever' is right." Kelly returned his attention to the bike. He tested the brake handles and adjusted the seat. When he turned back around, William was gone. Kelly exhaled. Maybe he really should let it all go, start having fun like William did. Then again, he'd come this far. Why quit now when his plan was so near completion? Satisfied he was set up correctly, Kelly stepped forward, counting down the row to where Jared was. Number seventeen. Ouch. He'd have to wait for eleven other swimmers to hop into the pool before he could give chase. That had to sting.

Soon they lined up according to number. Coach Watson had one more lecture for them before they were allowed to begin. "Play nice out there. If you need to pass someone in the pool, tap their left foot. If someone taps your foot, once you reach the end of the lane, let them go ahead of you. This isn't a game of tag and it's not a demolition derby. If I see anyone playing rough out there, I'll pull you out of the race and you can go home. Practice good sportsmanship. Your friends and family are watching you. Make them proud."

That's exactly what Kelly intended to do by being first across the finish line. He felt a little less confident when Anna splashed into the water. She was a little chubby, but this didn't seem to hinder her as she practically glided across the pool. Then came William, churning along like some kind of machine. He was already four lanes over when Kelly stepped up to the edge of the pool. Just before the whistle blew, he saw William steal the lead from Anna.

Then Kelly was swimming, trying to remember everything William had taught him. Nice and steady. That made sense because twelve lanes was a lot, and he'd still need plenty of energy for the rest of the race. Besides, he already had a strong lead. He only needed to maintain it, hop on a bike, and afterwards do what he did best. Kelly focused on his technique, feeling surprisingly calm as he proceeded. He was in the tenth lane when his hand brushed someone. At the end of the lane, the other swimmer grabbed the wall, trying to catch his breath as Kelly moved ahead. Fourth place now! Just two lanes to go!

Finally it was over. Kelly climbed out of the pool, accepted the towel offered to him, and dried off while rushing toward the bikes.

"No running, no running!" Coach Watson shouted.

"Not yet," Kelly murmured to himself, feeling cocky. Soon there would be some *real* running!

He felt a little less confident when he reached the bicycles. The guy in third place was still getting dressed, but Anna and William were already gone. Kelly rushed, putting his shirt on backwards but catching his mistake before he had both arms in. Just a few seconds lost, but those could add up quickly. Another person joined him at the bikes. Then another and another. Kelly struggled to get his helmet on correctly. Once he finally did, he hopped onto his bike, glancing over once and seeing Jared just reaching his. Ha! Way too far behind!

Kelly abandoned his insecurity and instead focused on the route ahead. The roads were blocked off for twelve kilometers— about seven miles—in a route that wove in a broad circle around the school. After that, a five-kilometer run would end directly on campus. Easy. Kelly's legs felt kind of funny after swimming, sort of like jelly, so he switched down to a lower gear.

Or he tried to. The gear released but didn't catch again, his legs freewheeling but not applying any force. He coasted forward like a car out of fuel, trying a few more times before the gear finally caught. He had no idea what it ended up on, but he was still pedaling like crazy and barely moving forward. Swearing, he kept fiddling with the gears. Finally it returned to something more normal. A few bicycles zipped passed him. How did he rank now? Fifth place? Sixth? Kelly leaned forward and pedaled harder, but he still didn't move as fast as he thought he should. When another cyclist overtook him, he decided to risk it and tried changing gears again.

This time it caught right away, but pedaling became extremely difficult, so he switched again. And again and again, trying to find one he actually liked. He cussed, wishing for the dirt bike he'd had as a kid. Pedal hard and you went fast. Simple as that. He passed a water station, but ignored the person who rushed out to meet him with a drink. Instead he kept fiddling with the gears, finally settling on one that seemed slightly less terrible than the others. He finished the rest of the route this way, groaning each time another bike passed him. He was dismounting and ignoring another offer of water when a bike skidded to a halt right next to his.

Jared. Kelly didn't hesitate, didn't waste any time delivering a one-liner. He just ran. Before Jared could get off his bike, Kelly was running. This was it. The real race began here, and the stupid bike had cost him his lead.

Three miles. Kelly kept repeating this like a mantra. Others were probably bemoaning the distance, wondering how they would ever make it, but to Kelly the number was hopeful. Three miles was long enough for the others to get tired and for him to make up for lost time. Sure enough, he caught up with and passed one person. Then another. He could win this! Of course Jared was probably thinking the same thing. Kelly glanced back once to see him not far behind. Not far at all. Then he faced forward and let the world melt away. Just a blur of cars parked on the side of the road, a barber shop on the corner, a little girl waving a rainbow pinwheel like a flag as her mother held her back. Another offer of water ignored, Anna Herbert standing there and shaking her head as he passed by. Carefully pruned trees, a cracked sidewalk, a confused old man yanking on his small dog's leash as Kelly leapt over the living obstacle. All these images were slightly distorted and fleeting, like a slideshow of impressionist paintings.

He rounded the corner, running out into a blocked-off street. Then the world came back into focus as Kelly saw three things: William, the school, and the finish line. He forced himself to maintain the same pace until he was closer. Even this was enough to bring him shoulder to shoulder with William. For a moment they ran alongside each other, William glancing over in surprise before smiling and saying two words. "Win this." Kelly grinned at him and nodded.

At that exact moment, Jared passed them both.

Kelly didn't let this deter him. He channeled his reserves, burning the last of his energy and shooting forward, catching up with Jared in just a few loping paces. The rest wouldn't be so easy. Kelly pushed himself, but so did Jared. Neither one was holding back now, having entered those last crucial moments. If one of them didn't pull ahead, they would cross at the same time. A tie! A lousy crappy stalemate! Neither would find satisfaction in that. Kelly dug deep, searching for some untapped source of energy, some hitherto undiscovered miracle juice.

"Ungh!"

An ugly sound, like a sack of meat hitting the ground and rolling. Kelly glanced over, but his rival was still there. Confused, he looked back, his mind screaming that even this might be enough to cost him the race. William was on the ground, curled up on his side. Kelly felt like he'd been punched in the gut. The wind left his lungs when he needed it most, his limbs locking up as he instinctively skidded to a stop. Then he kept running, but in the opposite direction. He reached William's side in seconds, surprised by just how close he was. That he'd been able to keep up at all was impressive.

William rolled over onto his back just as Kelly knelt over him. He groaned and held up one arm, the skin raw and bleeding.

"What happened?" Kelly asked.

William's eyes went wide. "What are you doing? Run!"

"What happened?" Kelly repeated. "Are you all right?"

"I tripped," William said. "It's just a scratch. Go!"

Kelly glanced up. Jared hadn't yet reached the finish line. There was still time. He'd have to kill himself trying, but there was still the slimmest of chances... and he didn't care. He looked back down at William, at the urgency in his eyes, and almost laughed. Let Jared win. Let him strut around the school with that stupid gaudy trophy, and let him successfully impress his father with it too. Kelly no longer cared about any of that. Heading toward the finish line had lost all appeal. What mattered most was right in front of him, lying on the ground and slowly sitting up while holding the injured arm aloft.

"You know," Kelly commented, "they say dogs have antiseptic saliva. I saw one not far back. If you want I can fetch it for you so it can lick your wounds."

William stared at him incredulously. "The race—"

"Doesn't matter," Kelly said.

William eyed him for a moment. "What about Jared?"

"Doesn't matter," Kelly repeated.

William's lips twitched, like he was trying not to smile. "What about me?" he asked.

Kelly grinned. "That's a very big question. One I'm not ready to answer just yet."

William got to his feet with a wince, waving Kelly away when he tried to help. "Come on," he said. "Let's finish the race."

Kelly shook his head. "You go ahead if you want. I never should have entered. You're here for the right reason. So is Jared. I'm not."

"You sure?"

"Yeah," Kelly said. "I'm going to join my family. Once it's all over, come find us. Okay?"

William nodded. Then he started hobbling along before he managed a decent jog. Another runner passed him, but he'd probably manage third place, assuming Anna Herbert didn't come tearing down the street like a tornado. Kelly strolled over to the sidewalk and slowly headed toward the crowd. He could see that Jared had already crossed the finish line. Martha was there, trying to hug him as he jumped around. Jared only calmed down when his father approached and offered a hand in congratulation. Today would probably be one of the best of Jared's life: a girl hanging off his arm, a proud father patting him on the back, and a big-ass trophy.

Kelly considered all of this. Then he smiled.

"Why didn't you finish?"

Kelly knew he'd be hearing this question over and over in the coming weeks. He'd have to invent a good excuse, since the truth was much too complicated. Luckily, the only person demanding an explanation at the moment was his little brother.

"Mind your own business," Kelly said, getting him in a headlock. Then he released him and smiled innocently at his father, who had raised his eyebrows in warning.

"Why'd you stop for that guy?" Royal asked, unabashed.

"Because he owed me money," Kelly said. "I got a twenty off him while he was still down."

This made Royal laugh, which would hopefully stem the tide of questions. At least their parents seemed to understand.

"That's him, isn't it?" his mother asked. "That's your William."

"He's not my anything. At least not yet. But yeah."

Laisha's face lit up, just like it did every time Kelly revealed he was interested in someone. "Do we get to meet him today?"

"Sure." Kelly strained to see over the crowds. "He probably has to receive his third-place medal along with the other winners. But afterwards, I'll introduce you. Just be discreet. He's still coming to terms with everything."

His parents nodded their understanding. Royal was oblivious, already lost in a handheld video game. As it turned out, they didn't have long to wait. William appeared just a few minutes later, patiently working his way through the crowd with his parents in tow. Odd, since Coach Watson could be heard announcing the winners.

"Fourth place," William explained, holding up a ribbon.

"Really?" Kelly asked in disbelief. "What happened? Anna Herbert?"

"Yup. Came out of nowhere."

They shared a laugh before remembering their families. Then the typical introductions took place, the adults stepping forward and exchanging first names. These always sounded a little odd to Kelly, who only thought of them as Mom and Dad. The adults engaged in small talk, complimenting each other's children, even though they didn't really know them well. William was praised for finishing so early, and Kelly for stopping to help him when he fell. All of this made him feel awkward, so he stepped aside to talk to William.

"You would have won," William said. "Before I went and ruined it all, Jared was falling behind."

Kelly shrugged to show it didn't interest him. "So what's the rest of your day like? Want to go out and celebrate?"

"Yeah," William said. "Except my parents said they'd treat me to dinner and a movie. Just look at them!"

Kelly glanced to where Mrs. Townson nodded at something his mother was saying, while Mr. Townson showed his father a business card. He didn't see anything special, so he turned back to William for clarification.

"They're getting along great," William said, eyes shining as he watched them.

Ah. "That's cool. Go have fun with them. Enjoy yourself."

"What about tomorrow?"

"Tomorrow is good," Kelly said. "I don't have anything going on. Besides my little youth group, that is."

"Oh," William said. Then realization dawned. "Oh!"

"I don't have to go," Kelly said. "Let's hang out."

"I could come with you," William suggested.

"Really?"

"Yeah! I'm curious."

Kelly supposed that was normal, although for some reason, the idea made him slightly uneasy. Regardless, this was a crucial part of coming out, since it was important to see that other gay people existed. They weren't alone. He just hoped William would remain interested after discovering how many options he had. A guy like him would be popular, meaning Kelly needed to express what he felt before it was too late.

The horn honked once, annoying and shrill. After a moment's pause, Kelly pressed on the steering wheel again. Then he got out of the car, motioning for William to do the same. "It'll be more dramatic this way," he explained.

William peered at the front of the house. "Your friend doesn't know I'm tagging along?"

"Nope. She won't mind, don't worry."

Bonnie appeared on the front porch, closing the door behind her before stopping to stare. Then she continued down the walkway, looking William over a few times.

"Who's this?" she asked.

"Hitchhiker," Kelly said. "I thought we could bring him to our special meeting. Try to convert him."

"Worth a shot," she replied, holding out her hand. "I'm Bonnie."

"William." He looked a little dumbfounded as they shook. "So you're really a lesbian?"

"Yup!"

"Wow!" William said with wonder, like someone discovering an honest-to-goodness dinosaur at a pet store. He must have realized how overboard this reaction was because his face turned red.

Bonnie beamed in return. "Oh, this meeting is going to be so much fun! Let's go."

She climbed into the backseat, despite William insisting she could sit up front. On the way to the church, she asked for details about the triathlon. Kelly had already told her most of it while texting last night, but of course in person he could make the story more dramatic. He left out his big revelation at the end. She already knew that part, and talking about it in front of William would be embarrassing.

Once they arrived at the church, Kelly's apprehension increased. As much as he liked these meetings, they could be a meat market. Especially when someone new arrived. Still, keeping William hidden away felt immoral, like obscuring the truth from a lover so he wouldn't leave. Too slimy. No, this was the honorable thing to do.

Five minutes later, Kelly decided honor wasn't so important. Already three different guys had walked up to William and introduced themselves. Layne—Mr. Everything is a Joke—had taken an interest in romance, hooking his arm through William's and dragging him away toward the refreshment table.

"Patricia May," Bonnie said from next to him. "You remember her?"

"Yes," Kelly answered tersely.

Bonnie explained anyway. "New girl at school, ridiculously pretty. She had that brownish red hair. Isn't there some sort of wood like that?"

"Rosewood," Kelly said, not taking his eyes off of William.

"Yeah." Bonnie sighed at the memory. "Then I had the stupid idea of bringing her here, and before I even had a chance to kiss her, she ran off with Christine. *Christine!* The girl who couldn't make it through a single meeting without farting."

Kelly smirked. "I wonder what happened to her. We did see her at that one party, remember? She said Patricia was crazy, that her family was mixed up in some kind of cult."

"Doesn't matter," Bonnie said. "I still would have liked to get her in the sack. That's what I should have done before I brought her here."

Kelly shook his head. "Young lady, you are unscrupulous."

"Thank you," Bonnie said. "So have you two bumped bare feet yet?"

"No. I just figured out how I feel, and all of this is new to him, so I figured we should take things slow. Besides…"

"Besides?"

Kelly shrugged. "What if he's just a rebound? I don't want to use him. Think what a crappy experience that would be for us both."

"Don't sell yourself short." Bonnie thought for a moment. "I'm pretty sure you have to actually be with someone before you can have a rebound. Jared doesn't count."

"No?"

"No."

"Oh." Kelly watched as Layne tried to hand-feed William a cheese cracker. Time to intervene. Kelly walked over and snatched the cracker from Layne. "I saved you a seat, William. Let's go."

Just as Layne opened his mouth to protest, Kelly popped in the cracker, silencing any rebuttal. The meeting began shortly afterwards. Today Phil lectured them on politics, talking about Stonewall, Harvey Milk, and other events and people that helped pioneer the modern gay rights movement. William listened with rapt attention while Kelly spent most of his time staring down anyone who looked at William. He wasn't usually the jealous type, but maybe Bonnie was right. Bringing William here without having staked a claim was foolish. Once the lecture was over, he stayed by William's side, which helped deflect would-be suitors. Lisa walked over and asked in her usual bashful tones if they were a couple, which caused William to blush. Kelly waited for a definitive answer and ended up witnessing a shy person standoff. When it was clear an answer wasn't forthcoming, Kelly pretended not to have heard the question.

Once the meeting was over, they went to a diner, sipping drinks with Bonnie at a table separate from everyone else. Kelly found himself waiting for William to grab his hand or compliment him or flirt or even attempt a clumsy kiss. Nothing. Maybe they needed to be alone, but after they dropped off Bonnie, the results were the same. Even in the privacy of William's room, all that happened was a little small talk, a pizza delivery, and three episodes of *Beast Wars*.

Perhaps Jared was right. Being black was a disadvantage or an undesirable characteristic. At least to some people. William wasn't racist, but maybe Kelly wasn't his type. Maybe William dreamed of a pale-and-pasty redhead—Patricia May as a boy. Or perhaps he was still debating if getting involved with a guy was worth risking a career in the Coast Guard.

"I should probably head home," Kelly said. "It's getting late."

William nodded. "I'll see you out."

The perfect opportunity for a parting kiss. Outside they stood next to Kelly's car, watching each other without speaking. This is when it would happen. Except it didn't. William opened the car door and Kelly got inside. Then he spent the entire drive home feeling certain that he'd lost at the game of love yet again.

Chapter Six

happy Birthday

Kelly read and reread the text message, searching for hidden meaning like he did with any of William's words or actions. Just a common phrase this time, but even it could be interpreted. No exclamation point, for instance. Did that show a lack of enthusiasm? Then again, there wasn't any punctuation at all. And why was 'birthday' capitalized?

Kelly rolled his eyes. The last three days had been hell. Not only was he overanalyzing the slightest interaction between William and himself, but avoiding Jared had become inconvenient. Kelly steered clear of his locker, his backpack overburdened with books. Lunches were spent eating outside. Alone. Even when it had rained on Tuesday. Of course this only delayed the inevitable. Once track season started in the spring, he'd have no choice but to be around him. Kelly wasn't giving up his Olympic dream just to avoid hearing Jared gloat about his trophy.

At least today was free from such problems. Kelly stretched out in bed and sighed contentedly. He'd never been to school on his birthday in his life. Not once. His mother always let him stay home to celebrate his big day. When he and Royal were younger, she would take the day off work to be with them. Today Kelly had the house all to himself. Already he had indulged in cheesy soap operas, surfed the Net for porn, and been as absolutely lazy as possible. Now the afternoon was winding down and he needed to make himself presentable. He rose to get started when his phone chimed again.

are you skipping? can't find you anywhere

Kelly smiled and texted back. *Eager to give me my present?*

you have no idea

Okay... *I'm at home. You coming over soon?*

yup

Kelly tossed the phone aside and headed for the shower. He'd taken a luxurious bath in the morning, but they never left him feeling as clean. Once he was dressed, he headed downstairs. His mother came through the door just as he was leaving, carrying a boxed cake. She instantly got sappy when she saw him, like he'd just popped out of the womb.

"My birthday boy," she said, misty-eyed. "I can't believe how big you've gotten."

"I'm the same size I was yesterday," Kelly teased as he pressed past her. "I'm headed out to pick up Bonnie."

"Don't be too long!"

"I'm not going to miss my own birthday, don't worry." He hesitated. "If William shows up while I'm gone, don't say anything weird."

His mother shook her head like he was being silly. Maybe he was. He knew the answer to all of his problems. This mystery was easy to solve. Even Bonnie stated the obvious when Kelly picked her up from her school.

"Just ask him," she said, adjusting her seatbelt so it wasn't crushing her boobs. "Better yet, make a move. Kiss him or hold his hand. Anything!"

"I can't," Kelly said. "Seriously. I can't handle any more rejection right now. Not after Jared."

"Fine." Bonnie glanced out the window. "Can I ask him? I'll pull him aside where you can't hear. If he likes you, I'll let you know."

"And if you don't mention the subject again, I'll know he doesn't!"

"He likes you," Bonnie said.

"As a friend, maybe."

She raised an eyebrow. "If it wasn't your birthday, I'd give you such a talking-to!"

Thank goodness for that. His mother already pestered him daily for details that didn't exist. With this in mind, he pressed on the accelerator and hurried home. His father's car was in the driveway, but no sign of William yet.

Once they were inside, Bonnie hung out with his mother in the kitchen, comfortable in her presence. His father forced a hug on him and offered his congratulations before getting distracted by Royal, who was bragging about a new high score. This left Kelly free to repeatedly glance out front. After the five millionth time—or so it felt to Kelly—William's car finally appeared. He wore yet another polo shirt, this one pale yellow with light blue stripes. Kelly normally turned up his nose at William's fashion sense, but today the colors complemented his fair complexion. He wasn't carrying anything, so no birthday present, unless it was small enough to fit in his pocket. A wedding ring, maybe?

Kelly laughed madly. Then he tried to calm himself and opened the door. William looked surprised for a moment before grinning. That's all it took for Kelly's insides to start doing back flips. He felt woozy. Maybe he needed one of those fainting couches Victorian women were always collapsing onto.

"—such a nice neighborhood," William was saying. "I didn't know you were rich."

"I try to keep a low profile," Kelly responded. "I get a lot of gold diggers after me."

He ushered William inside and started doing introductions before he remembered it wasn't necessary.

"We're just waiting a moment for the ice cream to thaw," Laisha said. "Then we'll have cake."

"Great," Kelly said, unnerved by how his mother kept looking between them and smiling. "Uh, I'm going to show William my room."

To his horror, her smile got even brighter. It's not like they were going to have a quickie. Although Kelly wasn't exactly against the idea.

"It's cool to finally see where you live," William said on the way up the stairs. "Makes me embarrassed of my place."

"I like your house," Kelly said. "Besides, I'm just as broke as you are. At least until I open my presents. My grandparents always send cash."

"Nice," William replied. "I'll give you my present later, okay?"

"You don't have to give me anything," Kelly said, but he glanced over at William, searching for a hint.

"It's in the car." William became distracted by the room they walked into.

Kelly stepped aside and let him take the lead, reassessing it all. The bedroom was about the same size as William's, although the vaulted ceilings made it seem larger. He didn't have a television, but the computer and large desk in one corner functioned as an entertainment center. He relied on the machine for almost everything; playing his music, watching illegally downloaded movies, or editing his photos. Like William, he had a dresser, but Kelly's fit in the walk-in closet. The only other substantial pieces of furniture were a queen-size bed and a shelf filled mostly with photography books.

"Sorry to disappoint you," he joked, "but I don't have any Transformers."

William shot him a quick smile before returning his attention to the room. He seemed most interested in the matted and framed photos on the wall.

"Are these yours?" William asked.

"Some of them," Kelly said. "Most of the black and whites are, although the smoking-hot guy pouring water over himself is by Will McBride. And this one—" he pointed to a shirtless man wearing drag queen makeup, his hand on the shoulder of another guy "—is by Nan Goldin. The sailor boy and captain obviously isn't mine. You're familiar with Pierre et Gilles, right?"

William shook his head.

"Oh. Well my photos aren't next to theirs because I think they deserve to be. I'm not that deluded. I only hung them up recently to help me compare what I'm doing. And to see what I need to learn or which direction I should go."

William glanced over at him. "My action figures seem even lamer now. I don't have anything artistic like this."

Kelly shook his head. "Sure you do. Someone had to sculpt that rhino figure, decide how it would be painted, and design the parts to move correctly. That's art too. Maybe even of a higher caliber, since all I have to do is point a camera and push a button."

"It's not that easy," William said. "Remind me to show you the photos on my phone. They're terrible. Oh."

That last syllable sounded strained. William had noticed a photo on the wall. Jared, smoking a cigarette. The morning had been cold, and when he exhaled, his breath and the smoke had woven together into a ghostly fog, like his soul was pouring from his body.

"I've been meaning to take that down," Kelly said. "Unfortunately it's one of my best."

"Yeah," William said. "In more than one way."

"Meaning?"

William glanced over at him. "I never found Jared attractive before. Now I know what you saw in him. This photograph reveals it."

Kelly considered it anew, feeling a little jealous himself. Did the man in the photo represent William's type? The messy hair in need of a cutting? The haunted gaze that stared into the morning light? Jared didn't look much like that normally, but Kelly found himself wishing he had already taken down the photo.

"Honey!" shouted his mother's voice. "We're ready!"

William flinched in surprise, causing Kelly to chuckle. "She should have been an opera singer instead of a lawyer. Let's go before she really gets loud."

The candles of his cake were already lit, and everyone was singing when he arrived. This never failed to make him smile. He realized halfway through the song that he didn't have a birthday wish prepared. He took such things seriously, as if once a year he was given a magic spell he could use for anything he wanted. So what did he desire? William? Yes, but wishing for that felt like cheating, meaning a more subtle approach was required.

"Make a wish!" his mother cried.

Kelly leaned over the cake, filling his lungs with air. *Whoever he is. Whoever I'm supposed to be with to make me feel complete, just let me find him. No matter how long it takes.*

He blew out all the candles with one breath. Not bad considering there were seventeen of them. Then came presents. Bonnie elbowed her way to the front of the crowd.

"Open mine first. That way if you get anything awesome, mine won't look bad by comparison."

Kelly tore off the wrapping paper to discover a handmade frame, complete with glass. Sure the wood was painted purple when he preferred a neutral black. And maybe the sides weren't exactly even, making the frame lopsided, but he loved it anyway because he could tell it was homemade. Or schoolmade, as it turned out.

"I built that in shop class," Bonnie said. "You'd think a lesbian would be good at carpentry, but no."

"You're battling stereotypes," Kelly said. "I'm proud of you."

"That's one way of looking at it. I know it's a disaster. I don't expect you to put any of your photos in it but—"

"Of course I will!" Kelly said. "Just try and stop me!"

"Well, thanks," Bonnie said. "If anyone laughs when they see it, tell them it's one-of-a-kind. The shop teacher had to custom cut the glass just to make it fit."

"I'll treasure it," Kelly said. But for now, he was hungry for more presents. While everyone else was eating cake, he kept ripping them open, although there were less than usual this year. Cards with money from both sets of grandparents, a videogame from Royal they could play together, and a book about studying for the SATs from a career-centric uncle. That just left a thin present the size of a magazine. Kelly opened it while trying to imagine anything so small that wouldn't be disappointing. The paper fell away, revealing a brochure for camera equipment.

"I had to wrap *something*," his mother explained. "We're taking you to get your telephoto lens."

"For real?" Kelly asked, delighted. "When?"

"As soon as you get a job and earn the money," his father said.

"Doug! Don't tease the boy on his birthday!" She squeezed her husband's arm playfully before addressing Kelly again. "Eat up. Then we can go. As long as it won't take too long. We have dinner reservations."

"Not a problem," Kelly said. "I know exactly what I want!"

He flipped through the catalog, found the telephoto lens, and showed it to his parents. His father groaned dramatically when seeing the price. Then they turned their attention to eating. Except for Royal, who had already finished his cake and was pestering William with questions.

"How big are your muscles? Have you ever measured them? You know you cost my brother the race, right? You ever been in a fight? How many guys do you think you could beat up at once?"

William took all of this in stride, realizing there was no point in answering truthfully since that would only disappoint Royal. Instead William started talking about the time an alligator had gotten into the school swimming pool, and how only he had been brave enough to dive in and wrestle it out. All the while, a puddle of melting ice cream was slowly spreading across his colorful paper plate.

"Finish your cake," Kelly said, nudging him. "I've got shopping to do!"

William shrugged apologetically at Royal before making short work of his food. When Laisha offered him seconds, William's face lit up before Kelly started tapping his foot impatiently.

"Can I get that to go?" he asked.

"Sure," Laisha said. "Just as long as you're riding in Kelly's car and not my van."

"Better head out," Kelly said, hopping to his feet. "We don't want to be late for dinner. Or shopping."

"You're like a little kid," William teased him on the way out the door.

"You're one to talk. Should we stop by Toys R Us on the way?"

"I love Toys R Us!" Bonnie chimed in. "I'm applying for a job there as soon as I get my license."

"Then you two will have plenty to talk about," Kelly said. "Wait up. I'll be right back."

He rushed upstairs to fetch his camera bag. Then he printed out a listing he'd bookmarked online that showed exactly what he wanted. When he returned downstairs again, everyone was outside.

"Should I drive?" William asked. "Let me be your birthday chauffeur."

"Thanks," Kelly said, heading for the blue Taurus. "That's sweet... but it doesn't count as my present, right?"

William shook his head mysteriously. "Wait and see."

Kelly and Bonnie got into the backseat together, pretending to be ridiculously rich, swirling imaginary snifters of brandy while directing William. "Driver, turn here! Pick up the pace, won't you? Please ask those pedestrians to go away. They offend me!"

In reality all William had to do was follow Kelly's family to the camera store. When they arrived, Kelly's heart pounded in excitement. Funny how a material object could cause such an emotional reaction. But it was more than that. He'd only owned one lens before. Getting a different kind would open up so many new possibilities. These hopes were soon dashed when the salesman told them the lens Kelly wanted was out of stock. However, the store did have another with slightly higher specs... and a higher price tag.

He turned a pleading expression on his parents. His mother smiled. His father shook his head. Five minutes later, Kelly was strutting out the door, clutching a box to his chest.

"I love you guys so much," he said. "I've mentioned that, right?"

"Yes," his father said. "You even told the cashier that you love her."

"Did I?"

"Yes," Bonnie said. "And then you kissed her hand."

"I didn't!" Kelly said, looking panicked.

"You didn't," William confirmed. "But you did make her blush. That was cute."

As they piled back into their cars, Kelly was glad William drove. He was too blissed out to focus on the road. He wished they could skip dinner so he could play with his new gear. He considered fiddling with it at the table, but he didn't want pasta sauce splattering the lens. Dinner went by in a blur, his mind full of clicking shutters and whirring lenses. When they were leaving the restaurant, he couldn't take it anymore.

"I've got to try this thing out while there's still light." The sun had already sunk over the horizon, but a residual glow remained.

"Why don't you three go out and have some fun?" his mother suggested.

"Actually," Bonnie said, eyeing William for a moment, "I need to get home. Think you can give me a ride?"

"Of course," Laisha said, all too knowingly. "You boys have a good time. Don't worry about a curfew."

"Try telling my mother that," William joked.

Soon they were alone. Kelly unboxed the long lens on the trunk of William's car and attached it to his camera with a satisfying twist and a click. "Hell yes," he whispered.

He picked up the camera and squinted through the viewfinder. The Italian restaurant they had just left now appeared much closer. He could even focus on the windows to see the patrons slurping up pasta inside.

"I can see what they're eating," Kelly said. "I shit you not."

He swung the lens around, pointing it at William for an extreme close-up. He had to take a few steps back to get a better view. Then he noticed something odd. Most people, when suddenly faced with a cold camera lens, either reacted bashfully or started grinning. William's expression remained the same. He continued watching Kelly calmly, his eyes a little shiny. Kelly snapped a photo, then lowered the device.

"You been in front of a camera before?" he asked.

William shook his head. "No more than anyone else."

"Go on, admit it," Kelly said, raising the camera again. "You're a supermodel, aren't you?" He started snapping photos, stepping back to keep William in frame. This summoned a smile, but he still didn't seem the least bit uncomfortable.

"Shouldn't we find somewhere more scenic?"

Kelly stopped playing around. "You're right. I need a view. This thing is made for distance."

William nodded slowly. "I think I know a place."

He drove them across Austin and through downtown, Kelly using the lens like a telescope at every stoplight. Their destination was familiar to him, although he hadn't been to Zilker Park since his childhood. He had fond memories of digging up fake dinosaur bones in a massive sandbox and riding with Royal on a miniature train, making him long for a more innocent time.

"I used to love this place," William said, perhaps having similar thoughts.

"Me too," Kelly said, "but I don't think the fun stuff is open this late."

"That's not our destination," William said, parking the car. He nodded through the windshield. "Ever been on the Pfluger Bridge?"

"Nope. Sounds contagious."

William smiled. "Come see."

They walked down the street, heading for a curved ramp that arched over the Colorado River. Kelly could already see the reason they were here. Off in the distance, Austin's skyline sparkled with multicolored lights. He picked up the pace, eager to get out to the middle of the bridge where they'd have the best vantage point. Once there, Kelly pressed against the rail to steady himself and raised his camera. The night had fully descended, the only light coming from lamps lining the bridge and the twinkling diamond-encrusted buildings across the river. A wide-angle lens would be better, especially for a panoramic view like this, but Kelly took delight in focusing on different aspects of it anyway. He'd never capture the true beauty, not even if the equipment and conditions were ideal. He didn't expect to. But if just one of his photos expressed a fragment of what he saw and felt now—that would be enough.

"So," William said, clearing his throat. "Is that thing digital, or do you have real film inside?"

"Digital." Kelly pulled his eye from the viewfinder, realizing that he'd been taking photos for the better part of fifteen minutes. "I used to have a film camera, but I blew through way too much cash on refills and development."

"Oh." William looked a little anxious. He patted his pockets, eventually producing a pack of gum. He unwrapped a stick and popped it in his mouth before holding the pack out to Kelly. Then his cheeks turned red. "Want a piece?"

"Sure," Kelly said, eyeing him a moment longer.

They chewed in silence as they took in their surroundings. William seemed most focused on the people, watching who was coming and going from both sides of the bridge. Then he spit his gum out into the paper wrapper. "I'm done," he said. "Are you?"

"I guess so." Kelly mimicked his actions, his pulse kicking into high gear. He had a feeling they were here to do more than just take photos. William kept taking deep breaths. Unless he was about to dive into the river for a swim, he seemed to be working up his courage. This was obviously a very big deal to him. His first? Forcing himself not to smile, Kelly detached the telephoto lens, placing it safely in its case and reattaching the normal lens. Then he snapped a quick photo of William looking all flustered and uncertain.

"I thought you were done taking photos," he said.

"I can be," Kelly said, "if you can think of something better to do."

William glanced around again and licked his lips. "I wanted to give you your birthday present."

Kelly smiled and leaned back against the rail. "I'm ready."

"Yeah. Good." William stepped forward, the toe of his shoe accidentally kicking Kelly's foot. "Oh, sorry."

"It's okay," Kelly said.

William steeled himself and brought his body closer to Kelly's. The camera lens poked him in the chest, causing him to look down in confusion.

"Sorry," Kelly said, unstrapping it from around his neck and carefully tucking it away in the case. "So. About that present."

William took another deep breath, seeming on the verge of tears. All amusement left Kelly, the vulnerability pulling him forward. He stopped just before their lips touched and left the rest up to William. He placed a hand on Kelly's face, his thumb stroking downward and stopping at the edge of his lips, as if to guide him. The rest happened so slowly, so carefully, as if William was determined to get it absolutely right. Their lips brushed together, not once but twice before William pressed them more firmly together. He held them there, exhaling through his nose, his breath warm on Kelly's cheek. Then William stepped backward, Kelly practically tumbling forward because he didn't want the kiss to end.

"That was incredible," he breathed.

William grinned, looking a little more self-assured.

"And here I was thinking it was your first time," Kelly said.

"It was."

Kelly's eyes widened in disbelief. "Then you're either a fast learner, or one of your pillows at home is covered in slobber."

"A little of both," William said. "So what do you think? Was that a good birthday present, or should I have actually spent money?"

"It's perfect," Kelly said. "Although I'm more interested in the implications. No, that can wait. What I really want is a rerun."

This time William was more confident when he stepped forward, even if he did nearly kick Kelly's camera into the river. If that had happened, the second kiss was incredible enough to have been worth it. Kelly was mildly aware of people walking past them, one couple conversing loudly, but this didn't bother him. Nor did it seem to faze William, who came in for more. They passed quite a few minutes this way, laughing when they finally pulled back.

Kelly bent down to pick up his camera, and when he rose again, William was considering him thoughtfully.

"What did you mean by implications?"

"Ah," Kelly said, feeling sheepish. "I wasn't sure if you were interested in me or not."

William's features scrunched up. "We're dating, aren't we? Of course I'm interested!"

"We're dating," Kelly repeated. He knew he should probably just enjoy the news and keep his mouth shut, but that had never been one of his strengths. "Since when exactly?"

"Since our first date," William said. "When we played pool together. Right?"

"Sure!" Kelly nodded quickly. "Yeah! Of course!"

"Oh my god," William said, his face flushing.

Kelly laughed. "It would help if we had actually talked about it. Or if you had made a move sooner."

"I didn't want you to think that I thought you were easy!"

"Sounds like you were thinking a little too much." He paused. "Maybe we both were. So are we just dating, or are we boyfriends?"

William blinked. "What's the difference?"

"Boyfriends means being in a relationship. Dating means you're playing the field, trying to find the right person. There is no commitment."

"Boyfriends," William said firmly. "If that's okay with you. I know what I want."

"I know too," Kelly said, slinging his camera bag over one shoulder. "So, boyfriend, how do you feel about holding hands in public?"

"I've never tried it before," William admitted, reaching out to touch Kelly's fingers. "But don't worry, I've been told that I'm a fast learner."

They pulled into the driveway of Kelly's house, William shutting off the engine and remaining still. And silent, which was odd, since they'd done nothing but talk as they strolled along the Colorado River.

"Don't tell me you're nervous about the goodnight kiss," Kelly teased. "You've had plenty of practice tonight."

William flashed him a smile before growing more somber. "Am I supposed to come inside with you?"

"Uh, you can if you want, but I know for a fact that my mom will be loitering around the living room, hungry for details."

"Oh." William looked relieved.

"I could probably sneak you inside somehow," Kelly said, just to test the waters. Sure enough, William tensed up. Kelly allowed himself a half-smile. "Then again, we don't have to rush anything."

William glanced over at him and exhaled. "You've done all this before, haven't you?"

Kelly chewed his bottom lip before he answered. "I don't have any first times left, if that's what you mean. I hope that's okay."

"Yeah," William said quickly. "It's just that everything is new to me. I've never even kissed a girl before. I had a girlfriend once, but that was freshman year, and neither of us really had a clue. We were more like friends. Super-awkward friends with nothing in common. So I don't know what I'm doing, but if I go too slow—"

"There aren't any rules," Kelly interrupted. "Whatever works best for you. For us, really. We'll figure it out together. And if I go too fast, well, I warned you about that when we first met. No one in the school is faster than me."

William laughed. "I wish tomorrow was Saturday. I want to spend the whole weekend with you. Do you have any plans?"

"I do now."

"Awesome." William sighed wistfully. "Too bad we don't have the same lunch period. Or some of the same classes. Let's make sure we do next semester."

"Now who's moving too fast?" But to show he was teasing, Kelly unbuckled his seatbelt and leaned over for a kiss. His entire body reacted, enough that if William wanted to come inside or stay right here for a little action, he wouldn't have said no. When the kisses felt more like sweet torture, he pulled away.

"I'll see you tomorrow?" William asked.

"Yeah." Kelly considered him a moment. "You're the best birthday present I've ever gotten. Hey, that's a first! No one's given me a white boy as a present before."

William laughed. "You're crazy."

"Yup. And now you're stuck with me."

"Good."

William's tone left no room for doubt. What they had together, it was good.

Kelly sat down at the lunch table the next day, no longer fearing the ridicule of his teammates. Or how Jared would surely rub the triathlon victory in his face. He could bear all of this negativity and more, because having William changed everything. Kelly had won in a way he had never imagined possible. Even if no one else understood that, their relationship gave him strength.

For the most part, everyone acted glad to see him. Kelly was just starting to relax when Jared showed up, Martha still at his side. Only then did one member of the track team open his big mouth.

"Hey, Kelly, you want a pillow to sit on? I bet your ass is still sore from the whooping it took in the triathlon."

There were a few laughs, but they were soon cut short. By Jared.

"Shut up," he said, glowering at the others. "He ran a good race. Better than any of you could have. As usual."

Kelly tried to mask his surprise. When he nodded his appreciation, Jared nodded back before turning to Martha, who beamed at him like he was a hero. Jared started talking with her, not looking in Kelly's direction again. So they wouldn't be friends, it would seem, but they wouldn't be enemies either. He took some comfort in this, but mostly he felt saddened.

Of course now he had the perfect way of cheering himself up. He knew where to find William after lunch. Just as before, a couple of girls had him cornered outside his biology class, their eyes shining as they chatted away. Kelly felt uncertain as he approached. They hadn't yet discussed how they would behave in school or how open either of them was willing to be. William certainly didn't show any apprehension when he spotted Kelly. His face lit up, matching those of the girls around him. They turned, mildly confused as they looked for the girl who roused this reaction. They got their explanation when William stepped forward and reached out a hand. Kelly stared at it for a moment, concerned about the consequences and nearly dumbfounded by just how sweet a gesture it was.

How could he say no?

In the hallway that day, two guys took hold of each other's hands. They didn't shake them or arm wrestle or anything else that young men are expected to do. Instead they simply intertwined their fingers and looked into each other's eyes, the level of emotion apparent to every witness there. In this way, they came out to the entire school without uttering a single word.

Like a cup of coffee or a hot shower, William's smile was the perfect way to begin the day. Before school, Kelly would often open the front door to discover that smile waiting for him. Or if it was his turn to drive, he would cruise over to William's house, park in the driveway and sit on the hood of the car, casually waiting for it to appear. And there it would be. That smile, lighting up the world and making Kelly's insides buzz. He'd had boyfriends before and even thought he'd been in love once or twice. Now Kelly dismissed all those failed relationships because this was different—more than just a hot body and a tumble on the mattress. This was William who was sweet and kind and made everything better just by flashing those pretty white teeth.

And not just in the mornings. Occasionally William would surprise Kelly between classes, or Kelly would seek him out, and although these trysts would scarcely last more than a minute, they were always worth it, mainly because of that happy face. So after nearly a month of this, when the smile failed to appear one morning, Kelly was so startled that he stood up from the hood of his car and took a few steps forward. William's eyes rose to meet his, but the light there had been extinguished.

"You okay?" Kelly asked.

William nodded, heading for the car with urgency, as if trying to escape rain. Kelly hurried to the driver's side, looking at him for an answer once they were both inside and seated.

"Just drive," William instructed. "Please."

Kelly backed out into the street, noticing Mrs. Townson standing at the front door, her lips pressed together with concern. What was going on? They were halfway to school when Kelly decided he couldn't take it anymore. He pulled into a shopping center, parking the car in front of a flower store.

"What's going on?"

For a moment, William stared ahead at a window display of colorful bouquets. His attention remained glued on the flowers, even when he spoke. "I was coming down the stairs this morning when I heard my parents arguing. That's been pretty common lately, even though they try to hide it from me. This time I spied on them, and they were talking about—" He stopped, clenching his jaw.

Kelly reached over to take his hand.

William squeezed it, then said the rest with desperate haste, like ripping off an adhesive bandage. "My dad doesn't want me to live with him."

Kelly shook his head, not understanding.

"They're getting a divorce," William explained. "I didn't hear them say that, but what else could it be? My mom kept shouting that I deserved a choice, and at first I thought my dad wanted to take me away from her." William's voice squeaked. "But the truth is, he doesn't want me. Even if I begged to live with him, I don't think he'd agree."

Kelly struggled to find something to say, some soothing words, but this was too far outside his realm of expertise. His parents rarely argued, and when they did, it was over something stupid like his dad making a mess in the kitchen. His boyfriend was sitting in the passenger seat, fighting to hold back tears, and all Kelly could do was stroke his hand. "I'm sorry," he managed at last. "Maybe they got caught up in the heat of the moment. People say things that they—"

"My mom is picking me up from school. She and my dad want to talk to me."

"Did they say why?"

William shook his head.

Kelly leaned back in his seat. "Maybe they're only taking a break," he tried. "Separating so they can work through things, but not splitting up completely."

"Maybe."

Kelly exhaled. "Let's skip school. We can go back to my place. We'll have the house to ourselves, and we can talk about everything. Or we'll just watch TV. Whatever you need."

William shook his head. "I don't want to get in trouble."

"It's the last day before winter break," Kelly said. "No one will care. Tons of people don't show up. In situations like these, you need to take care of yourself. Give yourself time to think."

William looked tempted, but then he steeled his jaw. "Things are already bad enough. Let's go. We're going to be late."

Kelly turned away so he could covertly roll his eyes and started the car. William was always doing the right thing, especially if someone else needed help, but rarely did he do what was best for him. What William needed today was to take time out and come to terms with everything. And really, if his parents were getting a divorce, Kelly felt they would cut him a little slack.

"Are you sure?" he tried again. "We could hit the mall. I'll buy you lunch."

William just shook his head sullenly. Usually he brightened the day, but today he brought the clouds with him, and Kelly found them hanging over his head too. He took every opportunity to see William between classes, but of course nothing had changed. Only after school did his boyfriend appear slightly more optimistic.

"I bet you're right," he said. "It's only a separation. They need a break. They've been together since before I was born. Everyone needs a vacation now and then, right?"

William even tried to smile, but his mother pulled up then, chasing his hopes away.

"Text me," Kelly said. "As soon as you know something, text me."

William nodded wordlessly and went to meet his mother.

Kelly's own family had plans, like they always did on Friday nights. Lately he had been bailing on them, choosing to spend time with William instead. Now he wanted to be near them to make sure nothing had changed. His mother was always fond of choir music at this time of year, associating it with the upcoming holidays. This meant sitting in a cold church and listening to music that made Kelly grind his teeth. He made the best of it anyway, repeatedly looking to his mother and father, who held hands throughout most of the concert. When he wasn't watching them, Kelly was checking his cell phone, but he didn't hear a peep from William. Not until late that night when the house had fallen silent.

i need to see you

Okay, Kelly texted back. *Where?*

can I come over?

Kelly hesitated. He didn't have a strict curfew, so long as he didn't abuse his freedom. But his mother preferred a quiet house at night. Even when Jared used to sleep over, they had to keep it down past a certain hour. Then again, he could hardly abandon his boyfriend at a time like this.

Okay. Drive safe.

He sat on the edge of his bed, deciding the news couldn't be good. Otherwise, William would have texted him something cheerful before making plans for tomorrow. After enough time had passed, he went out to the driveway. A familiar car pulled up soon after. Kelly expected William to look downtrodden, but instead he glowered openly, as if angry with the world. Kelly even took a step back when William marched toward him. So much for his smiling saint. This was someone new.

"He's gone," William said, his voice much too loud. "The bastard took off while I was in school."

"Easy," Kelly said, glancing around. "Let's go to the backyard. And try to keep it down, okay?"

"Fine," William huffed.

He continued to do so as Kelly led him around to the gate in the privacy fence. Their property included a yard that could best be described as long and narrow. This was good, since it put distance between them and the house. They walked all the way to the end, where trees and bushes obscured the other properties from view. An old swing set rusted away in one corner. William headed for it and sat on one of the plastic seats. Kelly joined him, thinking of all the times he and Royal had competed to see who could soar highest.

"They're getting a divorce." William gripped the chains so tight that his knuckles lost color. "My dad's been cheating."

"Oh shit," Kelly said. "I'm sorry."

"It's not your fault," William snapped. "He's the one who needed some woman—some *girl* nearly my age—to make him feel young again. It's fucking pathetic! He didn't even have the guts to face me. He and my mom were supposed to talk it over with me after school. Remember what I heard this morning? How I should have a choice? I don't think my dad wants to be reminded that he has kids. I wouldn't want to live with him anyway. I hate him!"

William's voice cracked. He turned his head away.

Kelly struggled to find some sort of advice. "All you can do is be there for your mom."

"Yeah," William said. "I won't abandon her. And if my father thinks we're selling the house, he can forget it! He's not a part of this family anymore."

Kelly hesitated. "Has there been talk about any of that?"

William exhaled. "I don't know. My mom kept saying I shouldn't worry about it. She put on a brave face, which only made me more pissed at him. How could he do this to us?"

"I don't know," Kelly said. "I really don't."

He reached out a hand and placed it over William's, which still clung to the chain. The second their skin touched, William jerked away, standing up and walking a few paces. A void opened inside of Kelly. He felt vulnerable, like his heart was exposed to the chilly night air. "What's going on?" he asked as he stood.

William kept his back to him. "Don't you get it? My parents used to love each other. You never got to see it, but they were always kissing and saying romantic stuff, even though my brothers and I acted like it was gross. But it wasn't. My dad always made my mom laugh when she was in a bad mood, and she always took care of him. Just look at them now! Hell, look at your own parents because mine weren't so different once. And look at us, because even though everything is new, this is our future too. No one thinks of that when first starting out, but it happens. More often than not, relationships fall apart."

Kelly walked up behind William, about to touch him before hesitating and letting his arm drop. "I won't let that happen to us. No matter what."

William spun around, his face crumpled. "I don't want to be like them!" Then he grabbed hold of Kelly, squeezing him tight. Painfully so, but Kelly took it, because it felt better than when William had pulled away.

"Stay the night," Kelly murmured.

William stepped back, uncertainty in his eyes. For a moment Kelly thought he'd say his mother needed him, or something self-sacrificing like that, but instead he nodded. Kelly reached down to take one of William's hands and led them toward the house. The back door was still unlocked, but he paused before opening the sliding glass door.

"We have to be quiet. Even once we're in my room."

William nodded his understanding.

On the way up the stairs, Kelly pictured how the night might go. Should he try to cheer William up? Maybe with some online shopping or silly YouTube videos? He couldn't imagine either being effective. William probably needed a sympathetic ear. Kelly could listen, but he already knew he wouldn't have any advice. If their situations were reversed, Kelly would be freaking out right now, like his entire world was falling apart. Obviously William felt the same.

Once they were in Kelly's room, he shut the door behind them, wondering if he should have headed to the kitchen first. "Are you hungry?" he asked. "Or thirsty? We have—"

He was turning when William's lips mashed into his. Kelly needed little time to recover. He rested his back against the door as William kissed him and pressed their bodies together. This was nothing new. They had kissed in every way possible in marathon make-out sessions that left Kelly aching with desire. William always retreated in the end, not quite ready. Except now, he didn't let up. He pawed at the wall next to Kelly's head until he found the light switch. Then the room went dark, except for the cold glow of the computer monitor.

William dragged him backward toward the bed, and once there, he sat on the mattress and started working on Kelly's belt. And although Kelly had been fantasizing about this moment for weeks, he forced himself to pull away.

"Hold on," he said. "Is this what I think it is?"

William nodded, looking hungry.

"Okay," Kelly said. "Uh, just give me a second."

William crawled backward onto the bed, a thick bulge in his jeans. Kelly wanted nothing more than to unwrap it and— Wait, that wasn't true. He wanted one thing more or he'd be tearing open a denim flap right now. Forcing himself to concentrate, he went to the desk and fetched a lighter from one of the drawers. Then he walked around the room, lighting candles that were normally nothing more than decoration. Once this was completed, he returned to the desk and shut off the monitor. Now the room was cast in warmer light. He was wondering if he should put on some music, just in case they were overheard, when William spoke.

"Kelly. Please."

He glanced toward the bed. Nothing had changed. William's expression still spoke of pure need. Kelly had waited so long for this, but with the moment now here, he didn't want to rush it. He wanted to spend the entire night slowly undressing each other, savoring every inch of skin as it was revealed. With this idea in mind, he went to the end of the bed and knelt down.

"Shoes," he said, reaching for the laces.

"Oh," William said. "Sorry."

"Let me." Kelly untied and loosened both sets of laces before pulling off the shoes simultaneously. Then he removed his own before hobbling into bed on his knees. William pushed himself upright into the same position. They met in the middle, William's lips on his, hands reaching for the hem of Kelly's shirt. He allowed William to pull it off before returning the favor. Then they looked at each other, which was silly considering how often they'd been bare-chested together at the pool. Still, here in the candlelight, the shadows subtly moving across every curve, their bodies were made new again.

William was first to reach out, placing a palm flat against Kelly's chest before sliding it across to his ribs and down to his hips. Kelly shivered, letting the tips of his fingers touch William's nipples and quietly laughing with him when he reacted like it tickled. Then he allowed himself to feel those pecs with both hands. He had never understood when Jared used to point out big breasts at the mall. For Kelly they held no appeal, but here, faced with William's enviable physique, he understood. He wanted to stare at those pecs, to trace the outline of each. And he wanted to feel them pressed against his bare skin, so he brought their bodies close enough to do so. William wrapped his arms around Kelly and started kissing his neck, one hand supporting the back of his head, the other grabbing his ass and pulling him even closer.

Close enough that their crotches rubbed together, both radiating with heat. Kelly couldn't wait anymore.

"Lie on your back," he said.

William shook his head. Then, muscles tightening around him, Kelly found himself being flung onto the mattress. Now he was on *his* back, William huffing as he looked Kelly's body over. His attention settled on one spot, so Kelly flexed, his cock pressing against his jeans as if begging to get out. William took this as his cue, reaching again for Kelly's belt. No holding back. Once the leather was unbuckled and the jeans were unbuttoned, he grabbed the waistline—underwear included—and pulled down.

Kelly ignored his own nudity and watched William's expression instead. Hopefully he wasn't expecting certain stereotypes to be true, although Kelly felt fairly good about what he had. His cock was long and narrow. A previous boyfriend had nicknamed it The Lance. Kelly tended to be a little longer than most guys he'd been with, but it could be that William was expecting something huge, like a zucchini on steroids. Or maybe not, since he was practically drooling as he stared.

"You can do more than just look at it," Kelly suggested with a smirk.

William pulled his eyes away. "Naw, I'm done. This is as far as I want to go." Then he laughed at Kelly's expression. "Want to see mine?"

Kelly nodded eagerly. "Show me what you've got, white boy."

It must be something good, because William didn't look at all insecure. In fact, he appeared smug as he unbuttoned and unzipped his jeans. William was more careful with his own clothing, tugging down the jeans first so that the meaty outline of his cock could be seen straining against his cotton underwear. Hooking both thumbs in the elastic band, he playfully wiggled the fabric, lowering it a smidgeon at a time. Eventually there wasn't enough material left to contain him, and his cock flopped out completely. He was every bit as long as Kelly, but thick too. Just like the rest of him really—one more pale muscle to complement the rest.

"Bring that thing here," Kelly pleaded.

William hobbled forward on his knees. The second he was close enough, Kelly reached out his tongue to tease the head. William moved closer, allowing him to take it in his mouth. He moaned a few times, thrusting some, but mostly he didn't need to because Kelly was doing all the work. Then he pulled back suddenly.

"Uh," he said, cheeks flushing.

"Close already?" Kelly asked.

William's face grew even redder. "That's usually not a problem."

"I'll take it as a compliment," Kelly said. "Get back here."

"No," William said. "I want this to last."

Then he found something else to occupy himself with. After kicking off his jeans, William lay on his side and snuggled close to Kelly, resting his head on his stomach. Of course he wasn't interested in cuddling. Instead his head was turned downward as he traced a finger along Kelly's dick, starting with the tip of the head and working his way down to the base. Then he took hold of it and pumped. Kelly sighed in pleasure, caressing William's hair or reaching over to knead a strong deltoid.

William scooted down, and Kelly braced himself for teeth or gagging or a clumsy first effort. Instead he felt firm lips followed by wet warmth. William proceeded with caution, his tongue lolling against the head of his cock, or twirling around it like a French kiss. Then those lips would come together, massaging, pressing, caressing.

Competing desires coursed through Kelly. He wanted to pull William up, to kiss him for real as their bodies lurched against each other. He wanted William in his mouth again. He wanted William inside of him in other ways too. Instead he gave in to the pleasure, writhing on his back as William experimented, using his hand or taking Kelly as deep into his mouth as he could manage. Now it was Kelly who needed to pull away. He whispered a warning that William should stop, but this only seemed to encourage him. And why not? Kelly remembered his first time, how what he wanted most was to make another man come. If that was William's wish, it was all too easy to grant. One more final warning and Kelly's hips started bucking with each shot. Eventually he had to push William away because it felt too good.

William didn't let this discourage him. He rose to his knees again, hurrying back to where he'd been before. Kelly was happy to comply. He took that fat meat in his mouth and sucked as if his life depended on it. William had one hand on the back of his head, the other on his neck. His body tensed and he started thrusting, Kelly barely managing to breathe. Then he was swallowing, not once but twice. Obviously poor William hadn't taken care of business for a while. After some barely stifled groans, William pulled out and looked down at him with concern.

Kelly smiled reassuringly and reached out his arms. William eagerly fell into them, pulling Kelly as close as possible and holding him there. His breathing evened out, enough that he seemed to have fallen asleep. Eventually he released Kelly and propped himself up on one elbow. His features were sad as his eyes travelled over Kelly's naked body.

"We won't fall apart," William whispered. "Promise me."

"We won't," Kelly said. "I know we won't."

William exhaled through his nose. "You sound so certain."

"Because I love you." The feeling welled up inside of Kelly. "I love you and I'll never stop. That's all it takes."

William studied his face a moment before he nodded. Then he settled back down, pulling Kelly close so they were spooning against each other. His breathing deepened, the breaths further and further apart, but before he fell asleep completely, he murmured something into Kelly's ear.

"I love you too."

Chapter Seven

Kelly awoke the next morning, surprised to find William's arms still around him. Somewhere in the night they must have gotten cold, because they were under the blankets. He remembered stirring a few times, not used to having someone in bed so determined to hold him. He wondered if William would always be like this, or if it was an expression of his anxiety over crumbling relationships.

Kelly remained motionless with his eyes open, trying to figure out how to politely disentangle himself, when he decided to simply enjoy the sensation. He'd stay in bed until William was ready to get up. At least that was the plan. When Kelly heard the front door open and close a few times, he realized one of his parents must have noticed the extra car in the driveway.

He quickly squirmed out of William's embrace, waking him in the process. Kelly was throwing on yesterday's clothes when murmured words asked him what he was doing.

"Stay here," he answered. "I need to talk to my parents."

William sighed in response, perhaps remembering what had happened with his own. Kelly didn't have time to comfort him. The last thing he wanted was his mom or dad to knock on the door and see a naked man over his shoulder. He glanced back longingly on the way out, William covering his head with his arm before thinking better and using a pillow instead.

Kelly met his mother as she was coming up the stairs. The question she asked was so obvious that he almost mouthed along with her.

"Why is William's car in the driveway?"

"He spent the night." Before she could react, he added in a whisper. "His parents are getting a divorce."

"Oh, that's terrible!" She looked past him at the bedroom door. "Does his mother know where he is? She'll be worried sick."

"I'll make sure he calls her."

"Good. The poor thing. He must have gotten here late."

"Yeah. His dad took off yesterday, and William was with his mom most of the night, trying to comfort her."

"And then it was your turn," Laisha said, her tones sympathetic. "How is he?"

Kelly kept his answer simple. "Better."

"Do you think he'd like an omelet?"

Kelly grinned. "I'm sure he would, but you better make double for him. Wait until you see him eat. It's scary."

"I remember from your birthday!" She spared him another worried glance before turning to head back down the stairs.

"Mom," Kelly said to stop her. He checked that his bedroom door was still closed. "You and Dad are okay, right? You'd tell me if something was wrong?"

His mother looked up at him solemnly. "Honey, quite a few marriages fail. That's a sad fact. But your father and me, we're forever."

He smiled in response, then watched her mosey down the stairs.

Forever. She made it sound so beautiful, so possible. As he headed back to his bedroom to rouse a grumbling lump from sleep, he prayed that it was.

Accompanying William back to his house had seemed like a good idea at the time. Kelly wanted to show his support, and for William to see that he'd be there for him through thick and thin. What Kelly hadn't counted on was how stifling the environment would be. The home had always felt so cozy before, in a cluttered sort of way. Now—while there was no sign that Mr. Townson had taken anything with him—an absence hung in the air. Something was missing. Kelly felt he would have noticed, even if he hadn't known the truth.

Mrs. Townson was in the kitchen, making cookies while Christmas music played in the background, but the most wonderful time of the year felt anything but. She greeted her son with a hug, as she always did, thanking him for his text message. Then William announced his intent to shower and get changed. Kelly's instinct was to follow him up the stairs, but William had other plans.

"What's she going to think if I'm in the shower and you're upstairs with me?" he said in hushed tones.

Kelly raised an eyebrow. "That you're gay?"

"Ha ha," William deadpanned. "She's been awesome about all of that, but I don't want to push my luck. Even my brothers weren't allowed to have girls over to... You know."

"What?" Kelly asked innocently.

"Get frisky," William said. "Shut up," he added when he saw Kelly's smile. "Besides, you think you can keep an eye on her? Baking cookies first thing in the morning is weird, even for her. Please?"

"Okay."

Kelly reluctantly headed back to the kitchen and sat at the breakfast bar. Mrs. Townson gave him a half-smile before returning to work. He watched her for a moment as she transferred cookies from a baking sheet to a wire rack. Then he glanced around the house again, noticing the Christmas tree in one corner, ripe with presents at its base. He wondered how many had been for Mr. Townson, or were gifts from him. How could they possibly expect to have a nice holiday this year?

He looked back at Mrs. Townson, who had put another loaded cookie sheet into the oven and shut the door, leaning against the counter next to it.

Kelly tried to find a cheerful topic of conversation, but ignoring what was happening seemed disrespectful, as if it were of no consequence. So he didn't.

"I'm sorry," he said. "About everything."

Mrs. Townson nodded. "I honestly didn't see it coming. You think you know someone..."

"Yeah," Kelly said, barely able to relate. He supposed Jared had turned out to be a lot less cool than he'd hoped, but running out on your family—especially at this time of year—was completely different. The thought made him shake his head. "He could have waited."

"What do you mean?"

"Mr. Townson. He could have waited until after the holidays. That would have been the decent thing to do."

Mrs. Townson crossed her arms over her chest. "He didn't have a choice. He was caught. I followed him after work and saw him pick her up in that stupid car of his. As soon as she kissed him, I laid on the horn. You should have seen their faces. I think she bit his tongue and—" She shook her head. "Are you saying I should have waited until after Christmas to confront him?"

"No," Kelly said, trying to keep up. "I was just thinking about William. He's going to have a bad Christmas this year."

"*I'm* thinking of him too," Mrs. Townson said. "His father

being here wouldn't have made the holiday any happier. No doubt he would have found some excuse to sneak off in the middle of opening presents. Does that sound like a merry Christmas to you?"

Kelly had no idea why this kept coming back to him, but he was getting annoyed. "All I'm saying is that if I had kids, I would fake it. No matter what was going on between me and my partner, I'd pretend we were fine until Christmas was over."

Mrs. Townson scoffed. "You try being married to someone, giving birth to three of his children, and giving him twenty-five years of your life. You do all that, and *then* see how you feel when he cheats on you!"

Kelly felt confused and frustrated. He hadn't meant for the conversation to turn so sour. "I feel bad for William," he finished lamely. "That's all."

"So do I," Mrs. Townson said. Then she turned around and busied herself with her baking. She kept her back to him until William returned downstairs. Only when he joined her at the counter did her shoulders relax somewhat.

"Everything okay?" he asked, grabbing a cookie.

"Fine," his mother said. "Your brothers are coming over today. They don't know yet. I thought you could help me talk to them."

"Yeah," William said. "Of course."

"This is a family matter," she said pointedly.

"I know," William said. Then he turned to Kelly and shrugged helplessly.

That was his cue. "I should head home," Kelly said.

"Take some cookies with you." Mrs. Townson met his eye briefly, but didn't smile. "For your family."

"Thank you," he said.

He watched in silence as William picked out cookies and his mother packed them in Tupperware. Then she turned and handed it to him.

"I really am sorry," he said, not sure if he was apologizing for the conversation or for the divorce. Either way she nodded curtly.

Once they were outside, he felt like he could breathe again.

"I think she likes you," William said.

Kelly glanced over at him to see that he was serious.

"Yeah," Kelly said. "We get along great."

* * * * *

"PARTY!"

Whoever shouted this sounded somewhat desperate. Surveying what little of the house he could see, Kelly couldn't blame them. William's friends—one of the girls who had a transparent crush on him, even now—was throwing a New Year's Eve soiree. Kelly had been excited when William first told him about it. None of the track team guys had anything interesting going on, except for a plan to find a homeless man downtown who would be willing to buy them beer. Classy.

So Kelly had leapt at this opportunity. No parental supervision. The end of the year. One last wild night before the next school semester started. So much could go delightfully wrong. And yet, Kelly felt like he was in a family-friendly sitcom where nothing truly bad or interesting ever happened.

No beer, no cheap fruit-flavored booze, not even a Jell-O shot in sight. No heavy clouds of smoke from cigarettes or joints. At least the music was pumping, but William's friend had a thing for the eighties, making Kelly feel like he was trapped in the car with his parents. Or worse, since the dining room furniture had been shoved to one side so white people could lurch stiffly in what might have been an attempt to dance. But for the most part, everyone hung around the living room, engaging in conversations that could have taken place anywhere, even in a classroom.

Kelly stifled another yawn, watching as two girls held pencils to their mouths and pretended they were puffing on cigarettes. Naturally this made them both giggle. Suddenly, that booze-buying bum didn't sound so bad. He glanced over at William, who appeared perfectly content. He even smiled as he watched the proceedings. Of course this was the guy who rushed home after school every day for cookies and an episode of *Beast Wars*. Kelly tried to roll his eyes and ended up sighing. He was dating such a nerd, but damn was he adorable!

"Okay, everyone," said their hostess, nearly shaking with excitement as all heads turned toward her. "It's time to really start having fun!"

She had a bottle in her hand, which was encouraging, but as soon as Kelly saw it was empty, he knew what was coming.

"Spin the Bottle!"

Kelly glanced around the room, realizing there were about

three lassies to every lad. Several of those girls were looking in their direction. He met William's eye.

"Okay," Kelly said. "Time for us to take our leave."

"I don't want to go yet," William said. "It's almost midnight." After a girl across the room waved at him he added, "But maybe we could find somewhere a little more private."

Kelly grabbed his backpack, which held his camera and something that might rescue the evening. Then he followed William upstairs. He seemed to know where he was going. Down a hall and to the right, they entered a room that was— feminine. That about summed it up. Pinks and pale yellows. Lace curtains, bottles of perfume and a makeup mirror on a little vanity table. Next to that was a small television set, its edges decorated with glitter paint and tiny plastic jewels. Overall the room felt comfortable and nice, rather than utilitarian like Kelly's or even William's room. Sure, maybe Kelly decorated with photos and William had his toy display, but everything here felt carefully chosen and arranged.

"Is it wrong that I like this?" Kelly murmured.

"The room?" William chuckled. "I always wondered what it would be like to have a sister. You?"

Kelly shrugged. "Royal is enough trouble. I never wanted to double it." He walked over to examine the photos on the dresser, which were mostly girls clutching at each other and smiling. One was of a much younger William wearing a bowler hat and holding a banana to his ear like a phone. Kelly picked it up and looked over at him questioningly.

"I was in drama freshman year," he explained. "Wasn't really my thing, but we had a lot of fun."

"Not a bad photo." Kelly set it down and glanced around the room. This is where the year would end. He never would have chosen such an environment, but he was glad to have William to himself. The holidays had been spent waiting for him to be free again. The Townsons had pulled together over Christmas, the three brothers gathering around their mother as if to guard her from further harm. Endearing as that might be, it left little room for Kelly. Only tonight did they finally have substantial time together, and he intended to make the most of it.

Kelly switched on the lamps at either side of the bed—pastel sketches of sheep leaping across the shades—and turned off the overhead light. This created a much cozier ambiance. Then he opened his backpack and took out his camera, making room for it on the dresser. He fiddled with the settings for a moment and pointed it toward the center of the room. Then he pushed a button and left it behind.

"My mom gave us a present," Kelly said, reaching into the backpack and pulling out a bottle. Unlike the one downstairs, this was still sealed shut. "She made me promise we wouldn't drink it until we're home again."

"Is that champagne?" William asked, walking over to see. He took the bottle, turning it to read the label, but Kelly watched his face instead, his body reacting already. But it wasn't just hormones. He loved William. He really did. Every little detail drove him wild. The way his brow furrowed as he read, the way he nibbled on one corner of his lip as he examined the foil-wrapped cork.

click

William looked up. "What was that?"

"My camera," Kelly said. "It's set to take a photo every minute. Most of them will turn out blurry, but I thought it would be a fun experiment."

"Okay," William said, trying to hand back the bottle.

"Open it," Kelly insisted.

"But you said —"

"You've never broken a promise made to your mother? You know what, don't answer that. Just make with the bubbly."

William grinned, and for the next five minutes, they bickered over the right way to open it.

"Don't do it over the carpet!" Kelly insisted. "Foam will spray everywhere."

"That's why I plan on putting my mouth over it as soon as the cork pops," William replied.

"Ever tried that with a can of cola that's too shaken up? It'll come out your nose."

"Then you better hold two glasses to my nostrils."

"Gross! Wait, we don't have glasses at all."

In the end, they opened the bedroom window and took out the screen. The plan was to hold the bottle outside the window until the foam drained off. William looked like he was handling hazardous materials as he enacted this plan, his cheek against the top window pane as his outstretched arms worked blindly. Then came the *pop!* and they both went still.

"Well?" Kelly asked.

"It's not overflowing," William said. "Maybe it was flat already."

But a nice curl of fumes came from the bottle when William pulled it back inside. Over the muted sound of Duran Duran downstairs, Kelly could hear bursting bubbles.

"Should I go find cups?" William asked.

"We can slum it and drink directly from the bottle."

"Okay," William said. "You first."

He held out the bottle, but Kelly didn't take it. Instead he stepped closer. William caught on, lifting the bottle and carefully holding it to Kelly's lips. William tilted the bottle slowly, bit by bit, until golden sparkles poured into Kelly's mouth.

click

Then Kelly had to pull away, because his cheeks were filling up and his nose was tickling. He swallowed in one big gulp, covering his mouth just in case.

"How is it?" William asked.

"Good! Now your turn."

"Oh no!" William said, dodging away from him. "I'm not letting you hold the bottle. You'll make me drink way too much."

"I won't," Kelly insisted. "Trust me."

Of course when William handed him the bottle, Kelly did just that. William nearly sprayed champagne all over the room, but he managed to swallow it without too much dribbling out.

"You're cruel," William said, shaking his head.

"I know," Kelly said proudly, taking another swig.

The door to the bedroom opened then, in the frame a hopeful-looking guy with his arm around a girl's shoulders. "Whoa!" he said. "Sorry. Didn't know anyone was in here."

"It's fine," William said.

The guy looked between them a few times. "We were searching for somewhere private. The master bedroom is already taken. Uh."

"Oh!" William said. "We can leave."

click

Kelly rolled his eyes and went to the door. "Try the laundry room downstairs. Or maybe the hall closet." He shut the door so fast that the couple had to jump backward to avoid being hit. After pushing the lock on the knob for good measure, he turned around.

"I may be cruel, but you're way too nice!"

"They wanted to be alone," William said.

"And we don't?"

William's cheeks flushed. "Right. Sorry."

"It's fine," Kelly said. "What time is it?"

"Just a few more minutes." William sat on the end of the bed, eyes unfocused. "What a shit year. I'll be glad when it's over."

Kelly sat down next to him. "It wasn't all bad. Was it?"

"No. It would have been one of the best. I met you. Then I came out, and it's like no one even cares. Except..."

Kelly nudged against him. "Don't worry about the name-calling at school. It's just random assholes."

"It's not that," William said. "I'm not sure if my mom is okay with it. Every time I mention your name, she kind of makes this face."

click

"Oh," Kelly said. "I'm sure she's okay with you. She and I just need to get to know each other better. Besides, she's probably worried you'll get hurt like she did."

"You think so?"

"Yeah," Kelly said, wishing it were that simple. Eventually he'd have to try to smooth things over, but right now he didn't want to dwell on the past. "So tell me about next year. What's going to happen?"

"You want me to make a prediction?"

"Sure," Kelly said.

William thought about it. "Everything's going to be perfect."

"Really?"

"Yeah. No more heartbreak. Not for my mom, not for us, not for anyone. And then... Vegas."

"Vegas?" Kelly asked.

"Yup. We fall so madly in love that by the time the school year is over, we head down to Vegas to get hitched."

"Wow," Kelly said. "Are you proposing to me?"

"Not yet," William said, "but give me another swig from that bottle and we'll see what happens."

Kelly laughed and handed it to him. A moment later, shouting came from downstairs. Outside the open window, someone started banging a pan. Two thousand eight had arrived. They looked at each other in surprise, William's eyes searching his. Then he leaned over, and with lips tasting of champagne, he gave Kelly his first kiss of the year.

click

"He's so… nice."

Bonnie placed her feet on a plastic chair, popped the last bite of a homemade brownie into her mouth, and considered him. "You say that like it's a cussword. *Nice.*"

"I'm simply stating the facts," Kelly insisted.

"And is his niceness the reason he's not here?"

"Sort of."

The gay youth meetings had descended into chaos lately. Phil, their group leader, hadn't shown up today. This happened on occasion when he was ill or some other emergency cropped up, but now he had missed three consecutive meetings. For better or worse, they were on their own. Kelly enjoyed it, since all they did was get together to socialize. William missed the structure and wasn't as eager to attend anymore.

"I've mentioned that Royal is totally crazy about him, right?" Kelly said. "Now he's decided he wants to be in the Coast Guard too, and today in Galveston they're having some sort of open house. On a boat. Or maybe an aircraft carrier. I don't know, but guess where my boyfriend is. He's driving Royal down there so he can see it."

"That bastard," Bonnie said without emotion.

"He's taking a road trip," Kelly stressed. "Without me."

"You couldn't go?"

"It wouldn't have been romantic with my little brother tagging along."

"I guess not." Bonnie shrugged. "Maybe the break will do you both good. Carpooling to school, classes together, a shared lunch period, and gee, what do you do after school?"

"Hang out."

"Together. Just you and him. No one else. That's pretty intense. I don't remember the last time you and I did anything."

"Sorry," Kelly said.

"I get it," Bonnie said. "I know what it's like to be in love.

But moderation and all that. Eat too much candy and you'll end up sick."

"Maybe you're right."

Bonnie put her hands behind her head and leaned back. "You should be happy. Most couples who spend that much time together argue nonstop. Sounds like you guys get along."

"We bicker," Kelly admitted. "Usually over stupid stuff. Like on Valentine's Day. We went out to dinner together and were halfway through the meal when the waiter asked if we could hurry up. I'd been saving my allowance for weeks! I made that reservation a month in advance too. The stupid waiter didn't want us to finish our food."

"Fuck that," Bonnie said.

"Exactly! It was supposed to be our big romantic night out. I got pissed and told the waiter that not only were we still eating, but we were planning on having a leisurely dessert afterwards. Of course William got all flustered and acted like I was being offensive. Then he ate even faster than usual and insisted he was full. He's *never* full. So no dessert. Just a rushed meal. Super-expensive fast food. When I suggested we shouldn't tip the waiter, he looked at me like I was being unreasonable."

Bonnie scrunched up her face. "Okay, so maybe that's a little too nice. But it's still better than him being a jerk. Would you rather William had leapt up from the table and put the waiter in a headlock?"

Kelly thought it about it carefully. "Yes. I would have liked that very much."

Bonnie laughed. "You'll be fine. Opposites attract."

"I suppose. I just wish we hadn't spent the rest of the night arguing about it. Definitely not a romantic Valentine's Day."

They noticed then that the youth group had quieted down. An adult had entered the room, one wearing a flannel shirt and round glasses. With his medium-length hair, the guy could have been a John Denver impersonator. "Settle down now, everyone."

Kelly and Bonnie exchanged glances. The party was over.

"My name is Keith, and I'll be leading these group meetings from now on. I've been asked not to talk about what happened to Phil, the previous group leader, but I feel that being open and honest is important. As you may have heard, Phil was asked to step down because he engaged in inappropriate conduct."

"You mean kinky sex?" Bonnie asked.

Keith reconsidered his words. "More of an inappropriate relationship."

"Wait," Kelly said. "Wasn't he married? He talked about going to Massachusetts with his husband just so they could get hitched."

"That's true," Keith said, adjusting his glasses nervously. "I don't want to go into details, but I thought you should know the general reason."

The room was silent. "What do we care if he cheated?" Bonnie said. "Has nothing to do with us."

"Unless one of us helped him cheat," Kelly said, meaning it as a joke.

In the corner of the room, Layne started coughing, waving away any offers of help. When he recovered, he tittered nervously, unable to make eye contact.

"And now we know," Kelly murmured.

"Anyway," Keith said, "with that out of the way, I'm afraid there will be other changes too. Meetings will now be biweekly—" A mixture of groaning and jokes interrupted him. "—but this will also free up the budget to allow activities outside the church. For the remainder of today's meeting, I thought we could discuss some of those possibilities."

Kelly rolled his eyes and tuned out the rest of the lecture. Or tried to. Bonnie seemed genuinely interested, even raising her hand when Keith solicited ideas.

"A camping trip," she said.

"I do love pitching a tent!" Layne chimed in. "With people my own age, of course. Um."

Other members of the group latched on to Bonnie's idea. Kelly shot her a glare, as if she had betrayed him.

"What?" she said. "It'll be fun. Just think about sharing a tent—and a sleeping bag—with William."

Kelly blinked a few times. Then his hand shot up. "Camping sounds good to me!"

Mosquitoes or the ghastly chemical smell that kept them at bay? Not the best of choices. Kelly slapped his arm, deciding that if he weren't hoping for action tonight, he would have gladly dunked himself in skunk spray to avoid any more insect bites.

He just hoped all this suffering would be worth it. He glanced over at William, who was still trying to get the campfire going. The sun hadn't gone down yet, but he insisted it would be easier to start now rather than fumbling around in the dark.

"You wouldn't believe how romantic he is," Layne was saying to a captive audience. His forbidden relationship with Phil was common knowledge now, but he'd been tight-lipped about the details. Until tonight. With Keith having wandered off to gather firewood, Layne was taking the opportunity spill the details. "I never would have guessed he has a foot fetish. That's sort of weird, but whatever. He sure knows how to make a guy feel special. Once Phil moves out of his mother's place, he says we can live together."

"You're sixteen," Kelly pointed out.

"So? That's legal in most states. I can't help it if Texas is so prudish."

"He's forty years old," Kelly said next.

"Thirty-nine," Layne corrected. "And you're just jealous that I have a lover with so much experience."

"Congratulations," Kelly said, "but you guys don't have anything in common. You can't."

"Leave him alone," William said.

Kelly ignored him. He knew Layne well enough to know he could handle a little teasing. "What do you talk about when you're not shoving your feet in his face or whatever?"

Layne pursed his lips. "He's going through a midlife crisis and wishes he could be a teenager again. I *am* a teenager, and I want school to be over so my adult life can begin. We spend a lot of time comparing notes."

"And other things, no doubt," Bonnie said. She had her arm around Shirley, a skinny new arrival with big teeth and probing eyes. The black makeup she wore only drew more attention to these features. Kelly supposed she was pretty, in an alien sort of way.

Layne considered them one by one. "You can't tell me none of you have lusted after an older man. Or woman. Come on! No hot teachers? No friend of the family who always wants you to sit on their lap?"

"You're horrible," Lisa said, covering her mouth.

"He's honest," Bonnie corrected. "And yes, there was

someone. My boss at my first job. She was nearly fifty. Of course I didn't know that at the time. She could have passed for twenty, I swear, and she totally fed into that. I didn't find out her real age until—"

Kelly slapped at his neck. Deciding he'd had enough, he stood and headed for his tent. Maybe once the fire was blazing, the smoke would drive away the mosquitoes. Until then, he would take sanctuary inside aluminum poles swathed in cheap nylon. Once inside, he zipped shut the entrance flap and surveyed their weekend paradise. The tent had enough room for two sleeping bags, a cooler filled with ice and drinks, and their backpacks, which contained a change of clothes and toiletries. And in Kelly's case, a little bit more, just in case things went further than before.

Flopping onto a sleeping bag, he reached for his cell phone before remembering it was still in the car. He spotted William's and swiped it, typing in the password and checking reception. One meager little bar connected them to civilization. Maybe it would be enough for some surfing. He opened the web browser, finding it on the page William had been viewing last. Google Maps. Nothing interesting. Kelly was about to head over to his Flikr account when he noticed the address. It wasn't just familiar. He knew it by heart because he'd been there himself. Countless times.

Jared's house. Why would William need to know where Jared lived? Kelly forced himself to stay calm and consider the possibilities. An affair? That was laughable. Kelly may have once deluded himself into thinking Jared was gay, but he harbored no such illusions now. Maybe William loved Kelly so much that he felt driven to pick a fight with Jared. But no, he was much too kind for anything like that.

Kelly wracked his brain but couldn't think of a single reason why William would need Jared's address. Not one. William's text messages and email revealed nothing. Finally, he got up and unzipped the tent. Keith had returned, the fire was nearing a roar, but Kelly had no intention of rejoining his friends.

"Darling?" he said. "Could you step inside for a moment?"

"Got a hankering for some hanky-pankering?" Layne asked. "No doubt my stories got you all riled up."

"That's right," Kelly said. "William, get in here so I can suck your toes."

He smiled at the laughs this summoned, but as soon as William was in the tent and the flap zipped shut, he became serious. "I didn't mean to snoop," he said, holding up the phone. "I was just trying to... What is this?"

William, sitting on his knees, peered at the screen before realization dawned. "Oh."

"Oh?" Kelly repeated.

William sighed. "I don't want to have another argument. This is supposed to be our special weekend together."

"No one is arguing!" Kelly said, his voice rising. Then he forced himself to take a deep breath. "I just want to know why you were looking up the address of someone who— Ugh. Forget it."

"Someone who what?" William asked, crossing his arms over his chest. "Broke your heart?"

Kelly gritted his teeth. "Someone who hurt me. And don't tell me you're still jealous of him!"

William sighed and let his arms drop. "He's in my sociology class."

"Since when?"

"The beginning of the semester. Ever since we changed our classes around. You know, so I could spend more time with my boyfriend and eat lunch with him every day." William offered a smile. "Remember that?"

"Yes," Kelly said, feeling a little better. "So why didn't you tell me?"

"Because I knew it would upset you."

"Damn right," Kelly said, but he did so softly. Crisis averted. Almost. "I still don't get why you have his address."

"We were assigned to work together on a project."

"So you had to meet after school? That must have been awkward."

William broke eye contact.

"What? Tell me."

"You were friends with him for a reason, right? He's a likable guy."

Kelly's jaw dropped. "Are you telling me that you're *friends* with him?"

"We talked a lot while working on the project. His grandfather was in the Coast Guard, and they still have a lot of his things so—"

"Are you kidding me? The fucking Coast Guard is your excuse?"

"No!" William said. "I don't need an excuse. He's a nice guy and we hung out. Don't act like that's a bad thing because you were his friend once too!"

"Yeah, before he made racist and homophobic comments. Has he mentioned that?"

"We don't talk about you," William said. "He started to once, but I felt it would be disrespectful, like talking behind your back."

"Disrespectful is sneaking around to hang out with someone I—"

"Still love?" William interrupted. "I know."

"No," Kelly said, jaw clenching. "That's not how I feel at all. And for someone you think I still love, you sure seem eager to spend time with him."

"I honestly don't think about it. When I hang out with Jared, everything is normal. It's only when you overreact like this that I wonder."

"Wonder what? That I don't love you?"

William shook his head reluctantly. "I don't know."

Kelly stared at him. "I get upset about you hanging out with a former friend, and that somehow equals me not loving you anymore. Great! That makes perfect sense! So what does not taking my feelings into consideration when hanging out with your new buddy mean?"

"This is exactly why I didn't tell you." William looked skyward in exasperation, head still shaking. "I totally saw this coming."

"Saw what coming?"

"This!" William gestured around them. "We're supposed to be having fun here, but instead you're freaking out. Lately all I seem to do is piss you off. And you know what? I'm sick of it! Maybe I shouldn't be around at all!"

Kelly was so shocked by this declaration that he couldn't think of anything to say. He found no words to stop William as he unzipped the tent and left. All he could do was sit and wonder if he'd just ruined everything.

Chapter Eight

Right or wrong? Kelly couldn't decide. He sat in his tent, changing his opinion so many times it made him dizzy. On one hand, he was hurt. William had known being friends with Jared would upset him, and he'd gone and done so anyway. Why? Because Jared was nice? Because he had some old Coast Guard medals or uniforms? There wasn't a good enough reason.

On the other hand, so what? Kelly wished he didn't care. He really did. Logically it shouldn't matter anymore. Jared was likable—or had been until the end. Even now he remained civil to Kelly during track meets. No homophobic jibes, no more flaunting his girlfriend. He knew about Kelly's relationship with William. The entire school knew. And yet Jared had still been okay with hanging out with William—hanging out with a gay guy—after school. Just not with Kelly.

That hurt.

Unless Jared had seen the error of his ways. Maybe he was trying to show Kelly they could be friends again. Or maybe this was all a big middle finger. Why was it okay for Jared to be around William but not him? Because of the feelings Kelly had once confessed?

Either possibility made him miserable. Kelly didn't want to be Jared's friend. Even after all this time, even with a handsome boyfriend who was wonderful and kind, the idea that they would be friends and nothing more still made him ache inside. What did that say about him? Or his feelings for William?

And yet he knew he loved William. He absolutely *knew* it. That's why they argued so much. Even the smallest thing that William did seemed hugely important. The littlest phrase or tiniest action had overwhelming significance because William meant so much to him. Kelly loved him, and he hated that a one-sided romance had returned from the grave to ruin what they had together. If only he could let go of the hurt, release all the anger he still felt when he thought about Jared. At times it seemed like he already had. Usually Kelly felt at peace, but William's new friendship had stirred things up again.

He had to find a way of fixing this. Losing William would leave him empty, hollowing out his heart. Kelly stepped outside the tent. Night had fallen. Not far away, hot dogs and marshmallows were roasting on sticks. A number of eyes turned to him. He looked at each, hoping to find a pair familiar and green.

"Want to bite my wiener?" Layne asked.

Kelly ignored him. "Has anyone seen William?"

"He headed for the woods," Bonnie said. "Looked pretty mad. That was awhile ago."

"But it's dark out." Kelly glanced toward the edge of the trees where everything faded to black.

"I think he borrowed some stuff from Keith," Layne said. "Supplies of some sort."

"Like he's going to camp in the woods alone?"

"No idea." Layne shrugged helplessly. "Sorry!"

Kelly rushed off to find their group leader, catching him leaving his tent with a guitar in hand.

"Everything all right?" he asked when he saw Kelly's panicked expression.

"William isn't back yet."

"From fishing?" Keith asked.

Of course! Kelly headed for the lake without answering him, soon wishing he'd brought a flashlight along. The night was dark, without even the moon to light his way. A shiver ran down his spine as something scurried through the underbrush to his right, like a bad horror movie come to life. He felt calmer when the trees opened up again, the lake ahead tranquil and quiet except for the gentle lapping of water. A silhouette sat on the dock, the shape of those strong shoulders instantly recognizable. Kelly hurried forward, his footsteps on the old wood causing William's head to rise. But he didn't turn around. Kelly hesitated as he neared.

"Catch anything?" he asked.

William didn't respond.

"Come back to the campsite," Kelly said. "It's getting cold."

"Are we pretending it didn't happen?" William asked.

"What?"

"The argument."

"No," Kelly said. "We can talk about it." He sat down, realizing the conversation was going to happen here or nowhere at all.

William continued to concentrate on the water. "Do you even like me?" he asked.

"I love you!"

"Yeah, but do you like me? Because I'm pretty sure they aren't the same thing."

Kelly shook his head. "I don't understand."

"The Coast Guard stuff," William said. "You always act like it's a waste of time or—"

"I was upset that it made you want to hang out with Jared!"

"I told you that wasn't the only reason. He's nice. He might have been a dick to you, but he's nice to me. And what about when I took your brother down to Galveston? You didn't even come along."

"I was pouting because I wanted to be alone with you." Kelly sighed. "I'm fine with you wanting to join the Coast Guard."

"It's not just that. Sometimes I get the impression that you think I'm weak. Just because I don't tackle anyone the second they give me trouble doesn't make me weak. I can take a lot, and yeah, sometimes I let people push me. I believe in second chances, sometimes even more. But when people push me too far…"

The sentence hung unfinished on the air. Suddenly Kelly wished very much for the amiable version of William to reappear.

"We're different," Kelly said. "But I don't think that's a bad thing. We're still getting used to each other. Sometimes I wish I was more like you. I can't keep my cool. I don't know how you do it. I don't think you're weak. I just don't understand your strength."

William was silent. Kelly didn't know what else to say. They sat side by side, staring out across the lake. Eventually Kelly's nose felt frozen, his stomach grumbling.

"Come back to the campsite," he tried again.

William shook his head. "I need to think."

"For how long?"

"I don't know."

Kelly held back another sigh. William was rarely in a bad mood, but when he slid into one, he got stuck in deep. "I'll give you your space. I don't want to, because I love you. *And* I like you. But if you need space, I understand."

William didn't respond. Kelly stood and trudged back to the campsite, no longer worried about monsters lurking in the trees. Let werewolves bite his flesh, let zombies grope for his brains, and let vampires lust for his blood. None of them were as scary as the idea of losing William.

* * * * *

Kelly lay on his back in the sleeping bag, staring upward. The campsite had gone quiet. He didn't know how late it was, but William should have returned by now. He alternated between wondering if he was out there freezing, or if he had driven home alone. When the tent zipper slowly travelled along its path, he sat up, nearly reaching out when he saw William's form.

"Are you okay?" he asked.

"Yeah," William answered, his voice gentle again.

"You can be friends with Jared," Kelly said quickly. "I don't care."

William stepped into the tent, zipping the flap closed again. "Yes you do."

"Maybe, but I'd rather you be friends with him than— I don't want to lose you."

"I don't want to lose you either," William said. He crawled over to where Kelly was, bringing their faces close together. "I'm sorry. I knew it would hurt you and I did it anyway."

Kelly shrugged. "That's the price of love, I guess. We'll hurt each other occasionally, but the good times outweigh the bad. At least I think so. I hope you do too."

"Definitely," William said, pecking him on the lips. "Now scoot over because I'm cold."

Kelly unzipped the sleeping bag for him while William got out of his shoes. Then he scrambled inside, Kelly rolling over so William could hold him.

"You should be holding me," William complained teasingly. "I'm the one who's freezing."

"Which is why you need to cuddle up with something nice and hot. Like me."

"Ha."

William wrapped an arm around him, pulling him close. It wasn't long before the temperature had risen considerably. Kelly casually moved his rump, feeling William's hardness pressing against him. That was good. Sometimes when emotions were unreliable, physical intimacy was needed to bring estranged hearts together again. Their thoughts must have been running along a similar course, because the moment Kelly rolled over, William's lips were on his.

They threw open the sleeping bag, struggling to get their

clothes off so their skin could touch. Rolling back and forth, they kissed and pawed at each other. Once William was on top, he began grinding his hips against Kelly. Finally! He had wanted this for months, but felt it best to let William take things at his own pace. Now seemed to be the right time. After coming so close to losing each other, the moment couldn't be more perfect.

"Hold on," Kelly said, reaching for his backpack. He dug inside until he found a miniature bottle of lube. He hesitated, thinking of the condom, but he'd been getting tested every six months since his first time. William hadn't been with anyone else, so they should be okay.

"What's that?" William asked.

"It'll help things go smoother," Kelly said.

"Oh. Uh…" William's features crinkled with concern. "How do we decide who—"

"Don't worry," Kelly said with a chuckle. "I know my place. In bed, at least."

William still looked conflicted, but that was probably just first-time jitters. They would take things slowly. Hell, it had been so long for Kelly that he had no choice. He made it as playful as possible, spreading lube on two of William's fingers before moving his hand downward. Sweet William was back, since he kept asking if he was hurting Kelly. The best way of reassuring him was to moan, even though this would cause plenty of amused commentary at breakfast tomorrow. If they were going to be overheard, Kelly intended to give them something worth talking about.

"Come here," he said, pulling William close. Holding on tight, he forced him to roll over, so that Kelly was on top.

"I'm confused," William said. "I thought you wanted me to—"

"I do, but this makes things easier on me, and you're not going to be so easy to take. Once we get going, you'll be able to do whatever you want."

William stared up at him. Kelly watched his face the entire time. The way his eyelids fluttered in pleasure once he was inside, how his breath became shallow as Kelly gyrated his hips, and most of all the realization that this was something completely different from what they had done before. In a physical sense, that was obvious, but the connection that had grown weak and weary

was now revitalized and strengthened. Maybe more than ever
before, because when Kelly rolled over onto his back, clutching
William to him as his thrusts intensified, that connection blazed
with light. Their love was safe, rescued by an act that intertwined
their souls together once more.

"Hello, Mrs. Townson. You look lovely today! So lovely that I
wish I was ten years older. And straight." Kelly hoped the flattery
came across as friendly, and not sarcastic.

Mrs. Townson seemed in high spirits today because she
smiled. "Try twenty years older," she said. "It's your lucky day
though because I happen to have a son your age. I believe he's
waiting for you." She stepped aside so he could enter.

"Thanks," he said. Then in more serious tones, "You really
do look nice."

"I've been working out back in the garden. It must be the
sun."

"You actually tan," Kelly noted. "William only burns."

"He gets that from his father." Her features tensed a little, but
it was clear that she was doing better. She hadn't started dating,
but William said she had found a new rhythm and was moving
forward. "Willy is upstairs."

"Thanks," Kelly said, adjusting his backpack. It felt odd
to be carrying it on a Saturday. No school today, but what the
backpack held was of much greater importance than textbooks.
Kelly's heart began to race on his way up the stairs, and not
from exertion. Today was special. So far he had kept the date to
himself, hoping William hadn't realized. Kelly wanted him to
be surprised.

Six months. The time had flown by. They were doing well too.
Sure they still bickered, but he knew now that William had a low
threshold for such things. Since the camping trip, when they'd
come so close to losing each other, Kelly tried hard to rein back
on his temper. They'd been given a second chance, and since then
it had been one long honeymoon. For him, at least. He could only
hope William felt the same.

Taking a deep breath, he opened the bedroom door without
knocking. William froze in the middle of getting dressed. A
crumpled tank top lay on the bed, the shirt he was putting on a
navy button-up. They had picked it out together, Kelly trying to

wean him off the polos William was so fond of. Even with the shirt hanging open and lose on his shoulders, he looked sharp. Did that mean he knew the day was significant?

"You're early," William said, shrugging the shirt the rest of the way on and fondling the buttons.

Kelly was tempted to ask him to leave it off, at least for a little while. "I'm not early. I said I'd pick you up before dinner."

"It's only five," William said, looking at the clock.

"Which is before dinner," Kelly replied. "If I'm early, it's because I wanted to give you this."

From out of the backpack, he took a wrapped present. He had found it at the store by complete coincidence. Royal had dragged him down the toy aisle, and once it caught his eye, Kelly knew it was the ideal way of showing his support for William's interests. In more than one way. Now he felt less certain.

"What's the occasion?" William asked, looking apprehensive.

"There doesn't need to be one," Kelly said. "I like showering my men with gifts. I also like showering with my men. Ha ha. Um."

He sat on the edge of the bed, William doing the same. Then he watched William carefully unwrap the present by peeling back the tape and unfolding the paper. Kelly felt like leaping forward to tear off the rest for him, just to get it over with. Eventually though, the toy was revealed.

"It's not an animal," Kelly said. "But I thought... Well, it's a Transformer and—"

"It's a Coast Guard helicopter!" William nearly shouted. "This is a Eurocopter Dauphin! An AS365!"

Kelly chuckled. "I'll take your word for it."

"Holy shit!" William said. "I didn't even know they made something like this!"

Kelly felt relieved. "I figured it's two of your hobbies rolled up into one. I know it doesn't match the rest of your collection."

"I love it," William said. Then he leaned over and kissed him. "I love you!"

"I'm glad to hear it. Now open it up. The helicopter mode has a little hook on a string that you can use to rescue drowning people."

He watched William free the toy from its packaging, looking very much like a kid on Christmas morning. While transforming the toy into robot mode, William gave him an enthusiastic lecture about the real-life helicopter and all the different ways it was used to save lives. His eyes were positively shining as he played with each gimmick.

"This is amazing," he said. "I want to do something like this for you too."

"Do they make a camera that transforms into an Olympic runner?" Kelly joked.

"I'm serious. Sometimes I don't feel like I deserve you."

"I know the feeling," Kelly said softly. "Just be my date tonight. That's already more than enough."

"Okay," William said, standing and making room for the new toy on his shelf. "But I'm paying."

"Good, because I booked the most expensive restaurant in town."

In truth they didn't have a reservation. Kelly still felt burned by Valentine's Day, so they decided where to eat impulsively. They chose a grill downtown, which was perfect because it wasn't far from their next destination. Once they were finished with dinner, Kelly drove them a little farther, parking the car on the opposite side of the Colorado River to maintain the surprise.

"Why do you have your backpack?" William asked as they strolled.

"You'll see," Kelly said.

William glanced around, searching for clues. As they were rounding the corner, just before the landmark came into view, he figured it out.

"The Pfluger Bridge!"

"Gesundheit," Kelly said with a smile.

William glanced over at him, mind working. "That's where we had our first kiss."

"Is it?" Kelly said innocently. "I must have forgotten."

"Don't play coy," William said, reaching over to take his hand. "You're just an old romantic. Admit it."

"You have no idea."

They ambled along the bridge, grinning goofily at each other, stopping when they came to the place where they first kissed. William moved in to reenact the moment.

"Not so fast," Kelly said, sidestepping him. "First you have to answer a trivia question."

"Seriously?"

"Yup. How long have we been together now?"

William's jaw dropped. "Six months?"

"To the day," Kelly said.

William's smile faltered. "Wait, I thought it was early November. We played pool together. Remember?"

Kelly rolled his eyes. "We weren't together then. I wasn't even sure it was a date."

"It was to me," William said.

"You can't date someone without their knowledge," Kelly countered. "I didn't know you liked me until we were standing right here. So it's six months ago today."

"Six and a half?" William said, like he was haggling.

"It'll be a miracle if we make it to seven," Kelly said with a sigh. "Now be quiet and let me work my magic."

From out of his backpack, he pulled a bottle of champagne the same size and brand as the one they had shared on New Year's Eve.

"Now you're going to tell me we weren't official until New Year's," William teased.

"Don't start," Kelly said. "Tonight is about celebrating our entire relationship. All the highlights that have made it special so far. Can you guess what we'll be reenacting later on?"

"You have a collapsible tent in that backpack?" William asked with a grin.

"Exactly. And no, I don't, but this time I remembered to bring glasses." They were plastic and disposable, but that was okay. He still had to drive, so he wouldn't be having more than a sip or two.

"I can't believe your mom buys you this stuff," William said as he took the bottle to open it.

"Begging was involved. My parents don't mind me drinking, as long as I only do so at home and I don't leave after I've started. It's only on special occasions really. If I asked them to buy me a six pack every week, there's no way they would."

"Might be worth a shot anyway," William joked. When the cork popped, they watched it soar into the air before it plopped into the river below. "I wonder where it'll end up?"

"Probably in our drinking water. Speaking of which, I'm parched."

"Coming right up." William tilted the bottle while Kelly held the plastic flutes. Then he set the bottle on the ground.

Kelly handed William his drink and recited the toast he'd been practicing for a week. "May six months turn into six years, and six years into six decades. You've made me incredibly happy, and I can't wait until—"

"Gentlemen?" a voice interrupted. "I'm going to need to see some ID."

Kelly froze in shock. Then he turned to find a police officer standing behind them. Of course they shouldn't be drinking in public, but they were in the middle of a pedestrian bridge. It's not like patrol cars were cruising by every few minutes.

"Now!" the officer said, mustache bristling.

William had already set down his flute and had his wallet out. Kelly didn't move.

"We didn't actually drink any," he said.

"I'm still going to need to see identification," the officer responded, sounding unimpressed.

Kelly rolled his eyes, set his glass next to William's, and got out his driver's license. He watched impatiently as the officer examined both IDs and stated the obvious. "Neither of you are old enough to drink."

"Busted," Kelly said. "So it's a good thing we didn't drink."

"You're also not old enough to possess alcohol, especially an open container."

"My parents bought it for me," Kelly said. "That makes it legal. Texas law."

The officer's eyes narrowed. "The law says a parent can buy their child a drink so long as it's consumed in their presence. *That's* the law." He grabbed the radio on his shoulder and said a few codes into it that sounded like gibberish. Then he looked back at them. "I'll need you both to come with me."

Kelly stared in disbelief, temper rising. "We didn't drink anything!"

"Kelly," William said warningly.

"What? My parents bought this for us." He faced the officer again. "I'm supposed to drink it in their custody? Fine! I'll go home and do so. Or take it away from us and I'll drink with my parents some other time. But we didn't do anything wrong, so there's no fucking way I'm going anywhere with you!"

A tense moment of silence followed. The officer seemed to be sizing him up, maybe wondering if he needed to break out the pepper spray or something. All Kelly knew was that if he did, he'd take his ass to court over it.

"You're only making it worse."

Kelly wished, more than anything, that these words had come from the police officer. But they hadn't. William had spoken them instead.

"I don't want to handcuff you," the officer said, "but I think it's for the best. Turn around."

"You're kidding me," Kelly said.

"Turn around!"

William had already done so. Sighing, Kelly did the same, tempted to jump into the river rather than let the metal close around his wrists.

"It'll be okay," William whispered. "They'll call our parents and it'll all get sorted out. Like you said, we didn't drink anything." Then louder, he added, "Can you give us breathalyzer tests please? We want it on record that we haven't consumed any alcohol."

"I'll be glad to," the officer said. "Thank you for cooperating."

This of course was only directed at William. As Kelly heard the cuffs click shut and felt their heavy weight, he realized he had lost his freedom.

The concrete walls were white, repainted so many times that they looked more like frosting covering a cake than barriers meant to contain prisoners. The only furnishings in the room were a large plastic outdoor table and six matching chairs. Kelly supposed the intent behind the flimsy furniture was that they couldn't bonk an officer over the head with it and escape into the rest of the police station. The only item of substance was a security camera high in one corner. That was a nice touch, although he felt disappointed by the lack of a one-way mirror.

"This is ridiculous," Kelly said as he paced the room.

William sat, appearing calm. Ever since the officer had brought them in here, taken off the handcuffs, and left them alone, William hadn't said much of anything.

"They're just doing this to scare us," Kelly said. "What would they charge us with? Intent? Possession, maybe, but when my mom gets here, I'm sure she'll explain that I had her permission."

"You can't argue your way out of this one."

Kelly spun around. "What?"

"Arguing isn't going to help," William said. "What happens next will depend on facts. Not your opinion."

"The facts are that we didn't drink anything!"

"You keep saying that." William sighed as if tired. "And yet here we are. No one is denying that we didn't drink anything, but for some reason you think repeating that over and over again is going to make a difference. Just sit down, okay?"

Kelly clenched his jaw, but the tension in William's voice made him clamp down on any snappy comeback. He took a seat across from his boyfriend and considered him. "So what do you think will happen? What's our punishment going to be?"

"If we're lucky, they'll let our parents decide. We're too young to go to jail, and juvenile hall seems a little extreme."

"So we're grounded," Kelly said.

"I know I will be. You said your mom will be understanding."

"Wishful thinking." Kelly exhaled. "You have to admit it's pretty silly. It's like being caught raising a hammer in front of a jewelry store window. Why didn't the cop wait for something to actually happen?"

William smiled. "I definitely would have let us drink first. Hell, if I was an officer and saw two hot guys getting tipsy and romantic, I'd take a few steps back and enjoy the show."

Kelly laughed, feeling a little better. "Then again, it probably would have been worse if he'd let us."

"Probably."

He reached a hand across the table, but before William could take it, the lock clicked and the door opened. Mrs. Townson. Kelly craned his neck to see if his parents were there too, but it was just her and the police officer. A moment later, and it was only her, shaking her head at the both of them.

"Tell me you have a reasonable explanation," she said. "You were walking across the bridge, you found an open bottle, and you picked it up at the absolute worst moment."

"I'm sorry," William said. "It was meant to be romantic."

His mother sighed. "Romance doesn't involve getting drunk. In public. In fact I'd say that's the opposite of romance."

"We didn't," William said. "Did the officer tell you about the breathalyzer tests?"

"Yes, and frankly, it doesn't make me feel much better. He

stopped you before you did something very stupid." She turned to Kelly. "How were you planning on getting home? Were you going to drink and drive?"

"No," Kelly said. "I was only going to have a few sips, maybe a glass at most. We weren't planning on getting wasted."

"It's champagne," Mrs. Townson said. "The sugar makes it go straight to your head."

"One drink is within the legal limit," Kelly responded.

"For an adult! You're just a child!"

"I'm seventeen years old!" Kelly shot back.

Mrs. Townson crossed her arms over her chest. "And hopefully in four more years, you'll have smartened up quite a bit, because most cities frown on stumbling around drunk in public. And when it comes to driving, you'll be lucky to keep your license."

"I wasn't planning on getting drunk," Kelly growled. "We were only going to have one fucking drink together and—"

"Enough!"

If Kelly had been growling, William had positively roared. Startled, Kelly glanced over at him, expecting to see him angry at them both, but he focused solely on him.

"Don't argue with my mother!" William said. "Don't argue with anyone else tonight either or you *will* regret it. Understand me?"

Kelly stared in shock before nodding numbly. Maybe he had crossed a line, but that woman really knew how to push his buttons. At least she didn't look smug as she sat down next to her son. Instead she stared down at her purse on the table, preoccupied by thought. William placed a hand on her shoulder, then reached across the table and took Kelly's hand, as if he could connect the two of them this way. They sat like this without speaking.

Kelly didn't do well with silence. He was a fighter. His entire life had been about fighting. Often these battles were internal. Accepting that he was gay or pushing himself to be the best athlete possible—neither had been easy. And sometimes the outside world challenged him too, usually in the form of racism and prejudice. Kelly didn't turn the other cheek in these situations. Nor would he ever. So he snarled and snapped and fought with his last ounce of strength to defend himself. Like tonight, which was supposed to be special. Someone had come along and ruined it. Why should he meekly sit there and allow that to happen? And yet, William didn't seem to admire his fighting spirit. Instead it made him unhappy.

The door opened again, his heart leaping. His parents had arrived. This time the officer remained in the room when the door shut again. Mrs. Townson stood, offering her hand to his parents. Peace had been made. Surely everything would be explained now. His mom and dad would make everything right.

"I'm sorry," Laisha said to Mrs. Townson. "I'm afraid this is my fault. I bought the champagne for Kelly, but it was never supposed to leave the house."

Mrs. Townson nodded in understanding. "William didn't exactly talk him out of it or refuse a glass, from what I understand."

Kelly slumped in his chair, accepting defeat. He had hoped his mother would defend her right to allow her son to drink, but the pursed lips and shaking head told him all he needed to know. He watched in a daze as they all sat down and the officer talked about court dates and possible repercussions. Mrs. Townson wasn't so far off the mark. Kelly might lose his driver's license. All sorts of terrible things were possible, but he tuned them out for the most part. Instead he kept thinking of where he should be. The hour was getting late. They would have gone home by now. Kelly would have put on some light music, lit some candles, and given all of himself to William. Maybe a few times, before the night was over.

He glanced over at his boyfriend, who was listening to the officer and nodding politely, as if he were also an adult. For one fleeting moment, Kelly wished he'd toss the angel halo aside and look miserable or roll his eyes or be anything besides perfect. But of course, Kelly wasn't sure he'd love him then. Regardless, a little commiseration would have been comforting. Teenagers drank. They would always drink. He had planned on doing so responsibly, but that didn't count for anything. Instead they were all wasting their time. This interference wouldn't change a thing. If anything, Kelly felt more like getting trashed than ever.

"Thank you," his father said, standing and offering a hand to the officer.

At least this signaled it was over. They were escorted outside.

Once in the parking lot, all Kelly could do was exchange a muted goodbye with William before they went in different directions. He was trudging along behind his parents, hating the world in general, when he heard footsteps running across the parking lot.

William. His mother was in the distance, not looking pleased, but that didn't matter. Kelly glanced over at his mom, who nodded grudgingly. Kelly broke into a sprint, meeting William between two cars. Standing before each other, his anger melted away. Instead he felt like crying.

"I wanted the night to be special," he said.

"I know," William responded. Then he stepped forward, wrapped his arms around Kelly, and kissed him. "Happy anniversary."

"Yeah," Kelly said. "It's been an amazing six months. Six and a half," he added quickly.

William looked exasperated. "It's been memorable to say the least. Listen, I'll probably be in a lot of trouble, so…"

Kelly grimaced. "Yeah, I know. We'll still see each other in school, right?"

"Right. They can't take that away from us. If only Romeo and Juliet had the same lunch period, the whole tragedy could have been averted." William hesitated. "Still, don't do anything crazy like showing up at my house in the middle of the night, okay? We should take things easy."

Kelly shrugged, not willing to agree. "Text me, okay?"

William nodded. After a half-smile, he turned to walk away. As Kelly watched him go, he couldn't help but think of that alternate reality again, where in a room lit by dancing flames, they were warmly wrapped in each other's arms.

The next time they saw each other was in court. Mrs. Townson had kept William out of school on Monday so they could consult with a lawyer. That seemed a little extreme to Kelly. Then again, maybe his own mother would have too if she wasn't a lawyer. She dealt in bankruptcy and not juvenile delinquency, but this made her feel comfortable with how their court date would proceed.

Kelly would start by apologizing, something he had plenty of practice with lately. At his mother's insistence, he had already apologized to her for breaking her trust, to his brother for being a bad role model, and even to Mrs. Townson in a written note.

Kelly said he could do so in person, but his mother just shook her head and handed him a pen and paper.

He expected to see William the next day, but when Tuesday's third period rolled around, William's seat was empty. Kelly skipped lunch that day, unwilling to eat alone. Then his mother picked him up in the afternoon, just as she had dropped him off, since he was no longer allowed to use the car. All part of the plan. Kelly was to inform the judge that he had lost permission to drive, which she hoped would circumvent his license being suspended. Kelly felt they could just pretend instead, but she was adamant. No car.

At home he changed into a suit before being whisked away to the courthouse. To lift his spirits, Kelly pretended he was headed there to get married; the fantasy strengthened when he saw William in a dress shirt and tie. No wedding bells though. Just grim-faced parents who watched with eagle eyes. Kelly and William approached each other cautiously, perhaps fearing if they showed any enthusiasm, this moment together would be taken from them as well.

"I don't want to kiss," William murmured under his breath. "Not in front of them."

"Save it for when we're in front of the judge," Kelly joked.

William didn't laugh. "I need this to go well, okay? I don't want this affecting my chances of getting into the Coast Guard."

Kelly resisted an eye roll. "I'll behave. You know, sometimes they sentence people to join the military instead of sending them to jail. Maybe I've just increased your chances. You'll probably be shipping out tonight."

This earned him a smile. Court itself wasn't as whimsical. The judge seemed bored more than anything. Kelly recited his speech, which involved him expressing regret and describing all he had lost already due to his error in judgment. William's words were more emotional, focusing on how he'd let his mother down. They didn't seem practiced, meaning they were probably sincere. At the end of this all, they were sentenced to thirty hours of community service and placed on a kid version of probation. Basically they couldn't get into trouble for the next six months and that was it.

Kelly thought the worst was behind them, but his parents appeared just as displeased as before.

"You think it makes me happy seeing you in court?" his mother asked. "This better be the last time!"

"What about jury duty?" he asked.

She answered by swatting him on the back of the head. He felt like they should all go out to celebrate or something, but of course that wasn't in the cards. When his parents went to speak with Mrs. Townson, he lagged behind so he could have a word alone with William, who also failed to look placated by the light sentence.

"Could have been worse," Kelly said.

"Speak for yourself. I'm grounded for a month."

Kelly winced sympathetically. "Two weeks. Unless my mom hears how long you're grounded for. Then she'll probably increase my sentence."

William glanced at their parents. "I should go. I guess we'll only see each other in school."

"Not true," Kelly said. "We have thirty hours worth of dates coming up. It's just that they'll be spent serving the community."

Chapter Nine

Kelly hopped from foot to foot in front of the door, wanting to stay in motion, even though he had reached his destination. The afternoon sun felt good on his back, the light breeze cooling the sweat on his skin. When the door opened, Kelly held his breath until he was certain who it was.

"You shouldn't be here," William said, eyes travelling down Kelly's body.

"Your mom is still at work, right?"

"Yeah. She'll freak if she finds you here." But he stepped aside anyway, allowing Kelly to come inside.

Little had changed in a week. No iron bars on the window or nanny cam on the bookshelf. He casually glanced toward William's feet, searching for signs of an ankle monitor. "How's house arrest treating you?"

"Ha ha," William answered, shutting the door. Then he turned to consider Kelly again. "I'm horny as hell."

"Me too. There's always the bathroom stall at school. Our parents have driven us to it."

"Yuck."

"How much time have we got before Mom gets home?"

"Half an hour," William said. "But you're disgustingly sweaty."

"Then you better hop in the shower with me."

They didn't last long, not just because they were short on time, but a whole week without sex felt like an eternity. Kelly had been on the verge of declaring himself a virgin again. Once back in his sweaty clothes, he towel-dried his hair as he inspected William's bedroom. The new Transformer stood in the midst of the animal figures, like some sort of robot shepherd.

"I love that thing," William said, pulling on a pair of jeans before sitting on the bed. "My mom walked in the other day when I was zooming it around in helicopter mode. Totally embarrassing, but so much fun."

Kelly grinned. "Are you looking forward to community service tomorrow?"

"I wanted to talk to you about that."

Kelly sighed and plopped down on the mattress next to him. "Not this again."

"I'm volunteering at the Food Bank. I've thought about it and—"

"Nooo," Kelly groaned. "You saw the video on their web site. We'll be packing boxes of food nonstop. It never ends. We won't have any time to hang out or have fun."

"Picking up trash is fun?"

"No, but the work isn't so relentless. We'll be together out in the sunshine and fresh air, keeping Austin beautiful. I'm bringing food along, so we can have a picnic together on our break."

"The Food Bank helps feed hungry people," William said. "That's more meaningful to me. Besides, it'll look better on my Coast Guard application. I'm going to keep doing this past the thirty hours too. I want to be seen as a volunteer, not someone who helps out only to pay off a criminal debt."

Kelly raised an eyebrow. "You'd rather look good than spend time with me?"

"No, I'd rather feel like I'm making a difference. Cleaning up the environment is nice, but I want to help people. That's why I'm becoming a rescue swimmer."

"Charming, but this is the only time we'll have together until you're ungrounded."

"Then spend it with me packing boxes of food."

Kelly clenched his jaw. "It's bad enough we're being punished for this. I'm not going to make it hard on myself by working my ass off."

William shrugged. "Then I guess we're volunteering separately."

"I guess so."

Kelly flopped onto his back, staring at the ceiling, wishing just one conversation with William could be normal. Jesus was great and all, but he would have made a shitty boyfriend. *No time for a romantic night out, my child. I've got starving orphans to feed and lepers to bathe.*

"I want to see more of you," Kelly said.

"You know where to find me. School or the Food Bank."

Kelly rolled over to face him. "Can you start picking me up every morning? I'm sick of riding the bus."

"I thought your mom was giving you rides?"

"Nope. She wants this to be as humiliating as possible." Kelly reached over and put a hand on his back. "Please."

"Okay," William said. "You better get going."

"So I won't see you again until Monday? You could at least try Keep Austin Beautiful with me. Just for this weekend. If you don't like it, you can go be a worker bee."

William glanced over at him. "I'm trying to turn something negative into a positive."

"So that's a no?"

"That's a no."

Kelly stood up, gave him a passionless kiss on the cheek, and walked out of the room without saying another word.

William smiling, crossing his eyes, laughing, sleeping, swimming, sitting with his hands behind his head and staring off into nothing. A dozen different Williams, all spread out on his bed. The idea made Kelly lightheaded. Too bad these were just photos and not the real thing. Regardless, his insides got all tangled up, as if he were looking at the man in the flesh. William drove him crazy in a lot of wonderful ways. And quite a few bad ways too.

"Maybe I'm just not good enough for him," he said to the sympathetic voice pressed against his ear.

"Or maybe he's just too goody goody." Bonnie sighed into the phone. "Remember that girl I dated briefly? The one who was saving herself for marriage. I kept telling her it would never be legal in Texas, and if it ever was, she'd probably be in her sixties by then. Nobody wants a wrinkly old virgin."

Kelly chuckled into the phone. "I remember. She even wore one of those purity rings, right?"

"Yep. And I was all starry-eyed because of it. I thought she was so noble, so full of integrity. Of course not being able to get into her panties drove me wild too. But eventually it got boring. She was a little *too* pure. She wouldn't even play poker with me."

"Was it strip poker?" Kelly asked.

"Well yeah, but come on. Live a little!"

Kelly considered the photos on the bed, rearranging a few. "William isn't that bad."

"But..." Bonnie supplied helpfully.

"But he's obsessed with doing the right thing. And the Coast Guard. Oh my god, don't even get me started on all of that. I want to run in the Olympics, and I will, but my entire life doesn't revolve around it. It will one day, but I don't live and breathe for that moment. I can either let myself have fun now, or shriek in terror every time someone offers me a candy bar."

"I'd like to see that," Bonnie said. "So what are you going to do?"

"What can I do? I love him."

"Then you'll just have to suffer in silence. Good luck with that."

"Thanks," Kelly said, not hiding his sarcasm.

"How'd volunteering go today?"

"Fine. Next to no supervision and beautiful weather. The cars roaring by every few seconds sucked, but I could have made it romantic."

"You coming to group tomorrow?"

"Nope. My battle with litter continues. Besides, I can't drive right now."

"I could have picked you up for once. How awesome would that have been?"

"Actually, you *could* pick me up and drive me to my stupid community—"

"Oops! Battery is dying. Can't talk!"

The line went dead. Kelly glanced at his phone questioningly before setting it aside. Then he went back to staring at his photos of William, because for the moment, they were all he had.

Miserable. The rain had come on Sunday and the heavy gray clouds had refused to blow away since then. Kelly had inhaled enough of the wet weather to pollute his spirits. He couldn't seem to shake his bad mood. Even William picking him up in the morning hadn't helped, perhaps because that sunshine smile was nowhere in sight. Instead he was quiet as he drove them toward school.

"So how was the Food Bank?" Kelly asked, his voice sounding snider than he intended.

"Great. The people there are really cool. We worked our butts off, but everyone is so pumped that it's kind of fun. My voice was hoarse at the end of the shift from talking so much. How was yours?"

"My voice?" Kelly said. "Silky smooth. I didn't talk to anyone. I just kept thinking of you. We could have had our picnic. It would have been perfect."

"Kelly—"

"Of course Sunday the weather turned to piss, so it's just as well you weren't there. I had to wear a trash bag to stay dry."

William glanced over at him. "Really?"

Kelly snorted. "Yes. I tore a hole in one of them for my face. And two little holes for my arms."

"I'm sorry I missed out."

"I bet."

The car was silent a moment before William spoke again. "You can still come to the Food Bank with me next weekend."

Kelly set his jaw. "And you can still join me for trash duty next weekend. Why do I have to be the one to compromise?"

"You really want me to answer that?"

Kelly raised an eyebrow. "Please do."

"Because none of this would have happened if— Never mind."

"No, say it!"

William shook his head.

Kelly stared at him. "You think this is all my fault? I was trying to make our anniversary special!"

"It's not that," William said. "It's your attitude. If you had been nice to the police officer, admitted that we were about to make a mistake, he might have let us go with just a warning."

"I doubt that."

"I don't, because you're right. He could have called your mom, verified that she bought you the alcohol, and that you had permission to drink it. At home. He probably would have taken away the champagne, slapped us on the wrist, and let us get on with our evening. Instead he ended up *handcuffing* you. You get why, right?"

"Gee, I wonder."

"This isn't because you're black!" William huffed. "It's because sometimes you behave like a monster. Instead of trying to reason with the other person, or charm your way out of rough situations, you fly off the handle. Of course the police officer handcuffed you! Hell, I felt like doing the same."

"Because I stood up for myself?" Kelly said. "Jesus Christ, I had no idea you were so subservient. I guess I shouldn't be surprised. You're desperate to join the Coast Guard where some jarhead will tell you what to do and how to think."

William looked over at him, eyes blazing with warning. "You

just love bringing that up, don't you? Enlisting means everything to me, and you never pass up a chance to make me feel shitty about it."

"Maybe you should!" Kelly said. "Especially if the Coast Guard is more important to you than spending the weekend with your boyfriend!"

"So what?" William thwacked the windshield wiper controls. The blades swiped faster as the rain increased. "You think eating sandwiches together while picking up trash sounds appealing to me? And really, why should I reward you for getting us into this mess?"

Kelly crossed his arms over his chest. "So it's all my fault?"

"Yes! How can you not see that?"

"Maybe because I'm not interested in placing blame. I didn't make you feel bad for costing me the race."

William appeared stung. "The triathlon?"

"Yes, the triathlon. I didn't give you shit just because you tripped and fell. You're not perfect either. You never will be, no matter how much you try, so come down off that high horse."

William shook his head. "It's not about either of us making mistakes. It's about how you react to them. You were cool during the race. Why couldn't you have been that way with the police officer?"

"With the pig?" Kelly snarled. "Maybe because I don't love him!"

William's voice was muted when he responded. "And do you still love me? All we do these days is fight. I think you did love me back then. I believe you. But something has changed because it's obvious I don't make you happy anymore."

"You do," Kelly said, feeling exhausted already. "But not when you put other things before our relationship. Not just other things. Everything! Your mom, the Coast Guard, and the needs of just about anyone who stumbles into your life. You're always thinking about them and not us. But despite all of that, no matter how much your chivalry makes me want to tear my hair out, you still make me happy."

The motors of the windshield wipers groaned as they worked overtime to send water flinging away. The thumping sound filled the car, the silence just as suffocating as the humidity outside. Instinct caused Kelly's stomach to fill with dread as he waited for William to speak.

"The thing is, I'm not sure I'm happy anymore."

Kelly's jaw dropped, even though he saw it coming. "What are you saying?"

William chewed his lip and glanced over. "I don't know. Maybe just a break. We can try being friends again and—"

"Because I messed up?" Kelly shouted. "Because I'm human and actually let myself feel anger? What's wrong with that? Why do you have to be such a fucking robot?"

"I'm not a robot," William grumbled, his jaw clenching.

"Sure you are. Just like your toys. That must be why you admire them so much because you want to be the same way. Plastic and unfeeling."

"I get angry!" William shouted back. "You *know* I do. But I also understand the concept of restraint. You flip out every five seconds like—"

"I do when I'm with you because you always—"

"That's why we shouldn't be together!" William snarled. "Something's wrong!"

Kelly narrowed his eyes. "You will never, *ever*, be in a relationship where you don't argue. Not that it matters. Where you're going, you'll never date again."

William glared at him. "And why's that?"

"You know why."

"Say it," William said, lips pulled back. "Say it one more time. I fucking dare you, because if you do, it'll be the last time I listen to your crap."

Kelly knew this was one challenge he shouldn't accept, but he was hurt and it was all over anyway and he wanted to make William cry so he wouldn't have to. "Once you're in the Coast Guard, it's back in the closet or your superiors will disown you. You'll live your pathetic robot life, sleeping on a cold bunk every night, sneaking off to a cruise park occasionally to suck—"

The car jerked suddenly, Kelly's body along with it. His voice cut off as the seatbelt squeezed painfully hard against his chest, the sound of screeching tires replacing his shouting as the vehicle spun. His insides felt as if they were doing horizontal cartwheels, like they had somehow driven into a centrifuge and gravity was trying to tear them apart. Then the car finally stopped. Kelly glanced over at his former boyfriend, saw his face twisted up with rage, and knew William was right. All this anger inside of him, all these battles he waged against the world, only made things worse. Not just situations, but people. He was ruining one of the best people he'd ever met.

"William—" he said.

More screeching tires, which was odd, since they weren't in motion anymore. Then a blast of impossible force. Shredding metal, splintering plastic, shattering glass, exploding air bags, and blinding light. Then a comparative silence. Just the pitter-patter of falling rain, the drops wet and cold on Kelly's cheek.

He tried to make sense of the world. He was still inside the car. Still seated, but leaning with his head outside the window, which was odd, since he hadn't rolled it down.

"Are you okay?"

He tried to move his neck, finding it stiff, but he managed an inch or two, allowing him to look into headlights. Squinting against them, he saw up-close the damaged grill of something massive, like a metallic dinosaur. A version of Godzilla constructed by the auto industry.

"Kelly!"

He sucked in air, the sound squeaky and shuddering. The rain was getting in his eyes. He needed to pull himself back inside the car to see if William was okay, because his brain was starting to catch up. They had been in a wreck. He struggled to put the pieces together, which was nothing compared to the effort it took to move.

"Stay still, stay still! Oh God! Where's my phone?"

William sounded frantic. Was he hurt? Wanting to check on him, Kelly grunted, pushing against the car interior with one arm, and managing to get himself upright. The cost of this was a throbbing ache, but he tried to ignore it as he turned. William's face was covered with blood, his eyes wide as he stared at Kelly. For some reason he was looking down and making little noises, single guttural syllables that didn't have meaning. Kelly gave up trying to understand, then followed his gaze. William reached out for his chin, as if to stop him, but it was too late. Kelly saw the truth.

He wasn't inside the car. The car was inside of him.

Or both, because flesh and metal and blood and plastic were all mixed together. He couldn't tell if shreds of cloth belonged to the clothing he wore or were remnants of the seat cover fabric. Discerning by color didn't help, since everything was drenched in wet sticky maroon. Kelly took in all of this, his brain registering one sensation above all others. Pain. It filled him, rising up from inside, forcing his head back and his mouth open. Then it poured out of him, manifesting as a scream. Like steam coming out of a kettle, it was the only way to release pressure. Eventually even this wasn't enough. The last he heard were shrill sirens and William pleading with him to "stay with me, stay with me, stay with me" before mercy came in the form of soft silent darkness.

The world approached and retreated in waves. Sometimes when Kelly opened his eyes, the pain was there waiting for him, along with people he didn't recognize. In these moments, all he had to do was close his eyes again. Other times the world was fuzzy and pink, as if he'd been wrapped in cotton candy. The pain would be gone and faces would fill his vision, all of them smiling to let him know it was all right. His mother, his father, even Royal, who didn't smile as much as he cried. Kelly kept listening to their message, repeating it when he could manage. "It's okay. I'm all right."

This was his world now. Pain he recoiled from, or moments of fluffy bliss that he tried to stay awake for. The more he opened his eyes, the more he understood. The strangers were doctors and nurses, the uninspiring backdrop a hospital. The expressions of his family eventually shifted, becoming less tearful and more determined. Only when a new face appeared, like Layne's, did the crying start again. Then Kelly would squeeze their hands and tell them what they needed to know. He was okay.

Eventually the worlds of pain and bliss melded and met somewhere in the middle. When he opened his eyes, he felt a distant ache and the buzz that kept it at bay, but Kelly no longer found it so hard to think. He was able to stay awake this time, and he remained still while doing so, staring at the ceiling.

The car accident. He replayed the memories, trying to arrange jumbled impressions into a coherent event. When he finally managed, he closed his eyes again, remembering how his lower body had been indistinguishable from the rest of the wreck. He slowly took stock of himself. The drugs numbing him made it difficult, but he could feel his arms, his torso, an unpleasant prickling sensation in his crotch, and both of his legs. Everything was still there. He was fine.

Except that his right leg was dangling over the mattress. That didn't make sense because Kelly could feel that he was on the bed correctly and not resting at an angle. The rails ensured he was. He even opened his eyes to confirm this. His legs were straight, one bent at the knee. So his lower leg was dangling *through* the mattress? Did they have a hole cut into it for some reason?

"Honey! You're awake again. Are you thirsty?"

His mother came into view. She placed a palm on his forehead as if to feel his temperature. He nodded, trying to sit upright.

"Hold on," she said.

An electric whir accompanied half the bed rising until Kelly was sitting up. He glanced around the hospital room, feeling dizzy and trying to focus on the straw his mother was aiming toward his mouth. Once he caught it, he sucked, tasting cold water.

"How do you feel?" she asked, setting aside the cup.

He nodded.

"Maybe I should call the doctor."

"I'm okay," he said quickly. "No need to make a fuss."

"You look good," she said, studying his face. "Your eyes are clear."

He nodded again, resisting the urge to close them.

"Do you remember—"

"Where's William?" he interrupted.

Laisha's lips tightened. "He's gone home."

"Is he okay?"

"Yes, honey." His mother pressed her hand to his cheek. "Do you remember the accident?"

He nodded.

"And afterwards?"

The question confused him, since this was afterwards. She acted like there had been more. Perhaps there had been. "How long have I been here?"

"Almost a week. How much do you remember?"

She kept asking him that, making him wonder if he had suffered a brain injury. "Is something wrong with my head?"

"No!" His mother's face nearly crumpled, but she was strong enough to force it into a smile. "We came close to losing you, honey. The doctors saved your life. It means so much that you're still here with us. I love you. Your father and brother love you."

"I love you guys too," Kelly mumbled.

She smiled while looking him over, her hand still on his cheek. Her eyes were welling up, and while much of this came from affection, he also recognized something was wrong. Something serious.

"Mom?" he asked, the panic escaping into his voice.

"You're okay, baby. But you were hurt pretty bad and they couldn't save all of you."

"What do you mean?"

His mother kissed him on the forehead, once, twice, and a third time. Then she looked into his eyes, her own wet with tears. "They had to take one of your legs."

Kelly glanced down at himself, wondering at first if this was all some cruel joke, because covered in blankets, everything looked normal. Except at the very end of the bed, where there should be two little mountains formed by his feet, he saw only one. But there was a reason why. He could feel that leg dangling over the edge, or through the mattress, or whatever.

He didn't hesitate. He pulled back the blankets, wanting to see the truth. A hospital robe and a tube sticking out near his crotch. The discomfort of that was overshadowed by his struggle to get the sheets off completely. He could see both thighs. That was fine. Maybe he had only lost a foot or—

"Honey, try to relax."

"I want to see," Kelly said, getting worked up. "Just help me! Please!"

His mother eyed him a moment. Then she moved to the end of the bed and helped pull down the sheets the rest of the way. Where Kelly's right knee should be was a bundle of bandages. Beyond it, nothing.

Kelly pushed the button on the remote control, over and over again. On the television screen, the picture changed every two seconds. He didn't really see the images, didn't care when his brother complained or his father asked if he needed anything. He simply stared unseeing at the television mounted on the hospital wall, because it was the only thing he had power over.

He was used to fighting. Kelly could do anything if he put his mind to it. Determination, hard work, and above all, no compromises. When he decided that victory was the only acceptable outcome, he made it happen. Grades, relationships, his athletic career—everything was within grasp as long as he tried his best. His mind kept telling him now that he should fight, that he should do anything and everything to fix this. And yet there was nothing to be done. His leg was gone, leaving him helpless. Powerless. Crippled.

"Kelly," his father said, placing a hand over his. And the remote. "Let's just leave it off. For now."

Kelly changed the channel a few more times. Then he shut off the TV and glanced around. He hated this room, hated the hospital. He wanted out of here. Now. But even if he threw a fit and hopped out of bed, he couldn't walk out of the room and run down the hall. He couldn't go anywhere anymore. Not without help. Speaking of which, his back was killing him. He wanted to roll over onto his side, but even that was difficult. His physical therapist was teaching him how to move again. Half a leg gone, and his balance was thrown completely off. Even the smallest task now took herculean effort. Still, at least the catheter was gone. What happened in the restroom was now private again.

He reached for the television remote, missing his cell phone. Another casualty of the wreck. No right leg, no phone, and no... Kelly swallowed. Over the past few days, the details had come back to him, and the words leading up to it. He didn't know where William was. That he had already been discharged from the hospital was all his mother would say. Then she would start rambling on about legal action, which seemed ridiculous to Kelly. William didn't have any money. What would they take from him as compensation? His toys? Kelly tried talking sense into her, but the mere mention of William's name caused her mouth to tighten and her eyes to narrow.

Sort of like the face she was wearing now. Laisha walked into the room, appearing flustered. "Honey, you're not in the mood for visitors, are you? I didn't think so. I told him that you needed—"

"Who?" Kelly asked, trying to sit upright. "Tell me."

His mother shook her head. "I bumped into William downstairs. He was asking the reception desk for your room number, but you're in no condition for visitors."

Kelly gestured to them. "You guys aren't visitors? Is he coming up here?"

"I told him you didn't want to see him."

"Mom!"

"Don't tell me you want to! After what he did?"

A soft series of raps interrupted them, four heads turning at once to the figure in the doorway. William stood there, withering under their gazes. He had a bandage across his forehead, and one of his cheeks was dark with bruising, but aside from that he looked okay.

"How'd you get here?" Royal said with venom. "Don't tell me you drove."

"I took my bike," William said sheepishly.

"They shouldn't even allow that," Royal spat. "They should cut off your legs so you'll never drive, bike, or walk again. See how you like it!"

Kelly waited for his little brother to be reprimanded, but his parents seemed content to sit and give William the evil eye. Kelly sighed. "I'd like to be alone," he said.

His mother looked vindicated. "I told you he wouldn't want visitors."

"I mean," Kelly said, fighting against the drugs in his system to muster some anger, "that I want to be alone with William. We need to talk."

"Son—" his father began.

"Now!" Kelly snapped, and it felt good. For the first time since he'd woken up completely, he didn't feel helpless. Not entirely. He watched with satisfaction as his family shuffled out of the room. It also gave him something to focus on besides William, because Kelly was scared he was about to be hurt all over again.

As soon as they were gone, William came and stood at his bedside. His eyes kept flicking down to where Kelly's leg was— or where it should have been. Then his face crumpled and he started crying.

"I'm sorry," William sobbed. "I wish I could undo it all. I wish I could give you your leg back and make everything okay somehow, but I fucked up. I ruined everything, and I don't know how to make it right."

Kelly watched as he cried, almost feeling bemused when William's grief brought him to his knees at his bedside. Maybe it was the drugs numbing Kelly and preventing him from crying too. He wasn't entirely indifferent though, because it felt good to see William again. That he was here and still cared… For this one small moment, Kelly could pretend they would make amends.

But that wasn't reality. William wouldn't want him anymore. Nobody would. Kelly was a cripple. A wheelchair awaited him, followed by crutches once his wounds had healed enough. Eventually he might get a prosthetic leg, but this would only obscure the truth. Even if he looked normal to the casual observer, in any relationship a time would come when the clothes came off. He couldn't expect anyone to find him attractive then. Not when they saw his stump. This was a fact he had already accepted, and not even the drugs could stave off the resulting sorrow.

"I just hope you still want me."

The words could have been Kelly's, but they weren't. He didn't hide his puzzlement as William reached out and took his hand, but he did force the hope rising inside of him back down. "What?" he managed.

"I did it on purpose, Kelly. In the car. I got so mad at you and I—" William's voice faltered, ending with a croak.

Kelly's emotions pulled back defensively. "What do you mean on purpose?"

"I jerked the wheel," William said. "I meant for us to pull over, but I also wanted to scare you, so I jerked the wheel and hit the breaks. With the rain and everything I didn't realize— I never wanted us to get in an accident. But I did want to—"

"—shut me up," Kelly said. "Apparently it takes more than a car wreck to do that."

William didn't laugh. He only seemed more miserable. "I didn't know this would happen. I never meant to hurt you. If I could take it all back or give you my leg or anything, I would. I swear!"

"I know that," Kelly said, placing a hand on his head and stroking his hair. Maybe it was the morphine or perhaps it was a testament to love, but he didn't hold the accident against William. Even in their darkest moments together, Kelly had never felt that William wanted to physically harm him. Or anyone else, for that matter.

"I'm going to keep my promise," William said, clenching his jaw.

"What promise?"

"In the ICU," William said. "After the accident. You don't remember?"

Kelly looked into eyes hard with determination and shook his head.

"You kept reaching for me. You kept asking me to stay with you."

Now Kelly's chest grew tight. "And what did you say?"

"I promised." William steeled himself. "I'll never leave you, Kelly. Not if you still want me."

Now Kelly cried, but they were tears of relief. He used all his strength to tug on William's hand until he stood and leaned over the bed. Then Kelly wrapped both arms around him, pulling their bodies close. Cheeks wet, he nestled his head against William's neck, breathed in his scent, and murmured his own promise.

"Of course I still want you. I always will."

Part Two
Austin, 2008

Chapter Ten

I am the butcher of the wind. My arms cut through it, increasing my speed. I can feel the air coursing over me, see it in my mind's eye as silvery airstreams flowing around every curve, every flexing muscle. I am the very essence of speed, and still it isn't enough for me. My shoes hit the earth over and over again, like a giant spinning the globe beneath his feet. I am running, and I am untouchable.

Kelly awoke with a start, arriving in a world almost as surreal as the one he'd just left. He was in the downstairs master bedroom, except the heavy oak dressers and widescreen television belonging to his parents had been taken away, replaced by his desk and computer. The sleeping form next to him wasn't his father—thank goodness—but William. The nightstand once typically held a portable Nintendo or a classic car magazine, but now a red helicopter robot stood guard over a pair of swimming goggles.

Married life at seventeen. Who would have thought?

Kelly lay in bed and stared at the ceiling, willing the dream to continue so he could bask in the sensation of movement again. He wouldn't have to pretend for long. Today was the day. Might as well get up and get ready, especially considering how long it took. Besides, he really had to pee, and he couldn't exactly rush to the toilet. Kelly rolled over and sat up with little effort, reaching for the forearm crutches leaning against the wall.

This was enough to wake William. "Need help?" he asked blearily.

"Nope." It was the same question every morning and the same answer, but he loved William for still caring after three whole months of this. If the roles were reversed, Kelly would have covered his head with a pillow and let poor William drag himself to the bathroom. Getting his crutches into position, he pushed himself up, barely swaying as he found his balance. He was improving, not that it would matter soon.

He hurried to the bathroom attached to the master bedroom, which was now his. Kelly's parents had made this sacrifice so he wouldn't have to deal with stairs. On mornings like these, when his bladder felt ready to burst, he also appreciated the nearness of the bathroom. Sleeping naked meant not having to fiddle with pajama bottoms. As soon as Kelly reached the toilet, all he had to do was turn around, carefully lower himself down while counterbalancing, and take a small leap of faith. He plopped down on the toilet seat and sighed. Oh how he missed the days when all he had to do was whip it out and point!

Once finished, he struggled to stand again, ignoring the bar his father had installed on the wall. Then he stared at the shower, debating how he was going to proceed today. Sometimes he took his crutches in with him, just because it made him feel slightly more normal to be standing. When it came time to soap up, he was forced to use the special flip-down seat. He despised this. Who took a shower sitting down? Glaring at the bathtub in general, he turned to the medicine cabinet, opened it, and grabbed his bottle of painkillers. Then he remembered it was empty. He'd been cut off two days ago. Kelly had agreed at the time, and while he wasn't hurting physically, he now felt emotionally vulnerable. He opened the bottle, just on the off chance one lonely pill sat forgotten at the bottom. There wasn't one, of course, but he did notice the film of powder that lined the inside. He was considering licking it when William padded through the door.

"You okay?" he yawned. Instead of waiting for an answer, he made use of the toilet.

Kelly glanced over at him, taking note of his body, the curve of his shoulders, the impressive pecs, and the little glimpse of his cock that could be seen past his hip. Being off the painkillers might make him feel raw inside, but it also brought back his sexual appetite. Not that their love life had died completely. Over the summer, Kelly would long to be close to William or worry about meeting his needs. On such occasions, he would make the effort, despite being too numb to enjoy himself much. Now his craving for sex had returned like a hungry demon, his skin tingling at the idea.

He turned and leaned against the counter, leaving his naked body in full view, including his erection. This didn't go unnoticed.

William glanced over at him and smirked. "Want to hop in the shower together?"

"I wish." Kelly glanced back at the plastic seat and frowned. "I swear, as soon as the prosthetic leg goes on, I'm never taking it off and I'm never sitting again."

William followed his gaze. "You don't like sitting in the shower? It's so convenient."

"Are you telling me that you've been using my cripple seat?"

"Don't call it that." William repressed a smile. "And yes. I do like it. Hell, I was thinking about installing a waterproof couch in there."

"You're so lazy."

"Maybe. You still haven't answered my question. Do you want to take a shower with me?"

"Who gets the seat?"

"Neither of us," William said. "Come on. I'll hold you."

Kelly hesitated. The offer sounded appealing, but he wasn't entirely nude. Not exactly. He still had on his shrinker sock—tight fabric that helped compress his stump, keeping the swelling down to ensure that what remained was a manageable size for his prosthesis. While he didn't need to wear it when he slept, he did so anyway. Anything to make sure that today went smoothly. He wanted his new leg to fit perfectly, returning him to the mobility he'd once cherished. And of course the sock hid his amputation. Kelly didn't like anyone to see it. He wasn't ashamed exactly, but for William especially, he worried about sex appeal. So Kelly normally had it covered, something that would be impossible in the shower.

"Was it something I said?" William came closer and cupped his hand over Kelly's cock, which was now drooping. "I promise I won't let you fall."

"It's not that," Kelly said.

William searched his eyes. "I love all of you. Even the parts that aren't there."

Kelly snorted. "Nice line."

"It's working," William said, rubbing his hand up and down.

"All right. You should probably get in first. Then I'll join you."

William kissed him and went to start the shower. Kelly balanced himself against the counter and took off his sock, glancing up to see if William was staring in horror, but he wasn't paying attention. The "residual limb" as the doctors tended to call it, didn't look so bad. No ghastly scars or twisted tissue. The shape put Kelly in mind of someone folding their arm to expose their elbow. His thigh simply tapered off into a rounded edge, all of it covered in healthy dark skin, just like the rest of him.

"Come," William said, holding open the curtain.

Kelly left his crutches where they were, hopping forward on one leg. This was a trick he was proud of. His balance had been off when he first returned from the hospital, but now he could hop all over the place without too much trouble. Of course he couldn't safely hop into a tub, but as soon as he was close enough, William wrapped an arm around his waist and helped him step in.

And it felt great standing up with both his hands free. William held him close, their torsos pressed against each other, and as horny as Kelly was, he felt more excited about taking a shower like he used to.

"Let me turn around," he said.

"Straight to business this morning!" William said.

Kelly rolled his eyes playfully. "Just hold on tight."

If William expected the ride of his life, he was in for a disappointment. As soon as Kelly was turned around, he leaned over and grabbed the bottle of shampoo. After a suds and rinse, he did the same with the conditioner.

"Uh," William said.

"Hold your horses," Kelly teased, reaching for the body wash.

"Does that make you my horse?"

"Ha ha," Kelly deadpanned, even though he was grinning. Maybe the body soap could wait. William was still hard and rubbing up against his ass cheeks. Kelly wasn't going to risk one-legged anal sex in the shower. That sounded riskier than juggling fire or swallowing swords. But he realized the seat in the shower might still be put to good use. A moment later he confirmed his findings. The perfect height. Soon William was thrusting in his mouth, Kelly taking care of himself with his free hand. Neither of them lasted long. Today was different, and not just because he was off the drugs. For the first time in months, their lives would return to the way they had once been. Kelly was excited, and William seemed optimistic too.

"I love you," he whispered, helping Kelly stand again.

"I love you too," Kelly said in equally hushed tones. "Are we trying not to wake my parents or something?"

William's features wanted to smile, but concern got there first. "Are they tagging along today?"

"I'm finally getting my prosthetic leg," Kelly said. "Of course they're going to be there."

"Do they have to be?"

Oh. He didn't need an explanation. His parents still hadn't

forgiven William. Royal had done so after Kelly had given him a pep talk, but his parents still made cutting remarks. They blamed William for the accident. Maybe it was his fault technically, but he hadn't meant for either of them to get hurt. Regardless, they seemed intent on punishing him. That William was there for Kelly day and night, tending to his every need, didn't seem to count for anything. Nothing he could do or say would ever be enough for them.

"I'll take care of it," Kelly said. "Today it'll just be you and me."

"Just me and you, huh?" William murmured.

"No complaining back there," Bonnie said, "or I'll turn this car around!"

She wouldn't, of course. Bonnie had been wonderful since the accident and had more than paid back all the rides Kelly had given her. Despite still possessing their driver's licenses, William was unwilling to drive and Kelly didn't think he was able. Switching to his left leg probably wouldn't be a big adjustment, but like William, the idea of being behind the wheel made him nervous. He knew now how life-changing one miscalculation could be. William didn't even enjoy being a passenger anymore, preferring to bike everywhere or take a bus if Kelly was with him.

"You boys just keep those hands where I can see them," Bonnie said, eyes narrowing in the rearview mirror. "No funny business in the Bitchmobile."

"There's nothing funny about my business," Kelly said. Then, more seriously, he added, "Thanks for the ride. I don't want you to feel used or anything. You know I love you, right?"

Bonnie's eyes softened as they flicked back and forth between him and the road. "It's no big deal." After a beat, she added, "Even though it is starting to feel like *Driving Miss Daisy* in reverse. You pumped?"

"About my new peg leg?" Kelly asked. "Hell yeah!"

"So am I. Maybe we can walk the mall in celebration afterwards."

"Why not?"

He nearly begged Bonnie to speed the rest of the way to the medical center. In the waiting room, Kelly wished he already had the leg so he could pace back and forth. He tried doing so using his forearm crutches before William made him sit down. Then his name was called. They were shown to a private room where the prosthetist met them with the prosthesis. He and William had joked about these terms during their visit two weeks ago when Kelly had been fitted. Especially 'prosthetist,' which hardly rolled off the tongue. Luckily, the prosthetist in question preferred to be called Michael.

"Here we go," he said, entering the room while holding an absolute treasure, even if the leg didn't look like much.

The wooden foot was especially primitive, but that would soon be covered in the extra shoe Kelly had brought along. A silver metal pole attached it to a knee joint, above this the socket—a clear plastic cup molded to fit his stump so perfectly that it created a vacuum seal. The cup was longer than Kelly had expected. After putting on a special sock, the socket was placed over it, the plastic covering most of his remaining leg and continuing right up to his pelvis. The edge of this hugged one hip, the back of the socket partially supported one butt cheek, and farther around, the plastic rim pressed into his crotch. Not exactly comfortable, but he focused on the positive: His new leg was attached. He was whole again.

"How does that feel?" Michael asked.

"A little tight," Kelly said. He was still sitting and already felt discomfort.

"I noticed that," Michael said. "Have you been wearing your compression sock?"

"Yeah," Kelly said, "even while I sleep. The only time I don't have it on is in the shower."

"Did you take one this morning?"

Kelly nodded.

"That could be it, especially if you were upright a lot. In the future you might want to only shower or bathe at night when temporary swelling won't matter."

"I can't use this thing in the shower?" Kelly asked, looking down at it. "What if I wrap the foot up so it doesn't get wet?"

Michael shook his head. "Not this leg. You need to keep it dry. Some of the components are prone to rusting. Ready to try walking?"

"Sure."

In Kelly's frequent fantasies about this moment, he was like a newborn foal. Once helped up, he would stumble around a few times before finding his feet. Then he would walk for the first time since the accident. Afterwards he would celebrate by tap dancing around the room. Maybe that last part wasn't realistic, but he truly believed the rest was possible.

Instead he found himself between two parallel bars, holding on to them for dear life as he tried to make his new leg do what he needed it to. Getting the knee to bend, relying on gravity instead of muscle, was alien to him. His weight rested not on the foot as much as the top of the socket by his hip. The prosthetist described it as sitting and walking at the same time. As if that made sense! After nearly an hour of coaching, he managed to walk, but only while keeping one hand on the rail.

"Takes some getting used to," Michael said as he helped Kelly sit again. "You'll do fine. Stick with it for a week, use your crutches while wearing the leg, and let yourself adjust slowly."

"I have school in two days," Kelly said. When it was clear Michael didn't understand the implication, he added, "I was hoping not to need my crutches by then."

"You'll always need them," Michael said. "When you're at home at the end of the day, you'll want to remove the leg. I'm told it's like taking off a pair of shoes. Even the most comfortable sneakers get old after a while. Or, if there are ever problems with your leg and it needs to get repaired—"

"Does that happen a lot?"

Michael exhaled. "The average leg lasts three years, but some I've built have lasted over a decade. With a lot of care and regular maintenance, you'll get a good amount of use."

Kelly looked down at the leg, feeling disappointed. This would be harder than he thought, but the end goal, that dream he'd had this morning, surely that was still in sight. "Once I get used to walking, how long until I can run?"

Michael raised his eyebrows. "Oh. I don't recommend running with this model. Uh, this is probably something you should talk over with your parents. Other prosthetics are available for specialty functions, and some amazing products are hitting the market now. But you need to be aware of cost, and what your insurance company will and won't cover. The good news is that someone your age should adapt quickly. With the right equipment and a lot of determination, you'll find very few limits to what you can do. But those specialty prosthetics—or even the normal ones—add up quickly and not just in the initial cost. You're looking at over half a million dollars in lifetime maintenance. So it's important to plan carefully and be selective about what you do and don't need."

Kelly just stared at him numbly. Half a million dollars? He looked to William and Bonnie, who quickly hid their shocked expressions. At least William did. Bonnie mouthed the words, "Holy shit!"

"Master this leg first," Michael said. "That's your goal. Running we can talk about some other time. See you next week?"

Kelly was quiet as he returned to the front desk, nodding at the offered appointment and allowing William to take the pamphlets and papers Kelly was supposed to review. His leg required a lot of care, like a pet, except it wasn't furry or cuddly. In fact, he was already beginning to hate it. Not only did he have crutches to deal with, but now he had dead weight hanging off one limb. And riding up on his butt uncomfortably. The optimism he'd felt this morning now seemed like childish naïveté.

"So what do you think?" William asked when Bonnie went to fetch the car.

Kelly sighed. "Can you call my doctor about getting a refill on my pain meds?"

"Does it hurt that bad?"

"Not really."

"Then why—"

"Those pills are good for more than just physical pain," Kelly said. "One more refill. Please."

William shrugged. "I can try. I don't mind, but why don't you call?"

"Because people really like you," Kelly said, managing a smile. "You're charming."

"Am I?"

"You can be."

William smiled back. Then he reached over and put a hand on Kelly's, which was gripping the handle of his crutch. "This is going to change everything," he said. "You'll see."

Kelly felt it already had. Just not in the way he'd hoped for.

Kelly remembered most first days of school, each of them full of the jitters. His mother dropping him off at Kindergarten and how he'd cried and cried. Grade school, which he'd faced bravely, feeling ridiculously grown up. Junior high, which had forced him to seek out new friends because everyone seemed scattered by this much larger arena. And high school, which had come as a relief, because people in his youth group had promised that individualism was more accepted there. Now, despite being a senior at the top of the high school food chain, Kelly felt nervous all over again. Especially when he looked in the mirror.

The black pants helped hide the folded fabric where one leg ended much too soon. The burnt orange dress shirt complimented his skin tone and brought out the gold in his eyes, the cut tight enough to show of his physique. He'd been knocked down, but he wasn't feeble and weak. If anything, his upper body was constantly getting an extra workout, compensating for what was missing below. From the waist up, he looked good. Not like a guy who had nearly lost his life at the beginning of summer.

"Damn," William said, coming up behind him and planting a quick kiss on his neck. "What's the occasion?"

"Everyone's going to be looking at us," Kelly said. "I'd rather they bite their bottom lips in lust than give me one of those awful pity smiles."

"You'll definitely be turning heads. Think I should change? Or maybe strut around shirtless?"

William stepped out from behind him. Yet another polo shirt, this one lemon yellow. If the pants were white instead of worn blue jeans, he'd seem like he was heading out for a day on the golf course. He looked good anyway. Throw a trash bag over that body and those curves would still bulge from beneath it, notching up the sex appeal. Maybe they had time for a quick—

"Uh, aren't you going to wear your prosthesis?"

Kelly took a deep breath, looking to one corner where the leg was propped up. "No, I'm not. I'll be late to each class with that thing weighing me down."

"You're supposed to wear it every day."

"Yeah, but not today. Let's go."

He spared one last glare for the leg, despising it for being such a disappointment. He had practiced with it, and even managed to lurch across the kitchen without his crutches, but at a tediously slow rate. At least with the crutches he could swing himself forward, getting a tantalizing taste of the speed he missed so much. Like a drug. Like those stupid pills that the doctors still refused to refill. He had found some old painkillers from when Royal sprained his ankle, but there hadn't been many. Kelly had already munched them all. Now he was facing the first day of school stone-cold sober.

At least he wouldn't be alone for the first half. The school had worked with them to ensure William shared as many of his classes as possible. One of the perks of being crippled. They shared the first three periods and lunch. Only in the afternoon would Kelly have to fend for himself.

Heading into the school building for the first time since the accident was intimidating, but less so with William at his side. He wasn't sure what to expect aside from lots of stares. He definitely got those, but he'd grown accustomed to them over the summer. The smiles took him aback. Mostly these came from girls. They weren't quite pitying. Supportive? He wasn't sure, but he found it disconcerting. Quite a few even said hello, calling him by name. He supposed he shouldn't be surprised. Their accident had been all over the news, both online and off. One web article had a comment section full of variations of "Oh my god! They go to my school!" And of course there were lewd comments about what he and William might have been doing to each other to cause the wreck.

"Hi, Kelly!" said a complete stranger in passing.

"Gosh," he murmured. "We're famous."

"Don't get used to it," William joked. "By this time tomorrow, you'll be old news."

"I hope you're right."

The weirdness continued throughout the day. Every teacher pulled him aside, letting him know they were there if he needed anything. In one period he was offered a seat up front, like missing a leg somehow affected his eyesight. Several people asked how he was doing, or oddest of all, said he was an inspiration. By lunch he felt unnerved. William was carrying two lunch trays, since Kelly couldn't manage one on his own, when they approached a table with many of his teammates. Kelly knew he could count on them to be insensitive assholes.

Or so he thought. Jared stood up, taking one of the trays from William. Then he hovered near Kelly as he sat, just in case he needed help. Once this humiliation was out of the way, and after some lingering stares, conversation resumed as normal. Mostly. Jared kept smiling at him and Martha watched him with shining eyes. Kelly practically counted down under his breath, just waiting for it. He'd already heard it enough times today. Once more wouldn't kill him.

"You're such an inspiration!" Martha gushed.

"Thanks," Kelly muttered, focusing on the flavorless rectangle of starch that was supposed to be pizza.

"So, did you guys see *The Simpsons* last night?" William asked.

"Yeah," one of the other guys said. "Why'd they show the Halloween special so early?"

"No idea," said another. "That show sucks anyway. *Family Man* is way better."

"It's *Family Guy*, dumbass. And both shows suck."

Kelly breathed out in relief. This was more like it! Stupid banter that would soon be forgotten. By the time Kelly had forced down his lunch, he was feeling much better. When two of the guys got into an argument about foreign versus domestic sports cars, he felt positively elated.

"Nothing is faster than a Lamborghini!"

"We're talking cars normal people can buy, not the toy of some rich old guy. And if you want to see fast, just wait until I kick your ass after school today."

"You think you can outrun me?"

"I know I can!"

The table went silent. Kelly glanced up in time to catch a number of uncomfortable expressions. Of course. Cross country season was just beginning, and a lot of the guys from track—Kelly included—treated it as training before track season in spring. He wouldn't be participating in either this year. Kelly had avoided thinking much about that, but now the truth was all too conspicuous. Even sitting at this table was a joke. He no longer belonged here. He was no longer a part of the team.

"Better get a head start," he mumbled, pulling his tray toward him before swinging a leg over the bench to stand.

Before he could, Jared shot to his feet, taking the crutches leaning against the bench and holding them out helpfully. Kelly felt his face burning and considered crawling under the table to die. He stood instead, Jared taking his tray and walking beside him toward the trash. William and Martha could only trail behind.

"You doing okay?" Jared asked.

"Never better," Kelly said, voice laced with sarcasm.

"Oh. Uh. Hey, if you ever want to hang out, you've got my number. Text me or something. We can go for a drive." An awkward pause, followed by a very hurried, "Or hit the mall or catch a movie. I don't know. I'm sorry about everything, okay?"

Kelly glanced over at him. Did he feel guilty now? After all this time, did seeing Kelly one leg down make him feel bad for what had happened between them? He took in Jared's smile and felt pathetic. How a friendly gesture could make him feel so small, he had no idea. But it did.

"Thanks," he managed as Jared emptied his tray into the trash. "I gotta get to my next class."

"Okay. Well... See you around!"

No chance of that. Tomorrow Kelly would find somewhere else to sit. He didn't want to be the loser who didn't make the team but still hung around with those who did, desperate to belong to the pack. Hell, even that sort of person had more going for them, since at least people would snub them. That took honesty. If Kelly showed up at the track, his teammates would probably applaud, even if he couldn't run.

He understood everyone was trying to be nice, but that wasn't normal. Random people didn't smile at him last year. Aside from his friends, most people ignored him and weren't overly friendly. He thought of Bonnie, how after the accident she had showed up at the hospital, looked him up and down as he lay in bed and said, "Whelp, this sucks." He loved her for that. No encouraging smile, no pep talk. Just the truth. Losing a leg sucked, but everyone acted like he'd done something brave.

"Hi," said a girl in sixth period. "It's great to see you here."

Kelly had no idea who she was, but she spent most of the class watching him. He did his best to ignore her. When the bell rang and he leaned over to grab his backpack, she stood and put it on his desk for him. Then she spoke words which set Kelly's teeth on edge.

"You're an inspiration. You know that?"

"How exactly am I an inspiration?" Kelly asked. "Do I make

you want to cut off one of your legs? Is that how I inspire you?"

"No," the girl stammered. "I mean that you're brave."

"Brave? I got hit by a car, blacked out from the pain, and woke up without my leg. How is that brave? Because I came to school, dared to show my disfigured form in public instead of hiding myself away in shame?"

The girl's face flushed. "I don't... I don't know what I mean."

"That's painfully obvious."

Kelly watched her flee the room, cheeks burning, and felt better. Maybe he wasn't being fair, but it felt good to bite back instead of swallowing any more pity. His vindication kept him going as he worked his way through the hall, glaring at any strangers who dared send sympathy his way. Head held high, Kelly made it outside and found William waiting next to the curb, his mother's car already there to whisk them home. William took one look at him and knew something was wrong. Setting his backpack on the ground, he stepped forward. Kelly didn't stop moving until he was in his arms. Only when his face was buried against William's neck did he squeeze his eyes shut, fighting to hold back the tears.

Chapter Eleven

They're coming for me. I try to run, but my feet are heavy. Made of clay. Lifting each takes monumental effort, cracks appearing in my terracotta legs. I can either admit defeat and allow them to swarm over me, their claws rending my flesh to shreds. Or I can keep running. My feet drag behind me, made of iron now, but I won't give up. I grit my teeth and force myself to lift one foot... and it's too much. My right leg shatters into pieces. The maddened laughter behind me grows closer.

Kelly awoke with a gasp, his throat burning dry, his body drenched in sweat as he glanced around the room. Little had changed over the last six months. William's slumbering form was next to him, no doubt ready to stir the second Kelly got out of bed. Then he would utter the same words he did every morning. Just the thought made Kelly's jaw clench. He was tempted to lie in bed the entire day to avoid another tiresome replay. Unfortunately his bladder had other ideas. Exhaling, he sat up as quietly as possible and swung his leg over the edge of the mattress.

William smacked his lips a few times. "You okay?"

Kelly could feel the pulse throbbing in his neck. He wouldn't answer today. What a stupid fucking question. Of course he wasn't okay!

"Kelly?"

"I'm fine," he managed. Then he pushed himself up and started hopping. Too bad the Olympics didn't recognize this as a sport because Kelly could hop like a pro these days. He headed into the bathroom, sat on the toilet seat, and stared into space as his body took care of the rest. He was hopping back toward the bedroom when William appeared in the doorway and gave him a goofy grin. He was rock hard and his muscles still radiated heat from being under the covers. Sexy, but lately Kelly hated mornings, because a good night's sleep seemed to refuel William's optimism. No matter how bad the arguments the day before, no matter how much they struggled to get along, he would present Kelly with a fresh chance the next morning. While that used to be endearing and generous and welcome, now Kelly knew it would only be a matter of time. His anger would show or some bitter part of him would unleash words to wipe the smile from William's face. And he hated it. Hated himself, hated how it made him feel, and sometimes he even hated William for setting himself up to be hurt. So much hate. It needed to end.

He stepped aside and leaned against the counter. William made use of the toilet, shooting Kelly a few suggestive glances as he peed. Kelly didn't return the compliment. Lately he only felt sexy when he was dressed and his body was covered.

"Wanna take a shower?" William asked.

"If you're referring to the golden variety, then no."

A little humor. Okay. So far so good.

William flushed the toilet. "Too late for that. Unless you wait while I drink a couple gallons of water."

Kelly snorted. "I'd prefer the water before it passes through your personal filtration system."

"Suit yourself. Come on. I'll hold you."

Kelly's molars ground together. William holding him in the shower had once felt sweet. Liberating. Now it only seemed pathetic. "You go ahead," he said. "I'm getting back in bed."

"Then I'll join you," William said, taking a step closer.

"If you're not going to shower then I will," Kelly snapped.

He wanted to close his eyes and take a deep breath. Instead he stared William down, too proud as always to admit he had once again lost control. The anger inside of him was growing every day. In his dreams he might be chased by unseen monsters, but in the waking world, the true enemy lurked within.

William slunk out of the room without another word. Kelly shut and locked the door after him and resisted the urge to cry or scream or just go completely insane. Something had to change. He needed help. As he stood there leaning against the cold marble counter, he realized what he needed most. He rushed through showering as much as possible. Afterwards he put on a robe and hopped back to the bedroom. The blinds were open, letting in the soft Sunday light. William sat on the edge of the bed, pulling on his shoes.

"I'm heading out for my swim," he said without looking up. "I'll shower at the YMCA. Afterwards I thought I'd check on my mom."

"Okay." The room was silent as Kelly fetched his crutches and went to the dresser. He took more time than he needed, eager for William to leave. Only when he was at the door did Kelly turn around. "Are you coming to group today?"

William's eyes darted over to him, then away. "I'm hardly home anymore. The lawn needs to be mowed and I'm sure—"

"It's fine," Kelly said. Then he swallowed, because even through all the anger, he still loved William. "Will you be here tonight? You know I hate sleeping alone."

"I'm sure Royal would be glad to snuggle up with you."

Kelly felt like snapping at him in return, but he caught himself and chuckled. "I'd rather sleep with you."

A little optimism returned to William and he nodded. "I'll be here."

Once he was gone, Kelly allowed himself to dwell on the feeling of affection in his chest, wishing it would always be there to keep his other emotions at bay. Then he remembered his idea and grabbed his phone. He sat on the bed and sent a text to Bonnie. Then a few more to get his point across. Afterwards he waited, and when she finally sent him a digital thumbs up, he knew he would be okay. By the time William saw him again tonight, all the hate would be purged from his heart.

"Is this what you're looking for?"

Kelly felt like swiping the bottle from Bonnie, but he restrained himself. The orange plastic cylinder, the small printed text that said *as needed for pain*, and best of all, the rattling noise when Bonnie shook it. Not just a few pills. Nearly a full bottle. He was salivating, literally, when she handed it to him.

Kelly turned the bottle over in his hands, reading it more carefully. Elise Rivers was the intended recipient. The date was fairly recent. Just a month old. "Is this from when your sister had her wisdom teeth out?"

Bonnie nodded. "Eli took one of them and ended up barfing. The rest should still be in there."

"Excellent," Kelly breathed.

"Okay... So is your stump hurting or something because I don't get this."

Kelly considered lying, but she was his best friend. One of the many things he loved about Bonnie was how he could be totally honest with her. "They make me feel good."

"High?"

"Yeah. You know how miserable I've been lately. Well, when I first lost my leg, I was pretty damn cheerful about the whole situation. Because of these." He shook the bottle. "My little friends here want to take me on a nice vacation."

"It'll be a short one," Bonnie said. "Those are the only painkillers in our house. If you're really that unhappy, maybe you should get to the root of the problem."

"I know the root. I'm missing a leg and I want it back. What's the solution?"

Bonnie thought about it. "Okay, I've got nothing. Including more pills. What happens when they run out?"

Kelly glanced over at her and smiled wickedly. "Have you had your wisdom teeth out yet?"

"Not a chance!" Bonnie said, eyes widening. "You know how I feel about dentists and doctors. I'm not going under the drill just so you can get high!"

"Worth a shot," Kelly said, opening the safety lid.

Bonnie put a hand over his to stop him. "Do me a favor and wait until after group. I don't want you acting all weird. Or barfing while I'm trying to mac on some hottie."

Kelly considered her and shrugged. He could wait. Just having the pills as an option made him feel happier. Besides, his mood was usually good during group. Everyone there was an outsider—different than the norm. When he first showed up after the accident, there had been hugs and relief that the wreck hadn't cost him his life. That was it. Gay people were survivors by default. They understood how useless pity was. Perseverance was part of the daily grind. So they treated Kelly as they always had. Sure, a few of them tended to fetch things he needed, and Layne kept asking for the unused shoe whenever Kelly bought a new pair. Lord only knew what he did with them all. Most likely he just thought it was funny, and that was fine. On with the show.

Kelly's spirits remained high throughout the meeting. Keith lectured them on the importance of family, and Bonnie complained about the lack of new lesbians joining. Her months-long dry spell continued. On the drive home she joked about hooking up with a feminine guy instead. "It's the next best thing," she insisted. "We won't be able to do more than dry hump with our clothes on, but I'll take what I can get at this point."

Kelly laughed, one hand in his pocket to fondle the little plastic bottle. Bonnie hung out with him and his family for a few hours. Video games, caramel popcorn, and some tunes in her car before she had to go. When she did, Kelly felt so happy he decided he didn't need the pills. Then he thought of William, wondering if he'd show up for dinner or wait until afterwards. Either way, just the thought of facing him again, of wanting to be perfect for him despite that no longer being possible... The happiness drained from Kelly like he'd been poked full of holes. He went back inside, grabbed a Coke from the fridge, and returned to his room. Once there he considered the pills.

Whatever they had given him after the accident had been strong. Way stronger than what they would prescribe a wispy girl barely in her teens. Kelly decided to double the recommended dose. Popping four pills into his mouth, he put on some music, sat on his bed, and waited. Twenty minutes later he felt an edge of warmth creeping into his system. Half an hour later and his head was humming like an air conditioner on a hot summer day. Kelly rolled onto his back, staring at the ceiling with half-lidded eyes. He felt like he was floating, his body listing gently back and forth. He thought of William, love bursting from his chest with such strength that it was almost overwhelming. The hate was gone. Kelly felt like reaching for his phone to call William, just to hear his voice. He'd apologize for everything. All the bad things. Kelly would excuse himself, and then tell William to hurry back so they could start over again.

But first he needed to close his eyes, just for a moment, so he could marinate in these waves of bliss.

Kelly wasn't sleeping. Not exactly. A trance? Is that what this was? His body felt far away, his mind happy to entertain thoughts and images with little form and even less purpose. Most of all he was content, which made it all the more jarring when someone shook him.

"Kelly? Oh Jesus! Honey, wake up!"

He opened his eyes a fraction, wincing against the volume of his mother's voice. Then his lids shot open because she was holding the prescription bottle, lips moving as she read the chemical name. Then she turned and shouted another name.

"Doug! Get in here! Something's wrong with Kelly!"

"I'm fine," he grunted. "Calm down."

His mother turned to him, her relief only fleeting. "How many of these did you take?"

"Just one," he lied.

"Why do you even have them?"

"Phantom pain," he lied again.

His mother shook her head. "These aren't for you. If you're having problems, we'll go see the doctor."

"They wouldn't give me any more painkillers. You know that."

"So you asked Bonnie's sister for these?"

Kelly sighed. He needed to keep blame away from that family. The last thing he wanted was his mother to start making phone calls. "I took them myself. I was looking for aspirin at her house when I noticed them."

"You stole these?"

"They were trash," he said. "They made Eli sick, and she didn't need them anymore."

"You don't either," his mother said. "You only need what the doctor gives you."

Kelly didn't agree, but what really upset him was his mother walking out of the room. With his pills. "Wait," he said, sitting up. "I'm fine. You know that, right?"

"I don't know that, but I'm getting your father."

"Okay, but hold on. Just leave the pills here, all right? You don't know what it's like. My leg hurts."

"Then we'll take you to the doctor."

"They won't give me what I need!" Kelly said, his temper rising, even through the fog of opiates. "If they do, it'll be the same pills, so there's no sense in them going to waste."

His mother looked him square in the eye. "I'm getting rid of these pills, young man." She turned to leave again.

"Fucking stop!" Kelly shouted. He tried to stand to go after her, and he made it a few hops, but his head was still swimming and he lost his balance. Before Kelly could right himself, he toppled over, slamming a shoulder against the dresser. The pain came slower than it might have usually, but it was still enough to make him wince.

"Doug!" his mother shouted, tossing the pills aside and kneeling to help him. Royal showed up first, then his father. Kelly, feeling humiliated, was helped to the bed. He rubbed his shoulder, ignoring his mother's tears and his father's questions. Instead he stared at the carpet, where the bottle of pills sat. Then he made himself look away, hoping they would be forgotten.

"I'm fine," he said, answering their questions at last. "Everyone is freaking out over nothing."

"Are you *really* overdosing?" Royal asked skeptically. "Wouldn't you be puking? Or convulsing."

"Exactly," Kelly said, grateful for his brother's big mouth. Now he just needed everyone out of his room. And away from the pills. "Isn't it dinnertime? Let's go. We can talk while we eat."

"What's going on?" William appeared in the doorway, took in the concerned expressions, and rushed into the room. His foot kicked the pills, causing a rattle. When he heard the noise, he stooped to pick up the bottle, face still concerned. "Is everyone okay? What happened?"

Kelly didn't answer. Instead he felt anger as his mother snatched the bottle of pills from William and left the room, shaking her head as if it were his fault. It wasn't, but Kelly couldn't help noticing that, once again, William had inadvertently cost him his happiness.

Allison Cross, LPC, NCC

Kelly kept glancing between the name plate on the desk and the actual woman. Allison was currently stapling together papers that his mother had filled out. While doing so, she idly chatted about last night's thunderstorm, which had brought down both trees and power lines. The words were mostly lost on Kelly, as he tried to decipher what the abbreviations after her name meant. Licensed Pill Curer? Narcs Can't Crave? Neither was remotely likely. He knew at least one "C" stood for counselor, because that's who he was here to see.

So far he wasn't impressed. Allison didn't have her own secretary. The small waiting room held only a few chairs, all of them empty. People weren't exactly lining up to have their heads examined by her.

"Ready?" she asked.

Kelly nodded. He didn't have a choice.

Allison opened the door to another room, this one larger and more impressive. Kelly swung in on his crutches, noticing two couches facing a table. To one side was the classic reclining-patient couch with a chair next to it. No way was he doing that. He headed for the couch, noticing that his mother had remained in the waiting room, the door to it shut now. He took a seat, Allison sitting directly opposite him on the other couch.

Kelly avoided looking at her, choosing instead to examine the many potted plants. Or the fat candle with three wicks, which seemed superfluous since plenty of natural light came from the large window on the far wall.

"Hello there!" The woman waved to get his attention. "I'm Allison. Nice to meet you."

"Kelly," he responded. Was this the first test because... "We already did intros in the front room."

"I know," Allison said, "but sometimes when I show up somewhere new, I get a little flustered and the details pass me by. Especially if I'm nervous."

"I'm not nervous," Kelly insisted.

"Great. How are you feeling?"

Aside from nervous? He considered the question. Allison watched him with wide eyes. She looked concerned and genuinely interested, but then again, that was her job. He decided to be honest. At least it would give him a chance to vent. "I'm upset," he answered.

"Okay. What about?"

"I don't want to be here. I shouldn't be because I'm not crazy."

"Definitely not," Allison said easily. "If you were, you wouldn't be talking to me."

"Why not?"

"I'm a counselor, not a psychologist. I'm not here to diagnose or prescribe medicine. I'm just here so we can talk. And maybe we can work through a few of your problems along the way."

"I already have friends I can talk to," Kelly said.

"Sure, but sometimes a fresh perspective can be invaluable. It's also nice to have someone you can trust with your secrets. Some things you can't say to your friends because the truth might hurt their feelings. You don't have to worry about my feelings, Kelly, and your secrets are safe with me."

He considered her again. This was all a trap, right? Then again, what did he have to lose? The worst of it was out already. "I took a few pills the other night," he said. "My mom found them and flipped. Now she thinks I'm a pill junkie like my Aunt Mary, which is ridiculous, because I'm pretty sure you need a steady supply of pills before you can become an addict."

"That would certainly make it easier," Allison said. "So what drove you to take those pills?"

"The pain," Kelly answered instantly.

"Your leg?"

Kelly huffed.

Allison studied him a moment. "Ah, that sort of pain. I can relate. I used to get pretty blitzed in college. In retrospect, I wasn't just drinking to feel drunk. I was drinking to stop myself from feeling other things."

"Like what?"

"The pain caused by my father's death. I'd get a little drunk, and usually start crying over it all, but I knew if I kept drinking, I wouldn't feel a thing. Well, besides plastered that night and hungover the next morning. But at the time I thought the discomfort was worth it. What about you?"

"I don't have any booze to get plastered with."

"No, I mean why do you take pills? The buzz feels good, but is there something you're trying to escape?"

"Myself," Kelly answered, his throat feeling tight. Allison nodded as if this made sense, but it couldn't, because Kelly barely understood it himself.

"If you could travel back in time one year and give yourself a bottle of pills, do you think the Kelly from back then would take them?"

"No," he said instantly. "I didn't need them then."

"Why not?"

"Because that Kelly had everything. Maybe I didn't realize it then, but I had it all."

"And now you don't?"

Kelly frowned. "Nope."

"Tell you what," Allison said. She slid a pad of paper across the table to him. Then she tossed him a pen, forcing him to catch it. "Why don't you make me a list of all the things you've lost in the past year. Take your time. I'm going to sit here playing Bejeweled on my phone. It's a dumb game, but personally, I can never concentrate if I know someone is staring at me."

"You want me to write down what I've lost?" Kelly asked incredulously.

"Yup." Allison already had her phone out and was pressing

buttons. "Oh! Be sure to write 'What I've Lost' at the top and underline it. That'll make it feel more official."

He stared at her, but she didn't laugh. In fact, she already seemed completely absorbed in her game. Well, she wouldn't get much play time out of him. This was going to be a very short list. He wrote out the title of the paper, just as she asked, then on the first line he wrote the first and last entry.

My leg.

Simple as that. He was about to hand back the pad of paper when he hesitated. Maybe it wasn't so simple. His parents had made him attend an amputee support group once, and some of the people were chipper and cheerful. He didn't understand how that was possible. He certainly didn't feel optimistic, so he added another line to the paper. Then another and another. Before he knew it, he had a list of eight. He reread it, feeling vulnerable by how much truth had been spelled out in so few words.

"I'm finished," he mumbled.

Allison pressed a few more buttons, then tossed aside her phone as if she'd been burnt. "Ugh! So addictive. And so very pointless. Let's see what you've got."

Instead of scanning the list in silence, she read each line aloud. "Your leg."

"It's no longer there," he explained patiently.

"Fair enough. Next one. Happiness?"

"That's right."

"You never feel happy anymore? Not ever?"

Kelly hesitated. "Maybe I should have written satisfaction instead. Or contentment."

"There aren't any wrong answers. I'm just trying to make sure I understand you. As for your handwriting, I *will* have to take points off your final grade."

Kelly raised an eyebrow. "What?"

"I'm kidding," Allison said. "Although your penmanship really is atrocious. A hyperactive monkey with a fistful of broken crayons could do better."

Kelly smiled at the visual image. Okay, so maybe he could still feel happy. But the rest of the list...

"Hope," Allison read aloud.

"I'm not going to get better," Kelly explained. "I'm never going to walk again. I tried a prosthetic leg and it's not for me."

"Yeah, but you should still have something to hope for," Allison said. "Just because you can't walk, doesn't mean you have nothing to look forward to."

"Maybe you should keep reading," Kelly said.

"Independence. Meaning others need to help you?"

"Yes," Kelly said. "There are little things I can't do by myself anymore. If I drop a bunch of pencils, how am I going to pick them up?"

"By getting on the ground, just like the rest of us."

Kelly rolled his eyes. "You don't get it. Everything is harder now, and I've got pride, okay? I try to manage on my own, but sometimes there's no choice and I need help, even if I don't want it."

Allison raised an eyebrow. "Same here. Same with anyone. Listen, I didn't have you make this list just to shoot it all down. The point isn't to prove to you that you haven't lost anything. But you'll have to do better than this. None of these justify you popping pills."

This time she wasn't kidding. He felt like grabbing the pad of paper back from her. Instead he nodded at it. "Keep reading."

"My dream," she said. "What's your dream?"

"To run in the Olympics. And don't start spewing crap about the Paralympics. Maybe they're a pale imitation, or hell, maybe they're harder than the normal kind and more worthy of praise. I don't care either way, because we're talking about *my* dream, and that's not what it was. I was going to be in the Olympics."

Allison studied him a moment. "I always thought it was bullshit that disabled athletes aren't allowed to compete in the Olympics. I hope that changes someday, because it smacks of segregation."

"Yeah," Kelly said. "It does."

"If that were to change, would you still want to compete? Or would you only want to win on your own two legs, like in your dream?"

"I don't want to answer that because it'll sound petty."

"It won't," Allison said. "There's nothing wrong with mourning a dream, so long as you don't let it stop you from finding a new one." She glanced back down at the list. "What's this about photography?"

"It was a hobby of mine."

"And now?"

"I can't hold the camera still enough. I could use a tripod, but the best photos are those you snap spontaneously. When you see something special, you have to act quickly before it disappears. A steady hand is crucial."

"You might be more limited now, but you could sit at street-side café and keep your eyes open."

"And be lower than the subject I want to capture? I can still take photos, but without total creative freedom, I'm no longer interested."

"Very well." Allison looked down at the list again, then back up at him. She did this a few more times and snorted. "Sex appeal? You've got to be kidding me. Hold on, I'll get a mirror, because—don't take this the wrong way, I'm a happily married woman—but you are ridiculously handsome."

Kelly couldn't help smiling. He felt pretty good about his appearance, but he hadn't said he'd lost his good looks. The problem wasn't that simple. "I don't feel okay about my body anymore," he said. "When I'm nude, I try to hide my amputation."

Allison waved a hand dismissively. "If anyone out there has a problem with it, send them packing. You'll soon find someone who doesn't mind. For some people it's a huge turn-on."

"I'm not sure I'd like that either," Kelly admitted. "I just wish it wasn't an issue. I never had to think about stuff like that before. I could just be me."

"But even then you probably had a feature you felt insecure about," Allison said. "Everyone worries about something. When I was little, I used to wish my hair was straight like the white girls. And lately I've been hitting the gym to make sure this booty keeps its bounce."

Kelly was surprised by this confession. Allison seemed in good shape to him.

"My husband keeps saying how fine I look," she continued, "and that flabby or firm, he'll still love my butt and the rest of me. Regardless, I keep looking in the mirror and driving myself crazy over it."

"I used to worry about my ass hair," Kelly confessed, mostly just to comfort her. "I even tried shaving it once and got such bad razor burn that I couldn't sit for days. At least you don't have to worry about that."

"That's what you think," she said with a wink. "You see my

point? Everyone worries about something, and most likely, that hang-up doesn't even matter to other people. Now you're worried about your amputation instead of your hairy crack. Believe me, the older you get, the longer that worry list becomes."

Kelly laughed. "Okay, fine. I'll try to keep that in mind."

Allison smiled back down at the list. Then her face grew more serious. Kelly was glad, because it matched just how twisted up his stomach felt, even before she spoke the name.

"William."

"Yeah," Kelly said, his voice hoarse.

"Tell me about him."

Oh boy. Where to even begin? Dancing around the truth seemed pointless. "How do you feel about gay people?"

Allison leaned back and exhaled. "How can I put this?" After a moment's thought, she continued. "You know when you first tell someone you're gay, and assuming they aren't a homophobic nitwit, they usually mention some other gay person they know? No matter how random it is, they'll mention a distant cousin, a family friend, the local butcher, or even some character on TV. And you know they mean well, but you're not sure how to react, because it's not like all gay people know each other. Am I right?"

Kelly laughed. "How do you know all that? Are you—?"

"No," Allison said. "My best friend is gay. Oh great, now I sound like everyone else! I was trying to prove I'm cool by flaunting my insider knowledge. The thing is, my best friend is more like a significant other. I might already be married to a straight man, but nobody—and I mean nobody—comes between me and my gay husband!"

Kelly grinned. "Well, I don't have a husband, but my boyfriend just happens to be gay."

"William? Tell me about him."

Kelly did, starting at the beginning. He smiled through most of the story. Then he reached the morning of the accident and hesitated, but Allison's expression was open, so he kept talking. As soon as he reached waking up to discover he'd lost a leg, he stopped, because he knew how Allison would react.

"William didn't mean to cause the accident," he said. "He didn't want to hurt me. It's not his fault."

Allison blinked. "Then whose fault is it?"

Kelly opened his mouth, but no words came out.

Allison studied him a moment before a gentle knock at the door drew their attention. She glanced at the watch on her wrist and sighed. "Out of time. I hate when that happens. One more question, the very same one I asked at the beginning of the hour. How are you feeling?"

Kelly considered the question and answered honestly. "Better."

Allison nodded. "I'm glad to hear it. I'd love to talk to you again. If you're up for it."

"Yes," Kelly said instantly. "Definitely."

"Good. Let's go speak with your mom."

His stomach sank as they stood and headed for the waiting room. He shouldn't be surprised. Allison would confer with his mother now, giving her a full report of his personal thoughts and feelings. That was the deal. His parents wanted to know what was wrong with him, and Allison's job was to figure it out and tell them. Already they were talking together.

" —another appointment this time next week." Allison was saying as she flipped open a book on her desk. "A little later actually, if that works for you. Four in the afternoon?"

"Yes," Laisha responded, seeming uncertain. "That would be fine."

"Great!" Allison smiled at Kelly. "I'm looking forward to it. See you then!"

His mother didn't move. "I thought we would have time to talk."

"Oh!" Allison said. "You want an appointment for yourself?"

"I mean now," Laisha said. "About all of this. About Kelly and the pills."

"He's doing fine," Allison said. "Sometimes it helps to talk things through, especially with the knowledge that anything you say will remain confidential."

"I'm his mother."

Allison nodded. "Yes, but there are some things we don't feel comfortable telling our parents. Otherwise he would have done so already. Maybe in some future session, if Kelly is okay with it, we can all sit down together. For the time being, I'd rather work with him alone. You have a wonderful son, Mrs. Phillips. We all wander off the path sometimes. Maybe he and I can figure out if it was the right path to begin with."

"Okay," his mother said, not sounding convinced. "Well… Thank you for your time."

They were at the car before his mother tsked and shook her head. "I don't know. All I wanted was—"

"Mom," Kelly interrupted. "It helped. Seriously."

She looked him over, her features relaxing somewhat. "I suppose that's all that matters."

They huddled together at the bus stop, the plastic roof above their heads too narrow to completely shield them from the drizzle. The weather was slightly chilly, but Kelly didn't mind, since it allowed him to nestle up to William for warmth. The evening had been nice. He'd given a lot of thought to the list he had made for Allison, and how much of what he thought lost was still right there. With that in mind, he'd invited William out for dinner and a movie. And they were getting along, proving that nothing between them was permanently damaged. A little bruised maybe, but they could heal.

As enjoyable as cuddling against William was, Kelly was eager to get home and warm up through more intimate activities. "I don't think the bus is coming," he said.

William glanced down the street. "I think you're right. It's what—twenty minutes late now?"

"When's the next one?" Kelly asked.

William twisted to check the sign posted behind them. "Ugh. Another forty minutes."

"Makes me miss driving."

William didn't respond.

"Let's call my parents," Kelly said. "It's getting cold."

"We could walk," William said. "Start heading the right direction but stay on the bus route. That will warm us up, and we can catch the next bus about halfway."

"Crutches and the rain," Kelly chided. "Not the best combination. Unless you want to carry me. No, I'll call home." He reached for his phone.

"Wait," William said, sounding tense. "It's been a nice night."

Meaning that being around Kelly's family would ruin it for him. He didn't take it personally. Rarely a day passed that someone in his family didn't make a slight at William's expense. Kelly was tired of that. Maybe they should have one big family session with Allison. Regardless... "One call, a quick car ride, and we'll be alone in my room."

William perked up. "I'll call my mom! She can give us a ride."

Kelly's stomach filled with dread. So maybe he understood William's reluctance. Mrs. Townson behaved as if Kelly had stolen her son away. "We *could* call her," he said carefully, "but it doesn't make sense for her to drive us to my house before returning to her own. That's an extra trip my parents won't have to make."

"So let's stay at my place," William suggested.

Kelly searched for an excuse not to, his jaw working. He had promised himself he wouldn't argue tonight, but he hated the idea of seeing Mrs. Townson's pursed lips, or watching her fawn over William, intruding on their personal time together.

"We can wait for the next bus," he said at last.

"I don't want to," William said. "I like the idea of being in my own room."

"Then maybe we should each call our parents and go our separate ways," Kelly snapped. He took a deep breath. "Sorry, I didn't mean that."

"It's okay," William said, not sounding angry. "We can't always spend so much time together."

Kelly glanced over at him. Something in his tone suggested this comment wasn't a general observation. "What do you mean?"

"I got a job," William said. "Part time, after school."

"Where?" Kelly asked, hating the panic in his voice.

"That juice place at the mall."

"Why would you do that?"

"For the money. Just think of the presents I'll be able to buy you."

All Kelly could think of was the additional time they would spend apart. Lately William had been waking up earlier than normal to go swimming. When Kelly opened his eyes in the morning, the bed next to him was already empty. Now the only hours they would spend together would be in school—when they couldn't really be intimate—and whatever meager time remained before bed. How was that a relationship?

William didn't appear apologetic, or worried about missing anything. He didn't even seem interested in discussing it further. Instead he stared down the road, but he was no longer searching for a bus. His eyes were unfocused, and he wasn't even looking in the right direction. Kelly watched him with a sinking sensation. That list he'd made for Allison? He felt certain he'd got one thing right. Somehow, he had lost William.

Chapter Twelve

"So he got a job," Allison said. "Big whoop. You'll still have weekends together, and really, not many people your age share a bed every night with the person they love. You're spending more time together than any of your peers."

Kelly shook his head. "I trust my instincts. William is distancing himself from me on purpose. I don't blame him. Lately I'm so damn pissy."

Allison didn't argue the point. Instead her brow furrowed as she looked over her notes. She hadn't taken them while he talked, meaning she must have written down her observations after their previous session. He wondered — if he asked — whether he would be allowed to read them or not. "I'm glad we're talking about William," she said. "Let's go back to the accident. Last time you said it wasn't William's fault."

"It wasn't."

"Okay. Do you feel like the accident was anyone's fault?"

Kelly nodded. He'd thought about this many times. "I pushed him," Kelly said. "Not just that morning in the car, but even before then. There's this part of me that feels vulnerable, and my reaction is to lash out. Well, I kept lashing out at William until he couldn't take it anymore."

Allison frowned. "You'd be surprised how often I hear the same thing, usually from women. They didn't fulfill their husband's needs or take his feelings into consideration or blah blah blah, and *that's* why he was forced to hit them."

"It was an accident," Kelly stressed. "William isn't abusive. I'm not a battered woman!"

"So the only way William could have reacted that day was to jerk the wheel and send you both spiraling into traffic? He couldn't have ignored you, or told you to shut up, or pulled over until he got his temper under control?"

Kelly sighed. "My mom got to you, didn't she? They hate William, and you're supposed to make me feel the same way."

"Nope," Allison said. "I'm not trying to break you guys up. Believe me, I know how impossible it is to talk sense into a lovesick heart. But I *am* trying to make a point. You blame yourself for what happened, right? Well, what if the situation was reversed?"

"Like if I had been driving that day?"

"And lost your temper, turned the car into oncoming traffic, and cost William his leg. Just think how that would have affected his life."

Kelly's head spun as he considered the implications. "No more swimming. At least not like before. And definitely no Coast Guard. William wants to be a rescue swimmer, and it's one of the most physically grueling programs out there. Hardly anyone graduates."

"In other words," Allison said, "a shattered dream. How would you feel if you had done all that to him?"

"Awful."

"And who would you blame. Him?"

"No!" Kelly said instantly.

"But he made you so angry! While you were driving! He pushed and pushed and—"

"Okay," Kelly said quietly. "I get it."

"You want to know why you harbor so much anger?" Allison asked. "Maybe it's because you haven't allowed yourself to be angry at the right person. You keep blaming yourself, and honestly, I'm not asking you to stop and blame William instead. You both made mistakes that day. You shouldn't have argued with someone who was driving. He shouldn't have reacted in the way he did. Even the rain is to blame, or the truck that collided with you. Maybe the driver could have done something differently—more sleep, coffee, or who knows what else. There are more factors at play than we can ever count, but the only finger of blame you're pointing is at yourself. That doesn't seem fair to me."

"So what do I do?" Kelly said. "Go home and yell at William?"

"There's been enough yelling," Allison said, "but maybe it's time to sit down and talk. Tell him what you're sorry for and what you regret about that day. If he's a good man, he'll do the same. He broke your trust. He was supposed to drive you safely. An accident is forgetting to check your blind spot and sideswiping another car. Wanting to scare someone just to shut them up, that's no accident."

"But he didn't want—"

"I know," Allison said. "He didn't want you to lose a leg, but he should have known the risk he was taking with your safety. Does William blame himself?"

"Yes," Kelly said. "Even though I wish he wouldn't."

"Let him accept responsibility. You denying he did something wrong when he knows he did can't feel good. You both messed up. Better acknowledge that before it tears you apart. You boys need to talk."

Kelly stared at her. "God I love your brain!"

Allison sighed wistfully. "Gay men always do."

"You're alive!"

Kelly spun around to face the parking lot—at least as quickly as his crutches would allow—and made sure to put on a suitably guilty expression. "Sorry," he said.

Bonnie shook her head. He wouldn't be forgiven so easily. She pulled out her phone, rested her weight on one hip, and read from the screen. "Last text message I got from you says, and I quote, 'Oh Jesus, oh Jesus, oh Jesus!' That's it. I've spent the last two days wondering if you were having an orgasm, or if you saw Godzilla just before getting eaten."

"I'm sorry," Kelly repeated. "You know all that stuff I've been talking about with my counselor?" He lowered his voice as two guys from the youth group passed them on the way into the church. "William and I finally had the talk."

"You did?" Bonnie dropped all pretense of being angry. "How'd it go?"

"Good," Kelly said. "William actually cried."

"For real?"

"Yeah, but more like he was relieved. We both accepted blame for what happened. Then we took turns expressing what we were angry about before we forgave each other. It felt… cleansing."

Bonnie snorted. "Cleansing? Please tell me you're not getting too deep into this self-help stuff. Pretty soon you'll be lighting incense and asking everyone to hold hands while sharing their positive energy."

"Laugh all you want, but William and I are enjoying our second honeymoon."

"Well, in that case I'm glad." Bonnie shot a wink at Lisa, who blushed before hurrying on her way. "Love those shy girls. So how did you get here without me giving you a ride?"

"That's one of the things we discussed," Kelly said. "William and I both feel uncomfortable around each other's parents, so to minimize that, no more bumming rides from them. We're trying to be more independent, which means taking buses as much as possible."

Bonnie shrugged. "I'm still available if you need me, but I think I understand. So you spent the last couple of days in bed together?"

Kelly grinned in response.

"I'll take that as a yes. Let's head inside and see if there are any new girls looking to do the same with me."

Kelly didn't keep tabs on the girls much, but all the faces seemed familiar. After grabbing a sparkling water from the refreshments table and deciding none of the snacks appealed to him, he took the seat William had reserved for him. Bonnie plopped down on an old love seat farther along, the space next to her empty, like she was tempting fate.

Keith was wiping down the marker board he adored writing on while lecturing them, a sure sign that the meeting was about to begin. Before it could, two late arrivals entered the room—a guy and a girl who were holding hands like Hansel and Gretel on their way into the dark spooky woods. Kelly resisted a chuckle, remembering how nervous he'd been his first time. Unless they were actually a couple. If so, he couldn't imagine what they were doing here. The girl—heavyset with a face more handsome than pretty—shook off the guy's hand. With a flick of her sunshine brown hair, she strutted into the room like she owned the place. This made the guy appear alarmed before he hurried to catch up with her. They went to the refreshments table and poked around, the entire room growing silent as they were observed.

"It's like an AA meeting in here," the girl muttered.

Layne, who was casually inching toward them, responded with, "You've got that right, honey, but it's not booze we're addicted to!"

Most people laughed. Kelly rolled his eyes, noticing how the new guy's shoulders tensed before he spun around, as if he intended to leave. Probably a closet case. Like a shepherd sensing one of his flock about to go astray, Keith blocked his path and offered a hand. When it became clear that the guy wasn't going to make a break for it, Kelly turned his attention to William, who was staring at the newcomers with his mouth hanging half-open. Kelly playfully put a finger beneath his chin and closed it.

"Someone you know?" he asked.

"No," William said, blinking before flashing a smile. "It's just been awhile since there's been anyone new."

"I know," Kelly said. Then in his best imitation of Dracula, he added, "Fresh meat!"

"Okay!" Keith said, taking a seat next to Bonnie. Kelly stifled a laugh. If she was hoping for a hot new love affair, it was off to a rocky start. "Today we're going to talk about relationships. But first, let's do a round of introductions."

Kelly groaned. He wasn't alone. Bonnie shot him a glare and mouthed "self-help" as if this was all his fault.

"Now, now!" Keith said. "Some new people are here today, and I could also use a reminder of who's who. Tell us your name and one thing about yourself."

Kelly daydreamed through most of this. He knew everyone in group so well that he could have done the introductions for each person. Layne wanted to be a makeup artist. Sarah was crazy about boy bands—which was weird since she dug chicks. Lisa wanted to establish an animal shelter for injured wildlife, and Bonnie loved her cello. Everyone had their thing. Then it was Kelly's turn. He opened his mouth to talk about his Olympic dream or his love of photography, before he remembered what Allison had said. He was mourning his lost dream, but he hadn't found a new one yet. His voice nearly caught in his throat until humor came to the rescue.

"My name is Kelly," he said. "And I'm very disappointed Lisa didn't bring brownies this time, since I skipped breakfast."

"Sorry!" Lisa replied from across the room.

Kelly smiled at her. "It's okay."

"I'm William," his boyfriend said, "and I'm glad there aren't any brownies since I ate way too much this morning."

Kelly was about to smile when the new girl cried out like she'd been struck. "Nyyyah!" Did she have Tourette Syndrome or something?

"Oh, go ahead!" Keith said.

"Sorry." The girl twirled a lock of hair around her finger. "All this talk of food got me excited."

Layne guffawed and slapped his knee. Even Kelly couldn't resist a smile.

"My name is Emma," she continued, "and I was born to love you. Unfortunately I can only love one of you, so let's keep things civil. No cat fights, please, but I do accept bribes."

The room laughed, all except Kelly, who leaned forward to look down the row at Bonnie. She was smiling appreciatively, her eyes half-lidded. That dry spell was about to come to an end.

"And who did you bring with you?" Keith asked.

Oh, this should be good!

"Jason," the new guy said. "And I... uh... heeeee."

That last bit was a wheeze. Kelly clenched his jaw to keep from laughing. These two couldn't be real! This was some sort of prank, or maybe they were clowns, here to announce the circus was in town. Or maybe not, since Jason's face had turned bright red. Was he still breathing? Maybe he had swallowed a piece of gum and was choking on it.

"That's okay," Keith said. "How about you, Lisa?"

Kelly kept his attention on Jason, who must have felt it because the guy made eye contact. And stared. Kelly stared back. Jason's hair was a mess and his cheeks still sunburn red, but those blue eyes were intense. And so penetrating that Kelly forfeited the staring contest, turning his attention to Lisa.

"—much more challenging than taking care of domesticated animals, since a wild animal doesn't want to be petted or comforted. In fact, the wildlife rehabilitator has to approach each rescue with—"

Kelly leaned back and got comfortable. Lisa was shy and quiet, but when she got going on this subject, she was assertive and wordy. Once she was finished with her micro-lecture and the rest of the introductions were made, Keith got started on the theme of the meeting. He began by challenging the assumption that men and women wanted different things, asking them what they desired in a mate. Kelly already knew that in a room full of gay people, traditional gender roles were null and void, meaning the answers would be interesting. Bonnie went first.

"I want to be understood," she said.

Kelly felt like rushing over to give her a high-five. Nothing was more frustrating than being with someone who didn't seem to understand you. He still felt that way with William occasionally, especially when he reacted to Kelly's anger like it was unreasonable instead of natural.

Keith wrote Bonnie's answer on the board. "What else?"

One of the circus clowns, Emma, went next. "I want to feel

appreciated," she said, looking across the room. At Bonnie. There would be some fast and furious texting tonight! Assuming Bonnie wasn't preoccupied by then.

"Excellent," Keith said, marker squeaking across the board. "Let's hear from the boys too."

"He has to be hot!" Layne called out.

"Goes without saying," Sarah replied.

"So," Keith said, "both sides want someone they are attracted to. Everyone has their own definition of hot, so this can be anything. What else?"

William raised his hand, causing Kelly to feel defensive. What if William named a trait he didn't have much of? Patience or kindness or something along those lines. "Commitment," he said. "Loyalty is important."

Kelly had that in spades, so he relaxed. "Trust," he said. "You should be able to trust the person you're with."

He looked at William, who appeared wounded. Kelly was trying to reference their recent conversation, not the accident, but even now it still loomed over everything. He wished it wouldn't. Regardless, William placed a hand over his, Kelly surprised to find his own balled up into a fist. He forced himself to relax so their fingers could weave together. Obviously they still had a few issues to work out, but they could get there if—

"Humility," Jason said, his voice clear and strong.

Keith's marker stopped squeaking as he turned. "Humility?"

"Yeah," Jason said. "I don't want some guy I have to impress or one who feels like he needs to show off. I just want someone who loves me that I can love back. Simple as that. That's all it takes."

Humility. God, if there was one thing Kelly didn't have, it was humility. He relied on his pride, depended on it to get him through life's rough patches. It even motivated him. Kelly wanted to be the best, and he was willing to work his ass off for it. That had nothing to do with humility. If this had been William's answer, Kelly would be in a blind panic right now. The current situation was nearly as bad, since William was nodding as he listened.

"I don't really care about honesty," Jason continued, "or being totally understood or any of the other stuff, because being human is all about messing up and breaking trust and telling lies.

I wouldn't want to be with someone perfect. Just some humble, totally normal guy will do."

Jason looked from person to person, those eyes blazing. He'd been shy before but this... this was something different. Forget circus clown. As Jason's fierce gaze locked with Kelly's, he wondered if he wasn't meeting the devil incarnate. How else could he have chosen the one trait Kelly felt devoid of? When Jason looked at William next, Kelly nearly leapt in front of him, just to break the spell.

"Humility," Keith said, sounding impressed. He wrote it on the board and took a step back. "So as you can see, we all have a lot of emotional needs, despite gender or sexuality. It's important not to give in to gender stereotypes or keep perpetuating them. Now let's pair up, boy-girl, boy-girl, and do some role-playing. Come on, everybody find a partner."

Kelly exhaled. At least this exercise would prevent Jason from making a move on William. Or so he thought. Jason remained seated, but his friend Emma walked right over to them. "You seem nice," she said to William. "Let's be partners!"

"Sure!" his boyfriend replied, amiable as ever.

Okay... Kelly turned to find Bonnie, spotting her on the other side of the room. Talking to Jason. What the hell was going on here? Lisa had her head down, too shy to ask anyone, so Kelly went to join her. He tried to focus on the exercise, which involved pretending to be the opposite sex while spewing unfair gender stereotypes. Seeing quiet Lisa pummel her chest or hold a finger under her nose to simulate a mustache—that was fairly distracting. Regardless, he couldn't help looking over at William, who was smiling and laughing with Emma.

Once the exercise was over, they were free to socialize. The first thing Kelly did was go to the restroom. He didn't have any pressing needs, but he figured leaving the playing field was the best way to reveal the moves of any potential opponents. While there he checked himself in the mirror, feeling confident, especially since the mirror was too small to show his whole body. The Kelly he saw reflected could very well have two legs and no clumsy crutches propping him up.

When he returned to the meeting room, he hovered in the doorway. Bonnie and Emma were talking now. No big surprise. As for Jason, he and William were on opposite sides of the room.

Not what he was expecting, but good news nonetheless. Jason was socializing with Layne and a few other guys, looking a little antsy. Elsewhere, William was flexing a bicep, inviting Lisa to hang off his arm as he did so. Kelly allowed himself a chuckle. Yup, he definitely needed Allison to help him with his insecurity.

He took a step forward, eager to rejoin his boyfriend, when William looked up. But not at him. Instead his gaze travelled across the room to Jason. Just like before, his mouth opened a little, as if in wonder. Jason wasn't even looking his way. In fact, his back was turned to the rest of the room, and yet William still stared. Then Lisa said something to regain his attention.

"I'm heading to work," Bonnie said.

Kelly flinched, not having noticed her approach.

"You okay?" she asked.

"Yeah," Kelly said quickly. "How'd it go with you?"

Bonnie gave a sly grin. "The bad news is that she's long distance. She lives in Houston. The good news is that she's all mine. Or at least will be."

"You've got a date?" Kelly asked.

"Yup. Next weekend."

"What about her friend?"

"Jason?" Bonnie smirked. "He's not my type."

"Does he also live in Houston?"

Bonnie shook her head. "He's local. Don't worry, though. He knows the deal."

"Meaning?"

"I made sure to mention that you and William are together."

"Did he ask?"

Bonnie put on her patient expression. "*All* new guys ask about one of you, usually both. Don't get jumpy."

"I'm not jumpy," Kelly said, trying to sound calm. "I'm good."

"Good."

"Good."

"Uh, as stimulating as this conversation has become, I really gotta get to work."

Kelly moved out of her way, then headed over to William. When he looked at Kelly, he seemed in high spirits. Too high?

"Let's head out," Kelly suggested. "If we don't catch the next bus, we'll be stuck here another hour."

193

William shrugged. "Okay."

Everything seemed normal. He was starting to think he'd overreacted, but when they reached the door, it happened again. In the corner of his eye, he saw William turn to face the room once more, looking toward Jason. Kelly shook his head, feeling his temper rising. They *weren't* going to argue. They hadn't for a week. He wasn't about to break that streak, but he was eager to leave.

He was already at the end of the hall, William rushing ahead of him to open the door.

"You know I don't need help," he snapped, brushing past him.

"I was trying to be romantic," William murmured.

Kelly pressed on. He just needed to reach the bus stop where he could calm down and think about everything. Guys looked at guys. That was normal, and expecting William not to do so was unreasonable. It's just that he *kept* looking, and seemed so damn enamored. That same star-struck gaze had once been reserved for Kelly alone, but now he couldn't remember when he'd seen it last. He heard flapping feet behind him, glanced over to notice William's absence, then stopped and turned.

His field of vision was filled with a very large girl and her grinning teeth.

"Hi!" Emma said.

"Hello," Kelly responded, trying to see past her.

She moved to block his view. "I was just wondering, are these meetings every week because I had a really great time. I sort of wish they were every day. Could you imagine? I'd never leave. Ha ha ha!"

"They're biweekly." Kelly barely spared her a glance, pushing himself up on his crutches to see over her shoulder. William was still at the church door, his back pressed against it to hold it open. Jason stood in front of him, their sideways profiles framed by the doorway, like an artist had placed them there intentionally. The scene would have had Kelly grabbing for his camera if he still carried it around.

"I don't see why they can't happen more often," Emma said. "Is it the church? Because my house is big enough to have everyone over. Of course that means a massive convoy of gay teens driving to Houston, but I'll make it worthwhile. I'll order pizzas. Real ones. Not the frozen kind."

Kelly stopped trying to see past her and fixed her with a stare. "Who are you people?"

"I'm Emma," she said, thrusting a hand out.

He pretended the crutches prevented him from shaking it. He felt like shouting, or maybe knocking her out of the way, but instead he forced himself to stay calm. He kept his voice level. "How about you do me a favor, Emma, and step aside."

She blinked, gave an empty smile, and very slowly stepped to the side. The door had closed behind William. He was facing Jason, who had his back to the parking lot, as if Kelly's presence there was of no concern. He couldn't tell if they were speaking, but it was clear Jason had William's full attention.

Okay. *Now* Kelly was angry. "Hey!" he yelled. "Are we going or what?"

That seemed to break the spell. Mostly. They still exchanged a few more words. Were they making plans?

"Nice talking to you, I guess," Emma said. "See you in a few weeks."

Kelly didn't humor her with a response. He watched her walk away, then focused on William. Kelly promised himself he wouldn't act jealous. Nobody found that attractive. "What was that about?"

William fought down a grin. "I think he likes me."

"You don't have to look so pleased about it."

William shrugged. "It's flattering, that's all. He'll back off once he finds out we're together."

That wasn't true because Jason already knew. Rather than press the point, Kelly stepped forward, hoping for a reassuring kiss. William placed a hand on his cheek, kissed him on the forehead, then moved past Kelly, heading for the bus stop. Kelly stared after him a moment, and for the first time in nearly four years, felt these meetings weren't such a good idea after all.

"I ran into Jason today."

Kelly glanced up from the back of the spoon where he'd been staring at a funhouse-mirror image of himself. William was beside him at the dining room table. For a moment, Kelly considered running through a list of Jasons they both knew, hoping it would be anyone but the guy with the haunting eyes, but William's expression was too open and frank for it to be anyone else.

"Where?" he managed.

"At the mall," William replied. "While I was working."

"He just came up to the counter or…"

"Yeah." William smiled. "He wasn't loitering off to the side or anything creepy like that."

Maybe not, but it seemed an awfully big coincidence. How long had it been since the last meeting? Ten days? And how could he have known where William worked? Unless Bonnie told Emma. He would have to ask her about that later, but for now, he needed to know exactly what had happened.

He started by expressing hope. "You probably didn't have much time to talk since you were working."

"It was my break, so we hung out briefly. Had a slice of pizza together. Or more like he watched me stuff my face. Ha ha!"

Kelly stared at him blankly, then looked across the table at Royal, who had just sat down, attention glued to the new cell phone William had bought him for his birthday. Soon Kelly's parents would enter with French onion soup and a mixed salad. Is that why William was doing this here and now? Did he think that Kelly wouldn't freak out, wouldn't shout and scream just because the family was gathered for dinner?

William needn't have worried. Kelly had already decided that getting angry again would push his boyfriend away, give him more reason to seek comfort in the arms of another man. "Well," he said in neutral tones, "if you should happen to see him again, tell him I said hello."

"That's the thing. He wants me to give him swimming lessons."

Royal glanced up from his phone. "How old is this guy?"

"Same age as us," Kelly said.

Royal snorted. "And he can't swim?"

"Weird, I know," William said, "but I thought this could be a good opportunity."

For his Coast Guard application? He'd already been accepted. Kelly didn't challenge this though, because he was sure William had some equally noble reason for wanting to help. To gain training experience, maybe. "Sounds great," Kelly said. "When?"

"I told him if he was serious, he'd have to wake up early and meet me at the Y."

That came as a relief. Kelly didn't know many people his age willing to get up at five in the morning, even for a handsome face. Still, he had to say something, no matter how small or delicately worded, to show he wasn't quite comfortable with all of this. "Just be careful." There. Simple as that.

"Don't worry," William said. "He knows about us. I made sure of that."

"Oh. Did he ask?"

"Nope, but I wanted to clear the air. Turns out he has a boyfriend too, so there won't be any false expectations."

"Cool."

Kelly's dad entered the room, carrying the first two bowls of soup, the cheese still sizzling on the floating toast. He supposed that ended the topic, so Kelly turned his attention to the spoon and considered himself again, feeling much less attractive than he had just a few moments ago.

"You'll be there, right?" Bonnie asked again, managing to sound more panicked than she had five minutes ago.

Kelly switched the phone to his other ear. "Of course."

"Bring your parents, okay?"

"Seriously? Why?"

"I'm worried no one's going to show up," Bonnie said, with a whimper in her voice. "I keep imagining myself on stage playing my cello with only one person in the audience. You."

"And William," Kelly said. "Oh, and the friends and family of the twenty other people playing at this recital. Did you forget about them? This isn't a solo performance, you know. You might be *my* star, but you aren't *the* star."

After a pause, Bonnie laughed. "Okay, so maybe I'm freaking out over nothing. Did I tell you Emma will be there?"

"No," Kelly said, trying to keep his tone neutral. Lately he felt like the world had gone insane. Or that he was missing something, because everyone seemed crazy about Jason and Emma. He could understand Bonnie's infatuation. When she fell, she did so like a sack of bricks dropped from a helicopter. Rubber bricks, because she bounced back incredibly fast. And often, few of her relationships lasting long. Except so far she had no complaints. Neither did his boyfriend, who had invited Jason along to Bonnie's recital. Less than a week's worth of swimming lessons and suddenly they were double-dating. Kelly felt reassured though, because that wasn't how cheating worked. You didn't introduce the spouses to each other.

"I gotta go!" Bonnie sounded as if she'd forgotten something. "Don't forget to show up! And bring your parents. Seriously. I need people to clap for me, even if I suck."

"I'm bringing along a couple of friends," Kelly assured her. "I've already reserved four tickets."

"Really?"

"Yes."

"You're the best. Bye!"

Kelly shook his head, made sure the call was disconnected, and set aside the phone. She hadn't bothered to ask who he was bringing, but that was fine. Let her share his puzzlement over these ever-present strangers who had so quickly weaseled their way into their lives, whether he wanted them to or not.

Chapter Thirteen

William paced while undressing, or sometimes while getting dressed. He kept marching between the walk-in closet and the full-length mirror in the bathroom, seemingly unsatisfied. Occasionally, like now, he would detour to where Kelly sat on the bed and give him a questioning expression.

"It's a music recital for gifted high school students," Kelly said. "This isn't a black tie event. The audience will mostly be parents in sweat pants, I swear." Of course this hadn't stopped him from putting on some of his nicest clothes. A black dress shirt with just a hint of shimmer and dark pants that sat low on his hips.

"Maybe I should wear something with more color," William said, pulling off the white sweater. "After all, this is an art thing, right? Artists like color."

"Not to mention that it's nearing summer. In Texas. You can put that sweater with the mothballs."

Not that they owned any. Or that William was paying attention. He'd already headed back to the closet, then marched to the bathroom, before returning once more. Now he wore a light-blue dress shirt that showed off his body. The khaki pants were a little cheesy, but he looked good anyway. "That's the one," Kelly said. "You're gorgeous."

William flashed him a smile. Then he bit his lip. "Maybe I'm trying too hard."

"*I* think you look good," Kelly stressed. Wasn't that all that mattered?

"Thanks," William said. Then he returned to the closet. When he came out, he had on a pair of pre-aged jeans that hugged him in all the right places. One in particular. William didn't ask what he thought this time. He seemed satisfied as he started fussing with his hair. Kelly sat on the bed, watching him, feeling like gravity was pulling at his mouth, his heart, his stomach, his hope. William wasn't getting dressed up for him. Or Bonnie. Maybe he was being paranoid, but Kelly now believed this was all for another person's benefit.

His mood didn't improve when they rode the bus to the Bates Recital Hall on the University of Texas campus. Kelly felt ridiculous looking his best on public transportation, as if he were showing up to a gala event on a hay-stuffed donkey cart. They were attracting more stares than usual, which made him tense. This feeling only increased once they had arrived and were waiting curbside for Jason and his date.

"So what do you know about this guy?" Kelly asked.

"Jason's boyfriend?" William shrugged. "Nothing, really."

"He doesn't come up in conversation much?"

"I know his name is Tim," William said, clearly grasping.

A honk made them both flinch, their attention travelling to the road, where a sleek silver car pulled to a stop. They could see Jason through the passenger-side window, raising a hand in greeting even though his expression seemed embarrassed. Kelly didn't look at him long, because the car was—

"Wow," William said.

Kelly made sure William was eyeing the vehicle and not the passenger. "Is that as expensive as it looks?"

"It's a Bentley," William said. When Kelly failed to react to this, he added, "It's pricey, yeah. Wow."

Jason stepped out of the car, the last shred of doubt dissipating from Kelly's mind. What William felt for this person still eluded him, but the indisputable fact was that Jason had feelings for William. More than lust, perhaps, because his eyes barely travelled over William's physique. Instead his focus remained on his face, Jason's eyes lighting up like he'd just stumbled upon the best thing in the world. Kelly felt a strange pang of envy, wanting to turn to William and see if he could still muster the same reaction.

Instead he watched those intense eyes move to meet his and become much more guarded. Jason looked him over, top to bottom, perhaps sizing him up. Then he walked over as the car behind him drove away.

Jason steadfastly ignored William, approaching Kelly instead and offering his hand. "Hi," he said as they shook. "Nice to see you again."

"Yes," Kelly replied. "How unexpected too. We didn't really talk at all during the meeting, and yet, here you are."

"Yeah." Jason blinked a few times and swallowed. Then he turned and shook hands with William. Kelly felt like swatting their wrists to break the physical contact.

"So," William said, "should we wait here while your boyfriend parks?"

"No, we can head toward the entrance," Jason said. "He'll find us."

That still confused Kelly. Why would Jason invite his boyfriend along? He thought of the car and imagined the sort of person who would own it. An older man, one who could give Jason everything he needed. Materially, at least.

"That's quite the car," Kelly said as they walked. "Expensive too. Is your boyfriend Richie Rich or is he an older guy?"

"He's a little older than me, yeah." Jason sounded upbeat about the fact rather than ashamed.

"Have you been together long?" Kelly pressed.

"We live together," Jason said, and as if trying to reassure him, he added, "It's pretty serious."

Kelly felt his jaw clench. "Now why should that concern me?"

Jason searched the horizon, perhaps hoping to find a change of topic there. "So, uh… How long have you guys been together?"

"A few years now," William replied.

"Wow! High school sweethearts, huh?"

"That's right," Kelly said, familiar emotions accompanying the memories. "It was love at first sight."

Jason glanced over at William, as if to confirm this, before asking another question. "How did you two meet?"

"We were training for a triathlon," Kelly said. "William is the school's best swimmer, and at the time I was the best runner—believe it or not—so we decided to team up."

"Not quite," William said. "You cornered me in the hallway and said no matter how good I was at swimming, that I'd never keep up with you on foot."

Kelly smiled. "And then you showed up at the track that afternoon to really start training. So I started showing up at the pool…"

"Not exactly love at first sight," William said.

"Speak for yourself." Kelly's stomach sank. Did these memories not fill him with the same warm nostalgia? They came to a stop in front of the music hall where a small line had already formed. "So, Jason, how did you meet your man?"

"Oh. Our story isn't nearly as good as yours."

Before he could say more, a guy walked up from behind Jason

and slung an arm over his shoulder. Kelly stared. This couldn't be him. The guy was older, but not by much. He was pushing thirty, if even that. His hair was jet black, his skin Mediterranean, like he'd just strolled out of Rome or Athens. The stubble, the muscles, the expensive clothes, and perhaps worst of all, the eyes like icicles melting in the sun. This couldn't be Jason's boyfriend. Absolutely not, because it would mean he already had the best and wanted William anyway. Or it could mean Kelly had been barking at shadows all this time, imagining someone was after his boyfriend, when in truth there was no threat at all.

"Hey sweet cheeks," the newcomer said, shining his teeth in Jason's direction and practically illuminating his face with their brilliance.

"Uh," Jason replied, completely affected by this.

Tim—that's who he had to be because of what happened next—pulled Jason closer and nearly pressed his mouth against his ear, murmuring amorous words too quiet to hear.

Jason smiled and tittered, clearly into this. Then he snapped out of it, remembering they weren't alone. "Kelly, William, this is Tim. My boyfriend. Tim, meet Kelly and William."

Kelly's hand was grabbed from where it hung limp at his side, nearly causing him to lose one of his crutches. Tim pumped his hand unmercifully until Kelly responded by doing the same. William already had his hand out, and as Tim held on to it, he seemed to size up William. Was he also confused about what was going on? If so, he quickly overcame any suspicion. And why wouldn't he? Just look at the guy!

"Okay, honey," Tim said rubbing his hands together eagerly, "where's that music you promised me?"

"Right this way," Jason said. "Darling."

Darling? Really? They sounded like little kids playing house. As they walked toward the entrance, Kelly met William's eye. He appeared equally puzzled.

"Male escort," Kelly mouthed silently.

William rolled his eyes, the hint of a smile playing about his lips.

Kelly nodded insistently, causing them both to glance back at the unlikely pair.

Then William gave a barely perceptible shake of his head.

Kelly raised an eyebrow, accepting his challenge. "So, Tim," he said. "We were just asking Jason how you two met."

Tim beamed and turned to Jason. "Do you want to tell it? No? Okay. It's a little embarrassing really. I was on my way downtown to do some shopping when I saw this handsome guy walking down the street." Jason was yanked closer. "So I parked the car as quick as I could and headed to where I'd seen him last. Luckily he had stopped to look at a window display, and I walked up behind him, checking out his reflection in the glass. He saw me too, and when he turned around—" Tim looked blissful. "We just hit it off!"

"Interesting," Kelly said. "Is that something you do a lot? Pulling over when you see a guy you find attractive?" He imagined it normally worked the other way around, people pulling over to pick him up, fifty bucks in hand.

"Never before," Tim insisted. "Not once. But come on! Look at him! Aren't his eyes intense? They sort of burrow into your soul, don't they? Or the way he clenches his jaw when he feels embarrassed. Or his messy messy hair." Tim ruffled it affectionately. "But really, those eyes are his best feature. Or maybe his lips, because man, the first time I kissed him... And if music is your thing, this boy can play the guitar! He's the one who should be up there on stage tonight. Then we'd be in for a treat!"

Nice sales pitch. Really, because Kelly now saw Jason in a whole new light. He *was* attractive, in his own way, and Kelly could easily picture how the tousled hair and penetrating gaze would come together nicely while Jason strummed a guitar. Like some sort of gay jukebox hero. If that's how William saw him too... Except his boyfriend looked a little irritated. At Tim's praise? Or maybe he finally agreed that something fishy was going on.

As they entered the recital hall and took their seats in the front, Kelly started to second-guess himself. Or triple or quadruple, because he no longer trusted his deductions. None of it added up. He didn't really believe Jason had hired an escort, although maybe Tim just happened to be one, and Jason was seeking a more wholesome relationship. Perhaps they were swingers on the prowl for other couples. Or maybe Kelly was just paranoid. He let himself seriously consider the possibility. He'd nearly ruined his relationship with William, and ever since he'd lost his leg, felt ridiculously lucky that anyone wanted him at all. He was insecure. So much so that he'd started inventing enemies which didn't exist. *That* was the truth.

Kelly sighed. William must have heard because he reached over and placed a hand on his. They would get through this. Allison could help. She had helped him overcome his anger. Now he would finally stop procrastinating and start addressing the next issue.

The lights dimmed and the curtain rose, Kelly taking comfort in the darkness. As the music began, he allowed himself to think it all over, stripping the recent events of his conspiracy theories, and gently chastising himself for being so foolish. Then Bonnie took the stage, hugging her cello and playing familiar music she'd practiced in front of him. She noticed him and smiled, as if knowing he needed reassurance. *Everything's going to be fine,* he could imagine her saying. *The drama was all in your head. No damage has been done.*

After the concert, when the curtain dropped and the lights came up, he felt reinvigorated. He intended to enjoy the rest of the evening. A double date! What could be more fun? He relaxed as they slowly worked their way up the stairs to the lobby. The atmosphere was electric, parents and friends congratulating the performers. He was looking forward to doing the same.

Tim didn't seem to be in such high spirits, although he had something similar in mind. "I need a drink," he said.

"You're the designated driver," Jason said pointedly.

"Then I'll have a very small drink."

Oh, trouble in paradise! Kelly politely averted his eyes and searched the crowd for Bonnie. There she was, strutting through the lobby with one arm stretched behind her so she could hold hands with her date. Emma was all gussied up and looked positively star-struck as she followed. Kelly felt a burst of happiness for his friend. He'd been so focused on his own fears that he hadn't stopped to consider how well this was working out for Bonnie. She finally had a girlfriend again, and from the looks of things, a fan too.

"Congratulations," he said, stepping forward to meet them. He was referring to the relationship more than the performance, but that had been damn good, which he made sure to tell her. "You were the best. Absolutely. All those other musicians shouldn't have bothered showing up. Next time it needs to be just you up on stage for two hours, because I can't get enough."

Bonnie grinned at his flattery, Emma tittering pleasantly. Kelly noticed her and shifted his weight to one of his crutches so he could offer his hand. "It's nice to see you again," he said, eager to make peace. "I've been hearing a lot of good things about you. I'm sure you can guess from whom."

Emma's cheeks flushed. "Thank you," she said.

He nodded, turning back to Bonnie to praise her more. William stepped forward, giving Emma a hug like they were old friends, and everything felt great. He was complimenting Bonnie on her bow work when she became distracted, looking away from him. "Sorry," she murmured, stepping forward and extending a hand to Tim. "You're Emma's uncle!"

Uncle? Kelly took in the scene. Emma had gone pale. Tim, one arm around Jason, was staring at her with his mouth open. Then he absentmindedly offered Bonnie one of the champagnes he had fetched. She barely noticed the glass as she took it, her attention on Jason now instead. "Hey! Sorry, I didn't recognize you at first. Wait, you're Emma's other uncle? The one who can sing?"

"No," Emma said, sounding confused herself. "You're thinking of Ben."

"And does Ben know you're here?" Tim asked, suddenly sounding a lot older than thirty. "Or your parents?"

Emma looked away. "They think I'm staying at a friend's house."

"Which she is," Bonnie said. "She's staying with me tonight."

"No," Tim said. "She's staying with us. I'll call Ben and tell him to come pick you up. He'll decide what to do."

"Uncle Tim," Emma pleaded. "Please don't! I'll be home tomorrow morning! It's not like it's a school night."

"You're fourteen years old," Tim said. "You're too young to be on your own in a different city."

"She's not on her own," Bonnie interjected. "Wait, what? Did you say fourteen?"

"You can't make me do anything!" Emma said, sounding on the verge of a tantrum. "You aren't *really* my uncle!"

"Then I'll call Ben," Tim said, digging in his pocket for a phone. "And we'll see what your *real uncle* thinks of all this."

"Hold up," Kelly said. "This is worse than reality TV. Who is related to whom?"

His plea for clarity was ignored.

"You know I'm still in the closet," Emma said, blocking the cell phone screen with her hand. "How am I supposed to explain why I'm here? Think about when you and Ben used to secretly meet."

Tim considered her words, put the phone back in his pocket, and chugged the glass of champagne. "Okay," he said. "Let's all just calm down and talk about this."

Kelly noticed Jason's reaction then. He looked as though everything had gone terribly wrong. How exactly, Kelly did not know, but he was eager to find out. "Over dinner?" he suggested.

Jason's eyes widened. "Maybe we should all just go home."

"You can't go!" Bonnie said. "It's my big night!"

"And I'm starving," Kelly said. "No, I definitely think some food is in order. Followed by what I imagine will be a very enlightening conversation."

Kelly felt positively high, and for once, no pills were required. His brush with humility, self-doubt, self-depreciation… All that had gone flying out the window during the muted drive to the Italian restaurant, because Kelly had solved the puzzle. The basic facts were the most important. Emma had two gay uncles. One of those had pretended to be Jason's date tonight. The exact reasons why could be deciphered and dealt with later. What mattered at the moment was everyone understanding the facts as he did.

Kelly felt like a detective at the end of a mystery. All suspects were gathered at the table. Bonnie sat at his right, hanging on his every word. Tim sat across from him, having undergone a transformation. He was still hot as hell, but he no longer fawned over Jason. Instead he seemed more like a mother hen, separating Emma and Jason by forcing them to sit on either side of him. And looking as displeased as any parent called in by the school principal.

The first order of business was protecting his friend. Kelly knew firsthand just how blind love could make a person, and he wanted to ensure Bonnie came out of this as unscathed as possible. He worried she would be hurt anyway, especially once she understood the kind of people they were dealing with.

"I think it's fair to say," Kelly said, "that there has been some very obvious misrepresentation of facts."

Tim stabbed moodily at tagliatelle in a mushroom crème sauce. "If it's so obvious, then why bother discussing it?"

"Because I have questions I would like answered. I don't think I'm the only one."

Bonnie looked resistant, so Kelly glanced to his left, where William gave a curt nod. His arms were crossed over his chest, and he hadn't touched his food. He didn't seem defensive though. He seemed angry and this—more than anything—mattered to Kelly because it meant William wasn't worried about getting caught. He was displeased with being deceived. This affair, if it could even be called that, was one-sided at best.

"Let's start with numbers," Kelly said. "Emma, I was under the impression that you are our age. Unless I misunderstood from the very beginning." He looked to Bonnie. "Did I?"

She inhaled deeply and shook her head.

"So basically, Emma told you, Bonnie, that she was sixteen, when in fact, she is only fourteen."

"Almost fifteen," Emma said. "Just a few more weeks."

"Congratulations," Kelly said dryly. "But 'almost fifteen' does not equal sixteen, which you claimed to be."

Bonnie stirred next to him. "I don't think she told me her age at all."

"That was me," Jason piped up. "I told you she was sixteen because I thought you wouldn't give her a chance."

"Of course she wouldn't have," Tim grumped. "Fourteen is too young to date!"

"Oh, absolutely," Kelly agreed. "But what I don't get is if you aren't her uncle—" He gestured first at Tim with his fork, then at Jason. "—and you aren't either, then where does this Ben guy fit in?"

"Ben and Tim are—" Emma began.

Tim raised a hand to silence her. "She has an uncle who lives here in Austin. I'm more of an honorary uncle."

Kelly nodded, certain that Tim was being duplicitous. "But you and Ben meet in secrecy sometimes."

"Not anymore. We used to in high school when we were a couple. Then we broke up."

This gave him pause. Was Tim outright lying? Or was he twisting the truth? He prodded further. "How odd. Bonnie clearly expected Ben to be with you. He's the one who sings, right? Or can you sing, Jason? That would surprise me because you've been very quiet recently."

Jason looked up from his plate of cold lasagna, eyes blazing.

"Tim's not my boyfriend."

"Obviously," Kelly said.

"Emma's Uncle Ben," Jason continued, "he's Tim's boyfriend. They're an amazing couple and are nice enough to let me live with them. And go along with my stupid ideas, like this one."

Kelly looked at William and raised his eyebrows. His boyfriend met his gaze, open to further persecution. Time to move in for the kill. "And why would you pretend to be with someone when you're not?"

Annoyingly, Tim chose to answer for him. "Haven't you ever been single? Haven't you been around other couples, ones you envy because what they share seems so incredibly wonderful that you want it for yourself? And, even though they might not intend to, don't those happy couples sometimes make you feel small and insignificant, like you aren't good enough to join their ranks?"

Kelly thought of Jared and Martha, and how crappy that had felt, but it wasn't a fair comparison. Jared had been single when Kelly had developed feelings for him. Kelly hadn't lied and wormed his way into Jared's life, trying to steal what wasn't his.

"I know," Tim continued. "I've been there before, and I didn't want Jason to feel the same way. He deserves to be loved. I meant what I said earlier about how handsome he is, but it's his personality that really shines. He's a survivor. He's been on his own since he was a kid, he's worked full-time since he was sixteen, and life *still* hasn't given him the good things he deserves. But he doesn't let that make him bitter. From what I can tell, he falls in love way too easily, but that's not a bad thing. I met a guy like him a long time ago, and I've been chasing him ever since. So maybe Jason is single now, but it won't be long before someone recognizes how special he is. *That's* not a lie. It's a prediction. Stick around and you'll see it come true."

Kelly didn't know what Tim did for a living. Maybe he was a spin doctor for politicians. If not, he should be, because he was gifted at making bullshit sound golden. Regardless, Jason had done all of this with an ulterior motive in mind. He didn't pretend to have a boyfriend to make himself feel less lonely. He had done so hoping William would let down his guard. Kelly didn't feel the need to press the issue further. Let awkward silence reign, the truth already laid bare!

"I don't care how old she is," Bonnie said suddenly. "I was

thirteen the first time I fell in love, and the woman wouldn't even look at me. I have to respectfully disagree with you, Tim. Fourteen is old enough to feel, and dating just means spending time with the person you love. Maybe she shouldn't be alone in Austin with me, but I'm not going to judge her by an arbitrary number. Emma, you're mature enough for me. That's all that matters."

Emma looked as though she wanted to swoon. Instead she risked a hopeful expression and turned to Tim. "Soooo. About tonight."

Kelly ignored the negotiations that followed, reaching under the table for his boyfriend's hand. When he found it, he squeezed. William squeezed back. They were okay. All this stuff with Jason had been a close call, but now William knew he had been duped. All that remained was politely letting the evening come to a natural end. From the excited banter Emma and Bonnie were exchanging, they wouldn't have to part ways tonight. Even Tim loosened up, ordering a beer that greatly improved his mood. Jason, on the other hand, mostly stared at his plate. Kelly felt a little sorry for him, but a lie was a lie.

Finally the meal was over. Bonnie asked to drive Emma back to her uncle's house, which sucked, because Kelly knew they wanted to be alone for romantic reasons. That meant taking the bus again... until Tim offered to give them a lift. Kelly eagerly agreed. An awkward car ride in a Bentley beat an awkward bus ride any day.

He had imagined sitting in the backseat with William, but Tim—who seemed a little tipsy—made a joke about playing taxi and hopped in the back. Jason was the designated driver, leaving them little choice but to split up.

"You take shotgun," William murmured. "Okay?"

Kelly hid his surprise and nodded. This was over. Well and truly over. Once on the road, Kelly fed directions to Jason piece by piece, while William went into nervous passenger mode and started talking nonstop. Tim seemed happy to accommodate him. During the longer stretches, Kelly felt like he should say something to Jason. *Sorry the evening didn't go as you hoped*, or *There are other fish in the sea that haven't already been hooked*. But really, Kelly didn't think any words could provide comfort. Hearts took their own sweet time to heal.

When they finally reached Kelly's house, he opened the car door and glanced over. William was in the back seat with his head bowed, his features lost in shadow. "Time to go," Kelly prompted.

William didn't move at first. When he finally did look up, he said, "I'm staying at my place tonight. I'm tired."

Vulnerability chipped away at Kelly's newfound confidence. "You can be tired here."

"I want to be in my own bed." William replied. "Besides, my mom misses me."

"Fine."

Kelly struggled to get out of the car, the crutches catching on something he couldn't see. At moments like these, he wanted nothing more than to smoothly slip out of the car and make his escape. Instead his exit was clumsy, his embarrassment compounded when William got out to help him. They didn't speak as they crossed the lawn. When they reached the porch, Kelly turned to face William, but he wasn't deluded enough to expect a goodnight kiss.

"He's a liar," Kelly said, trying to keep his voice from rising, but this only made it sound like a hiss.

"You made that painfully clear at the restaurant," William said.

"Can you blame me?" Kelly asked.

William didn't answer.

"Tell me you understand," Kelly said, hating how desperate he sounded. "Jason has a thing for you. All of this is because he wants to be with you!"

William's features remained impassive. "I know."

"Then why get back in the car with those people?"

"I need to be home. I need my space."

Tonight of all nights? They should be pulling together, talking this through. Obviously William felt differently. Maybe he didn't want to go home at all. Maybe the reason he kept looking back to where Jason had parked, jaw clenching, was because he couldn't wait to return there.

"I guess the apple doesn't fall far from the tree," Kelly spat.

William's head whipped around. "Meaning?"

"That you're more like your father than you care to admit."

William looked as though he'd been slapped. "That's not who

I am," he growled. "I don't lie, and I don't cheat!"

Kelly shook his head. "Then what are you doing?"

William didn't answer with words. Kelly wished he had, because his reaction was so much worse than anything that could have been spoken: William looked uncertain. He didn't know what he was doing, hadn't decided yet, but he felt pulled in more than one direction—that was for sure.

"Stay the night," Kelly said, a lump in his throat.

"I'll see you tomorrow."

As William turned and walked away, Kelly laughed bitterly. To think he had felt so victorious at the restaurant, when in truth, he had already lost. No matter what he said or did, he couldn't win anymore.

"Are you okay?"

Allison's eyes were wide with concern when she entered the waiting room. She looked Kelly over, as if expecting to find him wearing a cast or clutching at a stab wound.

"I'm fine," he said. "Why wouldn't I be?"

"When you called this morning, you said it was an emergency."

"Oh." Kelly grimaced. "Maybe I should have said personal crisis instead."

Allison didn't relax just yet. "You sure sounded upset."

"I was." Upset? More like locked in the bathroom and sobbing. "I'm feeling a little better. But I'd still like to talk to you. Please."

Allison gestured to her office door. "Come on in."

He took his customary spot on the couch, struggling to find a good place to begin. He hadn't seen Allison for months, and since then, Kelly's entire world had fallen apart.

"How's your anger?" she asked.

"Better. At least it was. Now it's back in full force."

"Any reason why?"

"Jason." Yes, that pretty much summed it up.

Allison checked her notes. "I don't remember us talking about him before."

"He's new. Showed up at one of our gay youth meetings, and long story short, he's infatuated with William. The more time goes by, the more I suspect the feeling is mutual."

"You're worried that William is cheating on you?"

Kelly hesitated. "Not exactly, but I'm near certain he wants to. William is... noble. He's one of those people who seems too good to be true, like he must have some hidden dark side."

Allison raised an eyebrow. "Doesn't he?"

"The accident." Kelly sighed. "I'm not saying he's perfect, but his father cheated on his mother before they got divorced. William is still angry with him over that, so I don't think he would do the same to me."

"It's normal to feel tempted," Allison said. "In any long-term relationship, there will always be someone new who comes along and seems fresh and exciting. Everyone has thoughts they don't act on, and that's okay. As long as you're certain William isn't cheating, it might be worth waiting to see if it all blows over."

"It's not that simple," Kelly said. "This Jason guy... I can't decide if he's a master manipulator or just plain lucky. What's certain is that he managed to tangle himself up in my life, and he used those crazy sailor knots, ensuring I can't shake him loose."

"That bad?"

"You have no idea." Kelly shook his head in exasperation. "Jason asked William for swimming lessons, which means they meet almost every morning. His best friend is dating my best friend, and about a month ago, William invited him on a double date to her cello recital."

"So Jason has a boyfriend too."

"Ha! No, that's the best part. He shows up with this hot older guy, but they were only pretending. Turns out that Jason's boyfriend, Tim, was actually Emma's uncle. Or the boyfriend of her uncle. Sorry, Emma is Jason's best friend. The one who is dating my best friend."

Allison stared at him incredulously.

"I know," Kelly said. "It's convoluted. Should I go back over it all?"

"No!" Allison grabbed her pen and started scribbling furiously. She didn't seem to be writing anything though. Was she doodling? Kelly supposed most people did that while thinking. "So what were the results of this extremely misguided ploy?"

"Nothing," Kelly said. "It's so frustrating. I exposed Jason as a liar, but he and William keep hanging out like nothing happened. They even went on a picnic together. William said it was a bike ride with a short break to eat, but come on! You better believe I flipped out over that one!"

"Can't say I blame you," Allison said. "I would have invited myself along."

"Crutches and bicycles don't go together real well. I did start tagging along with William during his morning swims. I started showing up at his work more often too. Not to catch him in the act, but just to scare Jason away. Nothing I do makes a difference. Then there's this stupid fundraiser tonight, and something about it stinks, but I can't figure out what, and I—" Kelly's throat tightened and he struggled to get the last few words out. "I feel like I'm going crazy."

Allison stood and opened her arms. "Come here."

The gesture summoned a longing from deep inside Kelly. He felt silly as he grabbed his crutches to stand, and as soon as he did, Allison stepped around the table to hug him. She also patted him on the back and gave him a little squeeze.

"That was very unprofessional of me," she said once they had parted, "but I can tell when someone needs a hug, and *that* was an emergency."

"Do you have kids?" Kelly asked. "Because that felt like a mom hug."

"Not yet, but I'm working on it." Allison gestured that they should sit back down. "Now tell me about this fundraiser."

Kelly took a deep breath. "William is going to be a topless waiter. I kid you not. Keep in mind this is a gay fundraiser, so it makes a twisted sort of sense. Of course it was Jason who asked William to do this because he also—surprise, surprise—will be a waiter. I figured they just want to spend time together, so I invited myself along. William didn't mind at all. No argument, no hint of frustration, nothing. He was perfectly fine with it. So I keep telling myself that maybe they really are friends and nothing more. Simple as that. I'm just being insecure. If only my gut would shut the hell up. I've gone in so many circles that I don't even trust myself anymore." Kelly let his shoulders slump in defeat. "Maybe the only thing that's wrong is me."

Allison was quiet as she considered his words. Then she stood. He thought another hug was incoming, but instead she headed for the door. "I need to make a call," she said. "I'm sorry. I'll be right back."

Kelly stared as she left the room. He had been on the verge of tears. Maybe she felt he needed privacy to cry? Was he supposed to now? He didn't feel like getting himself worked up. He was tired of pitiful tears. What he craved was advice. If he couldn't figure out which direction was right, he needed someone else to guide him.

"I'm sorry," Allison said once she reentered the room. "I know that probably seemed rude, but it couldn't be helped."

"It's fine," Kelly said.

Allison sat down, looked him square in the eye, and sighed. "You're not crazy. Most people who suspect infidelity are picking up on signals without even realizing it. Unfortunately this makes it easy to second-guess ourselves, when we should be listening to our instincts. That having been said, people who have been cheated on previously tend to expect it to happen again, which can lead to a lot of unjustified suspicion."

"I've never been cheated on," Kelly said.

"Good. As you said, it could be that nothing has happened between Jason and William. But I'm willing to bet your gut is right, and that something is off balance. I suggest you ask William to be honest with you. No accusations, no anger or sorrow, just ask him to be honest with you. Talking to each other is the only way this is going to get better."

Kelly swallowed. "And what if I'm right? What if he wishes we weren't together so he could be with Jason?"

Allison took a deep breath. "Just before the car wreck, when you and William were arguing, didn't he try to break up with you?"

"He was angry," Kelly said dismissively. "We both were. A lot of things happened that morning we both regret."

"The accident, sure, but maybe your relationship was coming to its natural conclusion."

Kelly's voice was terse. "He promised to stay with me."

"As you said, William prides himself on his nobility. Breaking up with the person you just put in the hospital is low. Lower than low. This is pure conjecture, but I can imagine William thought he was doing the right thing. Past the trauma of that event, now that you've both healed as much as possible, you need to ask yourself what has really changed. If you weren't compatible before, why would you be now?"

214

Kelly thought about it. He was less happy these days, less confident. William hadn't changed much aside from an added edge of guilt to his actions. Neither of them had been improved by what had happened. Maybe she was right. Maybe the accident had delayed their breakup and nothing more.

"Talk to him," Allison said. "Before the party tonight, give him a chance to be honest. If he still isn't, trust in yourself. Understand me? No matter what happens, you listen to your gut because you're right."

She sounded so certain. Kelly didn't see how she could be, but that confidence was infectious. Tonight, one way or another, he would get his answer.

Chapter Fourteen

Confronting the truth could be like walking toward one's own execution. Sure, this can be faced with a heart full of bravery and a head held high, but at the end of that march is still something so unpleasant, most people would avoid it. Had they a choice.

Perhaps that was why Kelly kept his mouth shut as William got dressed, not that there was much to put on. A pair of black slacks, dark shiny shoes, and a simple bowtie. He looked more like a stripper about to begin his shift than a waiter. Kelly didn't ask any questions when Tim drove up wearing the same outfit, nor did he bother with cutting words for Jason, who sat in the passenger seat. Kelly simply climbed in the back and allowed himself to be taken for a ride for just a little longer.

When they arrived at what could only be described as a mansion on the outskirts of Austin, he dismissed it as one more crazy wonder that Jason had conjured from his limitless bag of tricks. Better to take it all in stride, because Kelly's only other option was to ask William to level with him about everything: his feelings, these strange places, what the evening's true purpose was…

At the very least, the fundraising party provided ample distraction. When they first arrived, more shirtless waiters than guests were wandering around the spacious ballroom. Everywhere Kelly looked, his eyes met temptation. Hot guys with muscles, cute boys with boney ribs, and even a few pleasantly plump teddy-bear types, ideal for snuggling up to on winter nights. The world seemed to be sending Kelly a message. *See how normal it is to be tempted? Gaze upon these delights and tell me you still blame William for wanting to wander.*

Except every time Kelly sought out his boyfriend in the increasingly congested crowd, all those other guys failed to compare. William was familiar. Comfortable. Or at least had been. Kelly wasn't sure he knew him so well anymore. When they made eye contact, Kelly waved him over. William bent his knees once at his side, tilting the tray of *hors d'oeuvres* to offer what he described as *Brandade de Morue au Gratin*.

"And what is that exactly?" Kelly asked.

"I think it's French." William shrugged, the tray wobbling.

"Some big guy in a tuxedo yelled at me until I was able to say it right. All I know is that it smells like fish." After looking around, he placed the tray on the table and crouched next to Kelly. "You doing all right?"

"I'm having a lovely time," he lied. Not that the evening had been dire. More than a handful of men had sent amorous glances in his direction, reminding Kelly that many people had once considered him pretty. He couldn't remember the last time he felt truly attractive. The one guy brave enough to sit at his table had been sent packing, Kelly telling him the empty seats were reserved.

"You should eat something," William said. "Go on, try one."

They glanced at the appetizers, which appeared to be blobs of white slime oozing over thin wafers.

"I'll eat one if you do," William bartered.

"Promise?"

"Yup."

Kelly smirked. "Okay. You go first."

William puffed up his chest as if inhaling bravery. Then he took one of the appetizers, tossed it in his mouth, and chewed. Despite his best poker face, his nostrils flared, giving him away. "It's good," he said, talking around the food without having swallowed yet. "Try one."

Kelly narrowed his eyes in suspicion. "It's disgusting, admit it."

"It's not!" William insisted, cheek bulging.

Kelly picked up one of the appetizers. "Then have another."

William snorted, covering his mouth to stop the food from escaping. Kelly grinned and offered him a napkin so he could spit it out. Once he had, William's face remained red from embarrassment. Feeling sorry for him, Kelly grabbed one of the ghastly things, popped it in his mouth, and chewed a few times before swallowing.

William's face twisted up in disbelief like Kelly had just eaten a worm. "Ugh! Gross!"

"It wasn't so bad. In fact, leave the tray. I'll finish these myself." In truth, the appetizers tasted like cold fish congealing in spoiled milk. Not a sensation Kelly would willingly subject himself to again, but choking down one was worth seeing William laugh, his green eyes wet with amusement.

Kelly's smile faltered. How easy it was to pretend, to get caught up in the moment and believe that everything was okay. And it had been once—every day full of little situations like these that Kelly wished he'd paid more attention to. Now he cherished them. He always would. No matter what happened, he hoped the memories would comfort him more than they hurt. The time to talk had come.

"William—"

"Your attention please!"

They turned to the front of the room, where a tubby man stuffed into a white tuxedo stood on stage. His voice was elegant, his gestures delicate as he continued his speech. "As you all know, the intent of this little soiree tonight is to benefit those who are unable to leave their homes, be it due to illness or other unfortunate circumstances. In order to understand how that feels, let's bravely go an hour without food, drink, or charming company. I'm going to ask all my waiting staff to kindly leave the room. As they go, please place any remaining beverages on their trays."

William stood and picked up the tray. "Sorry. You'll have to finish these later."

Kelly just stared at him. William wasn't smiling anymore. He seemed—tense, worried, horny, anything but casual. Eye contact had ceased.

"See you soon," he said, heading with the other waiters for the kitchen door.

"Never fear!" the portly man on stage continued. "One handsome face will remain, besides mine of course. The rather dashing fire marshal here will oversee our safety during the shut-in, and despite his good looks and charming outfit, I assure you he isn't a stripper. Now then, as the doors close, please find a seat and give your attention to my dear friend Mr. Wyman, who for some reason has put his shirt back on. What a pity. Regardless, he shall regale us all with tales of how last year's money was put to good use. So please, take a seat, but before you do, remove those wallets and checkbooks from your pockets. You'll soon have need of them."

Kelly stared as Tim took the stage and hugged the man in the white tuxedo before nervously shuffling papers on the podium. The seats at Kelly's table were filling up, the lights lowering as a video projector was turned on for some sort of presentation. He shook his head as if to clear it, then reached for his crutches and stood, instinct driving him toward the closed kitchen doors.

That's what all of this was about. The plan was just as convoluted and ridiculous as Tim pretending to be Jason's boyfriend. Playing waiter, volunteering here tonight, all of it for one hour alone, safe from Kelly's prying eyes so they could... what? Stare longingly at each other? Kiss? Fuck? Or maybe they just wanted to talk. Kelly couldn't decide which scenario would sting most, but he wanted to witness it for himself. Doing so would make saying goodbye so much easier.

He reached the kitchen door and yanked on the handle, surprised it was truly locked and that the shut-in wasn't merely symbolic. He yanked again, just to be sure.

"Can I help you?"

A shadow detached itself from the wall and strolled over to him. Kelly glanced up. The man was tall and had the unmistakable vibe of a bouncer. What sort of a charity event was this?

"I need out," Kelly said, pulling on the handle again for emphasis.

"Didn't you hear the announcement?" the man asked. "Hey, are you listening to me?"

Kelly looked over at him again. In the darkness it was hard to make out much. Currently the distant light from the projector was reflected in the man's eyes, making him appear supernatural. He had a strong jaw covered in stubble and broad shoulders that he not-so-casually used to wedge himself between Kelly and the exit.

"Even if this door wasn't locked," the man continued, "it leads to the kitchen, which is off limits. Are you looking for the restroom?"

"Yes," Kelly said, leaping on the excuse.

"Other side of the room."

He didn't budge except to lift one of his crutches, drawing attention to them. "Is it handicap accessible?"

The man's brow furrowed. "I don't know. I'm sure you'll be fine."

"I need support bars mounted on the wall," Kelly said. "Lots of space too. A normal restroom won't work for me, so let me out and—"

"I'll support you."

Kelly stared. "What?"

"I'll accompany you to the restroom, and if need be, I'll hold you up."

Kelly's jaw dropped. "Do you have any idea how offensive that is?"

The man shrugged and crossed his arms over his chest. "I don't care. You're not getting through this door. What is it that you really want?"

Kelly sighed. "There's someone in there that I need to talk to."

"Need?"

"Yes! Need!"

The man huffed. "Trust me, there isn't anyone you need."

"Oh really. How would you know that?"

"Because I've put a lot of thought into the subject. Hold on."

The man took some keys out of his pocket, unlocked the door, and slipped inside. Kelly counted to three under his breath before trying the door again. Locked. Powerless to do anything else, he stood there and stared at the wooden surface. God how he wished he still had both legs! If he did, he could dart past the bouncer when the door opened again and run so fast no one could catch him. Instead, when the door opened, he didn't even try. There was no point. The man was already locking the door again, and when he turned around, one of his large hands held two glasses by the stems and a dark bottle by the neck.

"What's this supposed to be?" Kelly said.

"Come find out." The man gestured with his head before walking toward the back of the room. Kelly stared after him a moment before following. He was led to an empty table in one corner. The man pulled out a chair for him, then sat down. He didn't ask Kelly if he needed help or look up when one of Kelly's crutches slipped and clattered on the floor. Instead he busied himself with a pocket knife corkscrew, one of his meaty fists twisting until the bottle was open.

"I'm not old enough to drink," Kelly said.

"Oh no," the man deadpanned as he poured. "I hope I don't lose my job over this."

"You could be arrested. Believe me."

"So be it." The man pushed a glass full of shimmering liquid toward him. "Drink up."

Kelly ignored the glass. "What kind of a bouncer are you?"

The man snorted. "I'm not a bouncer. My name is Nathaniel, and I'm the coordinator of this event. Are you enjoying yourself?"

"No."

"Good. Now shut up and take a drink so I can have one too. Otherwise, you'll think I'm rude."

Kelly watched him a moment longer. Then he picked up the glass. He supposed a toast was in order, so he lifted it and said, "Here's to not getting what you want."

Nathaniel nodded appreciatively before taking a swig that drained half the glass. Then his eyes moved to the front of the room, where Tim had stepped aside for a video of people who benefitted from previous donations. Kelly took the opportunity to have a couple sips. White wine. He wasn't a connoisseur, so any subtleties in flavor were lost on him. Not that it really mattered, his sips becoming gulps. Soon his belly felt warm, his prior urgency ebbing away. He worked on emptying the glass, thankful for the emotional reprieve the alcohol granted him. As a consolation prize, it wasn't bad. Nathaniel could have chased him away. Instead he'd invited Kelly for a drink. Weird, especially since Nathaniel didn't seem eager to fill the silence. Maybe they weren't supposed to talk during the presentation. Still, Kelly felt he should say something.

"It's great what you're doing here," he tried, hoping it sounded generous and not sarcastic.

Nathaniel's eyes shifted to meet his. "And what is it that you're doing here? Are you someone's date?"

"No," Kelly said, not feeling it was a lie. He was pretty damn sure that he was the third wheel tonight. "I'm not rich either, so don't try hitting me up for money."

Nathaniel's eyes sparkled in amusement. "Then I ask again, why are you here?"

"It's a mystery," Kelly said, preferring to be vague. "I'm afraid you'll never find out. We'll share this drink together, go our separate ways, and that will be the end of our story."

Nathaniel nodded. "Fair enough. Of course the drink isn't over quite yet." He reached for the bottle to refill their glasses. Then he leaned back, his attention split between the presentation and Kelly. When they did lock eyes, Nathaniel seemed comfortable, but Kelly felt more and more like squirming, because the guy sitting across from him was kind of handsome. Probably an effect of the booze Kelly kept downing. Or the low lighting. Even in the shadow it was clear he was older. How much so? Five years? Ten? Once the lights came up, all the wrinkles and crags would surely reveal themselves. But for now...

"So what about you?" Kelly asked. "Are you someone's date?"

"I already told you, this is my job."

"Yes, but it's not like you can't bring your boyfriend along. If I was dating you, I'd insist on coming just for the free food. Except for those fish things. Those were gross."

"*Brandade de Morue au Gratin,*" Nathaniel said with a perfect French accent.

"Exactly," Kelly said, sliding his half-empty glass across the table for another refill. "Whoever put those on the menu needs to be fired."

"I put them on the menu," Nathaniel said.

"Oh. Well maybe not fired. Uh..."

"It's perfectly fine," Nathaniel said, tilting the bottle and pouring. "I was disappointed too. We had to switch caterers at the last minute. I won't be using them again. And for the record, if I had a boyfriend, I wouldn't bring him here. Topless waiters, rich old perverts, and bouncers who ply underage boys with booze. Not the most wholesome of environments, is it?"

Nathaniel smiled slowly. Kelly couldn't help joining him, even if the gesture was fleeting. In the back of his mind, he still worried about what Jason and William were doing. Then again, he was powerless to stop them. Even if he talked Nathaniel into opening that door, they would find some other place and some other time. Kelly was through fighting the inevitable.

"Watch this one," Nathaniel said, nodding to the front. "It's good."

Kelly turned just as a new video segment started. An old woman described her increasing agoraphobia, and how she couldn't even be in her backyard anymore without being crippled by anxiety. Ironic, since gardening had been her passion. Then the charity foundation had come and built a winter garden—a sort of greenhouse that attached directly to her back door. In this way she was able to be outside again to continue gardening.

"That last shot," Nathaniel said, "the soil passing through her gnarled old fingers... Beautiful stuff."

"You like photography?" Kelly asked.

"Something like that." Nathaniel pushed away from the table. "I'm afraid our time together is over."

"My glass isn't empty yet," Kelly said.

Nathaniel picked up his own and drained it, which seemed a little cold.

Elsewhere, the heavyset man had swept onto stage again. "At least take it off while you're collecting money!" he said in a stage whisper, tugging at Tim's shirt. Then he pretended to notice the audience for the first time. "Oh! You're all still here. How marvelous! And generous. Speaking of which—"

"I have to help collect donations," Nathaniel said.

The lights had come up again, and all the wrinkles and gray hairs Kelly had imagined were nowhere in sight. Definitely a good-looking guy. Just his type. Sort of like William, but more mature, more masculine. Maybe that's how William would look in ten years or so. Not that Kelly would be around to witness it.

"You'll be all right," Nathaniel said as he stood. It wasn't a question, but he waited for an answer anyway.

"Yeah," Kelly said. "Just fine. Especially if you leave the bottle."

"Not a chance." Nathaniel picked it up and started to head away before he hesitated. "You never told me your name."

"Kelly."

"Well, Kelly, I'd say it's nice meeting you, but I guess this is goodbye."

"I guess so." He gave his best smile, the kind he was always slinging around when he used to feel invincible.

Nathaniel's eyes sparkled in return. They were hazel, Kelly noted, just before they left his life forever.

He remained seated, toying with the stem of the glass, twirling it around and watching the liquid swirl in response. He didn't worry about William or watch the kitchen door, waiting for it to open again. He was over it. As much as possible anyway. Eventually, the shut-in came to an end and the waiters poured back into the room, rewarding generous donations with more food and drinks.

"There you are!" William said, walking around the table to face him. Then his eyes widened. In a hushed voice, he said, "Is that wine?"

"Sure looks like it."

"You're going to get in trouble!"

Kelly smirked. Then, doing his best impression of Nathaniel, he said, "So be it."

William shook his head. "I'll get you some water. Or maybe a Coke and something to eat."

Kelly waited until he was gone. Then he chugged the rest of the wine, got up, and headed for the exit. Once out in the night air, he caught sight of an older gay couple walking toward their car.

"Excuse me," he said, making sure his crutches were in plain sight. "If you're heading to Austin, would you mind giving me a ride?"

Five minutes later, Kelly was in the back of a luxury sedan, his head still spinning from the alcohol. He stared out the window, the streetlights and trees zooming by. Feeling more liberated than he had for months, Kelly leaned back, made himself comfortable, and closed his eyes.

A muted day. Hardly a word spoken between them. Perfect for an overcast Sunday. Kelly had fallen asleep in a blissful buzz before William had gotten home, and by the time he awoke, the other side of the bed was slept in and unoccupied. When William did show up, he smelled of chlorine, which came as some relief. Without the optimism of alcohol buoying him, Kelly didn't feel so ready to let go. The idea of William sneaking off with Jason made him feel foolish and vulnerable and somehow less of a man.

But as the day wore on, the silence between them thickened and solidified like gelatin in the refrigerator. Throughout the day, William spoke more to Royal than he did to Kelly. As the afternoon wore on, Kelly found himself doing the same, using his little brother as an unwilling mediator. Maybe that's why Royal left to visit a friend, leaving awkward tension in his wake.

Now they were getting ready for bed, their teeth freshly brushed and the covers pulled down. But tonight neither of them had undressed. Not yet. It felt wrong, somehow. Instead they sat on the end of the bed, perched on the edge, as if even this had become too intimate.

"Kelly—" William began.

"I'm ready to talk about it," he interrupted. "Just promise me you'll be honest and we can get through this."

William glanced over at him. But he didn't promise. His elbows were resting on his knees, his hands hanging limp before him. "I don't make you happy anymore."

"That's not true!"

"Are you sure? Because we can't seem to get through a day without you snapping at me or rolling your eyes or—"

"I'm a bitch," Kelly said. "I get pissy. You take it too personally."

William shook his head. "That's not how it was when we first met. I don't remember you getting so grumpy with me. Not all the time."

Kelly sighed. "Since the accident, I've been a little—"

"Not since then," William said. "It started *before* then. That's why I wanted to break up. I was tired of feeling like I constantly pissed you off. I didn't make you happy then, and I know I don't make you happy now."

"You're wrong."

"I'm not. Just think about it. Open yourself to the idea and ask yourself if it's true."

Kelly wanted to argue, but that would only prove William's point. So he sat quietly, just for appearances, but ended up thinking about it anyway. He loved William, that much was certain. But damn if he wasn't too noble and too nice sometimes! These might be wonderful traits, but they made Kelly feel bad about himself by comparison. And really, he didn't think there was anything wrong with snarling at the world occasionally, or even at each other. That was perfectly normal. Except William didn't seem to have that in him. He seemed to function by a different set of standards, and yes, this often drove Kelly crazy. To be fair, his own standards frustrated William just as much, except instead of getting irritated with Kelly, he got hurt instead.

"Maybe we're not the most compatible," Kelly admitted, "but they say opposites attract."

"They might attract, but they don't stick together."

Kelly raised an eyebrow. "What are you saying?"

"That I don't make you happy anymore, and if I'm honest, I haven't been happy for a long time."

"If you're honest," Kelly said, his voice rising, "all of this is actually about Jason Grant!"

"Not all of it," William said, "but yeah. Meeting him made

everything complicated. I promised you I would stay. In the emergency room, I swore I would never leave you because I wanted to do the right thing. And I still do, but now I'm worried that if we keep going like this, I'm going to do the wrong thing."

"With Jason," Kelly spat.

"Yes, with Jason! I'm through denying it. I love him."

Kelly felt like he'd been shoved backward, arms flailing to catch hold of some support and finding only empty air. That they found each other attractive was no surprise. That temptation existed—the allure of something new—all of that he already knew. But love?

"I never wanted to hurt you," William said, "and I didn't do this on purpose, I swear. Just… just think about the morning of the accident and pretend I didn't screw up and cost you your leg. If none of that had happened, do you really think we'd still be together?"

Kelly ignored this. "You *love* him? How far have things gone?"

William glanced over. "Isn't that far enough already? I want to be with him, but I also made a promise to you. I can keep that promise, but it seems insane, because you're not happy and I'm not happy, and now that you know the truth, do you really think that's going to get better? Is there anything we can say or do to fix this? Because if not, I'm scared I'm going to end up hating you."

Kelly's mind raced to find a solution, but he already knew William was right. What satisfaction was there in holding on to someone against their will? Part of him was still tempted, because the idea of being alone—no, of being broken and knowing he'd never find someone else to love him—that scared the hell out of him. But he hated feeling pathetic, and nothing was sadder than clutching at an unwilling lover.

"Okay," he said quietly.

"Okay?" William repeated. "What do you mean?"

"You kept your promise to me long enough. You stayed by my side." Kelly swallowed, the next part the hardest to say. "You're free. Go be with him."

William didn't move. "I hope we can be friends. I still want you in my life."

Kelly laughed bitterly. "Well, we don't have much choice. We share almost every class in school, so for the next few months, you're stuck with me."

"I can ask to be transferred to other classes," William said. "If you want."

"No," Kelly said instantly. "I really don't." They looked at each other, exchanging pained expressions. "I hate that everything ended up this way."

"Me too," William said. "I wish we had quit while it was still good, before it got tarnished by… *everything.*"

Kelly nodded, glancing around at the room in disdain. All the happy memories they'd made were upstairs. They had left all of that behind nearly a year ago. The room they sat in now was stale with old struggles and slowly disintegrating feelings. The large space would feel twice as empty without someone to share it.

"I need your help," Kelly said. "One last favor."

"I should probably head home before it gets too late," William said, putting on his shoes.

"I don't mean tonight. Tomorrow. Maybe the next day too."

"Oh."

Kelly rolled his eyes. "Just a couple more afternoons with me. Then you can spend your entire life with that floozy."

William looked surprised.

"That's right," Kelly said, "I called him a floozy. And you know that's me being nice. I can think of numerous other terms that would be more appropriate, such as—"

"All right, all right," William said with a wry smile. "I'll help you." He stood and stretched, turning to Kelly and seeming at a loss. "I guess this is it."

Kelly felt a lump in his throat. "I guess so."

William just stood there, eyes getting wetter, his features becoming more vulnerable by the second. "You were my first everything," he said.

Including his first breakup, and Kelly knew from experience that at this point, he probably needed an extra push. "From the sound of things, I won't be your last. Good night, William."

"Kelly, I really did lo—"

"Good night," Kelly repeated, looking away. He kept his jaw squared until he heard the door open and close. Then he let go, his lip trembling. "I loved you too."

"Oh, wow!" Bonnie said.

"Yeah."

They surveyed the room together, squeezed into the doorway.

Kelly had one hand on Bonnie's shoulder for support and tried to shake the feeling they were on the threshold of a museum exhibit. Since no red rope held them back, Kelly hopped forward, setting his crutches aside and turning to sit on the office chair. Bonnie followed him, glancing around as she headed for the bed.

"It's like a time machine or something," she said.

That it was. Kelly's room had returned from the past. His real room, not the master bedroom of his parents. He was upstairs again, and everything had been restored to where it once was. Mostly. There weren't any photos of Jared or William on the wall. Kelly hadn't done this to turn back the clock. Not exactly. The accident had happened. He accepted that, but instead of getting bogged down by self-pity, relying on pills to make him feel happy, or clinging desperately to William, Kelly was moving on. Yes, a lot of bad things had happened, but he was marching forward.

"I like it," Bonnie said as she sat, "but I don't get it. If my parents were ever foolish enough to give me their bedroom, they'd have to burn the house down before I'd give it up again."

Kelly shrugged. "It felt weird. Besides, they've put up with enough without having to be crammed into this room."

"Why not?" Bonnie said. "It's big enough for two." Then she winced.

Kelly felt like doing the same. He had shared this room with William on more than one occasion, and it certainly had been large enough. At times he wished it had been smaller, forcing them to be near and touch even more than they had.

"How are you doing?" Bonnie asked.

Kelly considered the question. "Like a doctor started doing open-heart surgery on me and wandered away halfway through the procedure."

"So no great feeling of liberation? Some breakups are like getting a second chance at life. Know what I mean?"

"Yeah. Maybe once I figure out what I want to do, I'll feel better. For now, I'd rather not talk about it."

Bonnie looked pensive. "It's just that…"

"What?"

"Does this mean I have to break up with Emma?"

Kelly almost laughed. Instead he kept his face stoic. "I didn't want to ask, but it would make things a lot easier. You'd do that for me?"

Bonnie crinkled up her features as if in pain. She hemmed and hawed, and Kelly let her squirm. Just before her head exploded from the pressure, he let her off the hook.

"Of course you don't need to break up with Emma. William and I are still friends. He's the one who helped move all my stuff back up here."

"Okay," Bonnie said hesitantly. "It's just that people always say they're going to be friends, even if they don't mean it."

"I mean it," Kelly said. "I think he does too. We have all those classes together, and pretty soon we'll be graduating."

"Think he'll still join the Coast Guard?"

"Why wouldn't he?" Kelly blinked. "Are you saying he only enlisted to get away from me? He better join!"

Bonnie laughed. "If he doesn't, just remember that my relationship with Emma has your blessing. You can't take it back!"

Kelly never would because now, more than ever, he knew what a treasure it was to have someone special. It was bad enough he had to be alone again. At the very least, he was glad his best friend had gotten something good out of this mess.

"There's another youth group meeting coming up," she said, perhaps having similar thoughts.

"I'll pass," Kelly said dismissively.

"Nope. You're going, and you'll keep on going until you and I are both tied down to someone and so happy that it's repulsive to outsiders. Deal?"

Kelly sighed. Then he nodded.

Life had returned to normal in every way possible. At school, most people had gotten used to Kelly's situation, so he was no longer treated with overwhelming courtesy. In fact, a few people made annoyed comments when tripping over his crutches. Kelly was fine with that, since it meant he'd returned to being just another student in the high school herd.

The days felt long as graduation drew near. With little doubt that he would be graduating with a decent grade point average, Kelly daydreamed through most of his classes. Or sometimes he would look to where his ex-boyfriend sat, but William never so much as glanced in his direction. Oh, they would talk before class or during lunch. That was never a problem, but those wistful little moments of regret belonged to Kelly alone.

The youth group meetings returned to normal too. No William or Jason. Just familiar faces, like Layne, who also bemoaned being single again and had taken to wearing running mascara to show how sad he was—or so he claimed. He still cracked jokes every chance he got. Newcomers came and went, none interested in Kelly. The feeling was mutual. Maybe his heart was all tapped out, drained of whatever it took to love, although it did experience a brief revival when William showed up at his door shortly after graduation. Alas, he wasn't there to beg for him back. He had only come to say goodbye.

"I'm shipping out," William said, puffing up his chest, but not in pride. Instead he looked on the verge of tears. "I just wanted to say thank you. For everything. Taking me in, letting me go, showing me what love could be. I'm happy, and I wouldn't be if it weren't for you."

Had it been anyone else, Kelly would have felt slighted. *Thanks so much for letting me dump you! Now I'm finally happy!* But this was William, who of course was only trying to be nice. Kelly allowed himself a sigh when William hugged him but made sure to roll his eyes when their bodies parted, as if he were annoyed by the whole display.

Then he smiled. "You're going to be amazing," he said. "The Coast Guard won't know what hit them. You'll be running the place by this time next week."

"I doubt that," William said with a goofy grin.

"What about Jason?" Kelly asked. "Did you talk him into enlisting?"

"No."

"But he's going with you somehow, right?"

William took a deep breath. "What I'm about to do, it's just for me."

"So it's a long distance relationship now?"

William bit his bottom lip. "I told him we should be apart. I need to focus on my dream. If I'm still with him, all I'll do is look back and think about going home, which will make—"

"—it impossible to become a rescue swimmer." Kelly nodded his understanding. "You and I were doomed from the start. You know that? If the accident hadn't happened, I would have given everything up for the Olympics, and you would have done what you're doing now. In some alternate reality where I still have my leg and we stayed together, we're probably standing here, saying goodbye. Just like we are now."

William searched his face, but his thoughts weren't on the past or even some other present. Instead he was concerned about the future. "Do you think I screwed things up with Jason? Did I make the right decision?"

Kelly shrugged. "How did he react?"

"He keeps saying he's going to wait for me."

"Four years?"

"Yeah."

Kelly snorted. Then he swallowed, because maybe this Jason guy loved William more than he ever could have. "I'm sure you'll be okay. If it's meant to be, you'll find each other again."

William tried to get him in another hug, but Kelly dodged backward as best he could and offered his hand. After a moment, William took it, but he didn't shake it. He just held it.

"Take care of yourself," he said. "Don't be surprised if a bunch of guys come chasing after you now that I'm out of the picture."

"In that case," Kelly said, "don't be surprised if we meet again and I struggle to remember who you are. So many lovers, so little time."

William smiled at his joke, and they both knew that's all it was. Kelly would never forget William. Not in a million years.

Chapter Fifteen

Nothing. That's all Kelly had left. He didn't let himself get depressed about it. He wasn't distraught. He simply accepted the fact. Empty summer days and vague plans about going to college, his parents certain he would find himself there. Kelly didn't want that, or anything else, and so he didn't do much of anything. As surreal as it sometimes seemed, his story had come to an end.

Bonnie still dragged him along to the gay youth group, feeling certain that love was the answer. He humored her, part of him even feeling optimistic as the chairs slowly filled each meeting. Today in particular brought a face he hadn't expected to see, although it was hardly a new one. Jason Grant, shuffling along behind Emma just as he had the very first time. Of course now everyone knew who he was and wanted to say hello again.

Once he finally took his seat, he noticed Kelly across the room and quickly averted his eyes. Kelly didn't return the favor. He wasn't angry. Just curious. Was Jason here because he too was trying to move on? What happened to waiting for William? Had Jason thrown in the towel already? But as Keith's lecture droned on, Jason didn't check out any of the other guys. When it came time to pair up for another exercise, Jason looked hopefully at Emma, who abandoned him to be with Bonnie. Then he appeared downright miserable.

Kelly pushed himself up and crossed the room, Jason noticing him halfway and reacting like a fox who had just seen the hunters and their hounds. Kelly didn't even risk a smile on his way over, feeling he would spook him further.

Around them, everyone was pairing up into couples, platonic or otherwise. According to the exercise rules, they were supposed to choose someone they didn't know well, since today was about understanding an unfamiliar perspective. "Want to be partners?" he asked as he sat next to Jason. "Although I think I know where you're coming from already."

"Do you?" Jason asked, still tense.

"Yes. After all, we both loved the same man, and he left us to go become a hero or whatever. I'm guessing you still love him as much as I do."

"Guilty as charged."

Kelly nodded and glanced over at him, noticing how his fists were balled defensively. "I'm not mad at you. Not anymore. William and me breaking up was the right thing to do. We didn't make each other happy. All we did was fight. Did you two ever argue?"

"Not really," Jason said, "but then we weren't together that long."

"The first time William and I met *was* an argument. That should have been a warning sign."

"I didn't want you to get hurt," Jason blurted out. "I'm not saying I didn't think some evil thoughts about you, but I was only following my heart. Ideally you wouldn't have been in the picture at all, if that makes sense."

Kelly nodded, no stranger to wishing things had gone differently. "Ideally he and I would have broken up that day instead of getting in a car crash. I assume he told you about that?"

"Yeah."

Kelly braced himself for pitying words, still bothered by the way people would say they were sorry, as if being one leg down was automatically a fate worse than death. For once, Kelly was joyfully disappointed because Jason simply sat there, waiting for the conversation to continue.

"I don't know about you," Kelly said, "but I haven't got a clue what to do with myself anymore. There's an entire summer before college, and without William, the world feels empty. *I* feel empty. When I lost my leg, I needed a long time to get over missing a piece of myself. How I feel right now isn't so different."

Jason finally relaxed, slumping down in his chair as he exhaled. "I couldn't have put it better myself. I keep wishing I had some of William saved up somehow. Maybe videos where all he does is look at the camera and talk. That way I could pretend we were having a conversation. I don't even have photos. I think the ones from prom got lost in the mail."

If the illusion of William was all he required, Kelly could provide. While there might not be photos of him hanging on the bedroom wall anymore, Kelly frequently scrolled through the images on his phone. "Here," he said, digging the device out of his pocket. "Give me your number and I'll hook you up."

"Okay. Uh." Jason rattled off his number, his body language tensing again. Kelly found this puzzling until landing on the first photo. A selfie. In it, Kelly was holding out the phone, arm stretched as far away as possible to capture both him and William on camera. Of course he had cut off most of William's face and a lens flare from the setting sun made anything else hard to see... but William's smile was still there on display, right next to Kelly's. A happy moment together. One of the first. Jason would hate seeing it, so Kelly kept going, making sure the photos he sent were of William and William alone. Then he studied Jason as he absorbed each image. Kelly could practically see the lump forming in his throat.

"Thanks," Jason said, voice hoarse as he wiped at his eyes.

Kelly had once dreamed of his photos causing emotional reactions, but never like this. "These are just the ones from my phone. I used to take real photos all the time. Sort of a hobby of mine. Give me your email address and I'll send you some."

Jason practically leapt at the offer. Kelly typed the info into his contacts, trying to remember the last time he needed to access them. These days it was just him and Bonnie, and she was usually preoccupied with Emma. The idea of having another friend sounded appealing. Kelly set aside the phone and took a deep breath. "Listen, I know I've been a bitch to you, but maybe we can hang out sometime. That way I can prove I'm not so bad after all."

Jason's eyes went wide. Then he nodded. "Yeah, why not? It could be fun."

"Or awkward," Kelly said.

After a pause, they both laughed, which felt good. Kelly hadn't been doing a lot of that lately. In fact, he hadn't done much of anything. Maybe it was time for that to change.

"It's kind of beautiful," he said with a sigh.

"What?" Jason asked.

"William. How he just let go of everything. Me, you, his mother, his past. I don't think we stopped meaning anything to him, but he somehow managed to release us all before floating away on the wind. I wish I could do that. Just think how liberating a fresh start would feel."

"No thanks." Jason shook his head. "I've had my fill of new beginnings."

"Really?"

"Yup. I've been in and out of foster homes my entire life."

Now the roles were reversed and Kelly felt like telling Jason he was sorry, but he paid him the same respect and remained silent.

"Even coming to Austin was a new beginning for me," Jason continued. "Hopefully the last. Maybe that's why I'm not packing my things and moving to Cape Cod to be with William. Part of me is tempted, but the rest feels exhausted by the idea. I have to put down roots eventually, right?"

Kelly chuckled. "No idea. All I've got is roots, and frankly, I feel tangled up in them."

"Oh. Maybe you just need to change a few things, not everything." Jason glanced down at the phone again, staring at an image of William at the YMCA. Behind him were only the lockers he leaned against. Kelly had made sure nothing else was in frame. Just a solemn William with arms crossed and a slightly rusty metal backdrop. "You ever think about turning that camera on yourself?"

"Me?" Kelly asked.

"Yeah," Jason said. "Professionally."

Modeling? Kelly almost laughed at the idea. Enough people had told him he was handsome, or at least striking, that the idea wasn't completely far-fetched. Regardless, one attribute would always disqualify him. "I'm pretty sure having a full set of limbs is required if you want to be a model."

Jason shook his head, as if he disagreed, and moved through the menus of his phone. Then he pushed a button and held it out to Kelly. "Talk to this guy for a minute, and he'll happily prove you wrong."

Kelly stared at the phone. Then he heard a click and a tinny voice say hello.

Jason gestured with the phone. "Go ahead!"

Kelly grabbed it, and not having a clue what was happening, pressed it to his ear.

"If you're not going to speak," said a husky voice, "you could at least breathe heavily. Give me *something* to work with."

"Hello," Kelly managed.

"Ah! Progress at last. What can I do for you? No doubt this is an ex-lover, driven by desperation to call me. The only remaining question is if amorous desire motivates you now, or a lack of funding instead. I'll cut to the chase and tell you now that you won't get a single penny out of me. No, sir!"

Kelly scoffed. "This is a joke, right?"

"Quite possibly," the voice replied. "Let's start over. Why are you calling me?"

"I don't know," Kelly confessed.

"Do we know each other? No matter. I have a marvelous ear. Had we met before, I would have recognized your voice by now. Why don't you describe your present circumstances to me? Start with your surroundings."

"Okay..." Kelly glanced over at Jason who nodded encouragingly, as if everything was going according to plan. "Right now I'm in a church basement surrounded by gay teenagers."

"Some immoral priest is squirreling away young men in his own personal dungeon? How scandalous!"

"It's a gay youth group," Kelly said. "I was just talking to Jason and—"

"Which Jason? Stewart? Grant? McMillan?"

"Grant."

The line went quiet a moment. Maybe the guy was consulting a crystal ball, because when he spoke again, he suddenly knew everything. "Kelly Phillips, how would you feel about your image being plastered all over the world? Don't ask any questions or trouble yourself with complicated details. Just consider fame and wealth, and give me a simple yes or no answer."

Kelly's mouth went dry. He craved change in his life. He still didn't know what was going on, or what could happen, but this was definitely something new. Taking a deep breath, he answered.

"Yes."

Kelly had made a deal with the devil. There could be no other explanation. He glanced over at the driver and felt certain. They were in the Bentley again, but this time Jason was behind the wheel. The person who could summon up super-hot guys as his date, or steal away boyfriends despite doing everything wrong. Now it all made sense. Jason had made a deal with the devil to get whatever he wanted. And now Kelly had done the same.

Jason sensed his stare and smiled reassuringly. "Feeling nervous?"

"No," Kelly lied. After a moment's hesitation, he added, "But thanks for tagging along."

"I'm looking forward to it," Jason said. "I've never seen a real photo shoot. Or Marcello's studios."

Just the name made Kelly squirm. Marcello. It sounded foreign, even though the voice on the phone didn't have an accent. Not really. Sort of pompous, maybe, like make-believe royalty. He knew little about the man, but Kelly had learned that he wasn't a complete stranger. The fundraiser where William had played waiter was Marcello's. The palatial home where it had taken place belonged to Marcello. The fat man who had been up on stage in a well-cut white tuxedo, graceful despite his large size, was Marcello.

These brief impressions intimidated rather than comforted, adding to Kelly's nerves as they pulled up to a massive square building without any windows. The only detail was on the door, written in unassuming black letters.

Studio Maltese

"Weird," Jason said. "Not at all what I pictured. Looks more like a movie studio. Oh! Oh."

"What?" Kelly said.

Jason cringed. "Don't freak, but Marcello doesn't just handle professional photography. His company also makes movies. For adults."

"Not a chance in hell," Kelly said firmly.

"I agree!" Jason said. "I swear he's only interested in you as a professional model. Tim would kill Marcello if he tried to get me or my friends involved in… that stuff."

"So that's how you know him?"

"Yeah. He and Tim are old friends. And before you ask, Tim hasn't been in any adult movies either."

"Too bad," Kelly murmured.

They shared an awkward laugh together.

"You ready?" Jason asked. "You can always bail if you want, although I don't think you should. Marcello is a little eccentric, but he's a good guy."

That remained to be seen. Kelly couldn't decide if he was being exploited, or if the money involved made it a respectable job. He wasn't just here to give nice headshots. Marcello was interested in other parts of him as well. But like Jason said, if he got uncomfortable, he could always leave. Steeling himself, he nodded. "Let's do this."

He and Jason had just reached the door to the studio when it swung open, the space filled by an imposing form. Marcello's suit was brown, the fine fabric nearly as dark as the eyes that scrutinized him with cold efficiency. Then he placed his palms on his generous belly and smiled, seeming much more harmless than he had mere moments ago. Just a balding, graying, older man who seriously needed to shed some pounds. And yet, he hadn't built his empire by chance. Kelly held on to the image of those hard dark eyes and promised himself he wouldn't forget who he was dealing with.

"So handsome," Marcello said. "The pair of you!" he added, opening his arms to Jason for a hug. After releasing him, Marcello considered Kelly again. "So glad you could join me here today. Now I see why you turned down my offer to have a car sent over. When it comes to good company, you can't do better than Jason Grant."

"Don't listen to a word," Jason said. "He'll flatter your pants off if you let him."

"Literally," Marcello said. "Please, come in. Let me show you around the studio."

He held open the door, meaning they had to squeeze past his bulk. The hallway beyond was the complete opposite of the luxurious home Kelly had visited. The walls were beige, or maybe just dirty, since the flickering fluorescent tubes above provided insufficient light to judge fairly. Aside from numerous doors, there was nothing else to see—no struggling house plants or burbling water cooler.

"Welcome to Purgatory," Marcello said, taking the lead. "Don't worry though, Paradise lies just ahead."

As they walked down the hall, Kelly strained to hear any hint of the illicit films Jason had mentioned. Thankfully—or perhaps not—he heard no trace of cracking whips or creaking bed springs. Regardless, the hallway alone managed to feel derelict, which didn't promise much for the room beyond the door Marcello opened.

Was he ever wrong! The large space was pristine, the spotless floors and walls painted a solid eighteen percent gray, just enough to neutralize light reflections without sucking up luminance completely. The ceiling was solid black, specialized lights hanging at different angles. Soft boxes and umbrellas were strategically placed, while tripods and crank stands held equipment so valuable Kelly felt scared to breathe. Backdrops, meters, and flood lights! Paradise was an apt description because Kelly felt like he'd skipped over all the dying stuff and gone straight to Heaven.

"It can be a little overwhelming at first," Marcello said, "but the staff is highly qualified, meaning none of this should concern you."

Kelly noticed the people for the first time, most of them gathered behind photography equipment, facing one person front and center. Who could blame them? The guy had a body sculpted out of clay, the unforgiving bright light revealing nothing but perfection. No unsightly hairs or the tiniest bit of fat. Just flawless skin, trained muscle, and an impressive package stretching white cotton briefs to their limit.

"He's terrible," Marcello said in hushed tones. "Absolutely abhorrent."

Kelly stared. If this guy didn't meet expectations, then he was doomed. Sure his upper body was still fairly toned, but Kelly didn't hit the gym like this person must do on a daily basis. The second he peeled off his shirt, who knew how many flaws would be revealed? Hadn't he found a pimple on his shoulder a few days back? Had that healed yet?

"I think you need glasses," Jason said, "because that guy is *smoking!*"

"His body may inspire fevered visions," Marcello said, "but those eyes are devoid of emotion. And really, once you see him among his peers between the pages of a magazine, muscular perfection won't make him stand out any more than the others do. A shame, since I hoped to get more use out of him. The photographer asked him to imagine his greatest passion, which only resulted in him mumbling something about football. His eyes never caught fire. I'm afraid he's destined to end up as a crotch on a box of underwear and nothing more. I only hope the client doesn't ask us to airbrush the finer details out, because the boy is truly blessed. Now then, shall we step into my office and talk business?"

They returned back to the hall and waited in front of elevator doors.

"Third floor please," Marcello said once they were inside.

Kelly reached for the numbers, only to discover a keypad. After chuckling mischievously, Marcello leaned over and punched in a code. The elevator responded, lurching upward. When the doors opened again, natural daylight filled his vision. Kelly hadn't seen any windows from the ground floor, meaning this space was probably an addition built above the roof. He took in the designer couches, the low coffee table, and the tasteful rugs strewn about the stone floor, and sighed. Must be nice to be rich.

Marcello avoided the desk situated near the far wall, inviting them instead to sit on the couches. He directed Kelly to one cushion in particular and for good reason. A contract sat on the coffee table, Kelly's name typed in a blank spot on the first few lines. He tried to ignore it once he was seated, looking at the ferns in wooden planters by the windows, or the marble bust of a male figure in one corner.

"Antinous," Marcello said, still not having taken a seat. "Emperor Hadrian's lover. When he drowned in the Nile, the emperor had him deified. What a gift! As if the immortal soul weren't enough, Hadrian decided Antinous should live on as a god. Do you suppose anyone worships him today?"

Kelly considered the statue. Even from here, he could see how handsome Antinous must have been. "People still worship beauty," he answered.

"Indeed they do," Marcello said. "Would you care for something to drink?"

Kelly shook his head. So did Jason.

"Very well." Marcello sat on the couch across from them and leaned forward. "I'm the sort of man who makes no qualms about what he wants, and I believe you are the sort of man who appreciates a direct approach. Am I correct?"

Kelly nodded.

"Excellent. Let's get right down to business. What you saw downstairs makes me weary. The commercial world has finally realized the value of male beauty, which means that anyone with a gym membership and a good orthodontist is trotted out in front of the camera. I'm tired of it and so are consumers. The world craves novelty, and there's no shame in that. I intend to fulfill that desire, and I believe you can help me."

Kelly considered him. "You think using an amputee as a model will create scandal and publicity?"

"No," Marcello said. "No scandal. I intend to show the world that beauty comes in many forms. I'm not making an appeal to the hearts of my fellow man. You've lost a leg. Fine. But you are also incredibly striking. Beauty sells, and yours is something special. You're not just another waxed frat boy who hasn't yet ruined his body through frequent inebriation. Even sitting here now, I'm tempted to take a photo of you. Do you often flex your jaw like that?"

"Only when I'm trying to control my temper, which is often."

"Have I insulted you?"

"I still feel like you're beating around the bush, even though you pretend you're not."

Marcello leaned back and nodded curtly. "Very well. You're handsome, but I have no shortage of handsome male models. Neither do my competitors. Your amputation will set you apart from the crowd. I'd like to take photos that include your amputation in plain sight. If you are comfortable with this, I'm certain I can reward us both with inordinate sums of money."

"Fine," Kelly said, "but only under certain conditions."

"Such as?"

"I have final say over which photos get used and which don't. Also, I want royalties. Jason says you deal in stock photography. It seems only fair that whatever you sell in the future, I get a portion of."

Marcello glanced over at Jason accusingly. "Did you advise him to be so cutthroat?"

"No," Jason said, "but I'm enjoying the show."

"This will come out of your finder's fee."

"That's not why I did this!" Jason said hurriedly. "I only wanted to help Kelly. You can keep your money."

Kelly rolled his eyes. He was starting to see why Jason and William got along so well. "He gets a finder's fee," Kelly said. "And I get final say and a fair share of sales."

Marcello considered him shrewdly. "I'll give you a two-day contract, in which you will be paid one hundred dollars an hour. Those photos will be a test to see if we are creatively compatible, and will be used only to gauge client interest. You won't have final say, but if you feel uncomfortable at any time during a session, you may speak up and those photos won't leave this studio. Once the two days are over, and if it is mutually beneficial, terms of a longer contract can be discussed. Do we have a deal?"

Kelly's mulled it over until satisfied. "Deal."

"Good," Marcello leaned forward and pushed the contract toward him. "Sign here."

Kelly realized that the compromises they seemed to have reached were actually the original terms of the contract. So much for his negotiation skills. He thought about playing hardball, maybe walking out of the office in the hopes Marcello would lure him back with a better offer. That would mean returning home to face another empty day...

Leaning forward, Kelly took hold of the pen and signed his name.

When considering the worst case scenario, Kelly imagined the photographers having him sit on a mat, his amputated leg stretched out before him for all to see. He'd be looking up at the camera, pathetically begging the consumer to buy whatever merchandise was being pushed. Or maybe they would have him lift the stump in the air, a pair of designer underwear dangling off of it.

Such schemes appeared even more plausible when in makeup, where Kelly was asked to strip down. Just about every inch of his body was powdered or plucked or somehow improved in places he never realized were a problem. This included the nub of his leg. Margie, the makeup lady, took it all in stride.

"Just be glad you've still got your briefs on," she said. "You wouldn't believe some of the things I've applied rouge to."

Kelly felt a little better once buttoned up in a stylish dress shirt and dark slacks.

"How do you usually handle the pant leg, honey?" Margie asked.

"I usually just fold it up with a few hair pins."

"Then that'll do just fine."

The first photo shoot was in a different studio area, one corner arranged to look like a Cambridge library. Kelly was directed to a high-backed leather chair where he was asked to sit sideways, his leg draped across one of the arms. The photographer—an older guy with just a few wisps of red hair left on his head— introduced himself as Rick. Then he quietly snapped a few photos and consulted the digital preview before looking up at Kelly again.

"You like boys or girls?" he asked.

"Men," Kelly responded.

"Fair enough. I know this might be a stretch, but I need you to pretend I'm the hottest guy you've ever seen. Your boyfriend, if you've got one. Is that who this is?" He gestured with his head toward Jason, who was standing in the corner of the room and now wearing a deer-in-headlights expression.

"Nope," Kelly said. "Not my type."

"Hey!" Jason protested.

Kelly smiled, which sent the camera flashing. Then he tried to get himself in the mood by thinking of porn stars or old crushes. He even tried thinking of Jared, but in the end, his stupid imagination settled on William. He pretended he'd been waiting up half the night, horny as hell, for William to come home. Now that he had arrived—in the form of an aging photographer— Kelly cranked up the sex appeal, trying with body language alone to get him to strip off his Coast Guard uniform. This little game must have worked because the photographer became more animated, dancing around Kelly and capturing him from different angles.

"Feel free to move," Rick said.

Kelly did so, rolling and twisting in the chair. He was just getting started when Rick lowered the camera and beamed at him. "Great stuff! Let's get to the next set."

Kelly was stripped down to his underwear, laid out on a couch, and tangled up in a blanket. As he squirmed, there were times his amputation was revealed, which of course was the point. Plenty of the rest of him was exposed too. Kelly found he didn't mind. The attention felt good. As the day wore on, he found himself looking forward to each new scenario. Every hour he became something new—a boorish jock, a proud-faced thug, a disinterested businessman. The only time he felt uncomfortable was when they tried dressing him up in army fatigues, as if he were a war veteran. That seemed disrespectful to actual veterans, and the moment he expressed his discomfort, they moved on to the next idea.

As much fun as he was having, when lunch break rolled around, he could see Jason was bored out of his mind.

"Nothing to do with your performance," he insisted over smoked salmon bagels. "You getting all sexy for the camera is very— Um. Yeah. It's just the never-ending moving around of lights, reading meters, switching lenses, and everything else that drives me nuts."

Kelly laughed. "That might be my favorite part!"

Every time the crew stopped to make adjustments, he paid careful attention, whisked back to the days when a camera was his best friend. Of course he could see how Jason would find the long waits during makeup and wardrobe changes tedious. "You can go home," he said. "I'll make Marcello call a limo for me."

"You sure?" Jason said, a little too eagerly.

"Absolutely. I was freaking out when we first got here, but I'm okay now. Thanks for tagging along. And for setting this up. That was really cool of you."

Jason smiled. His good deed done, he left once lunch was over.

Kelly reported back to the makeup room where Margie had a long white robe waiting for him, the sort that might be worn in the desert. "This isn't a statement about the war, is it?" he asked. "I'm not okay with anything like that."

"Nope." From one corner of the room, Margie grabbed a long wooden pole with a hook at the top.

"A shepherd?" he asked.

"Yup. Think you can stand with only this to balance you?"

"Easily," Kelly said. "I'm just surprised that shepherds concern themselves with the latest fashion trends. Or that they exist anymore."

Margie snorted. "You'd be surprised how much modeling has nothing to do with selling clothes. This might be used for cologne, or an expensive watch, or maybe even life insurance. Sex sells."

"Yeah, but shepherds aren't exactly sexy."

"This one will be. I need you to hop in the shower. Get all that makeup off you. Then we're going to oil you up."

O-kay. Kelly did what he was told, trying to imagine what was coming next. The second he stepped out of the shower, Margie was standing there with a towel. "I have sons nearly twice your age. You haven't got anything I haven't seen, or that I'm interested in."

Thankfully she didn't intend to dry him off, but she did have a swatch of white fabric that she wrapped around his pelvis and tied at the front, creating a primitive sort of skimpy underwear.

"No complaints," she said. "If it's good enough for Jesus, it's good enough for you."

As promised, she slathered him in oil. Or at least certain areas of him, like the front of his torso and neck but not his shoulders. Once he donned the robe, he found out why. It wasn't as long as he initially thought, the fabric ending somewhere around his knee. It also lacked a belt, meaning it was left hanging open. Margie stepped back to consider him before applying oil to a few places she'd missed. Then she swatted him on the rump and told him he was ready.

As soon as Kelly entered the studio and saw the light setup, he knew what sort of photo this would be. The background was white and the illumination levels cranked up. This combined with his white clothes meant that his freshly oiled skin would look darker than ever. High contrast was the theme. Like Charlotte March's photos of Trevor in *Twen* magazine, this involved a black model against a white background and an abundance of light. Kelly was looking forward to the end result, even if it had been done plenty of times before. With black models. He'd like to see a pasty white guy greased up and shoved in front of a dark background.

"I love that smile," Rick said. "I won't pretend it's sweet, but it sure makes the camera happy."

"No need to butter me up," Kelly responded. "Between the body oil and all these lights, I'll be deep-fried by the time you're through."

"I hope not," Rick said. "Into position please."

Margie brought him the shepherd's crook and took away his crutches. Kelly hopped a few times to get his balance. Even more lights were switched on. He faced them and tried not to squint against their brightness.

"What's my motivation?" Kelly asked. "Am I horny for my sheep?"

"Give me sultry," Rick said. After a few minutes of photos, he changed his mind. "Try stoic. Pretend you're standing on a hill, surveying your flock. No pride, no contentment. Just an acceptance of your duty."

Right. After Margie stepped in to mop the sweat off his brow,

Kelly tried putting himself in this mindset. He was a shepherd. He'd been doing this his whole life, the safety of his flock routine rather than extraordinary. Kelly stared into the distance, seeing only shadowy forms beyond the light: Rick moving back and forth, the lighting technicians making slight adjustments. Margie's stooped form. Marcello's silent bulk; His potential employer had been observing him the entire day, rarely offering any direction or feedback. Then there was the hulking shadow standing next to him. That one was new.

Kelly squinted to see better before Rick chastised him.

"Eyes on the flock!" he said. "Don't let those sheep get away."

Kelly returned his attention to the forefront, only glancing toward Marcello again when Margie came to sponge up more of his sweat. Whoever it was, the guy was big, since Marcello didn't look so large anymore.

"Ready?" Rick asked.

"Yeah," Kelly said. "Uh, wait." He hopped and shifted his weight, leaning more on the crook. And facing a little more in Marcello's direction.

Rick seemed okay with this, because he was snapping photos again. Now when Kelly stared off into the distance, he saw two forms. One rotund, the other a seductive silhouette. He snorted at the idea. Rick complained, but Kelly couldn't help it. Who'd ever heard of a sexy shadow? But the broad shoulders, the round deltoids, even the casual posture as the man leaned against the wall, one foot pressed against it… Kelly could make out some of the facial features, the shadows deep beneath the heavy brow. Then the figure stepped forward, reached for one of the lights, and turned it off.

"What the hell do you think you're doing?" Rick said, spinning around. "Oh! I didn't realize it was you. Sorry, Nathaniel."

Kelly's jaw dropped. He might not have remembered the name if Rick hadn't spoken it. Their brief encounter had been blurred by emotion and alcohol, but Kelly hadn't forgotten him. From the way one corner of Nathaniel's mouth jerked upward, he hadn't forgotten Kelly either.

"You're doing great," Nathaniel said to him. "Keep it up, and there might be another bottle of wine in it for you."

Then the light was switched back on. Kelly blinked against it before he said, "Can I get that in writing?"

"He's probably serious," Marcello grumbled.

"Gentlemen," Rick said, voice strained. "If I may continue?"

"By all means," Nathaniel said.

Kelly tried to focus on the task at hand, wanting to prove how professional he could be, but his mind was racing. What was Nathaniel doing here? He had arranged the fundraiser for Marcello, but that had little in common with a photo shoot. Maybe he had come by to discuss business with his boss and had stopped to stare. Lustfully.

"There's that smile again," Rick said. "I don't think I've seen anything naughtier in my life."

"I have," Marcello replied. "Shall I draw you a picture?"

Rick ignored this to give Kelly more instructions. The photo session dragged on, and soon all Kelly could think of was getting away from the lights and cooling down. By the time the lamps finally shut off, he saw ghost images that practically blinded him. When his vision cleared, only the technicians, the photographer, and his would-be employer remained. Nathaniel was gone.

"Well done," Marcello said, approaching with a hand outstretched. He thought twice when he saw how sweaty Kelly was. Instead he fetched Kelly's crutches and handed them to him. "We're finished for today. No need to come to the studio tomorrow. I thought we'd entertain ourselves with some location shooting. If you're agreeable, I'll send a car around to pick you up. Say, seven in the morning?"

"Fine," Kelly said. "Speaking of which, I need a ride home."

"I'll make arrangements immediately." Marcello looked him over. "Perhaps you should treat yourself to a shower first."

Kelly didn't need to be asked twice. When he got in the shower, he made sure the water was cool, but by the time he was finished, the small room was full of steam. Once he stepped out, he discovered he wasn't alone. Like Jack the Ripper lurking in the London fog, Margie stood there, a fresh towel held at the ready.

"Sounds like you're riding home with me," she said. "I hope you don't mind sitting in the smoking section, because that's all my car has."

Kelly snatched the towel from her, covered himself, and sighed. So much for his stretch-limo dreams.

Chapter Sixteen

Five in the morning. That's how early Kelly woke up. Now he wished he hadn't bothered. After taking a shower, he didn't have anything to do. He only ate an apple for breakfast, worrying more would make him look bloated. The text he'd received from Marcello last night insisted he remain as natural as possible.

No hair products, and certainly no makeup!

As if Kelly used either. Once ready, he sat around the breakfast table and yawned, the last twenty minutes full of temptation, thanks to his mother's French toast. Kelly glanced at the microwave clock, the first digit changing from a six to a seven.

Ding dong!

"I'm out of here," Kelly said, standing up and heading for the door. Then he stopped and considered his parents. "Or is that too eager? Maybe I should have one of you answer."

"I'm not pretending to be your servant," his mother said.

His father was already on his feet. "I've always wanted to be a butler!"

Kelly watched in amusement as his father headed for the door. He strained to listen. Would it be a limo driver? Or a taxi at least? Or maybe just Margie again. When his father returned to the kitchen, his eyes were wide. A limo! It had to be!

"I think you're going to enjoy this," he said. "Best of luck, son!"

"Thanks." Kelly swung toward the front door so fast he nearly left his crutches behind. Of course this made it all the harder to stop when he saw who was waiting for him.

Nathaniel stood just outside the glass door. His back was turned, but the build was unmistakable. Kelly slowed and reached for the handle. Nathaniel turned, looked him up and down through the glass, and made no effort to open the door for him. So much for helping the crippled guy. Not that Kelly really needed it. Switching one of the crutches to his other arm, he got it open and hopped outside.

"Good morning," Kelly said.

Nathaniel's brow lowered. "Don't speak. I'm serious. Just get in the car."

"Okay," Kelly said. "Are you hungover or something?"

Nathaniel just glared at him in return.

Not hiding his smile, Kelly headed for the driveway. No limo, but the black sedan was a step up from the hunk of junk Margie drove. Once again, Nathaniel didn't seem concerned with opening the door for Kelly. In fact, he was already seated behind the wheel by the time Kelly reached the car. Charming. He made sure that his crutches clattered together as he got himself settled. Once buckled up and in motion, he considered everything.

Light electronic music played just loud enough to be heard. The beat was pretty mellow, which seemed to ease Nathaniel's sour expression somewhat. The interior fabric was dark, the windows tinted against the sun. Maybe Nathaniel was a vampire. Kelly glanced over at him, noticing the natural highlights in his light brown hair, the tan on his forehead and nose, and the scruff on his chin that was platinum blond in places. No enemy of the sun. Just not a morning person. Or maybe he was irritated that he'd been sent to fetch Kelly. Marcello seemed to save money by having his employees act as taxis.

Kelly settled back and relaxed, waiting to see where the photo shoot would be located. On the banks of the Colorado River? Or maybe a downtown street, Kelly posing in front of expensive shops while Rick shot photos. Or how about a completely average pancake house, because that's what they parked in front of. He looked around for signs of the crew, or some cordoned-off area where they would be working.

"Come on," Nathaniel said, already halfway out of the car.

By the time Kelly was standing in the parking lot, Nathaniel had closed the trunk, a camera bag slung over one arm. When they entered the restaurant, he expected Nathaniel to announce them to the greeter. Instead, when she asked if it was just the two of them, Nathaniel grunted in acknowledgement. Soon they were seated.

Kelly glanced around. No sign of Rick or Margie. Or Marcello, not that Kelly could imagine him visiting such a humble restaurant. Maybe they simply hadn't arrived yet. He turned his attention back to Nathaniel, feeling a thrill at sitting across from such a handsome guy. God that was sad! Kelly blamed it on a lack of action. Not a drop since William, in fact, and even then they hadn't slept together for that last month or so. Not after Jason had wedged his way into the picture.

Nathaniel felt his gaze, the hazel eyes swiveling to meet his. "You eaten breakfast?"

Was that even a complete sentence? "I had an apple."

"That's not breakfast. You don't have body image issues, do you? If so, get out of the modeling business now."

Kelly shrugged. "I thought a big breakfast might make me look bloated."

Nathaniel snorted. "A hotdog eating contest will make you look bloated. An omelet will make you look like a normal human being." Then he winced, due to the arrival of their waiter.

"Good morning! It's going to be a lovely day! What can I get for you fellas?"

"Coffee," Nathaniel grumbled. "And the triple slam dunk breakfast."

The waiter scribbled on his pad before turning to Kelly. "And for you?"

"The same," Kelly said, smiling slyly. "Especially since I no longer have to worry about my figure."

"He'll have the single slam dunk," Nathaniel told the waiter. "No sense in wasting food."

"I'll be right back with that!" the waiter chirped cheerfully.

Nathaniel watched him go, then glowered at the other patrons. Not a morning person then. Kelly decided to let him stew, their time together spent in silence. This soon grew dull. With nothing to do, Kelly found his attention repeatedly returning to the man across from him. The impression from the first time they met remained. Nathaniel really could be some distant cousin of William's, or perhaps some future version of him, grizzled and embittered. Or maybe he just really needed some caffeine.

"Where's that coffee?" Nathaniel said, sounding weary.

What had it been now, fifteen minutes? Kelly could see multiple pots steaming at the nearby serving station. Pushing himself out of the booth, he grabbed one of his crutches, leaving the other behind so he'd have a hand free to carry a pot. Coffee cups were on the table already, along with cutlery, meaning they would be good to go. Kelly made it to the station and grabbed one of the pots before a waitress noticed him. She scowled, about to complain, but noticed the crutch and empty space where a leg should be. Then her face softened considerably.

"Need any help, hon?"

"Nope," Kelly said. "I'm all right. Uh, this isn't decaf, is it?"

"You've got the right one."

"Thanks."

He returned to the table, feeling victorious, especially when Nathaniel's eyes lit up.

"You're a godsend!" he said, grabbing the pot and pouring them each a cup. He held on to his for dear life as he slurped repeatedly and very slowly appeared to defrost. Or at least he ceased glaring at anyone in the near vicinity.

Kelly tried his own, overwhelmed by the bitter tang. Was it supposed to taste like aspirin? Nathaniel didn't appear disgusted and was already halfway through his cup, so Kelly had to assume this was normal. He took another sip, hoping his repulsion wasn't evident.

Nathaniel raised an eyebrow. "Do that again."

"What? Take a drink?"

Nathaniel nodded, digging around in the camera bag. Kelly took another sip, trying to make it a small one.

"Again," Nathaniel said, the camera out and pointing at him now.

"Do I have to?"

"Drink!"

Kelly slurped at the coffee and the camera flashed.

"One more time."

"It's hot!" Kelly complained.

"I agree."

Oh! That spurred Kelly on. He took not one, but three more sips, the last one ending with him declaring "Bleh!" and sticking out his tongue.

Nathaniel captured this on film and laughed, the sound deep and pleasant. "How long have you been a coffee drinker?"

"About five minutes," Kelly said.

"That's what I thought." Nathaniel set aside the camera. "You know what we're supposed to be doing today?"

Kelly shook his head.

"Your friend Jason convinced Marcello that photos need to be more spontaneous and less polished. That's called amateur photography. If people wanted that, they wouldn't yawn their way through tourist photos. Anyway, we're supposed to purposefully put you in a number of natural situations. You see the inherent flaw in that idea?"

"You can't be spontaneous on purpose," Kelly said.

"Correct. But maybe we can get close. Take a look."

Nathaniel pushed a few buttons on the camera and turned it so Kelly could see the display. It wasn't the most recent photo, thank goodness, but one of Kelly squishing up his face behind a cup of joe. And it looked good. Odd as it sounded, there was a certain appeal to it.

"Gorgeous but relatable," Nathaniel said. "Who would have thought?"

Kelly felt his cheeks flush. "So it's really just you and me today? No fussy technicians or little old ladies oiling me up?"

"Just us," Nathaniel said. "Doesn't sound so bad, does it?"

It certainly didn't, but before Kelly could respond, their waiter had finally returned. Empty handed.

"Can I get you anything else?" he asked. "If not, you can pay up front when you're ready."

"We're still waiting on our food," Nathaniel said.

"Oh!" The waiter took out his pad of paper, like they hadn't already ordered. "What can I get you?"

"A new waiter," Kelly snapped. "Preferably one who knows how to do his job!"

And there it was. Kelly sighed inwardly. Just as well that Nathaniel reminded him a little of William, because this was the exact situation they had found themselves in so often. Something dumb would happen and Kelly would react with anger. No doubt Nathaniel, much like William, would keep his cool and—

"Excellent idea," Nathaniel said. "While you're at it, send your boss over here. Better yet, have *him* bring us our food, because if he can't bother hiring competent staff, then he needs to get off his lazy ass and do the work himself."

Music should have swelled. In a puff of heart-shaped glitter, the waiter should have turned into Cupid and fluttered away. Then Nathaniel would clear the table with a swipe of his arm and take Kelly right then and there. Instead the waiter made a strangling noise before marching off. Shortly afterwards, the waitress Kelly had spoken to before came and apologized, taking their order once more and promising to rush some emergency carbs out to them.

"I'm still talking to the manager," Nathaniel said when she had gone. "I'll tell him to fire the other loser, and give that woman a raise."

Kelly rested his chin on splayed hands. "Can I watch?"

"Of course. Feel free to join in."

Before Kelly could propose, two stacks of pancakes landed on their table. Their real meals didn't take much longer, leaving them with more food than they could eat. Or so he thought. Nathaniel very steadily devoured any food Kelly left untouched. Afterwards, he leaned back and finally seemed at ease.

"That was a close call," Nathaniel said. "You almost saw me in a bad mood."

"Almost?"

Nathaniel grinned. "I can't stand mornings. Or morning people. Nothing personal."

Kelly shrugged. "Why would that offend me?"

"You're the one who insisted on an early start. Normally I don't get out of bed until ten."

Kelly blinked. "Marcello told me when I needed to be ready. It wasn't my decision."

Nathaniel exhaled and shook his head. "That motherfucker." Then he chuckled. "I am so going to make him pay! I hope today's assignment isn't also a joke."

"So do I," Kelly said, feeling vulnerable.

"It's not," Nathaniel assured him. "And even if it was, we're going to bring back photos so amazing that the poor bastard breaks down in tears. Hey, speaking of which, let's go find that manager."

"After you," Kelly said. When he was certain Nathaniel wasn't looking, he allowed himself the dreamiest sigh ever.

As fun as fawning over Nathaniel during breakfast had been, the time had come to start working. Kelly was curious as to how they would proceed. They returned to the car and stood outside it rather than getting in, Nathaniel glancing around the parking lot.

"Are we waiting for someone?" Kelly asked. "You said it was just me and you."

"It is," Nathaniel said. Then he pinched the bridge of his nose and growled. "This assignment is driving me crazy! Marcello sprung it on me yesterday, and I was up half the night trying to figure out what to do. If I spontaneously ask you to climb a tree, once you're up there, you're still going to look like someone who climbed a tree so he could have his photo taken."

Kelly searched for inspiration. "I could spread myself out on the hood of your car. Or wait, maybe I should just do it instead of talking about it."

"Won't make a difference," Nathaniel said. "Would still come across as contrived."

"In that case, you should drive me home so I can play video games with my brother. That's what I'd be doing if it weren't for this assignment."

Nathaniel perked up. "Maybe you've got the right idea. Video games are boring, but what else would you do today? It's Sunday. Church?"

"Sort of. I have a gay youth group every couple of weeks. There's one this afternoon."

Nathaniel shook his head. "I can't see that being too exciting. Unless I'm wrong. I'm picturing an AA meeting except with nervous gay teenagers instead of tired old alcoholics."

"Pretty much. You're probably way above the age limit anyway. How old are you? Thirty?"

Nathaniel scowled. "Twenty-three. How old are you? Twelve?"

"Eighteen."

"Great. So what else do nervous gay teenagers do for fun?"

Kelly shrugged. "Hang out with my friends, usually at their place, or in my room. Or at the mall."

"Gosh," Nathaniel said. "If that's your idea of a good time, I'd hate to hear about your bad days."

Kelly thought about it briefly. "Actually, you're on to something. Come on."

He got in the car, and before Nathaniel could ask where they were going, he started giving directions. Before long, they were parked outside the high school. Summer break made the place feel abandoned. Nathaniel surveyed the empty parking lot and the soulless brick building, nodding slowly. So far, so good. He had the camera out of the bag as Kelly led the way to the sports field.

They passed the track by circling around it. Kelly wouldn't allow himself to step onto the rubbery surface anymore. He no longer considered himself worthy, treating his former arena as if it were sacred. This was slightly marred by the middle-aged guy currently using it to jog, but even he was more in touch with speed than Kelly these days.

Leading the way to the bleachers, Kelly climbed a few steps and walked down the aisle until they were exactly in the middle. This is where he always sat when feeling morose. Just being here was enough to bring him to that state. Not even the presence of a hot guy with an expensive camera helped.

"What's the story?" Nathaniel asked.

"Same as Icarus when he flew too close to the sun. If you delight in something too much, the gods punish you for it. Icarus got his kicks flying, and I got high off running."

"You were on the track team?"

Kelly nodded. "Fastest guy in school. I even planned on making a career of it, Olympic dream and all that. Sounds arrogant to say it now. I probably would have learned a hard lesson when meeting the pros, but I would have preferred that to this."

"Huh."

"That's it?" Kelly glanced over at Nathaniel. "That's all you've got to say?"

Nathaniel shrugged. "You don't strike me as the self-pitying type."

"I'm not," Kelly said, returning his gaze to the track. "I used to be, but not anymore. Now I just miss it. I sit here because it's as close as I can get. I even wondered if I should be some sort of coach, you know? Professional boxers always have an out-of-shape dude telling them how to punch. You don't have to be the champ to make a champ."

"Is that something you're interested in doing?" Nathaniel asked.

Kelly shook his head. "Not really."

He watched the middle-aged guy stumble to a stop and wipe his brow before he started up again. His posture was terrible, his clothing wrong, and his gait an absolute joke—and still Kelly envied him.

"I left the flash in the car," Nathaniel said. "I'll be right back."

Kelly nodded, keeping his attention on the track and his thoughts on the past. Eventually, the middle-aged guy stopped running, cooling down by walking a lap. Then he wandered off toward the nearest houses.

The bleachers creaked as Nathaniel returned. "Got some good photos of you," he said.

"I figured."

"You knew?"

Kelly shrugged. "I know that a flash is near-useless in broad daylight." He nodded at the camera. "Especially when you're using a telephoto lens. What's the maximum range on that thing? Three hundred millimeter?"

"Five."

"Impressive."

Nathaniel considered him. "It felt sleazy as hell, taking photos of you looking sad. Too exploitative."

"I wouldn't have brought you here if I had a problem with it. I thought we'd go to a shoe store next, followed by a dance club." He cracked a smile, prompting Nathaniel to do the same. "For what it's worth, I think your tree-climbing idea is cool. You'd be surprised how mobile I am when not stuck on the stupid ground. As long as you're snapping photos of me in action, we might get something good. Besides—" Kelly flexed an arm muscle playfully. "—it'll allow me to show off some upper-body."

Nathaniel nodded. "Okay. Let's give it a go."

"Would you mind coming home with me?"

Wow! Kelly felt the photo shoot had gone well. Just not *that* well! They had driven out to a wilderness preserve where they were less likely to be interrupted and where the trees weren't pruned, allowing them to find one with low branches. Kelly had scurried up it, having a grand ol' time and easily forgetting the camera was there. Now they were taking a break beneath the tree, the sun high in the sky, both of them sweating. Or were they hot and bothered? Ha ha!

"Kelly?"

He blinked away the swirling fantasies. "Sorry. What did you say?"

Nathaniel got to his feet. "I need to run home. There's someone I need to check on. That all right?"

"Yeah, perfectly." With a little struggle, Kelly managed to get up. He refused to look at Nathaniel to avoid any offers of help. He didn't want to appear pathetic. Once back in the car, they didn't have far to drive. Nathaniel brought them to a fairly average apartment complex on the edge of town, which was surprising. Kelly had assumed everyone associated with Marcello was rich and gay, but now he wondered if Nathaniel was either.

And who was this person he needed to check on?

"You should probably wait down here," Nathaniel said after they had parked. "He tends to knock people over when he's excited."

Please let it be a dog and not a hyperactive kid or a socially awkward boyfriend. Not that Kelly had anything against children or people having relationships. It's just that someday he wanted those things too. "If you're going to leave me in a hot car," he said, "be sure to crack a window."

"I'm not that inhumane. There's an area for grilling around the corner." Nathaniel nodded toward the end of the building. "Should be plenty of shade. I'll meet you soon."

Kelly left the car and walked around the corner, finding a few picnic benches, a metal trashcan, and a cluster of trees. He stood beneath one of them and tried to look inconspicuous. A few minutes later, panting preceded Nathaniel's reappearance. Either he was really eager to see him or...

A dog. Kelly breathed out in relief. Or a wolf, because it had a gray coat and silver eyes and was huge. The dog spotted him. They considered each other for a moment. Then it broke loose, tearing across the yard toward him. Kelly missed his running legs more than ever as he stood there helpless. He supposed he could thwack it with one of his crutches, but Nathaniel was already chasing after it with pure concern etched into his features.

Sighing, Kelly tried bracing himself as much as possible. It didn't do much good. The dog leapt into the air, pushed him over with his front paws, and laid Kelly out flat. Then it circled him, sniffing every part of his body so quickly the dog sounded like it was hyperventilating.

"Zero!" Nathaniel was shouting. "Heel! Sit! Stop! Ugh... Fuck off, you stupid mutt!"

This got the dog's attention. It whipped its head around and ran back toward its master.

"Sorry," Nathaniel said, approaching with the dog in tow. "As a puppy, he was trained to sniff out drugs, but they only ended up creating a monster."

"No problem," Kelly said, waving away Nathaniel's hand as he struggled to his feet. "I'd love to see him in action at an airport. That would thin the crowds."

Once Kelly was up, he considered the dog warily, who was

now panting happily and looking like he wanted to do it all over again. "What sort of breed is that anyway? Hell hound?"

"Close," Nathaniel said with a chuckle. "Siberian Husky. The sled-pulling dogs. I'm tempted to hook up Zero to my car and put it in neutral. Maybe the exercise would finally get him to chill."

As if in response, the dog raced off, running around the park area in wide arcs that eventually returned to Nathaniel before Zero took off again.

"Usually I chase after him," Nathaniel explained.

"By all means," Kelly said, but Nathaniel shook his head.

"Let him do his business and blow off a little steam. Then we can escape inside to air conditioning. I'll even cook for you."

"Sounds promising," Kelly said, heading for one of the benches and sitting. "Are we done working today?"

"Oh, right." Nathaniel lifted the camera hanging from around his neck and snapped a few more photos.

Kelly raised an eyebrow. "Somehow I don't think those are going to make an impression."

The camera clicked again. "That one will. You look hot when you're being snarky."

Which was different than saying he actually was hot. Straight guys could tell if another man was good looking. Especially if they were photographers. Kelly was over waiting and hoping. He wanted to know right now.

"What's your girlfriend going to think when she comes home to find you cooking for another woman?"

"Subtle," Nathaniel said with a smirk. "If any girl of mine comes home, it better be a dude in drag, because I don't swing that way."

Thank goodness for that! "You're probably dying to know if I'm straight or not."

"Nope," Nathaniel said, becoming distracted. "Zero, if you chase that squirrel, and *especially* if you eat it, I'll wire your damn mouth shut!"

"Gosh," Kelly murmured, "you really love your dog."

"More than anything in the world," Nathaniel said, fixing him with a stare to prove how serious he was. "Besides, he talks back to me in his own way. If I annoy him too much, he'll chew up one of my Blu-rays when I'm at work. Just the case though. If he didn't love me back, he'd ruin the disc too."

"You like movies?" Kelly asked.

"I have a dog named Zero, don't I?"

Kelly wracked his brain, trying to catch the reference. *"Nightmare Before Christmas?"*

"Very good. And I'm not into movies. I'm into cinematography."

"There's a difference?"

"Anyone can point a camera and start filming, just like anyone can smear paint on a canvas. But very few are capable of true art."

Kelly's smile was subtle. "I'm a big fan of Michael Bay myself."

"I hate you."

"Or M. Night Shyamalan's later films. Those are a real treat."

"Go away. Right now. I mean it."

"Ah, but you promised me lunch," Kelly said.

Nathaniel sighed dramatically. "I suppose I did. Come on, Zero. Time to open a can of dog food for our guest here."

Kelly was curious if the apartment had a sprawling floor plan or was finely furnished. Upon entering, he saw a hall that led past a bedroom on one side and a bathroom on the other. The living room had a balcony overlooking a stretch of grass that ended in a wall of trees. To the left was a small dining area and a narrow kitchen. Aside from the huge television and surround sound system, the home seemed average. The couch—which Zero quickly hopped up on—was worn, the wooden coffee table nicked, and decoration sparse. Maybe Marcello didn't pay well. Then again, how much did a photographer earn? One who occasionally managed charity events.

"What exactly do you do for a living?" Kelly asked.

"Whatever Marcello wants me to." Nathaniel opened the refrigerator and bent to dig around. Then his head reappeared above the door. "Wait, that sounds perverted. I don't mean it like that. Marcello is a very successful man who has his fingers in quite a few pies. That can get complicated, and when he needs help, he knows he can rely on me."

"So you're not normally a photographer."

Nathaniel tossed a pack of ground beef on the counter before he continued digging. "Nope. I've got a good eye and I know my way around a camera, but Marcello has plenty of professionals working for him."

"So how come I'm standing in your kitchen right now and not Rick's?"

Nathaniel closed the refrigerator, hands full of produce. "I was wondering that myself. I have a few theories."

"Such as?"

"Remember when Rick asked you to pretend he was a hot guy?"

Kelly nodded. "Yeah."

Nathaniel's smile was slow. "With me, you don't have to pretend."

Kelly recovered quickly. "Actually, I do."

"What?"

"Yup. All day. I keep picturing this cute Asian guy. Short, slender, has a shy smile. So adorable!"

Nathaniel narrowed his eyes. "That's your type?"

"Oh yeah!"

"Your loss." Nathaniel frowned. "Not that it would have mattered if I *was* your type."

"Of course not."

"Right."

Kelly smiled. "Need help dicing that onion?"

"That would be great."

They started cooking together, Nathaniel working on a salad. After confirming that they'd be having burgers with it, Kelly washed his hands and worked on making patties.

"How did you become Marcello's right-hand man?" he asked.

Amusement tugged at Nathaniel's features. "I pulled his ass out of the fire. After that, it didn't take him long to realize how useful I can be. Hey, make sure not to put onions in two of them. They give Zero gas."

"I didn't realize we were cooking for the dog. And anyway, stop changing the subject. How exactly did you save Marcello?"

"The past belongs in the past," Nathaniel said dismissively, turning on one of the burners. "Would you mind setting the table?"

"Sure." Kelly felt puzzled while opening drawer after drawer to find the silverware. Why was the past so off-limits? How was he supposed to get to know Nathaniel if they were only allowed to talk about the present? His hunger to learn soon turned into a more traditional sort when the smell of cooking meat filled the air. He watched as Nathaniel flipped burgers while also working on vinaigrette for the salad. A grumbling came from below, one a little too low to be his stomach. Kelly glanced down to see Zero at his side, attention focused on Nathaniel as he cooked.

"He puts on quite the show, doesn't he?" Kelly murmured to him.

Once they were seated—Nathaniel and Kelly that is; Zero had to eat on the floor—he decided to pry again. "Do you like working for Marcello?" he asked. "I'm not sure what to make of him."

Nathaniel nodded as he chewed and swallowed. "Marcello is very good at giving people what they want, and even better at finding people who want the same as he does."

"So what's he give you that you want?"

"Something to do. I know from personal experience how destructive downtime can be. I also get bored easily, so I need work, and I need variety. Marcello understands that, and it's probably the real reason he has me playing photographer today. Otherwise he would have found an adorable Asian guy to keep your attention."

Kelly smiled. "Do you think I'm doing the right thing? Like you, I was looking for something to occupy myself with, but I don't know if I want to be a model. I don't know if I can be."

"Really?" Nathaniel stood and fetched the camera. When he came back, he sat next to Kelly instead of across from him. After pulling his plate close and taking another bite, he started pushing buttons on the camera, occasionally turning the display screen for Kelly to see.

Kelly wasn't arrogant. At least he didn't feel that way, but the photos were good. Much of that was due to Nathaniel's skill. He had a natural instinct for lighting and object composition. But also, for someone halfway up a tree, face sweaty and cheek dotted with a few scraps of bark, Kelly had to admit he looked pretty good. He struggled to remember the last time he felt that way about his appearance. Even the photos where he was clearly missing a leg didn't dash his confidence.

"You still unsure about modeling?" Nathaniel asked. "Maybe it's not your dream, but don't doubt for a second that you can do this."

"I'm starting college in the fall," Kelly said. "No idea why. I don't have a master plan. I don't know if I want to be a model, because I don't know what I want to do at all."

Nathaniel set down the camera. "So keep modeling until the end of summer. If you like it, great. If not, you'll leave with an excellent business contact and some cash. I know people twice my age who still aren't sure what they want. For most, it changes as they go along."

"So when did you figure it all out?"

Nathaniel shook his head. "I told you, the past stays in the past."

Kelly scrutinized him a moment. "You don't have any big dark secrets. I bet your past is so boring that you decided to act all mysterious just to make yourself seem more interesting."

"Is it working?"

"Nope. I'm not falling for it. You're dull, dull, dull."

Nathaniel's jaw clenched. "Nice try."

Kelly pantomimed a yawn.

"Fine. I'll give you one last piece of advice. Don't be afraid to make mistakes, because you can always start over. There came a point in my life when I felt like everything was ruined. So I put it all behind me and started fresh. I promised myself not to look back, and *that's* why I don't."

Kelly didn't tease him this time. The emotion in Nathaniel's voice made clear the topic was serious. They finished their meal in silence. When they were finished, Kelly said quietly, "Okay, so maybe you are a little interesting."

"Very generous of you." Nathaniel stood and collected their plates, taking them into the kitchen.

"I'll do dishes," Kelly said. "You sprung for the food and did most of the cooking."

Nathaniel stifled a yawn. "You don't have to."

"Go relax. I'll take care of everything. Besides, all I have to do is throw them in the dishwasher, right?"

Nathaniel didn't need more coaxing. He went to sit on the couch, Zero hopping up next to him. Kelly did a lot more than just putting the dishes in the machine. He made sure the pans were rinsed first, wiped down the counters, and got a pot of coffee brewing, even though he wasn't sure how many scoops to use. When he was finished and felt like the ultimate housewife, he looked into the living room. Nathaniel was still on the couch, except now he had rolled over onto his side and stretched out. Zero had too, his back pressed against his owner.

Were they spooning? Seriously? As quietly as he could, Kelly crept over. Zero stirred and kept a wary eye on him, but Nathaniel didn't budge. The guy had on a faded T-shirt, a pair of old jean shorts, and even passed out with his face half-buried in cushions, he looked good. The broad chest, the killer shoulders, the fine hair on his lightly tanned legs... Kelly even liked the white tennis socks covering his big feet. That summed up Nathaniel nicely. Big. He wondered if that was the case all over, but Kelly would gladly let that remain a mystery if it meant getting to cuddle up with him instead.

"Lucky dog," Kelly whispered. "I'll make you another burger if you trade places with me."

Zero huffed and closed his eyes. Proposition denied.

Rather than stand there and drool, Kelly explored the apartment, which didn't take long. The bathroom had a cheesy safari theme, and the bedroom wasn't too interesting: an unmade bed, a couple of houseplants, and a book about Alfred Hitchcock, opened to the middle and face down on the side table.

Kelly didn't remain in this room long, feeling a little creepy. Actually, he was okay with that. He just didn't want to get caught. Instead he returned to the dining room area and sat at the table. He admired the camera and played with the settings. Eventually he pointed it at the couch. After considering the image in the viewfinder he stood. He kept checking the framed image, not pushing the shutter release yet. He'd only take one photo, and when he did, it had to be perfect. That was the game.

After moving around and carefully considering the shot, he pushed the button. The camera clicked, Zero moved his head to follow the noise, and Nathaniel stirred. Kelly quickly returned the camera to the table and sat.

"Ugh," Nathaniel said, raising his head and letting it plop back into the pillow again. "Do I smell coffee?" came his muffled voice.

"Coming up!" Kelly rose to fetch him a cup. "If you're tired, we can call it a day."

Nathaniel pushed himself up. "Nope. We have to hit the pool before it gets dark."

"The pool?" Kelly asked.

"Yeah. Marcello wants a swimsuit shoot. He didn't tell you that?"

Kelly paused at the kitchen counter. "No. I don't have a swimsuit."

Nathaniel sighed. "That was probably intentional. How do you feel about nude photography?"

Chapter Seventeen

"So did you do it?" Bonnie asked.

"The naked photos?" Kelly asked. "Or do you mean frisky time?"

Bonnie hit the turn signal and gunned it past an elderly driver. "Either."

"Nope. I wish."

"So what happened?"

Kelly sighed. "A disaster. We went shopping for a swimsuit, but all were too short to hide my stump. For some reason I got freaked out about him seeing it, so we ended up buying a pair of jeans. I still went shirtless—"

"That had to get his attention."

"I guess, but I also got quiet. Like I couldn't think of anything to say."

"Damn. I hate when that happens."

"Yeah. I made everything awkward. From the department store on."

Bonnie shot him a glance. "You've got nothing to be ashamed of."

"Easy for you to say."

"You have a beautiful nub."

"You're a horrible person."

"I mean it!" Bonnie insisted. "It's not like it's all gnarled and twisted. The surgeons did a great job. And I hate to point out the obvious—"

"You love to."

"—but it's not like he doesn't know. This isn't a zit you can hide until it goes away. Unless you're expecting that leg to grow back, you sort of have to get past this. That, or become a nun."

"He's just so perfect!" Kelly moaned. "You should see him. There's no way he's interested in defective merchandise. Maybe I should aim lower."

"Or maybe you should get over it. Show some pride. Next time you meet, shove that stump right in his face!"

Kelly grinned, then told Bonnie to take the next left. "If there is a next time. I haven't heard a peep since Sunday. What is that, three days now? We didn't exchange digits or anything, but I figure he has my number through work."

"Maybe he'll be there today."

Kelly hoped so. He had made sure he was looking his best before Bonnie picked him up. Now, as they were pulling into the parking lot, his stomach filled with a mob of rioting butterflies. The front doors buzzed and unlocked when they rang the intercom bell, Marcello's disembodied voice instructing them to proceed to his office. The elevator doors opened as if by magic, closing again and delivering them upstairs automatically.

"Very James Bond," Bonnie commented.

Kelly supposed it did feel that way, especially when they marched into the office. Marcello remained behind his desk, gesturing for them to approach. After introductions were made and they sat down, Marcello slid a manila envelope across the ebony surface.

"My next assignment?" Kelly asked.

"The results of the previous," Marcello said. "You can keep those, but first tell me what you think of them."

Kelly opened the folder and removed the photos. Each was as large as a piece of notebook paper, but he found only around ten in total. "Is this all?"

"Quality over quantity," Marcello purred. "In this instance, at least. Three unattractive men can do things one gorgeous man cannot."

Kelly tried to picture what he meant and instantly regretted it. Then he turned his attention to the photos, considering each before passing it to Bonnie. He had expected Marcello to choose the most sexually charged images, but most were artistic. In one he stood behind a chair, his hands on its back. The photo was taken at a low angle, and at first glance, everything appeared normal, except that only one foot was visible beneath the chair. He liked that one, since it reminded him of those old picture tests for kids where the reader had to compare similar images and find what was missing. Also included were photos of him playing shepherd or looking sultry while tangled up in a blanket. Some of the second day's photos were in there as well: Kelly appearing unamused—Zero in the grass behind him with his head cocked as if questioning why. Kelly hanging from the limb of a tree, positively beaming at the camera. Or at the man behind the camera. He couldn't remember ever looking so happy. Overall Kelly was impressed with the quality of the set.

Then he got to the last photo. A dimly lit room, which wasn't ideal, but the subject matter...

"Is that him?" Bonnie said, snatching it away.

His eyes followed, unwilling to leave the image. Nathaniel sleeping on the couch, one arm wrapped around a Siberian Husky.

"How did that get in there?" Marcello asked innocently. "Better yet, how did it get taken? I'd love to hear the circumstances preceding it, or perhaps what followed."

"There's nothing to tell," Kelly said defensively.

"If one digs deep enough," Marcello said, "a story can always be found. I shouldn't need a shovel for this one. I have a right to know, since this photo was taken with company equipment while on company time."

"He has a point," Bonnie said gleefully.

"There really isn't anything to tell," Kelly said. "I'll kill you both if you ever repeat this, but I wish I did have something to brag about."

Marcello became much more somber. "Did Nathaniel flirt with you at all?"

He considered the question. There had been some banter, but nothing solid. "Nope."

Now Marcello frowned. "And did you flirt with him?"

"I don't know," Kelly said with a huff. "I'm a little rusty, okay? And why is this any of your concern?"

Marcello sighed. "I hate to see a good man go to waste. When it's two good men, we're entering the realm of tragedy."

"I'm sure Nathaniel could have anyone he wanted," Kelly said, hating how defeated he sounded.

"That's precisely the problem. Nathaniel has convinced himself he doesn't want anyone at all. I hoped that alone time with my new star model would cause him to reconsider." Marcello glanced at the photo Bonnie still held, even though he could only see the back. "Well, don't blame yourself. You can't drink from a glass that's already broken."

"What's that supposed to mean?"

Marcello shrugged, seemingly done with the topic. "Would you say these photos do you justice?"

Kelly glanced down at the desk, where Bonnie had laid out all of them. "Are you kidding? They make me look way hotter than I actually am!"

Marcello smiled pleasantly. "I disagree. And when the world sees you on the red carpet, I have no doubt they'll share my opinion."

"Wait," Bonnie said. "Is he going to be famous?"

"The potential is there. All your friend has to do is grab it." Marcello opened a drawer, pulled out some clipped-together papers, and gently set them on top of the photos. "I took the liberty of drawing up a contract. All you need do is sign it, and together we can take the world by storm."

Kelly didn't bother picking it up. "I'll show it to my lawyer," he said.

Marcello raised an eyebrow. Then he chuckled. "You're a little young to have a lawyer."

"She's also my mother, and trust me, that makes her way scarier than normal lawyers. Speaking of which, did you work in those royalties we talked about?"

"There are never royalties on back catalog material," Marcello said, voice sounding gruffer than normal.

"Just a token amount," Kelly said. "The kind reserved for— what did you call me? Your new star model?"

Marcello smiled at him. Or at least he bared his teeth. "I'll run the contract by legal again one more time before you leave."

"No problem," Kelly said. "Just have some lunch sent up for us, and we'll stay out of your way."

When envisioning his new life as a model, Kelly's imagination whisked him away to exotic locales. The pristine beaches of Greece to model a fedora, or the rocky coasts of Scotland to help sell a new windbreaker. When Marcello called him for his first gig, describing it as a city shoot, he felt certain they would travel to the fashion districts of Rome where police blockades would protect him from his adoring public. Instead, he ended up in downtown Austin on a Sunday.

One of the intersections was blocked off, at least. And a police officer was present to redirect the occasional car or pedestrian. That felt special, as did the makeup trailer... until he learned it wasn't just for him. Margie had a slew of extras she needed to primp and powder. Kelly soon discovered the crowded trailer was the last place he wanted to be. Once dressed in an expensive suit, he headed outside and watched the crew get set up.

Nathaniel was among them, a fact that would have been more exciting had they interacted at all. Instead he seemed preoccupied with talking to everyone *but* Kelly. Only when they were ready to go did he head over, giving him a quick upward nod in greeting.

"Elliot wants to know if you can balance on one foot," Nathaniel said.

"I don't have much choice," Kelly responded. "Who's Elliot?"

"The photographer, and he's being a douche about talking to you directly, so you're unlikely to see him again after today. The shoot calls for you to be in the crosswalk, standing still while pedestrians swarm around you. We planned to give you a stylish cane, but now there's concern it sends the wrong message. Think you can manage without?"

"I'll try."

He led Kelly to the middle of the crosswalk, where an assistant held a chair ready. Then everyone else got into place. When it was time to shoot, he stood, the assistant fled with the chair, and Kelly did his best to summon mystique. While balancing on one leg. In public. Across the street a small crowd of curious onlookers had gathered. Kelly soon found himself wishing for the privacy of the studio.

"Stop!" Nathaniel shouted. "Everybody back to the starting position. You! If you're going to just stand there, give me the fucking chair!"

A moment later Nathaniel set down the chair next to Kelly. Rather than sitting, Kelly only used the back to balance himself.

"Might as well get comfortable," Nathaniel said. "The crosswalk light is still running like normal, meaning all those photos we just took show it in red."

"And green sends a better message to the consumer, since it means money and it means go."

Nathaniel patted him on the shoulder, like a student who had answered a question correctly. Of course Kelly felt ridiculously thrilled by the physical contact. He watched Nathaniel walk away to speak with one of the city workers. Once the issue was sorted out, he held up a hand, gave a nod, and the crew scrambled back into place. Obviously he ran a tight ship.

Kelly tried to make him proud throughout the rest of the day. Thankfully this didn't require imitating a flamingo the entire time. Some shots involved him cockily reclining in the chair, or holding out his crutches like wings, blocking the pedestrian flow. They went through all sorts of ideas, some repeated due to costume changes.

When lunchtime came, despite his stomach rumbling with hunger, he avoided the catering truck. Instead he casually headed over to the street corner where Nathaniel stood with one finger in his ear, a phone pressed against the other. Kelly's timing was good, since the call ended just as he neared.

"Better eat something," Nathaniel said. "That was the city. We've got less time than we thought. Lunch is only ten minutes today."

"I'm not hungry," Kelly lied.

Nathaniel glanced at his phone once more. Then he pocketed it. "You're doing great. I've known pros who don't try half as hard."

"I won't either when I'm famous," Kelly said. "The crew will be forced to visit my bedside for photo shoots. What's the point of making your way to the top if you've got to keep working?"

"If you love what you do..." Nathaniel said.

"Good point." Kelly's eyes darted over him briefly, taking in the strong brow, the tight dress shirt—sleeves rolled up— and the stubbled chin that always jutted out slightly. All of this hit him like a drug and made it hard to think. Or talk. Fearing another awkward silence, he scrambled to find some topic of conversation. "How's Zero?"

"Good." Nathaniel nodded. "Doing real good."

"Great."

"Yeah."

Ugh, now they sounded like they had already dated, called it quits, and ended up on the same elevator by accident. Kelly had promised himself—promised Bonnie, actually—that if Nathaniel were here today, he would ask him out. Just a simple date somewhere, like a movie, dinner, or even a visit to the dog park. No big deal. All he had to do was ask.

"Dog dinner," he managed to say. Then he winced. "Sorry. What I mean is, I thought maybe you and I could... Uh. What are you doing this weekend?"

Nathaniel considered him, lips twitching. "Dog dinner?" he repeated.

Kelly glared at him.

"I'm not doing anything," Nathaniel said. "Besides feeding Zero his breakfast. And his lunch. And his—"

"Shut up," Kelly said before laughing. "What I meant to say, is that maybe we could take Zero to the dog park. Afterwards, we could grab a bite to eat. If you're not busy, that is."

"No, I'm not busy." Nathaniel's smile faded, which was nearly enough to make Kelly's heart stop. Then his phone rang. Nathaniel rolled his eyes, dug it out, and held it to his ear. Then he covered the mouthpiece. "Saturday," he whispered. "Dog dinner."

Kelly nodded and headed for the catering truck as quickly as he could, mostly to prevent Nathaniel from seeing the stupid smile that had spread across his face.

"Come on, come on, come on!"

Kelly hovered by the front room window, waiting for company to arrive. Not that he was alone. His mother kept finding excuses to join him. First she dusted, then she returned to vacuum. Tellingly, he didn't hear the vacuum cleaner running in any other room. Afterwards he chased her off by snapping at her. He knew this wouldn't last for long, which is why he needed Nathaniel to show up. Now. Despite his mother's wishes, Kelly intended to meet him in the driveway, where she couldn't embarrass him. Unless she followed him out there.

er-eee er-eee er-eee

Kelly spun around, trying to pinpoint the source of the squeaking noise. It didn't sound like mice. Someone polishing a drinking glass? Or washing the windows to either side of the front door. Sighing in exasperation, Kelly headed for the hallway. Sure enough, his mother was absentmindedly wiping one window with a cloth while staring through the glass.

"Mother!"

"Oh!" Startled, she tackled her task with renewed vigor. "So hard to get these streak-free."

"I'm moving out," Kelly said. "College dorms, Bonnie's couch, or under a bridge somewhere. Anywhere is better than here."

"You can't afford it," his mother said dismissively. Then she did a double take. "Oh, wait, I guess you can."

"That's right," Kelly said, "so either you go away or I will. Permanently."

"You wouldn't survive a day," his mother scolded. "If you want to be independent, you can start by doing your own laundry."

"Mom!" he pleaded.

"Fine." She picked up the glass cleaner and was turning to leave when something outside caught her attention. Then she stared, which wasn't a good sign. Kelly hurried to her side, looking through the window above hers. Nathaniel had just pulled into the driveway.

"Who is that?" his mother asked.

"Who do you think?"

She looked again before turning to him. "Your father said he was handsome."

"He is," Kelly said.

"Well, yes, but I was picturing..." She pursed her lips and shook her head. "You've developed a taste for white chocolate."

"Guilty as charged," Kelly said. "Now will you please go away?"

"Let me tell you something first. The older you get, the more you appreciate comfort. You're still young. You're out there tasting everything the world has to offer, and that's fine. But when you get older, you'll want your mother's apple pie, not some half-burnt crème brûlée."

"Are we talking about men or food?" Kelly asked. "Either way, this conversation is making me exceedingly uncomfortable."

"I'm just saying—"

Her words of questionable wisdom were interrupted by a light knock. Kelly's expression became pure anguish, which finally caused his mother to buckle. She kissed him on the cheek and hurried down the hall. Chances were she would still peek around the corner, but that was better than her staying to inform Nathaniel of what kind of dessert he was.

Luckily, his date didn't seem keen on meeting the parents. As soon as Kelly opened the door, Nathaniel jerked his head, instructing him to follow. That probably appeared callous or controlling. No doubt his mother would have something to say about it later, but he didn't care. Nathaniel was cool and smooth. Like a milk shake, he supposed.

"You'll have to wrestle Zero for the front seat," Nathaniel was saying.

"I can sit in back," Kelly said. "I don't want him to think I'm a home wrecker."

"You'd really do that?"

"Sure!"

Nathaniel flashed him a smile. "Thanks. But you're not sitting in the back. And why am I picking you up again? You don't drive?"

"One leg," Kelly said.

"Last I checked, that's all it takes. You know how?"

"Yeah."

Nathaniel held out the keys. "Perfect solution. You drive, Zero gets to stay where he is, and I'll sit in the back."

Kelly felt a jolt of discomfort at the idea, but it didn't last long. Technically he still had his license. Not driving was a habit left over from being with William. Nothing was holding Kelly back now. Of course his driving foot was long gone, but using his left leg instead shouldn't be much different.

Once they were seated in the car, Zero sniffed his face, exhaling through his nostrils a few times before sniffing some more. This left Kelly's face damp, but afterwards the dog eagerly stuck his head out the passenger window.

"I think we're ready," Nathaniel said from the back. "You know where we're going?"

"Yup," Kelly said, turning the key.

The radio came to life, playing something dancey and more than a little gay. He was tempted to lower the volume so he could concentrate better, but left it turned up instead. The accident was a blip on the radar, one he had put behind him. Now it was time to drive again. Kelly put the car in gear, reversed into the street, and grinned. Maybe this was one way of recapturing the speed he missed. He glanced over and noticed the seatbelt across Zero's chest. Then he put the car in drive and hit the pedal. Hard.

"Aaand we're never doing that again," Nathaniel said once they reached their destination.

"I am," Kelly said, still grinning as they got out. "Tell Marcello I need a company car. Something with a lot of horsepower."

"How about an old mule instead?"

"Or Zero could pull my sled," Kelly said, watching as Nathaniel opened the passenger door for the dog. Then he grabbed his collar and attached a leash. After that, they were ready. The scene they entered was idyllic, dogs politely sniffing each other's rears or prancing around in the afternoon sun. Their owners gathered in small groups, the sound of friendly conversation carried along with the light breeze. Past the big open field were a cluster of trees and two small ponds, although no ducks were foolish enough to land there.

Kelly took a deep breath and exhaled again. "Peaceful, isn't it?"

"Yup. Very." Nathaniel stretched out the arm holding the leash, unclenched his fist, and dropped it. "Watch this."

Mere seconds later, Zero realized he was no longer restrained and took off like a bullet. He headed for the nearest group of dogs, plunging into their midst, growling and snapping at the air. This caused similar reactions in the other dogs. Half of them panicked, trying to flee or hide behind human legs. The others fell in line behind Zero, charging the next group of dogs. Soon those owners were stumbling over each other and getting tangled up in leashes in an effort to keep their animals under control. Too late. The chaos spread further, a few dogs leaping into the water to escape the whirlwind of fur that was Zero's pack.

"I love that beast." Nathaniel sighed. "Come. Time to pretend this was all an accident."

Kelly chuckled and followed him. As soon as they reached the first group of owners, Nathaniel whistled shrilly, and Zero raced over to sit dutifully at his side.

"You need to keep that dog on a leash!" an older man complained.

"He is on a leash," Nathaniel pointed out.

"Then learn to hold on to it!" a woman scorned. "I should call animal control!"

"My fault," Kelly said quickly. "I was holding the leash, and well—" He gestured with his crutches. In an instant, the angry mob became much more sympathetic. Or at least more restrained.

Mostly. An old man mustered one last scrap of irritation. "You should enroll him in behavioral training."

"I agree," Kelly said, glancing at Nathaniel instead of Zero. "He won't be getting any treats tonight, I promise you that."

Nathaniel took Zero's leash, and they headed toward one of the ponds. A few dogs followed, clearly enamored by the Husky. Like father like son, Kelly supposed, because he loved the way

Nathaniel kept chuckling to himself and rubbing tears from his eyes.

"So where did you find Zero?" he asked. "A bullfight?"

Nathaniel's grin broadened, causing creases to appear in his cheeks. "He found me. Or at least he chose me."

"How? Did he put a classified ad in the paper? '*Ill-behaved dog seeks unscrupulous owner.*'"

"Hey now, that dog is a saint! And my hero." Nathaniel's tone grew serious. "He saved me from a very dark place."

"What do you mean?"

Nathaniel watched as Zero plunged into the pond, the other dogs giving chase along the shore. His strong brow knotted up in the middle. "Someone once told me that a dog is the best cure for a broken heart."

Kelly's breath nearly caught in his throat. Was he finally opening up? "And is it?" he asked.

Nathaniel watched as Zero barked at the other dogs while treading water. Finally, a few mustered enough courage to jump in the water after him. This seemed to appease Zero and caused his owner to smile. "All of us have an undeniable urge to be loved and to give love in return. In that regard, you can't do much better than a dog."

"I suppose," Kelly said, "although there are some comforts a dog can't provide."

Nathaniel glanced over at him and raised an eyebrow. "Such as?"

"Zero probably gives a lousy foot rub."

"Oh, you'd be surprised. When he's passed out in front of the couch, he makes a nice rug."

"I bet he can't cook you breakfast in the morning."

"He once tore into a carton of eggs I was unpacking from the store. That's pretty much scrambled eggs right there."

Kelly sighed. "I give up. I just wish I'd known you were already spoken for before coming on this date."

Nathaniel's body language stiffened. He *did* know this was a date, didn't he? They weren't just friends hanging out. Kelly refused to accept that, but it would make little difference. Contrary to popular belief, it doesn't take two to tango, but it sure looks a lot less ridiculous when another person is present and willing.

"I could definitely use more friends," Nathaniel said. "Zero isn't the best conversationalist."

Ugh. Misinterpreting that statement was near impossible. Kelly clenched his jaw, fighting down his frustration. "Friends, pets, significant others... Whatever form it comes in, you can never have enough love."

Nathaniel glanced over at him. "Maybe you're right."

A ray of hope? Perhaps. Kelly wasn't quite ready to throw himself on the bed and cry himself to sleep. The evening still held potential. "So what were you thinking for dinner?"

"Sonic," Nathaniel replied. "Or some other drive-thru, so Zero can stay with us."

Charming. "How about we get Zero his burger and put him to bed early? Then you take me out for something less greasy." He tried his most seductive smile. When it failed to cause the reaction he wanted, he sneered instead.

Nathaniel laughed. "Yeah, okay."

"You've got a thing for bad behavior, don't you?" Kelly asked. "If so, you're with the right guy. I'll give Zero a run for his money."

"I'll hold you to that," Nathaniel said. "We'll have an award ceremony at the end of the night to see who the winner is, although you've got some catching up to do."

He nodded to where Zero was trying to dunk another dog under water. Or maybe he was just trying to mount him. Either way, the other dog's owner stood at the shore with hands held to her face in horror.

"Want me to push her in?" Kelly murmured.

Nathaniel grinned broadly. "Nah. It's the thought that counts. This time, anyway."

Dinner was going well, despite taking place at a buffet—a word rarely used in the same sentence as 'romantic.' But maybe it should be, since no waiters came to disturb magical moments. They were able to try a little of everything and comment on what they thought. That was nice. Mostly though, Nathaniel seemed interested in talking about movies. He wasn't a snob who restricted himself to the golden age of Hollywood or obscure indie directors or anything like that. His tastes welcomed everything from low-budget films to the latest blockbusters. Not that he didn't have strong opinions.

"There's no point in watching a superhero movie," he was saying, "because you know the main character isn't going to die. Sure you might get caught up in the action, but in the back of your mind, you know the hero will emerge victorious. Where's the suspense? Like a bad sitcom, the end of the story always rushes back to the status quo, paving the way for the next generic installment. You know what I want to see? Let Batman die. Really, really die. No tricks, no resurrections. Just dead. If they want to film another installment, have Robin take up the mantle. That would be cool."

"What I'd like to see," Kelly said, twirling a spoon through melting ice cream, "is a black superhero. And I don't mean cheesy creations like Black Panther, Black Vulcan, Black Lightning, or any other character with 'black' in his name. No, I want to see a black actor cast as Spider-Man. Most spiders are brown, not white! Or how about putting the dark into the Dark Knight? Or best of all, let's make Superman, the face of America, look a little more like the people he represents."

"I'm pretty sure he's an alien," Nathaniel said, eyes sparkling. "But I agree. Superhero movies don't take chances."

"Wonder Woman should be Hispanic."

"And a lesbian."

"And give her an Irish accent, just to screw with people's heads." Kelly sucked on his spoon thoughtfully. "We should make our own movie. Gay superheroes. I'll star and direct, naturally. I'll even let you be my sidekick."

Nathaniel laughed, his gaze lingering. For a guy who had just eaten three full plates of food, he sure looked hungry. "Let's get out of here," he suggested.

"Sounds good," Kelly said. Unless he was reading the signals wrong, things between them were heating up. He went to use the restroom, mostly so he could check his own appearance, and when he came back, he found the bill had already been settled.

"My treat," Nathaniel said.

"Just like a date?" Kelly asked, grinning shamelessly.

Nathaniel shook his head ruefully, but a hint of a smile betrayed him.

They headed out to the parking lot, Kelly feeling giddy. Once they were both seated in the car, the keys dangling unturned from the ignition, Nathaniel stared at the steering wheel a moment before looking over at Kelly.

"You wanna come home with me?"

Kelly's body became a nucleus of reactions. He was nervous about being naked and exposed until hormones hit his system, begging him for release. His head felt light, his breath short, and his skin tingled at the idea of Nathaniel touching him. Was this too fast? They hadn't even kissed yet!

"Yes," Kelly said, surprised by the sound of his own voice.

"Good." Nathaniel flashed him a smile, before uncertainty wiped it away. "Listen, I don't want any mixed signals here. I'm good for a fling. That's about it."

Kelly shook his head in confusion. "You think that's all I'm after?"

"I'm not sure," Nathaniel said, "which is why I want to clear the air. I'm not the relationship type. I'd love to wake up next to you, but it wouldn't change anything. I'll make you breakfast—or maybe Zero will finally master scrambled eggs—and then we'll carry on just like before. Does that make sense?"

Yes, but it wasn't what Kelly wanted. Well, he *did*, because the idea of having sex with Nathaniel and afterwards pressing up against him as they slept... that sounded heavenly. But he also wanted to feel like he belonged to someone. He wanted to talk about their future and argue and make up again and get to know each other so well that being together was irritating and wonderful at the same time. All that good stuff. Not just sex followed by a complimentary breakfast.

"I want more," he said.

Nathaniel studied him, jaw clenching a moment later. "Then maybe I should take you home."

"I guess you should."

The atmosphere in the car turned stuffy and silent. Kelly second-guessed himself a million times during the drive, but always came back to the same conclusion. He wasn't interested in another one-night stand. Not without a chance of it leading to something more. And yet, when they pulled into his driveway, he felt like taking the consolation prize. Fortunately, he'd never been short on pride.

"Thanks for the evening," he said, opening the door. "It was a beautiful fantasy."

Nathaniel didn't respond. Whatever emotions played out on his face went unseen, because Kelly didn't even look at him. He just headed for the door, feeling mixed emotions when he heard the car back out and cruise away.

Chapter Eighteen

Another damn studio shoot. Kelly used to love them, since being out in public always came with complications and delays. Now every time he reported to work, he hoped to be dragged out to a theme park or dance club or anywhere that would require someone to manage the chaos. Someone like Nathaniel. Two weeks and four shoots later, Kelly was still trapped in the studio.

Today he was sitting in front of a plate of cake and plastic ice cream. He could smell the sugar, so he knew the cake was real. And a constant source of temptation. The decorative curls of frosting on the edges were blue—his favorite—and he could tell by sight alone it was the super-rich butter cream kind. The cake itself was marbled chocolate and vanilla, the best of both worlds. He would very much like to fall face-first into it, which probably wouldn't please the photographer, so instead he tried to focus on the plastic ice cream. He supposed it had to be fake so it wouldn't melt under the studio lights. All around him were beautiful teenage girls, smiling and giggling for the camera. They annoyed Kelly, mostly because they didn't have to wear a stupid birthday hat. Or the heavy thick-framed glasses these images would advertise.

"No need to scowl, darling," the photographer said. "It's your birthday, and you're not exactly turning forty. Give us a smile!"

Kelly pushed aside his irritation and tried to pretend Marcello had just given him a mansion for his birthday. He'd been grinning so long his jaw was starting to ache when he noticed a familiar figure in one corner of the room. Currently two of the female models had their arms draped around his neck and shoulders—skin sticky from sweat where they touched—which made turning his head difficult. He didn't really need to. Like a sixth sense, he knew Nathaniel was there. But why? This shoot was straightforward enough. Maybe he was only passing through on his way to more important business.

But no, half an hour later when lunch break was called, Nathaniel was still standing there, staring. His default expression was sort of grumpy, slightly narrowed eyes beneath a strong brow, like he was debating snapping someone's neck. Now was no different. At least until he winked, which made Kelly want to smile, cry, and scream all at the same time. Instead he headed into the break room.

Someone had bought donuts, the models descending on them like hungry seagulls. He wondered what their secret was. Or maybe, like him, they had been going crazy all morning staring at a piece of cake they couldn't have. Kelly was reaching for a blue frosted donut when he was interrupted by a voice he had longed to hear.

"How about I take you out for some real food?"

He didn't look. Instead he pulled back his hand and sighed.

"Or some ice cream?" Nathaniel said. "Of the non-plastic variety."

Kelly glanced over to see a lopsided smile. "If you want to treat me to something, how about an explanation?"

Gravity took hold of Nathaniel's features. "Fair enough. I'm a jerk. Satisfied?"

"No!" Kelly shouted. "How about you explain why I'm good enough to sleep with, but the idea of being on a date with me makes you squirm."

Nathaniel glanced around the crowded break room. "Maybe we should talk in my office."

Kelly shrugged. "Fine."

Nathaniel led them to the elevator and punched in a code. The ride was short, the doors opening to a dimly lit hallway. At the end of this, Nathaniel unlocked a door and gestured for Kelly to enter. Unlike Marcello's office, the space wasn't sprawling. Set on the corner of the building, the office featured adjacent windows which provided light for a large desk. Around it was the usual arrangement of chairs. Kelly went to the desk but remained standing, examining the carefully positioned stacks of paper. Pens and pencils sat in perfectly parallel rows. The keyboard and computer mouse were wireless, preventing clutter. Everything boasted of efficiency. Except for a handful of photos carelessly strewn in the middle of the desk. All of them of Kelly.

Nathaniel quickly leaned forward, arranged them in a stack, and turned them facedown. Then he gestured to one of the windows, where two chairs and a small table awaited.

"I'm fine," Kelly said.

"It's going to be a lengthy conversation," Nathaniel said.

"My lunch break isn't long."

"It's as long as I say it is."

Oh how Kelly loved it when Nathaniel threw his power around! Trying to hold on to his anger, he headed for the seats. Once they were both settled, Nathaniel leaned forward, elbows on knees, hands clasped together.

"You didn't do anything wrong," he said. "You're damn near perfect, and any guy would be lucky to have you. Including me. That's not the issue. You're not the problem. I am."

Kelly raised an eyebrow. "'It's not you, it's me'? Seriously?"

Nathaniel grimaced. "That sounds lame, I know."

"Then tell me something that doesn't. And please don't follow that tired old line with one about a fear of commitment."

"If that worried me, I wouldn't be okay with taking care of a dog or being married to this job." Nathaniel's eyes darted away. "But I do fear getting hurt, or even worse, hurting someone I care about."

"That's love," Kelly said. "Someone always gets hurt in the end."

Nathaniel looked surprised. "If you really believe that—if you really understand the implications—then I don't see how you or anyone else could willingly seek out a relationship."

Kelly cocked his head. "You don't think the pain is worth it?"

"Have you ever been in love?"

"Yes."

"And have you ever had your heart broken?"

Kelly shrugged. "Sure."

"I don't think you understand," Nathaniel said. "Have you ever been so devastated by a breakup that you didn't eat or leave the house or even want to go on living? Has anyone damaged you so completely that you felt broken, inside and out? No rebound, no silver lining, no learning from a bad experience and putting it all behind you. Just pure agonizing hell."

Kelly swallowed. "I would never do that to you."

Nathaniel laughed bitterly. "No one ever thinks they will. The guy who hurt me made a lot of promises. We both did. All the pain we put each other through started as love. *That's* why it's so dangerous. The most powerful forces always are. Curiosity and passion drove Rutherford to split the atom, and I have no doubt that in his giddy success, he saw nothing but the potential benefits to mankind. Do you think he ever dreamed of Hiroshima?"

Kelly crossed his arms over his chest. "As bombastic as you might be in bed, I'm pretty sure we won't be blowing up any cities."

Nathaniel shook his head. "You don't understand. Maybe that's for the best. Or maybe I'm crazy. But I hope I've convinced you by now that I'm the problem here. It sounds cliché, but it really is me, not you."

Kelly clenched his jaw. "So because someone broke your heart, you're going to spend the rest of your life alone?"

"Why not? I know Hollywood tries to convince everyone that it's not an option. A movie isn't complete without an onscreen kiss, apparently. But that's bullshit. Trust me when I say I've given this thought. I even told you when we first met. I don't need anyone. Neither do you. Nobody does."

"Then why am I sitting here?"

"Because I still like to have fun, and I really enjoyed hanging out with you. If I were a betting man, I'd wager you'll never talk to me again once you leave this office. But if there's any chance of us being friends..."

Kelly dropped his arms and sighed. "Who broke your heart? I'm assuming he has a name."

"Caesar."

Kelly snorted. "And if I find this Caesar person and beat the living hell out of him, would it make you feel any better?"

"Nope."

"What if I bring you his severed head?"

Nathaniel appeared to mull it over. "Nah."

Kelly shook his head slowly. "What happened between you two?"

"The past is the past," Nathaniel said. "While it might affect the present, there's no sense dwelling on what can't be changed."

"Right. There's no way of escaping the past. I get it. But have you tried getting really drunk, or having a good cry in the bathtub? Or doing both at the same time?"

"Kelly..." Nathaniel said.

"Fine." He rolled his eyes. "You're a broken man and there's no hope for you. Anything else you want to tell me?"

"I want to know if we can still be friends."

Kelly looked him over. Past the handsome face and awesome body, he found plenty to like in Nathaniel. At times they felt like kindred spirits. At others Kelly saw a person he wished he could be more like. Nathaniel had his shit together. Maybe not emotionally, but Kelly admired his unapologetic strength. And his naughty side, which he could only imagine would come out in full force in the bedroom. The most calm, collected guys were always freaks behind closed doors.

Heart, body, and mind, Nathaniel was his kind of guy. Being his buddy and nothing more would only be a constant reminder of what he wanted but couldn't have. Even just sitting here was torturous. Kelly would gladly give up a year's wages in exchange for just one kiss.

"I don't know," he said at last. "I need to think."

Nathaniel's features became strained, but he nodded. "Let me take you to lunch. We'll see how that goes."

"No," Kelly said, pushing himself up. "I'd rather get this photo shoot over with. And afterwards, no matter how stale it has become, I'm eating that goddamned piece of cake."

"He's such a jerk."

"Most people don't sigh dreamily when saying that." Allison Cross peered at him. "Or get a little sweaty and flustered."

"I'm not flustered," Kelly countered. "It's the heat."

They both paused, listening to the air conditioner steadily blowing cool air through Allison's office.

"Maybe it's menopause," Kelly tried. "Hot flashes?"

"If that's the case," Allison said, "then you need to see a medical doctor, not a counselor."

"Okay, so he's a jerk and I love it. I used to be dating the nicest guy in the world. Then he exploded with pent-up aggression and sent us spiraling into traffic, so I think I'll take my chances with someone who openly vents. Or at least I would if he'd let me."

"Mm-hm." Allison's pen scribbled on her yellow pad of paper.

"You sure are taking a lot of notes this time."

"Oh, I'm not taking notes," she said. "I'm doodling."

"You're doodling?"

"Yup." She glanced up, appearing shameless.

"I'm paying for this session, you know. Not my parents."

"You can afford it," Allison said. "I saw one of your magazine ads, by the way. Very sexy."

"Thanks," Kelly said without sounding grateful, "but maybe

you can set aside your artistic impulses and give me some advice."

"Donkey with a jet pack!" Allison said, holding up the drawing. Then she tossed the pad of paper on the coffee table and grew serious. "Listen, the reason I'm not hanging on your every word is because men like Nathaniel are a dime a dozen. They all have a different sob story or some bulletproof reason for not settling down, but it all boils down to them not wanting to commit. You came here for advice, but I already know you aren't going to take it."

"Try me," Kelly said.

"Run away," Allison said. "Turn around and run so far in the opposite direction that you never have to see him again. Find some smoking-hot boy without all the baggage, fall in love, and never look back."

Kelly bit his lip. "What's Plan B?"

Allison reached for her paper. "Donkey with a jet pack gets a space helmet."

"Please!"

"Fine." Allison looked at him squarely and shook her head. "I'll tell you what you need to do, but you also have to listen to what I *know* will happen."

"Deal," Kelly said eagerly. "So what's the magic spell?"

"He was willing to sleep with you, right? I'm assuming that hasn't changed. You've shown him it's all or nothing, but what you should do is ease him into the idea. Be his buddy, keep being eye candy, take things further than you would with any ordinary friend, and when you have him more hooked than ever, reel him in."

"You think I should sleep with him?"

"I think you should get him in a relationship without calling it that. We spend time with our friends, we confide in them, we rely on them. Love is certainly there too, but when you add sex to the equation, everything changes. Usually. Some people can be casual with their bodies without consequence, in which case, you'll end up hurt."

"Or maybe he'll wake up one day and realize he's already in love with me," Kelly said.

"Could be. If so, it'll probably be your last day together."

"What? Why?"

"Because guys like him get spooked." Allison's expression was sympathetic. "I've seen it happen to one of the dearest people in my life. Not being able to have what you want hurts, but I promise you, getting what you want and losing it hurts more."

"So you agree with Nathaniel? We should avoid taking risks just because we could get hurt?"

"No, but we should weigh those risks, especially when we see danger ahead. And maybe—just this once—you should listen to someone who has more experience in such matters."

"Okay, so what happened to your broken-hearted friend? Never left the house again? Became a man of the cloth? Lives a life of celibacy?"

"No." Allison's expression softened. "He lived happily ever after."

"See?" Kelly said. "There's nothing to worry about. I can handle this."

Allison sighed. "For your sake, I hope you're right. If you're not, you know where to find me."

Kelly stood in front of the apartment door, heart racing. This would lead to rejection. His hand had been played, his intentions made known. Nathaniel's scowling eyes would see through his ruse in an instant, stripping him bare, and not in the way he desired. But oh that hunger! If Nathaniel shared even a tenth of this desire, he wouldn't be able to turn Kelly away. Not tonight. The air pressure was thick, a thunderstorm having come and gone, but the tension remained. The water evaporating off the streets only added to the humidity, the very air sweating in anticipation.

But Kelly no longer perspired. His pulse steadied with new-found certainty. They both wanted this. He knocked on the door, just a few raps, hard enough to draw attention. Light appeared through the peephole, footsteps approached, and then shadows covered the tiny round glass. When the door swung open, Nathaniel stood there wearing a maroon bathrobe that sat crooked on his shoulders, as if thrown on in haste. Kelly could see fine straight hairs near the top of his chest where it hung loose.

"Kelly?" Nathaniel blinked a few times. A moment later his leg shot out to prevent Zero from escaping. "Back to bed, mutt." The dog grumbled and retreated down the hall, Nathaniel watching him go before turning forward again. "Any idea how late it is?"

"Two in the morning," Kelly said. "I finished thinking. What we talked about, I reached a decision."

Nathaniel's brow furrowed. "Oh yeah?"

"Yeah." Kelly took a step forward. "Just friends. Nothing more."

Eyes searched his. "Strictly platonic?"

"Strictly?" Kelly leaned forward. "I don't think so. How about no strings attached?"

Nathaniel's gaze intensified just before he grabbed Kelly's head in his hands, bringing their lips together. No tenderness, no hesitation. Their tongues touched moments after their lips did. Nathaniel tasted of toothpaste, his breath a little stale from sleep, his upper lip salty from the night's heat. Kelly didn't care. He loved it. The combination should be bottled into some sort of cologne or artificial flavor and be labeled *hot guy stirred from sleep*.

Kelly leaned into him so much that he almost stumbled forward when the kiss broke. They panted a few times, eyeing each other. He noticed that Nathaniel's bathrobe was now starting to tent toward the waist. The feeling was completely mutual.

"You're not going to make me drive home, are you?" Kelly said. "Any idea how late it is?"

"Two in the morning," Nathaniel said with a grin. "I should be in bed."

"I was hoping you'd say that."

Nathaniel stepped aside so Kelly could enter. He stopped in the doorway to kiss him again. Nathaniel reciprocated. For a moment, at least. Then he murmured against Kelly's lips. "The dog."

"Oh, right." Kelly entered the apartment, praying Nathaniel wouldn't offer him a drink or sit at the kitchen table expecting conversation. He didn't. Instead he walked down the hall to the bedroom door and stopped there. Good.

"You're sleeping on the couch tonight," he said.

"You'd better be talking to Zero and not me," Kelly replied.

Nathaniel looked him over. "That depends on how you do."

"Challenge accepted."

Kelly headed into the bedroom as Nathaniel struggled to get the dog out and the door shut. The sheets were tangled up, like the former occupant hadn't been sleeping well. Kelly considered taking off his clothes and diving in, but he felt Nathaniel's breath on the back of his neck first. Lips kissed the spot that had just been warmed before Kelly was turned around. They kissed as Nathaniel wrapped an arm around Kelly's waist and lifted him, leaning back so far that Kelly was almost on top of him. He let his crutches fall to the sides, freeing his hands to touch Nathaniel's hair, stroke his ear, caress his neck.

Then Nathaniel tossed Kelly gently onto the bed, where he landed on his back and sat up to enjoy the view. And what a view it was! Nathaniel slowly untied the robe, something thick and hard flexing as the fabric fluttered open. Kelly didn't look directly at it. Not immediately. He was too transfixed by the gorgeous pecs that stretched as Nathaniel shrugged off the robe completely, revealing powerful shoulders and arms thick with veins. His stomach had a slight paunch—a gentle curve rather than a beer belly—but even this was undeniably masculine. If Kelly wanted to see six-pack abs, he could look in the mirror. What he wanted was someone who made him feel slight, and right now he wanted Nathaniel's weight pressing down on him.

First Kelly admired the light covering of hair on Nathaniel's chest, which gave way to smooth skin beneath his pecs. This resumed again just below the belly button in a wisp that led down to—

He sighed. Some guys were like art, and should be cast-molded and kiln-fired into sculpture for the entire world to see. Not that he'd invite his grandma to this exhibition. Nathaniel's cock was just as thick as the rest of him, and judging from the bunched-up skin just past the proud ruby head, uncut. If that weren't delightful enough, he had the most amazing set of balls Kelly had ever seen. Heavy and pendulous, they would probably slap against Kelly's butt and all sorts of other places, depending on the position. Sure, the solid thighs were nice too, and that chest was demanding Kelly's attention again, but he couldn't tear his eyes away.

"You're making me feel like a piece of meat," Nathaniel said, dropping forward and placing splayed palms on the mattress to either side of Kelly's head. "And I mean that in a good way."

He dodged a kiss so he could reply. "Just as long as you don't expect me to compete with that thing."

"It's not a contest," Nathaniel said, "but I wouldn't mind judging."

He kissed Kelly, pressing their chests together before lifting up again, their stomachs touching next, then their hips before the motions were repeated, like the world's sexiest wave. Kelly's brain was overwhelmed with choice as Nathaniel gyrated against him. So much he wanted to touch and taste and cling to. How could he possibly decide? Luckily Nathaniel seemed comfortable taking the lead. After a few more kisses, he hopped up and kneeled, sitting on Kelly's crotch. Please don't let him be a bottom!

Nathaniel started working on the buttons of Kelly's shirt, but after the first, he grabbed fabric in both fists and tore it open. "I'll buy you a new one," he said before Kelly could complain. He tugged the remaining scraps off his arms, then relaxed his weight onto Kelly's hips while tracing a finger around each nipple, down to his belly button, back up along one arm. Nathaniel's eyes were glazed, already high from the rush of hormones. When he leaned over to kiss Kelly again, warm balls brushed his stomach, while further up, something hard and wet poked at him.

Kelly moaned in pleasure as Nathaniel ran a tongue along his bottom lip, and almost groaned in agony when Nathaniel's weight lifted off him. He had moved off the mattress, kneeling on the carpet and reaching for Kelly's belt to undo it. Eager to shed this last bit of clothing, Kelly felt his cock twitch, wanting to break free. But of course when the jeans came down, they would slide off one leg much easier than the other.

"Wait," Kelly said, grabbing Nathaniel's hand, just as the belt came loose.

"I told you it's not a competition."

"It's not that…"

Nathaniel studied him a moment before he understood. "If I had any doubts about what I wanted, we wouldn't have made it this far. Your move."

Those hazel eyes still smoldered, so Kelly reached to undo the button and rip down the zipper before he leaned back and put his hands behind his head. Nathaniel was more than willing to do the rest. Kelly closed his eyes as his underwear was tugged down, feeling a stubbled cheek against his cock, a tongue licking one of his hips as Nathaniel pulled off the jeans completely. Any lingering concerns he had were lost to an assault of endorphins as Nathaniel took him in his mouth.

That's not all he was doing. Those hands still explored, stroking the side of his ass, the underside of his thigh, the center of his chest. Everywhere. Even there. Nathaniel seemed intent on touching every single part of him, not avoiding any, and not lingering in any one place. Indiscriminate and impartial. Kelly wished they weren't denying their emotions, because the pleasure his body felt was overshadowed by the warmth in his heart.

The attention ceased. Kelly looked down to find Nathaniel grinning. "What?"

"I've been dreaming about those lips every night. Or at least right before bed."

Kelly smiled seductively, but not with his teeth. "What did you dream I'd do with these lips?"

"Stay right there and I'll show you."

Nathaniel climbed up, putting a knee to either side of his chest before flopping forward, holding himself up with his arms. Kelly opened his mouth in invitation, taking Nathaniel in as deep as possible before the thrusting began. He glanced upward at the bucking body, the flexing arms, the dark armpit hair, and occasionally the face twisted in ecstasy when Nathaniel let his head hang loose instead of holding it back and moaning. Kelly thought they would end this way, even thought he could explode right then and there.

But soon Nathaniel rolled over and propped himself up on his elbows. "Come sit on me."

"Condoms and lube," Kelly said. After a moment, he added. "And a few more nights like this, because I'm not ready yet."

"That's fine," Nathaniel said. "That's not what I meant anyway. Come here."

Kelly scooted up to be on his level, then threw a leg over him and sat his rump down on what felt like a scalding hot sausage.

"I love your face," Nathaniel said, grabbing his hips. "So many expressions."

He shifted Kelly downward a little, and then sat upright. Now he got it. Kelly readjusted, wrapping his thighs around Nathaniel's waist and bringing their cocks together. A warm meaty hand wrapped around both of them and stroked. Then they took turns spitting until the hand was able to slide. Locking eyes, they moaned. Nathaniel kept stroking, seemingly tireless as they stared into each other's souls. The tension built, Nathaniel bucking a few times before bringing his face close, his breath a puff of warm air when he spoke. "Come with me."

Kelly bit his bottom lip and nodded. Nathaniel's grip tightened, and he started pumping faster. Then he growled, and Kelly felt something hot and wet splatter into his chin before he let loose himself. Howls, clenched muscles, hisses, and finally sweet relief. Endorphins spilled into Kelly's bloodstream, pure and perfect in a way that painkillers never had been. Then Nathaniel leaned back, taking Kelly with him, holding him tight to his still-heaving chest. Eventually his breath steadied and his grip relaxed.

Kelly rolled over to his side, and instead of melting into blissful sleep, he became aware of another sort of tension. Unless a second storm was brewing outside, this couldn't be good.

"Kelly—"

Before Nathaniel could continue, he sat up, swung his leg over the mattress, and reached for his shirt. Or the remains of it, at least.

"What are you doing?"

"Just friends," Kelly said. "I'm totally cool with that. Don't worry. Besides, I sort of stole my mom's car and should probably get it back."

After a pause, Nathaniel murmured. "You're really okay with this?"

"Yeah!" Kelly said, sounding chipper.

"In that case," Nathaniel grabbed his shoulder and pulled him backward. "Friends have sleepovers too, you know."

"I suppose they do," Kelly said, keeping his face turned to hide his grin. "And I suppose when my mom finds both me and the car missing, she won't call the cops right away."

"Exactly."

"How about a towel," Kelly said. "You're a human geyser!"

"Sorry," Nathaniel said, sounding anything but. "Be right back."

When he returned, Zero was slinking along behind him, as if hoping he wouldn't be seen.

"The dog isn't sleeping with us, is he?" Kelly said, forcing down a smile.

"It's actually his bed." Nathaniel tossed him the towel. "Zero got a part-time job to pay for it and everything. If we're lucky, he'll let us share it with him. It's either that or the couch."

"I suppose we'll have to make do." He watched Nathaniel flop into bed, pull up a sheet, and pat the space next to him. Kelly wasn't sure if that was directed at him or Zero. "You sleep naked with the dog?"

"Don't worry, he's naked too. No collar, see? He'll let you wear it if it makes you feel more comfortable."

"That's all right." Kelly finished wiping himself off and slid beneath the sheets. "When in Rome…"

Spooning with Nathaniel would have been a nice end to the evening. Unfortunately, a small wolf squirmed his way between them. Not that it felt so bad. Kelly reached out to stroke the dog's fur. A moment later, his hand bumped into Nathaniel's. Their fingers intertwined, and hands still resting on the dog, all three of them slowly drifted off to sleep.

Kelly awoke to find the bed next to him empty, but considering he was in the other guy's apartment, Nathaniel probably hadn't run off in the middle of the night. He groped around for his underwear, then picked up his crutches and headed into the hall. He found Nathaniel in the kitchen, already showered and fully dressed. On the counter was a plastic shopping bag, a quart of milk sticking out of the top.

"Morning," Nathaniel said. "I hope you like pancakes."

"Absolutely" Kelly glanced over at Zero, who was already drooling. "Do I have time to get cleaned up first?"

"Sure. There's a fresh towel by the sink. Think you'll need anything else?"

The question seemed innocent enough. Nathaniel could have been asking if he needed a washcloth or a back scrubber. In reality, he wasn't sure how his guest would manage in the shower with just one leg. Kelly would have to sit on the bottom of the tub while doing so, which wasn't ideal but also not a big issue.

"I'll manage," he said.

Nathaniel nodded. "Cool."

Simple as that. No wringing hands or concerned expression. No well-meaning offers of help that Kelly would have to repeatedly decline. No helpful suggestions. Nathaniel had already returned to whisking the batter.

As Kelly scrubbed himself, the warmth of the shower matched his thoughts. He loved how casual Nathaniel behaved toward his disability. Especially since lately it no longer felt like an impairment to Kelly. Sure he was missing a part, but he no longer considered himself incomplete. Only when others reminded him of his difference did he feel uncomfortable. But that never happened with Nathaniel. He treated Kelly just like anyone else.

These thoughts were still on his mind when he sat down at the dining room table. "You never asked how I lost my leg," he said. "That's one of the first questions out of most people's mouths. Especially kids."

Nathaniel chewed and swallowed. "I already know."

"You do? How?"

"Marcello had me do some research on you. But even if I hadn't, I would have let you tell me in your own time."

Kelly took a few bites while mulling this over. "Seems a little paranoid, Marcello requiring background checks on all his models."

"Normally he doesn't. Marcello takes his models at face value, as he's so fond of saying. His escorts are another manner."

"Of which, I am not one," Kelly said pointedly. "So why was he poking around in my past?"

Nathaniel paused in his chewing, looking puzzled. His features relaxed again as he swallowed. "He wasn't doing a background check on you. He asked me to research William Townson."

Hearing Nathaniel speak the name of his former boyfriend was beyond surreal. Kelly was pretty sure the blood drained from his face, but it soon rushed right back as he put the pieces together.

"I doubt Marcello screens his waiters either, so why would he bother?" Unless someone asked him to. As a favor. But who would want to know more about William's past? The answer came all too quickly. "Have you ever heard of Jason Grant?"

Nathaniel took a sip of coffee, hand just as steady as his gaze. But even after he set the cup down again, he remained quiet.

"The night we met," Kelly said, replaying the events in his

mind. "You wouldn't let me into the kitchen. I always wondered what that was about. Did they really go through all that trouble just to have an hour alone? It's not like they couldn't meet at the mall while William worked. I know they did sometimes, and that seems way easier, so why?"

"I'd rather you remember that night for the drink we shared," Nathaniel said easily.

Wouldn't that be nice? But Kelly was too close to an answer now, and he knew he wouldn't have to drag it out of Nathaniel like he would other people. Nathaniel didn't pussyfoot around sensitive issues.

"Tell me," Kelly said.

"They weren't just hanging around the kitchen. Marcello arranged for them to have a private room. I wasn't there and can't say what happened, but I'm sure we can both guess."

"You knew!" Kelly said accusingly. "All this time, you knew!"

"Yes," Nathaniel said. "Are you going to hold that against me?"

Kelly tried suppressing his emotions and thinking about it logically. "You stopped me from discovering the truth."

"I stopped you from getting hurt. At least I wanted to. You could have torn through Marcello's home and caught them in the act, but I suspect you already knew what was happening, even if you didn't want to admit it to yourself. Instead of a very ugly scene, we sat down and enjoyed a bottle of wine together. When I saw this Jason Grant person later, I told him to stop with the secrecy."

"You did?"

"Yes."

Kelly took a shuddering breath. "William wouldn't have cheated on me. I figured maybe a kiss at most, but he never would have—" He shook his head. "Why does this matter? If William had shown up at my door yesterday and begged for me to come back to him, I would have said no. We're not meant for each other, I get that. But learning all of this, it still hurts!"

"Love is vicious," Nathaniel said. "Relationships and all the expectations that come with them—people are only setting themselves up to fail. What I told you that night still stands. You don't need anyone. You might want someone, but at the end of the day, only you are responsible for your own happiness. And until all this unpleasantness resurfaced, you seemed a lot happier without William in your life."

"I was," Kelly said. "I am. But part of me needs to know the truth before I can put it all behind me."

Nathaniel stared at his coffee. "Only two people in the world know what happened that night. You could always ask one of them."

Kelly nodded. "Then that's exactly what I'll do."

Chapter Nineteen

"Aren't they adorable?"

Kelly looked to where Layne had pointed. Bonnie had Emma pressed up against her car, their kisses so intense that one was liable to swallow the other. He was glad to see this, not just because it meant his best friend was happy, but also because it implied a certain someone was here. Jason rarely attended the youth meetings these days. Normally he only did so when Emma was in town, and that was just an excuse for her and Bonnie to hook up, Jason playing the role of apathetic chaperone. Kelly didn't attend so often either, but he'd been at every meeting for the last six weeks hoping for a chance like this.

Of course he could have texted William and asked to speak on the phone, but Kelly wasn't sure he could handle hearing the truth from him. Somehow that would hurt more. Just last week Kelly had stopped by William's old house to pick up some camera equipment he had left there. Seeing Mrs. Townson again made him oddly nostalgic, but that changed when he was allowed to go alone into William's old room. Once there, he noticed the shelf of animal action figures, now covered in a thin layer of dust. Maybe that's how it worked with the things William loved. Maybe he left them all behind without a second thought. Then again, the rescue helicopter Transformer hadn't been found. Kelly had even searched for it, but to no avail. He liked to think that William had taken that small piece of their past with him when he left.

"Geez," Layne was saying, attention still focused across the parking lot, "look at those two go! Do you think lesbians are better kissers than gay guys? Maybe I should go undercover— dress in drag and find some butch beauty to rock my world."

"Sounds like a plan," Kelly said. "Where's Jason?"

"He had to use the little boys' room." Layne crinkled his nose. "I guess the ride was too long for him. Hey, I wanted to ask… Is he single?"

Kelly thought about it. "Ever see that movie about the dog who kept waiting for his dead owner to return home, even though years had gone by?"

Layne pressed his hands to his cheeks. "Oh my gosh! That's so sad!"

"Yes, it is. Hopefully he gets a happier ending, but for now, don't waste your time."

"Oh." Layne peered at him. "Are *you* single?"

Kelly laughed. "What exactly is this about?"

Layne rolled his eyes, exasperated. "You wouldn't believe me even if I told you. Actually, it would make a phenomenal television drama, starring Robert Pattinson as yours truly. It all started when—"

"Excuse me," Kelly said, moving away. Jason was coming out of the church building, blinking in the afternoon sun. Kelly forced himself to remain calm as they neared each other. He had promised himself not to cause a scene. What would be the point? Of course not being emotional about this subject was nearly impossible, but he had to try.

"Hey!" Jason said, offering a smile. "Long time no see! Although I did see you in an advertisement at the mall. You were wearing that black suit and walking next to a panther. Did you really get to—"

"Photoshopped," Kelly said, cutting him off. "Listen, I need to ask you something, but I want you to know ahead of time that I'm not looking to reopen old wounds."

"Oh. Okay."

"The night you and William played waiter..." Kelly said. He felt he didn't need to make his point clearer. The way Jason's expression became guarded convinced him he was right.

Jason didn't answer immediately. He kept taking deep breaths like he was about to speak, but then those intense eyes would search his before darting away. Finally he exhaled. "When I first met William, he wouldn't talk about you. The subject was off limits, but not because he wanted to pretend you weren't there. Once I finally got him talking, it would always boil down to him wanting to do the right thing. For you. Regardless of his own feelings or mine, you were like this moral roadblock I couldn't get around. He made promises to you, and he intended to keep them."

"But then?"

"But then I decided to fight for him. Not at first. I didn't set out to wreck your relationship. I tried keeping my distance, emotionally at least, but I fell for him so hard. I still wanted to see him and be around him, even if he would never be mine. One day

I realized that I loved him and eventually I discovered that he…"

"Loved you," Kelly said. "I'm fine with that. In fact, it makes what happened more forgivable."

"He loved you too," Jason said. "I really think he did or he wouldn't have struggled with leaving you. It wasn't a decision he made lightly. He wanted to make you happy, and he wanted to keep all the promises he made."

"But that night at Marcello's home, what really happened?"

"That's what I'm trying to answer. I could give you details. If you really need them, I'll tell you, but what matters most is that William regretted what happened. He made sure to tell me that more than once. It was wrong, and I agree. Kind of. If I hadn't forced William to break at least one of the promises he made to you, then I think he would still feel bound by them. Even today."

Kelly supposed that was all the answer he needed. Part of him felt like asking Jason to say it outright, just so there couldn't be any shred of doubt remaining. After all, he still didn't know if it was a simple kiss that had broken the spell or something more. But he *was* certain that it no longer mattered.

"You didn't force him to do anything," Kelly said, "and honestly, if I had to put up with his virtuous ass for much longer, I probably would have gone insane."

Jason looked puzzled. "Really? I like that about him. He's so—"

"Noble?" Kelly shook his head. "You two are made for each other. I don't mean that as an insult. I really hope this long-distance thing works out, because you guys have more potential than he and I ever did."

"You're not angry?" Jason asked.

Kelly shook his head. "Nah. I've got mine."

Jason's surprise turned into interest. "Who's the lucky guy?"

"We're keeping it on the down low," Kelly said. "For now."

"You tease! Sounds kind of romantic though. Someday I want to hear all the juicy details." Jason glanced over Kelly's shoulder and appeared confused. "Uh, why is Layne talking to himself?"

Kelly glanced back and sighed. "I believe he's in the middle of telling his life story. If you're feeling charitable, we should probably go pretend to listen. Someone should be there to catch him in case he forgets to breathe."

* * * * *

Kelly stood in a dark corridor, fluorescent tubes flickering occasionally. Normally dim during the daytime, at night the hallway was positively gloomy. All those lights in Marcello's studios must burn a crazy amount of energy. Maybe the idea was to compensate by keeping the public areas dim. If so, Kelly wished they wouldn't because he was getting spooked. He jabbed at the elevator button again, willing the doors do open. "Come on, come on!" he grumbled.

"You have a meeting with Marcello in a few minutes."

"Gah!" Kelly spun around—not an easy feat on crutches, which was why he stumbled.

Nathaniel caught him, gaze still penetrating.

"I know I have a meeting," Kelly said, straightening himself. "What are *you* doing here?"

Nathaniel let go. "You can handle yourself. You know I believe this."

"Yes. And?"

"Marcello is the exception to every rule in existence." Nathaniel's brow furrowed. "Or at least he's broken every rule possible. You don't know who you're dealing with."

"The devil?" Kelly suggested. "I'm fine. Remember when he wanted me to wine and dine that sleazy client and I brought my parents along as chaperones?"

"Yes," Nathaniel said, resisting a smile.

"Or the photo shoot with the appalling fur coat, and how I showed up wearing a fake bear trap on my stump."

"The fake blood was a nice touch," Nathaniel admitted. "Marcello was distraught until I suggested we sell the photos to PETA. Then he thought it was funny. He was less amused about the incident with the fake rash. We almost lost a major contract over that one."

"So major that my image would have been in magazines nationwide. Selling *acne cream*. I didn't want the entire country associating me with zits. Besides, the rash Margie created using makeup was amazing. Especially the pus. She should work in horror movies."

"The rash was impressive," Nathaniel conceded. "Sending a repulsive photo of yourself to the company president, blaming the acne cream, and threatening legal action—that was a little extreme."

"Maybe. They made sure to choose a different spokesman, didn't they? My point is that I know how to handle Marcello. At least I could if this stupid elevator wasn't broken."

Nathaniel reached around him and pressed the button. The doors opened immediately.

"How did you do that?"

Nathaniel shrugged. "I guess you need me after all." He followed Kelly into the elevator and started pushing numbers on the keypad."

"You know the code to his office?"

"Of course."

"Tell me!"

"Not a chance in hell."

Kelly wore a pout until the elevator doors opened. Then he put on his business face because as much as he hated to admit it, Marcello really did keep him on his toes. Currently the man himself was standing next to the couches, three glasses of freshly poured champagne awaiting them.

"Nathaniel!" he said, clapping his hands together. "What an unexpected surprise!"

Nathaniel only shook his head. He walked to one of the couches and plopped down. Kelly did the same after Marcello had greeted him and reached for one of the glasses.

"Not a drop," Nathaniel said.

"Oh, let the boy have his fun," Marcello said, sitting across from them.

"Not until negotiations are over."

"Negotiations?" Kelly said. "You already have me under contract."

"Yes," Marcello said pleasantly, looking between them. "How wonderful to see you side by side. Such a handsome pair! You've become close while working together?"

Kelly felt like leaping across the coffee table to silence him. Was he trying to spook Nathaniel? Then again, they had been doing this for months now. Kelly turned his head to gauge his reaction.

"Somebody has to keep him in line," Nathaniel said.

"And I can think of nobody more qualified." Marcello toasted them with a glass before sipping from it. "Of course, one's personal life has a direct effect on their performance at work, so

I imagine if you really wanted to guide him, you would have to put in... extra hours."

The muscles in Nathaniel's jaw flexed a few times. "That's what friends are for."

"For good times, for bad times," Kelly deadpanned. "Why exactly am I here again?"

"They grow up so quickly," Marcello declared with a twinkle in his eye. "I can scarcely believe that we're sending you off to college next week."

"I couldn't have done it without you," Kelly lied, still not understanding where this was going.

"It makes me think wistfully of my own college days," Marcello said. "The wonderful adventures I had and all the friends I made. Of course there's a fair amount of grueling work, tedious classes, and professors with severely inflated egos, but I'm sure you'll weather all of that commendably. No, you're probably better off studying rather than lounging around Cancún."

"Cancún?" Kelly repeated.

"Oh yes, you know, beaches made of diamonds, water like liquid sapphire, an exotic culture in a foreign land you've never set foot upon. What did I read on the Internet earlier? One of the world's most renowned tourist destinations? How tiresome this must sound to you compared to sitting in a classroom day after day."

Kelly stared at him. "Okay, you've shown me the bait. Now where's the hook?"

"No hook," Marcello said, "unless you're not willing to play hooky. Ha! It's short notice, but the photo shoot would be next week."

"So I'd miss my first week of school," Kelly said. "That's not a big deal."

Marcello smiled. "Wonderful, my dear boy! How very generous of you. Let's drink to our mutual pleasure, shall we?"

"No," Nathaniel grunted. "Not until we're done with business."

Marcello drank anyway, scornfully gazing over the glass in Nathaniel's direction.

"There's more?" Kelly asked.

"Mm," Marcello said, nodding while he swallowed. "Your

reputation has sailed across the Atlantic. The Pacific too. How would you like to see New Zealand? Or Venice? We're still in negotiations, but Tokyo is likely as well."

Kelly worked very hard not to let his jaw drop. His eyebrows might have shot up, but he soon coaxed them back down. "Sounds nice."

"It does," Marcello replied with a heavy sigh. "What could have been. But no, your education is of more value."

"I'm still available on weekends."

"To fly to Tokyo and have a team of professionals photograph jetlag's new poster boy?" Marcello shook his head, jowls wobbling. "No, I'm afraid that simply won't do. You go become a learned man. In four years, if time has been merciful, I'm sure some lingering interest in your image will remain."

His intent was transparent. Marcello wanted him to continue working full-time rather than go to college. What Marcello didn't know is how little higher education interested Kelly at the moment. He still hadn't settled on a career choice. Rock star, astronaut, coach, or teacher—whether outlandish or practical, nothing sounded quite right. The same with being a model. He couldn't do this his whole life, and yet—

"You could always swing that handsome hammer now," Marcello said, "strike while the world's iron is still hot for you. In a few years you'll have earned enough to pay for your college tuition in full. In addition to a nice little nest egg, I would imagine. You don't realize how young you are, how much time you have at your disposal, how rare opportunities like these are."

"I already paid for my first semester," Kelly said.

"I can do amazing things with a telephone," Marcello said. "I'd have your money refunded to you by tomorrow."

Kelly's head swam like he'd already been drinking, but he didn't have to think hard about this. A year or two of travelling the world before he settled down to face life's realities. What could be better? He was reaching for the champagne glass when Nathaniel spoke.

"Kelly would be doing the studio a great favor," he said. "How many international contracts did we lose in recent years? And now they're coming back, all thanks to him."

Kelly glanced up to see a flash of panic in Marcello's eyes. Then he leaned back, leaving the glass where it was. "Of course I do have a few conditions."

"Naturally," Marcello said, shooting daggers at Nathaniel. "Let's hear them."

"I'm creating a college fund for my brother. He wants to be a doctor, so it won't be cheap. Whatever I put into the fund, I want you to match it, dollar for dollar."

"He wants me to put a doctor through college," Marcello said to the room in general. "Really now!"

"Well?" Kelly pressed.

"Is that your only demand?"

"No, I also want to get behind the camera again. I used to love taking photos, and lately being around all the equipment has got my shutter finger twitching. I want back in."

"Very touching," Marcello said, "but I can't put a hobbyist on a paid assignment. There's too much at stake."

"Then give me access to the equipment after hours. And get one of your photographers to show me the ropes. Preferably Rick, since he's nice. I'll build a portfolio, and you can judge it as you see fit."

Marcello turned to Nathaniel. "Will insurance cover any damage to the equipment?"

"Absolutely."

Marcello nodded. "Very well. To both conditions."

"Good," Kelly said. "In that case, I'll think about it."

Marcello's eyes narrowed so much that he almost appeared to have fallen asleep. Only the increasingly red hue of his skin suggested otherwise. Then he leaned forward and grabbed the bottle to pour himself a refill.

"We'll need another of these," he said. "Nathaniel, if you would be so kind."

"Sure." Nathaniel rose and headed to the other side of the room where a wooden cabinet hid a refrigerator. Marcello ignored both him and Kelly, reaching for his cell phone and typing with his thumb. Then he set it aside.

A moment later, Kelly felt a rumbling in his pocket. He pulled it out and saw a new text message. From Marcello, of course.

If you're nervous about international travel, don't be. Nathaniel will be with you every step of the way.

Kelly glanced up. Marcello nodded cordially and turned his attention to one of the potted plants, looking as innocent as a cherub.

Nathaniel returned with a bottle and got settled on the couch again. As he did so, Kelly imagined long waits at the airport together before even longer flights, where the only entertainment they had was each other's company.

"It's not like the University of Texas won't be there when I get back," Kelly said.

"Even if struck by a meteor," Marcello said casually, "there are plenty more like it."

"With that in mind—"

"You don't want to think about it?" Nathaniel asked.

Kelly took one look at him and, for once, had no doubts about what he desired. He leaned forward, took his glass, and held it up.

"Here's to knowing what you want and getting it."

"I believe I have that tattooed somewhere," Marcello said, reaching for his own glass.

Nathaniel considered them both and shook his head. Then he gave in and joined their toast, Kelly's gaze wandering longingly to the muscles of Nathaniel's neck as golden bubbles poured down his throat.

Ah, Paris, the city of love! Or was that Venice? Or Dublin, or even that small town in Utah, which was little more than a gas station and a Dairy Queen? Regardless of where his career took them, travelling together worked wonders for Kelly's relationship with Nathaniel. Not that he dared call it that, even six months deep.

When in Austin, they conducted themselves in a specific manner. At work they were complete professionals. After hours they would often while away their time like good friends. But the tension would build between them, culminating in mind-blowing nights, some of which left Kelly trembling. And overwhelmed with emotion that he didn't express verbally. Even little gestures like sharing casual kisses or holding hands seemed forbidden.

But when they travelled, all these rules were tossed aside. Nathaniel would lovingly stroke the back of Kelly's neck as they stood on the Pont des Arts and looked out over the river Seine, or kiss him playfully in a dark corner of an Irish pub. Only terms of endearment remained muzzled. No relationship titles, no silly pet names, and definitely not the 'L' word. But what their relationship lacked in spoken syllables, it compensated for with an emotional intensity Kelly had never known before. Crushes could be one-sided, but feelings like these had to be mutual, making it easier for them to remain unspoken.

Of course returning home again—like now—was always a bittersweet experience. Their physical affection for each other would be toned down, and that also meant their feelings would accumulate and explode again, like some sort of emotional orgasm.

"Is your brother picking us up?" Nathaniel asked, arms stretched behind him as their suitcases followed along faithfully.

"I can't remember if I gave him the flight arrival times," Kelly responded. "If not, we'll take a taxi. My treat."

"At least until we present Marcello with a list of business expenses."

They chuckled together, stopping next to an airport newsstand so Kelly could dig out his phone. "No new texts. I'll send him one real quick to ask if he's coming."

"Ask if Zero is okay," Nathaniel said, sounding as close to whiney as he ever got.

"He was fine when you had me ask yesterday," Kelly said, rolling his eyes playfully. "And the day before. The day before that you got a video of him scarfing down food."

"Just ask," Nathaniel pleaded.

Kelly glanced up while typing. A woman his mother's age had stopped outside the store and was opening a Diet Coke. She was watching him as she did so, and when she offered a friendly smile, he returned the gesture. Then Kelly focused on finishing the text. When it was sent, he noticed she was still standing there looking at him.

"I have a son your age," she said.

"Oh," Kelly responded.

"He's in the Marines."

Oh geez! Not this again.

The woman came closer, eyes already watering as she put a hand on his shoulder. Kelly felt like running because this happened more often than he liked, especially when his hair was freshly buzzed.

"Thank you," the woman said. "Thank you so much for your service to our country."

Kelly never knew how to respond to this. He couldn't accept

her gratitude, since he didn't deserve it, and calling her out would only make her feel stupid. Then again, maybe she had it coming, because it was awfully damn presumptuous of her. Young people could lose a leg to an accident or infection or diabetes or vascular damage. But no, she had this grand fantasy of him running across a field of landmines while waving an American flag.

"Best of luck to your son," Kelly managed.

The woman patted him on the arm, misinterpreting his miserable expression. "Your sacrifice will not be in vain."

"Great," Nathaniel snapped. "Now if you'll excuse us, we have to catch a flight to Washington and have dinner with the president."

"Oh!" The woman clearly couldn't tell if this was a joke or not, but at least she wandered away after giving Kelly a few more affectionate pats.

"That was beyond awkward," Kelly said. "I'm going to start wearing long flowing dresses to hide my secret shame."

"You've got nothing to be ashamed about," Nathaniel said, still fuming.

"It was a joke."

Nathaniel glared. "Aren't you sick of this?"

"Yes," Kelly said. "Of course. What can I do about it? Become a scientist and develop a cure for stupidity?"

"You've got options."

Kelly stared at him a moment. "Hate to break it to you, but I'm not doing this for kicks. The leg is gone for good."

Nathaniel continued to glower. "What about prosthetics?"

"You know I already tried that. We've talked about this. It was uncomfortable and—"

"—you gave up after a week. Or did you even make it that long?"

Kelly felt his temper rising, but at least he didn't have to hold back in this relationship. "Tell you what, genius, why don't I saw your leg off above the knee and we'll see just how cozy a fiberglass shell crammed halfway up your ass feels. Then you can lecture me all day long about—"

"Shut up."

"—about how easy it is to pop on a peg leg and prance around the room. And if you think I'm changing who I am because the occasional idiot mistakes me for a veteran, and because *you* think

I'm incomplete, you can shove it up your—"

"Kelly! Shut. Up. Now!"

His mouth snapped shut and he resisted a smile, loving it when Nathaniel got so authoritative.

"When have I ever said you were incomplete, or treated you as if you were helpless or anything but perfect?"

Kelly thought about it and came up blank.

"News flash," Nathaniel continued, "I want the best for you. If you were smoking, I'd be pressuring you to quit. If you started snorting white powder, or throwing your money away, or eating fast food three times a day, I would step forward and ask you to think about what's best for you. That's all I'm doing right now. You tried once while in the throes of trauma. Maybe it's worth another shot."

"I'm fine how I am," Kelly said. "Except for the occasional embarrassing assumption, I'm good."

Nathaniel nodded. "In that case, pull your own luggage."

That was his challenge? No problem. Sure, maybe it meant the luggage lurched along now instead of rolling smoothly, but Kelly could manage just fine, and he made sure to prove it.

"Good," Nathaniel said, walking alongside him. "Now take out your phone and call your brother to see what's going on."

Kelly stopped to get at his phone.

Nathaniel kept walking. "Come on," he said, "I don't have all day. Let's go."

Kelly glared at him and kept moving forward. He pinned one crutch under an armpit, freeing a hand. This meant he had to hop, and with the luggage yanking on him and a hand in his pocket digging for his phone, he soon lost his balance and stumbled.

Nathaniel was there in an instant, grabbing him by the shoulders to support him. "What if you were on your own and about to miss your flight?" he asked. "Or worse, what if some crazy asshole is chasing after you and you need to call the police? Homophobes are cowards by nature, and if they perceive you as an easy target…"

Kelly was about to retort, but the wild fear in Nathaniel's eyes stopped him cold. That's what this was about. Nathaniel was worried for Kelly's safety—that something might happen to him. The thought alone was enough to summon the panicked expression Nathaniel now wore.

In this moment, Kelly felt surer than ever that he was loved. "If anyone comes after me," he said gently, "I'm probably faster on my crutches than I would be a on a fake leg."

"It's not just my stupid fears," Nathaniel said, "and it's not about how other people perceive you. I don't know how to express it without it sounding trite, but there are times when I want to give the world to you. Everything good in life, I want you to have it. I think this might be one of those things."

"Have you done your research?" Kelly said. "Prosthetic legs are like buying a car. Past the hefty price tag, there's maintenance and repairs when things break, and even then it won't last forever."

"If money wasn't an issue..." Nathaniel said.

"There's not going to be a fake leg under the Christmas tree next week, is there?"

"I'm serious."

"So am I, and money is *always* an issue."

"Just for the sake of argument, if it wasn't, would you at least give it another try?"

"Yeah," Kelly said, "but—"

Whatever he was about to say was interrupted by a familiar voice. Then a dog plowed into Nathaniel, nearly knocking him over. Soon Nathaniel was on his knees, rubbing Zero's neck scruff affectionately. Kelly looked up to see Royal smiling apologetically as he trotted over to them. Jogging. Squatting. People sure took such things for granted. Watching them now, Kelly envied them both. He'd gone so long without the ease of such simple actions that he'd convinced himself he wasn't missing anything.

Maybe it was time to see how much of that former life he could reclaim.

"Oh ho ho ho!"

The sound was reminiscent of a demented Santa, one who had partaken of a little too much eggnog. But the holiday season had come and gone months ago, and unless Mr. Claus had decided to vacation in Austin, someone else was downstairs. Kelly strained to listen as he finished tying his shoe. He heard his mother's voice, then his father's, before the laugh came again.

"Oh ho ho! Goodness me!"

The voice was familiar, but it couldn't be. Not in his parents' home. Kelly couldn't imagine such a person in so ordinary an environment. He rolled off the bed and pushed himself into a standing position. The horrible prosthetic leg—the one William and Bonnie had once taken him to fetch—was back. Kelly had resolved to practice with it, even though the socket no longer fit properly. He had to add layers of socks to achieve a vacuum seal, which soon made his stump hot and sweaty, but he remained determined to do this. If not for himself, then for Nathaniel. Besides, later today he should be strutting around wearing something more comfortable.

Maybe not strutting, since Kelly was slower than ever, having to hold the stair rail with both hands and take each step one at a time. The laughter hadn't stopped when he finally made it downstairs. There, in the dining room, sat a very large man. In one hand he held a photo, in the other he swirled a glass of apple juice as if it were champagne. Gathered around him like groupies were Kelly's parents and brother.

"Marcello?" Kelly said in disbelief. "What are you doing here?"

"Enjoying the company of your magnificent family," Marcello purred, waving the photo. "And discovering why you're so resistant to the idea of nude photography."

Kelly sighed, hobbling forward while glaring at his mother, her cheeks rosy with motherly love. Once close enough, he snatched away the photo from Marcello, barely glancing at it in confirmation. Sure enough, it was *the* photo. In it, Kelly was three years old and standing on a beach. At the time, his mother had recently given him a mohawk, making him look like Mr. T's illegitimate child. The new style must have bolstered Kelly's confidence, because his lips were puckered, his chest was puffed up, and his fists were placed firmly on his hips as he glared at the ocean. He resembled a wee king. Or an emperor with no clothes because Kelly was naked, and as proud as he appeared, there was little to see between his legs. *Very* little.

"It was cold outside!" Kelly harrumphed. "And I'll have you know I'm all grown up now."

"Kelly!" his mother chastised. Then she giggled. "Of course, if you take after your father, then I'm not surprised."

He stared at her, aghast, before turning an accusatory glare at Marcello. "Debauchery follows you wherever you go."

"It's a gift," Marcello said with a smile. He gestured to the other family photos on the table. "Such beautiful people," he said to Kelly's parents. "It's no wonder your son is in such high demand. Why, I could probably book all of you as a group, an entire family of supermodels. Wouldn't that be something?"

Laisha lit up at the compliment; his father looking proud. Royal chose this time to roll his eyes and wander off. Kelly set the photo facedown on the table. He was tempted to rip it up, but the last time he'd done so, his mother had used the negatives to have more copies made.

"Is everything okay?" Kelly asked. "Nathaniel was supposed to pick me up. Why are you here instead?"

"An apt question," Marcello said. "Nathaniel was to bring you to your appointment, wasn't he?"

"My prosthetist, yes. I need to get going."

"And tomorrow you're flying to Germany, aren't you?"

"You know the answer to that," Kelly said, feeling exasperated. "There's a photo shoot in Berlin."

"Good." Marcello glanced over at Laisha. "Is he all packed?"

"He is." She appeared strangely emotional, gesturing at her husband, who stood and fetched a large suitcase from the kitchen.

"What's going on?" Kelly asked.

"We're sending you to live on a farm," his father said with a wink.

"I'm afraid you're needed in Germany today," Marcello said.

"But my appointment—"

"There is no appointment," Marcello interrupted. "Well, there *is*. Just not when and where you expect one." He took a sip of juice, nostrils flaring as if the substance was alien to him, but he managed to swallow it anyway. "I made a few calls, and there's a small company called Ottobock in Germany. Ever heard of them?"

"Small company?" Kelly chuckled madly. "Ottobock keeps coming up in the research I've been doing. They have these computerized knees called the C-Leg that are perfect for transfemoral amputees."

"C-Leg," Marcello said with a dismissive toss of his head. "Ha!"

"Ha?"

"Ha!" Marcello repeated.

"What are we 'ha'-ing about?" Kelly asked.

"Genium is the new buzz-word, and the latest technology from Ottobock. From what I understand, it's like comparing the first wheel a caveman carved out of stone to a nice plump Michelin tire."

Kelly vaguely recalled reading about the next generation of prosthetic knees, but as far as he understood… "Those aren't on the market yet."

Marcello waved a hand. "I made a few calls. Now then, a car with a well-stocked bar awaits. I suggest we share a toast over this happy announcement while being whisked away to the airport."

Kelly still had unanswered questions, but his house had become a bustle of activity. His father was carrying his luggage outside, his mother kissing his cheeks and telling him to behave, like he was still a child. Then he followed them outside to find a six-passenger limousine parked parallel to the house. One of the doors was open, his teenage brother leaning over with his head in the car. When he stood upright again, a large dog hopped out after him.

Zero saw Kelly and raced up the driveway for a quick greeting—nearly toppling Marcello in the process—before rushing back to Royal's side. That could only mean one thing. Kelly reached the car and stooped to look inside. Nathaniel sat there, already assessing Kelly to make sure he was okay with this turn of events.

"Marcello wanted it to be a surprise," he said.

Kelly just smiled back, because for some reason, he felt like crying.

His mother had no reservations about weeping. She hugged him, then grabbed Marcello and did the same to him. After a teary goodbye, Kelly escaped into the car, eager for some quiet so he could consider all that was happening. Of course there was a reason monks didn't hop into fully-stocked limos when wanting to meditate. Kelly marveled at the interior, feeling it was excessive to ride in such a large car. At least until Marcello squeezed in next to him.

"Lovely people," he said. "Shall I ask the driver to crack the whip?"

"Sure."

Nathaniel raised his hand to stop Marcello. "There's nothing else you need?"

"I'm ready." Then Kelly thought twice and stuck his head out the window, shouting at his brother who had just reached the front door. "Royal, run upstairs and grab my crutches!" He leaned back in his seat and knocked on his prosthetic leg "There's no way I'm wearing this sucker on an international flight."

"You might as well leave it behind," Marcello said. "Soon you'll have no need of it."

Kelly mustered up a smile, but as they waited for his brother to return, he felt increasingly uneasy about the implications. Once he had his crutches and the car was in motion, he decided to speak his mind before it was too late. "Listen, this is all really exciting, but even a normal C-Leg is fifty thousand. I'm not sure what my insurance will cover, especially if I'm abroad, and—"

"You'll be field-testing the Genium model," Marcello interrupted. "Why, you'll practically be doing Ottobock a favor."

"But does that make it free?" Kelly pressed.

Marcello raised an eyebrow. "Nothing in this world comes free except for heartache and death. Now, on that happy note, let's have a drink. That juice left the strangest taste in my mouth. How can I describe it?"

"Healthy?" Nathaniel suggested.

"That must be it." Marcello appeared disturbed by the concept. "Thankfully, the cure for most ailments can be found sitting in a bucket of ice. Who would care to join me?"

Nathaniel shook his head. "We talked about this. From now on you're waiting until a respectable time of day before you start drinking."

Kelly grinned. "You're making him wait until dinner?"

"Until lunch," Marcello snapped, "but brunch isn't so far away and is damn near the same thing."

"As soon as we're dropped off at the airport," Nathaniel said, "I'm instructing the driver to take you to the nearest Alcoholics Anonymous meeting."

"You'll find it's no use," Marcello said with a casual shrug. "I've been banned, nationwide, from all such meetings."

"You're full of it," Nathaniel said, crossing his arms over his chest.

"I'm not! They accused me of being the most prolific enabler the world has ever known, to which I replied that Jesus has me beat by a few thousand years."

Nathaniel scowled. "Too bad he's not here, because he could turn water—and that's all you're getting—into wine."

Kelly nudged Nathaniel with his foot, pleading with his eyes. Sure, it might be eight in the morning on a Monday, but today they had reason to celebrate. And a tediously long flight to sleep through. After that, who knew what the future might hold?

Chapter Twenty

Germany had never really been on Kelly's radar. In grade school, he had met a girl whose family had recently immigrated to the States. She seemed perfectly ordinary except for her accent. Kelly knew of the Berlin Wall, and of course the shadow of World War II still loomed over the globe. He remembered first learning about the Holocaust in school and seeing photos so disturbing that he wished such horrors were impossible. But they weren't. So aside from key historical events and a very friendly third-grader, Kelly knew little about the land they had arrived in.

On the flight over the Atlantic, he had imagined a country based on German efficiency and design—the buildings smooth and white, the people slim and dressed in black. No nonsense, just productivity and competence. So when the taxi drove them through the center of Berlin to their hotel, what he noticed first was spray-painted graffiti. Few surfaces weren't covered in at least a primitive tag of some sort: the long stone apartment buildings that filled entire blocks, the trains and streetcars that ran alongside traffic, street signs, phone booths, bus stops—all seemed to have been marked by the most prolific artist in the world. Or artists, since the graffiti ranged from ridiculously amateur scribbles to astoundingly skillful murals.

The German people were just as varied as the art. Sure, he spotted a few thin-faced individuals who appeared to be perpetually sucking a lemon, but he also saw punks straight out of the eighties, hot young guys in the most generically popular fashions, and pretty girls wearing thrift-store finds. Middle-aged women here often had an androgynous charm, and the elderly didn't seem averse to walking or biking. Those were just the people Kelly could fit into specific categories. Most seemed to be doing their own thing without worrying about any specific sense of style.

Closer to Berlin's center, the scenery became much more polished. Most cities put on a pretty face for tourists, which is exactly what he and Nathaniel were. No photo shoot awaited them. That had just been a ruse. Their vacation started today in a hotel designed for extended stays. This meant a larger living space beyond the bed, and a small but fully equipped kitchen filling one wall. As luxurious as this no doubt was for the region, Kelly found it—like most accommodations in Europe—somewhat cramped. Not that he minded Nathaniel and him being on top of each other. Or rather, Nathaniel being on top of him. Maybe a quick shower and then...

He glanced over at Nathaniel, who was seated on the small couch and staring at the television. Like everywhere they stayed, he would soon complain about the screen being too small, or the built-in sound system being inadequate, or worst of all, the television not being properly set up for high definition. Currently the screen was covered in multicolored text, like something from a primitive computer system.

"Weird," Kelly said. "What is that?"

"No idea. I must have hit the wrong button." Nathaniel stared a moment longer and then grunted. "That's the date in the corner, right?"

Kelly peered at the numbers. "Yes."

Nathaniel sighed. "I'm always doing this."

"Time change?" Kelly asked.

"Yup. We left on a Monday, we arrived on a Tuesday."

"That's okay, isn't it?"

Nathaniel looked over at him. "Your first appointment is in thirty minutes."

"I don't even have time to shower?"

"Nope."

Kelly groaned. "Okay. Gross, but okay. I doubt much will happen today besides them taking a cast of my stump. Should be easy, right?"

"Of course. I don't suppose you speak German?"

"Does anyone?"

Nathaniel raised an eyebrow. "I'm guessing the locals do."

Kelly shrugged. "So all we have to do is show up smelly and tired at one of the most technologically advanced corporations in the world and grunt in primitive English while gesturing at my leg. Or where a leg should be."

Nathaniel nodded. "That about sums it up."

Kelly flopped facedown into bed. "In that case, I'm not going."

"You are," Nathaniel insisted.

Kelly closed his eyes. "Reschedule or something."

"You're going."

Kelly ignored this, smirking into his pillow. He felt the mattress shift before an arm wrapped around his waist. Cuddle time? But no, Nathaniel hoisted him up, carried him to the hallway, and lowered him to the carpet. A moment later his crutches clattered to the floor next to him. Then the room door swung shut.

"Twenty-five minutes and counting," Nathaniel said. "Don't make me drag your ass down the sidewalk. You saw how much snow was out there. More like slush really, and no, we aren't taking a taxi, so hurry up."

Kelly sighed and rolled over onto his back. "You're so good to me," he said, staring at the ceiling. When he heard the elevator ding from farther down the hall, he decided he'd better follow. Especially since he had left his hotel key on the coffee table. It was either sleep in the hallway, or follow a handsome man out into the cold Berlin weather.

The next morning, for the second day in a row, they stood outside the Science Center Berlin. Kelly saluted to shade his eyes from the morning sun, considering the Ottobock-owned building with a clearer head. International flights always made him feel a little delirious, due to him rarely managing more than brief unsettled naps. He never handled sleep deprivation well, and so his first impression of the building had surely been skewed. Especially since he recalled a building transported from the future—a tall rectangle constructed from thick white ribbons and dark waves of windows.

That impression didn't make much sense, but standing here now, after a full-night's sleep and with a hotel breakfast in his belly, he saw his memory was absolutely correct. If the architecture was meant to convey a state-of-the-art facility, then it succeeded in excess.

"We're half an hour early," Nathaniel said.

"Good," Kelly replied. "I want to check out the exhibition."

He led the way inside, feeling again as if he'd stepped onto the bridge of the starship Enterprise. Polished white surfaces, round curves instead of sharp corners, and display panels everywhere they looked. An older man sat at a reception desk to the right, his dark suit and wrinkled face a strong contrast to the polished perfection surrounding him. After a brief conversation, they were allowed to enter the exhibition area. Much of it consisted of flashy interactive displays designed to get visitors involved. Nathaniel was drawn in by these, placing his arm on a flat surface that then projected an image of bones and muscles onto it.

Kelly barely paid attention, moving instead to the exhibitions that utilized actual prosthetic limbs. The arms and hands were fascinating enough, but when he stood in front of a cabinet with a real Genium knee and leg, he felt like a kid with his nose pressed against a toy store window.

"One of those is waiting for you upstairs," Nathaniel said, coming up behind him. "It's almost time. Let's go."

Kelly followed him to the elevator, eyeing the stairs longingly. He could take them, but it would slow them down, and right now he felt like rushing. The Germans didn't waste any time either. He couldn't believe that the custom-fitted socket had been prepared overnight instead of requiring the weeks of waiting he'd been through back home. Almost two years ago, he realized.

"Nervous?" Nathaniel asked.

"Yes," Kelly said.

That didn't begin to express it. They reported to the Competence Center—as it was called—Kelly fighting against rising hope, not wanting to be hurt when his unrealistic dreams didn't come true. The Competence Center was just as modern as the downstairs areas, but practical rather than flashy. Here they were shown to a room with balancing bars, small sets of steps for training, and other obstacles that normally wouldn't challenge anyone older than a toddler.

"You've got your angry face on," Nathaniel pointed out.

"Sorry," Kelly said as he took a seat at the end of the parallel bars. "That happens when I get anxious. Or when I get angry, obviously."

Nathaniel smirked. "Or in bed, just when you're about to—"

"*Guten Morgen, Herr Phillips! Herr Courtney!*" The woman who entered the room, Inga, was barely older than Kelly. Her hair was medium length, and she didn't bother with makeup, possessing a natural beauty that Kelly found appealing. He was amused as she formally shook hands with both of them, but he became a lot more serious when he saw the case she was carrying.

"Is that my leg?" he asked.

"Yes," Inga replied. She, like all the other Germans they'd met so far, had a strong grasp of the English language. Her phrasing was a little awkward at times, but devoid of the stereotypical accent movie villains were often burdened with. "Are you ready to try it on?"

"Hell yes!" Kelly said.

Inga smiled while setting the case on a low side table. Then she sat on a short rolling stool in front of him. "We'll start with the socket," she said. "And then, *icks tsfy*."

He glanced over at Nathaniel, who shrugged. Whatever *icks tsfy* meant, Inga had said it quite a bit yesterday too. He kept trying to figure it out in context, but so far the meaning eluded him.

As Inga fit the socket over his stump, he had flashbacks to the little clinic in Austin. William had stood there with an encouraging smile on his face. Nathaniel was almost in the corresponding spot, standing off to the side with his arms crossed. His expression implied he was ready to break something if this didn't work out. That made Kelly chuckle, easing his nerves somewhat.

"How does that feel?" Inga asked, tugging on the socket.

"Good," Kelly said, shifting his weight. "Actually, this is great!" Unlike the socket he already owned, this one didn't ride up on his ass. The material felt softer and more comfortable too. That might change once part of his weight was resting on it, but so far... "It fits like a glove!"

Inga looked puzzled a moment, then smiled. "Ah! *Handshuh*."

"Hand shoe?" Kelly repeated. "Is that what Germans call gloves? Shoes for the hand?"

"Yes," Inga said, returning his smile. "It makes sense!"

"I guess it does," Kelly admitted. "So what do you call pants? Leg shoes?"

"Leeder-hosen," Nathanial said. "Even I know that one."

Inga looked amused. "Lederhosen," she corrected, replacing that long "e" sound with a short one. "When you say *Liederhosen*, it sounds like musical trousers. Normal pants are just called *Hosen*."

Kelly shook his head. "Maybe we should stick to English."

"I agree," Inga said with some degree of pride.

"Why is this one so short?" Kelly asked, looking down at the socket. It only covered his stump, leaving most of his upper leg free. "The socket I had before always rode up on my junk."

"Junk?" Inga asked.

"Uh, that's difficult to translate," Kelly said quickly. "I mean it went all the way up to here."

Inga watched him gesture at his hip and looked surprised. "You didn't have a sub-ischal socket?" When he looked clueless, she added, "You have enough leg left that I don't believe you need so much support. Would you like to see if I'm right?"

Kelly nodded. The socket came off again, and he watched in fascination as she connected the leg to it. The prosthesis was a thing of beauty, deceptively simple in appearance, gunmetal gray and sculpted to resemble a natural calf muscle. All that technology packed into one efficient package. It truly was a marvel, and if the promises were accurate, soon it would allow him to do everything he could before. Well, besides swimming, showering, and the one activity he missed most.

"Ready to stand?" Inga said.

"Okay."

He grabbed hold of the balancing bars, but barely needed them as he stood. Inga encouraged him to take half a step forward. Then back again. She was blocking his way, one hand held out as she coached him on how to bend the Genium knee. This practice session dragged on, Kelly tempted to politely shove Inga and her rolling stool away so he could try walking for real.

"Stay patient," Nathaniel said, reading his expression.

"Yes," Inga said. "You must be patient. But I think you are ready."

She rolled backward to the end of the bars. Finally, path clear, Kelly took one step forward, then another. His concentration was focused downward at first, his hands hovering just above the bars, touching them occasionally. By the time he reached the end, he turned around without thinking about it. Inga called out, telling him how to turn correctly, but the technology was so damn good that he managed just fine. He looked up as he walked to the other end, catching sight of Nathaniel. His jaw was clenching, his face increasingly red, and he was breathing through his nose. The big lug was on the verge of crying!

Kelly smiled at him, too happy for tears at the moment. He reached the end and turned again. Inga stood as he got near, holding out her hands but stepping away from the bars. "Would you like to try without support?"

Kelly was barely touching the bars anyway. Without

hesitation, he walked to the end of them. And beyond. Without crutches, without a cane or any other kind of aid, he was walking. Inga stood and stayed in front of him, walking backward in case he needed assistance, but he was fine. So much so that Inga's back bumped against the wall.

"Very good!" she said with a laugh. "You're a quick learner."

"By the end of the day, I'll be running laps," Kelly joked.

"Jogging?" Inga asked, looking surprised. Then she saw his smile and relaxed again. "Not today. Maybe in a week, you can try."

His brow furrowed. "Not on this leg. The Genium doesn't support running."

"*Icks tsfy*," Inga responded.

"I don't know what that means."

"Oh! I'm sorry. The leg you have, it's a… uh… X2."

"I still don't know what that means," Kelly said.

"The X2 leg is designed in cooperation with the United States military." Inga guided him back toward the bars. "Right now it is for soldiers, but in the future, there will be a civilian release too."

"But what you're saying," Kelly said, "is that I can run on this leg. The one I've got on right now."

Inga nodded. "Yes. Of course. Just not now."

"Not now because it hasn't been developed fully, or—"

"You must learn to walk," Inga stressed. "You must train. Once you have, you can run with the leg you are now wearing."

Kelly glanced at Nathaniel, who nodded in confirmation while still trying to clamp down on his emotions. Kelly didn't hold back. For the first time in a very long while, both his hands were free to wipe away joyful tears as they spilled from his eyes.

"I need to sit down," Kelly said.

Nathaniel glanced over at him with something nearing concern. "You all right?"

"Yeah, just normal tired."

The day had been spent walking. Kelly couldn't get enough of it. They strolled the artsy shops of Kreuzberg and walked the length of the Berlin Wall—or at least what remained for tourists to gawk at. For lunch they ate a kebab from a fast-food truck that didn't offer seating. Then they took the S-Bahn through the middle of the city, stopping at random stations to see what they would discover. Most recently they had walked down a busy shopping street, the sidewalks so packed that they felt shoved along by the crowds. Kelly almost missed the excessive courtesy his crutches often earned him. But not really. Being on his feet all day had been wonderful, and now he wanted nothing more than to sit.

"Let's grab a beer," Nathaniel said, pausing in front of a restaurant door and triggering irritated grunts from the pedestrians around them.

"Sounds good," Kelly said, pushing open the door, "but let me order, okay?"

"Feeling brave?" Nathaniel asked.

"Yup!"

The restaurant was dark and cozy, lit by orange lamps that gave the illusion of firelight. The booths were wooden, only thin cushions providing any comfort. Kelly remained silent as they sat, not wanting the waiter to hear they spoke English. Sure enough, he came over and plopped down two menus, both of them covered in indecipherable text.

"Was zum Trinken?"

Whatever that meant. Kelly spoke the two words he felt he'd pieced together. *"Tsfy beers."*

The waiter raised an eyebrow. *"Zwei Bier? Welches denn? Pilsner? Hefe?"*

Kelly stared in response.

The waiter stared back a moment, then took a menu, opened it, and tapped a finger on one section. *"Welches?"*

Kelly glanced down at a list of brands, choosing one with Berlin in the title. People were always raving about local beer, so he figured it was a good choice.

The waiter leaned over to see and asked, *"Himbeere oder Waldmeister?"*

Kelly nodded hopefully in response.

"Na gut," the waiter said. *"Beides."*

Thankfully he then went away, Nathaniel chuckling as he did so. "Very impressive!" he said.

"Shut up," Kelly said. "I managed, didn't I?"

"Hopefully. Who knows what you really said. The guy might be on his way to call the police."

Kelly waved a hand dismissively. "Then it's a good thing

I'm equipped with a military-grade leg. This thing probably has secret deployable missiles, so don't mess with me."

"I wouldn't dare," Nathaniel said, eyes twinkling. "How does it feel? As good as the real thing?"

"Almost," Kelly said. "One of my butt muscles keeps twitching on that side."

"Maybe something needs to be adjusted. You'll have to tell them tomorrow."

"That'll be a fun conversation." Kelly frowned. "Listen, I'm really grateful for all of this—"

Nathaniel raised a hand. "Thank Marcello, not me."

"I definitely will, but between you and me, I'm worried. Having a leg of this caliber is wonderful. It's only the first day and already I feel like I've been given a second chance at… everything, really. But no prosthetic leg lasts forever, and I'm dreading the day this one breaks down. I plan on calling my insurance company as soon as we're back and opening a separate savings account, but if I ever need an entirely new leg, I'm not sure I'll be able to afford it. I know they say it's better to have loved and lost, but in this circumstance, I hate the idea of returning to the life I knew."

"Was it so bad?" Nathaniel asked.

"No," Kelly said. "Of course not. The accident could have been much worse. Day to day, I was happy. I don't know what I'm trying to say, other than getting what you want can be scary, because then you have to face the idea of losing it again."

Nathaniel stared at him, frowning slightly. "I know exactly what you mean."

"*Zwei Berliner Weisse*," the waiter said. He set down two drinks on the table. "*Noch was dazu?*"

Kelly shook his head instinctively. The waiter wandered away. That was good, because at the moment he was struggling to find words. Instead of mugs, they had received comically squat versions of wine glasses. The beer—if that's even what it was—came in two different colors. One was red, the other green. Sticking out of both were fat black straws.

"Wonderful," Nathaniel said, "you somehow managed to order us clown beer."

Kelly stared a moment longer before laughing. "This is some sort of joke, right? Something they do to stupid tourists who think they can speak German?"

Nathaniel shrugged and peered at the printed image on the glass. "It looks like a little kid sitting in a beer mug. Maybe this is the beer Germans give to their children."

"Is that even legal?"

"In Germany it probably is." Nathaniel pushed one of the glasses toward him. "Here. You drink the green one. I figure it's the most likely to be poisoned."

"Thanks," Kelly said. He sipped gingerly on the straw. The flavor was sweet. He still wasn't sure if it was beer, because it mostly tasted like some sort of fruit syrup.

"Not bad," Nathaniel said, after half-emptying his glass with one swig, the straw resting on the table. "I'm not sure I'd want to get wasted off them, but it's kind of good."

Kelly nodded and made them swap glasses so he could try the red kind.

Nathaniel watched him grab the straw from his old drink and used it to sip from the new one. "You don't have to worry," he said. "If anything ever happens to your leg, you'll get another."

"How?" Kelly asked.

Nathaniel took a deep breath and shook his head. "I honestly don't know. But I'll make it happen, no matter what. I promise."

Kelly smiled with his eyes as he continued to sip. The two tiny beers didn't last long. Rather than stick around and suffer any more awkwardness with the waiter, they used the menus to figure out what they owed and left the money on the table.

Not too far from the restaurant was a department store with impressive window displays called KaDeWe. Not the most catchy name, but he probably didn't know how to pronounce it correctly. He wondered if German tourists ever stood outside Walmart and shook their heads in puzzlement. Not that Walmart could be compared to a store like this, since what they entered was clearly a high-end store.

"I need new shoes!" Kelly declared. "And maybe a nice pair of jeans. I won't have to fold one leg anymore! Oh my god! Do you have any idea how exciting this is?"

Even if he didn't, Nathaniel smiled in response. Maybe the beer had loosened him up a little, because as they were riding up the escalator, he reached over to take Kelly's hand. Such a simple pleasure, and a maneuver that would have been complicated just a day before. Nathaniel didn't let go when they reached the next floor, and even when Kelly shook him loose to try on shoes, the second he was finished, Nathaniel sought out his hand again.

He was forced to let go when Kelly stepped into a dressing room to try on some black slacks that had caught his eye. He grabbed a jacket on the way in. Both were much more form-fitting than those he usually found back home, but Kelly liked that. He stared into the mirror and felt like he was dreaming. He had just dressed himself without struggling or hopping around. Now he was standing there, and to the naked eye, he looked just like anyone else.

"You almost done in there?" Nathaniel asked.

"Come see," Kelly said. He continued staring into the mirror as the curtain behind him opened. Nathaniel came close, put his hands on Kelly's hips, and considered their reflection. "What do you think?"

"Handsome as always," Nathaniel said.

"Thanks," Kelly said, "but I mean… I look normal!"

Nathaniel smiled at him from over his shoulder. "Normal? I don't think so. You're the most beautiful man I've ever laid eyes on."

Kelly felt like swooning into his arms. Instead he smirked and said, "You're just saying that because of the new leg."

Nathaniel shook his head, his gaze unwavering. "Take it off and throw it in the next dumpster you see. I don't care. Go back to your crutches if that makes you happy, or let me carry you anywhere you want to go. I'd do anything for you, Kelly. Absolutely anything, because I love you. You know that?"

Kelly nodded numbly, too shocked to respond in words.

Nathaniel appeared less certain. "Is that okay?"

Kelly remembered to breathe and spun around. "Is it okay that I've been in love with you for a ridiculously long time?"

A smile tugged at Nathaniel's lips. "Since when?"

"Gosh," Kelly said, casting his mind back. "Somewhere between the second and third glass of wine."

"At the fundraiser?" Nathaniel asked. "That far back? Wow! Must have been some potent moonshine!"

"It was," Kelly said with a grin. "Honestly, I don't know when it happened, but I've been keeping it a secret because I was worried that—"

"Kelly," Nathaniel said gently.

"Yes?"

"I need you to stop talking."

"Why?"

Nathaniel smirked, then drew him in for a kiss. They kept kissing long enough that Kelly was wondering if his new leg could handle hopping up and wrapping itself around Nathaniel's waist. Before that could happen, someone cleared her throat. They turned to find an older German woman with arched eyebrows who wore a department store nametag. She nodded meaningfully at the clothes Kelly was dressed in.

"Just doing a quality control test," Nathaniel said with a smile. "Don't worry, I plan to take it all home with me tonight."

The woman looked Kelly over again, and in lightly accented English said, "Would you like me to gift wrap him for you?"

By the time they entered their hotel room, they were both groaning like old men. Nathaniel sat on the edge of the bed, one shoe and sock already off as he wiggled the toes of a massive foot.

"Feels so good," he said. Looking over at Kelly, he nodded upward. "You said taking off your old socket felt like getting out of your shoes after a long day. Is it the same with this one?"

"Yes," Kelly said. "It's definitely more comfortable, but I can't imagine wearing it to bed."

Nathaniel took off his other shoe with a gasp. "Then why are you still standing there?"

"Because something occurred to me." Kelly bent the artificial knee before very carefully lowering himself down, resting his weight on it. Then he matched the position with his natural leg. "You have any idea how long it's been since I could kneel?"

"Neat, but are you planning to spend the whole night like that?"

Kelly looked at him pointedly.

Nathaniel's eyebrows shot up. As they came back down, a slow smile appeared. Then he stood and strutted over to Kelly with an exaggerated swagger that made them both laugh. He didn't stop until his belt was eye-level with Kelly.

Oh how he'd missed these little pleasures! Not that there was anything little about what Kelly intended to unwrap. He worked on the belt, then the button and zipper, revealing bulging underwear. Kelly grasped the cotton briefs and pulled them down in one smooth motion, Nathaniel's cock pointing at him expectantly. Kelly looked upward and smiled, enjoying this vantage point. He took Nathaniel's heavy balls in his palm, gently caressing them, then reached forward with just the tip of his tongue to tease the ring of foreskin.

Nathaniel gasped in pleasure, putting a hand on the back of Kelly's head and drawing him closer. Kelly kept looking upward even as Nathaniel's cock filled his mouth all the way to his throat. He'd lost touch with his gag reflex ages ago, so this wasn't a problem. As long as Kelly could still occasionally breathe in, Nathaniel could use him in any way he saw fit. He seemed eager to, eventually lifting up Kelly by the armpits and helping him to his feet so they could kiss.

Kelly took advantage of having his hands free, first by undoing his own pants, and then by pressing their cocks together, gripping them tightly and pumping. Nathaniel's eyes were half-lidded as he shook his head in awe, as if this was all too good to be true. Kelly agreed. He was happy to stay right where they were, but once again, Nathaniel had his own ideas.

"Get naked," he said, stepping back to shrug off his remaining clothes.

Kelly was shirtless and sitting on the bed to take off his pants when Nathaniel kneeled to help him. "All of it," he said, reaching for his socket. Kelly shrugged and leaned back, letting him do the work. Being free from its weight felt good. Both stripped bare, they scooted into bed together, Nathaniel crawling on top of him and kissing Kelly. Then he reached for the side drawer, but paused before opening it.

Kelly nodded. Now was as good a time as any. He toyed with Nathaniel's nipples as he worked on getting the condom wrapper open. He reached down to stroke those nuts as Nathaniel put it on. Then Kelly was flipped onto his stomach, grinning against the pillow and arching his back when he felt the cold lube between his legs. He closed his eyes as Nathaniel slipped one of his thick fingers inside, already wondering how anything could feel better. But he knew from experience just how much higher they could get together.

When he was finally ready, Nathaniel poised himself above Kelly and very carefully lowered himself, pressing against him until he was inside. He took it slow, just as he always did, watching Kelly so carefully that he never had to speak or give instruction. Once he was hilt deep and Kelly wasn't hissing in warning, Nathaniel lowered his weight. Then, still inside Kelly, he rolled them onto their sides.

This was different. Nathaniel had one arm wrapped around him as if they were spooning, which felt sweet and tender, at least until his hips started pumping. Then all the intense sensations—both physical and emotional—rose up inside Kelly, delivering him to euphoria. He grabbed Nathaniel's arm, clutching it to him, desperate to be closer than they already were. Nathaniel responded, tightening his grip so much that Kelly almost couldn't breathe, but he didn't care. Kelly would gladly give up oxygen to continue squirming against that muscled chest, for those hips to keep slapping his ass, to prolong the ragged breaths panted into his ear.

"I love you," Nathaniel was saying. "I love you. Ung. I love you so much!"

Part of Kelly felt like laughing, since his words sounded like someone had dubbed over the typical trash talk of a porno movie with the sappiest dialogue possible. But he also understood. He'd waited so long to hear those words, to be free to speak them aloud, that he felt like doing the same. At the moment though, he really was having trouble catching his breath. It wasn't just the toned bicep and forearm squeezing his torso like a python, or the way they both had to stretch their necks to kiss. Something else was building inside Kelly. Nathaniel was hitting him just right. Kelly wasn't even touching himself, and as he began to whimper, he realized he wouldn't need to.

"Yeah?" Nathaniel asked.

Kelly nodded, no other signal needed. Nathaniel started thrusting harder, slamming himself against his rump, which was all it took to send them both over the edge. Thought shut down completely as pleasure permeated Kelly's body, causing him to convulse. Nathaniel held on tight, lost in his own throes. Then they both exhaled long breaths and relaxed. Kelly's muscles melted like butter in sunlight. From the heaviness of Nathaniel's arm, he could tell he felt the same way. Eventually he glanced down at the sheets and saw multiple streaks of moisture in the fabric.

"When the maid sees the bed tomorrow," Kelly said, "she's going to flip."

"It's a guy," Nathaniel murmured, "and from the way he was checking you out in the hallway this morning, he'll probably ask you to autograph the bedspread so he can frame it."

"In that case, I'm glad I forgot to put up the 'do not disturb' sign."

Nathaniel raised his head. "I don't do threesomes."

"Which is why I'll wake up early and hide in the maid's laundry cart. Won't that be a nice surprise for him?"

A pillow thwacked Kelly in the head. After he pushed it away, he said, "Don't worry. You're the only one for me. And just for the record... I love you too."

Nathaniel squeezed him closer, tangled up their legs together, and celebrated this news by falling asleep. Kelly lay still a moment, basking in the wonderfulness of it all, before closing his eyes and giving chase.

Chapter Twenty-one

The wind whips around me, welcoming me back, inviting me to race off into infinity again. I pick up the pace, gyrating my hips to compensate, the artificial leg jutting off to the right. I'm tottering at high speed, bouncing along the track like a rubber ball, and the wind laughs... but not mockingly. The sound is joyful, because we are together again, the wind and I, rushing through space. I laugh too as a dog cuts across my path, nearly tripping me. I watch as he zips down the lane ahead, skidding to a halt before racing back toward us. And that's the best part. Us. Not just me and my elemental friend, but a real companion, jogging beside me and scowling at his dog. Then he looks over at me, wipes the sweat from his brow, and smiles.

Kelly's foot landed wrong—the biological one, ironically—causing him to stumble and tumble to the ground. Rolling to a stop, Kelly ended up on his back. Then he started laughing. Zero rushed up to give him a few sloppy licks before tearing off again. Soon after, a large form blocked out the sun.

"You all right?" Nathaniel asked.

"I think I skinned my knee," Kelly said, pointing at the artificial limb.

Nathaniel shook his head. "You better hope not, because we're not going back to Germany to get another one. Not until the snow melts there."

He offered Kelly a hand out of courtesy more than need. He knew Kelly could get up on his own these days. Once he was standing, Kelly shifted to the right, letting the sun warm him again. Being back in Austin felt good, especially now. They were standing on the track of his old high school, which had seemed a practical choice since the material was softer and would hurt him less if he fell. But running here again had another unexpected advantage. Kelly felt like he'd returned to a place of despair to conquer it with triumph.

"Keep grinning like that and people will think you've gone insane," Nathaniel said.

"I don't care," Kelly replied. "That felt too damn good. Ready for more? I'll race you!"

Nathaniel ran his fingers through damp hair. "Only if you promise to slow down."

"That was nothing. Just wait until I get my running blade. Then you'll really see fast."

"I'd rather see fast food." Nathaniel checked his watch. "It's past lunch time."

"Save your appetite," Kelly said, reluctantly heading off the track to where he had set up a tripod and camera. "The party will have plenty of food."

"Isn't that tonight?"

"No, in just a few hours." The camera took one more automatic photo before he turned it off.

"Kind of early for a party," Nathaniel said, watching him work.

"It's a birthday."

"For who? A little kid?"

Kelly handed him the folded tripod. "Geez, chill out Mr. Nightlife! Things happen during the day too, you know. And for the record, it's Layne's birthday. He's a friend of mine from the youth group."

"Youth group. As in teenagers."

"Yes. Tons and tons of teenagers who are eager to meet you for the first time. Prepare yourself. You'll probably have to give everyone piggyback rides."

"Sounds like a real cool party," Nathaniel grumbled. "Super neato."

He was sure it would be. Once back at Nathaniel's apartment, they showered and dressed, Kelly eager to head out again. He pictured the party taking place in a finished basement with low lighting and pumping music. But when they arrived at the house and were guided to the backyard by Layne's parents—what he saw there made his jaw drop. Tables, benches, and an impressive buffet were set up to one side. That was fine, but the rest of the yard was taken up by an inflatable monstrosity, the kind for kids to jump around inside of. This one was industrial-sized, multi-colored, and shaped like a cartoon castle. Kelly glanced over at Nathaniel, who shook his head and snorted.

"Welcome, welcome!" Layne said, approaching them with arms spread wide. "How kind of you to be here on my special day. My *very* special day."

"Eighteen is quite the milestone," Kelly said.

But Layne was no longer paying attention to him. Instead

he noticed Nathaniel, pausing to look him up and down before stepping forward for a hug. "It's so nice to meet you at last! We've heard so many wonderful things, some of them about you. What's your name again? Oh, it doesn't matter. You're so warm!"

"Okay," Kelly said, tugging on one of his arms. "Let go. Seriously."

"Fine," Layne said. He turned to Kelly for a hug before it finally clicked. "Oh. My. God!"

Kelly did a little jig. "No more crutches!"

Layne covered his mouth with both hands. Then he grabbed Kelly by the arm and dragged him forward. "Everyone, look who's standing on his own two feet!"

Almost everyone present was from the youth group, meaning they were practically family. Kelly hadn't attended a meeting in months, but seeing everyone felt good, as did their reaction. Most were smiling, a few looked emotional, and when Layne started clapping, everyone joined in.

"Thank you," Kelly said, waving them into silence. "I just want you all to know that it's incredibly insensitive to draw attention to my handicap like this, even if I do have an amazing bionic leg now. You are all horrible people."

He was assaulted by groans, turned backs, and a few middle fingers. Ah, they knew him so well!

"I think it's fabulous," Layne said, looping arms with him and Nathaniel, steering them toward the party. "Speaking of which, did you bring my present?"

Nathaniel held up a long gift-wrapped box. "You mean the bottle you're still three years too young to drink from?"

"That's the one!" Layne said, releasing them and snatching the present away. "This should liven things up!"

Kelly nodded toward the inflatable castle. "You might want to think twice about getting people drunk and shoving them in your ball pit."

"It's not a ball pit," Layne said, eyelashes fluttering. "It's a bounce house, and it happens to be my most ingenious plan yet. Just imagine me and a handsome boy jumping around in that thing, bumping into each other and getting all handsy until he falls on top of me and… well, paint your own picture."

Kelly grinned. "So who's the lucky guy?"

Layne nodded to one corner of the yard where three guys

were hanging out. Kelly didn't recognize any of them. Two had deep tans and jet-black hair. Unless he was mistaken, they were twins. Chatting with them was a lanky guy with pale skin and dark red hair.

"Which one are you after?" Kelly asked.

"Any of them will do," Layne said. "Or all of them. I'm hedging my bets. I figure I'm tripling my odds by inviting all three here."

"Are they from the youth group?" Kelly asked.

"Imported," Layne said proudly. "God bless the Internet!"

"Hungry," Nathaniel grumbled.

Kelly patted his arm affectionately. "If you'll excuse me, I have to go feed my man-beast."

Layne smiled pleasantly. "Have fun, you lucky bastard."

Kelly led Nathaniel to the buffet, positioning him in front of the deviled eggs and a giant bowl of potato salad. This kept him preoccupied enough that Kelly was able to mingle, catching up with people he hadn't seen recently, and one he saw plenty of.

"You guys look amazing together," Bonnie said with a heavy sigh. "I swear the sun came out when you two showed up here."

"Arguing with Emma again?"

"Do you see her here?" Bonnie asked, sounding more upset than angry.

Kelly winced. "Sorry. I'm sure you'll patch things up."

"Nope!" Bonnie said. "I'm back on the prowl, looking for my next great love. It could be anyone, even you. Wanna make out?"

"Seriously?"

Bonnie's shoulders slumped. "No. I'm so not over her."

"You two have always had your ups and downs," Kelly said carefully.

"Meaning?"

"That you've been here before and managed to get back into her good graces."

"That's true." She perked up a little. "Ever notice that when one of us is lucky in love, the other isn't?"

Kelly laughed. "It does seem that way."

"So me fighting with Emma means you and Nathaniel are doing good."

Kelly nodded happily.

"Have you used the 'B' word yet?"

"Boyfriend?" he asked. "Totally."

"And?"

"He was cool with it. When I first said it, he did this slow cocky grin thing that always drives me wild. Of course it was sort of gross, because I was on the phone with my mom, but I hung up and—"

"Heartbroken," Bonnie reminded him.

"Sorry," he said. Then, with more humility, he added. "Yes, we are doing quite well."

She punched him on the shoulder playfully. "I'm happy for you. Seriously."

"Thanks."

"Gather 'round, my precious guests!" Layne called. "Bring those singing voices with you because it's time!"

Everyone reconvened around a cake blazing with candles, sang the usual song, and watched as Layne rubbed his chin theatrically while trying to decide on a wish. Once he'd blown out the candles, he appeared expectant.

"Did it work?" he said. "Are you all madly in love with me?"

"Yes," they groaned obediently.

Layne looked pleased as he glanced around. Then he froze, his face filling with mock terror. "My beautiful palace!" he cried. "It's shrinking!"

Kelly turned, trying not to laugh when he saw one of the colorful towers flopped over like an impotent penis. For some reason, the castle was slowly deflating.

"This is worse than the Hindenburg disaster!" Layne said, rushing forward. "Oh, the humanity!"

"The air pump motor is still running," Nathaniel murmured from next to him. "The connection probably came loose."

"Think you can fix it?" Kelly asked.

Nathaniel puffed up his chest. "I'll try."

"Best boyfriend ever." Kelly smiled after him as he went to investigate. Then he turned back to the cake. Guests were still lingering around, eyeing it hungrily. Wanting to prevent a second disaster, he decided to cut slices before an angry mob formed. As he slopped cake onto paper plates and handed them out, the crowd began to thin. He decided to plate more servings so Layne wouldn't have to do the work later. He'd need one for himself too. And one for Nathaniel.

"I recognize you," said an unfamiliar voice.

Kelly glanced up and found one of the twins standing there. His eyes were cocoa brown, the tanned skin his natural tone, implying he might be of Latino descent. His teeth were bright white as they flashed at him. Kelly found himself smiling back automatically. Whoever he was, the guy was cute.

"I don't think we've met," Kelly said.

"No, but you're on my wall."

Kelly allowed himself to appear slightly concerned. "Excuse me?"

"You're a model, right?" the guy said. He offered a hand. "I'm Rico."

Kelly set down the cake knife so they could shake. "I'm Kelly."

"Kelly Phillips!" Rico gripped his hand tighter. "I'm right, aren't I?"

"Yeah," Kelly said, gently pulling away. "You recognize me?"

"Like I said, you're on my wall." Rico's smile was lopsided. "I hang up magazine ads of hot guys. You're actually on there twice."

"Which photos?"

"You're like a sheep herder in one. The other really freaks me out right now, because you're sitting in front of a cake like it's your birthday."

Kelly glanced down at the plates full of cake and laughed. "I promise this isn't my norm. Modeling and frosting don't go together well."

"Hey, I wanted to ask you about that," Rico said. "What do you think of this?" He lifted the front of his T-shirt, revealing a chiseled six-pack, smooth skin, light-brown nipples, an adorable bellybutton, and nicely toned pecs.

Kelly's eyes darted over all of this before the fabric dropped again, hiding it from view. "Uh," he responded.

"I want to be a model," Rico explained. "Think I've got what it takes?"

"You'll need more than just a good body," Kelly said. "You have to be patient. Photo shoots can be grueling, and some people are more photogenic than others, no matter how good they look in real life. Have you ever worked with a professional photographer?"

"Naw," Rico said. "I figured I should get into better shape before I try any of that. So you think it's a fun job? You get to travel and stuff, right?"

"I like it," Kelly said, turning his attention to the cake again, "but it's definitely not for everyone."

"It's just that my brother says I'm too ugly."

Kelly furrowed his brow as he cut another slice. "Aren't you guys identical?"

"To most people, yeah, but we can see the difference."

"Well don't listen to him, because you're gorgeous. In fact, I can give you the contact info of a guy who's always looking for fresh talent."

"You really think I'm gorgeous?"

Kelly raised his head. "Don't sound so surprised. No one's ever told you that before?"

Rico's teeth were brilliant against his brown skin. "Well, yeah, but not a model. Not one of the guys on my wall."

Kelly took in the half-lidded eyes, the shit-eating grin, and quickly turned his attention back to the cake again. Time to casually mention his boyfriend and let his admirer down easy. Before he could speak, Rico did so first.

"You've got something on your face. Like frosting."

Kelly glanced up, rubbing at himself. "Where?"

"Right here."

Rico reached out a hand, as if to help him, but hooked it behind Kelly's head. Their lips mashed together a split second later. He felt a tongue try to press into his mouth just before Rico was jerked away with such force that Kelly stumbled forward. His head was still spinning in confusion when he saw Rico being thrown to the ground. Then Nathaniel's massive bulk crashed on top of him and only Rico's legs could be seen, like when Dorothy's house landed on the Wicked Witch of the East.

Nathaniel's arm pulled back, ready to punch, and Kelly had a brief vision of police cars, a court date, and jail time. He lurched forward and managed to grab Nathaniel's bicep just as he was swinging. Kelly wasn't able to hold it back completely, but he did slow him enough that Rico could dodge. The bastard rewarded him for this rescue by popping Nathaniel on the chin. Now Kelly felt like clambering over Nathaniel so he could beat up Rico himself. He let go of Nathaniel, who didn't waste time slugging Rico's face and making his nose bleed. If he'd get out of the freaking way, Kelly intended to claw the kid's eyes out.

Bonnie skidded to a halt on her knees, pushing Rico down with one hand and raising the other to ward them off.

"Break it up!" she said, eyes wide. "Come on, guys. You don't want to do this!"

She was right. Kelly pulled on Nathaniel's shoulders, getting him to stand, while Bonnie continued to hold Rico down. Soon Layne rushed over, crouching next to him protectively.

"My poor Rico!" he cried. "What have you monsters done to him?" He gave them a theatrical wink before bending over Rico and dabbing at his face with a napkin. "Don't worry, baby, I'll make sure they don't hurt you again."

"I guess that's our cue," Kelly said, tugging away Nathaniel, who still looked hungry for violence. "Happy birthday, Layne. Sorry about all of this."

Layne had a hand on Rico's cheek and used it to turn his head away so he could mouth the words, "You're a genius!" Then he went back to fussing over his patient.

As long as he was happy. Kelly dragged Nathaniel out the side gate rather than through the house. He worried that someone had called the police, and he wanted to get away before they arrived. Releasing Nathaniel's arm, he reached instead for his hand, but it was knocked away.

Kelly stared in shock. "You *know* I didn't want to kiss him, right?"

Nathaniel just glowered, leading the way to the car.

"I'm driving," Kelly said, rushing after him. "You're way too emotional right now."

Nathaniel dug in his pocket for the keys and tossed them to him. They still weren't speaking. Maybe that was for the best. They both needed to calm down first. Once they were home again, they would talk this through and get it all sorted out.

But when they entered the apartment, Nathaniel went to the bedroom and shut the door behind him. Zero pawed at the wooden surface before looking up at Kelly in confusion.

"I guess it's just you and me," Kelly said. "Come."

Together they went outside so Zero could take care of business. When they returned, the bedroom was still sealed. All they could do was retreat to the living room and sit on the couch, waiting for a closed door to open to them again.

* * * * *

The sky was growing dark before Nathaniel came out of the bedroom. Kelly was in the kitchen cooking dinner because his mother always insisted most problems in the world could be fixed by a grilled cheese sandwich and a bowl of tomato soup. He hoped the smell would lure Nathaniel out, and if not, when he was ready to eat he could dunk his cold sandwich in the hot soup to warm it up again. Zero leapt up when the bedroom door squeaked, and followed Nathaniel into the kitchen, tail wagging.

"Hungry?" Kelly asked.

Nathaniel shook his head, eyes red from either crying or sleep. "We need to talk."

"Okay." Kelly turned off the burners and moved the skillet to a cool spot. His own appetite had fled now that he was faced with the unknown. They sat across from each other at the dining table, Kelly eager to plead his case. "I did *not* kiss him. I was just talking to the guy when he practically jumped me."

"I know," Nathaniel said. "I saw."

Kelly scrunched up his face. "Then why have you been shut in your room this whole time?"

Nathaniel broke eye contact. "It hurt. Seeing another person kiss you..." He shook his head. "You have no idea how bad that hurt me."

"I'm sorry," Kelly said. "Believe me when I say I didn't like it either."

"It's not your fault," Nathaniel said firmly. "That's what's so fucked up. I knew when I started falling for you that someone might get hurt, but I promised myself I wouldn't be the one to hurt you. And I trusted you would try your hardest not to hurt me. Today didn't break that trust. Neither one of us is at fault, and yet we still got hurt because we love each other."

"That's right," Kelly said. "And it sucks. There's nothing we can do about it, so we should have dinner together while badmouthing the guy. Or are you really going to let something this stupid tear us apart?" Nathaniel locked eyes with him, which was enough to make Kelly's blood run cold. "You better tell me what you're thinking," he said, voice shaking a little. "Right now!"

"This *will* happen again," Nathaniel said. "Even if we manage not to hurt each other, eventually one of us will get sick, or get bored, or someone else will get in the way. Maybe they won't mean to. Maybe my mom will need me when she's older and I'll have to go to her—"

"I'd go with you," Kelly said.

"—or maybe one of us will die young, or maybe you'll fall out of love with me because emotions can't be controlled. Or maybe we'll get to a point where we want to hurt each other. I know that's hard to imagine now, but relationships only get more complicated as time goes by."

"So we better avoid them?" Kelly snapped. "Why do you even leave the house? Why aren't you constantly scared of getting hit by a car or shot by some random lunatic?"

Nathaniel exhaled. "I never was before. Not until I fell in love with you. Now the idea of you being hurt, even just because I am—I hate it. I don't want to hurt you, but I'm going to now, because if I wait any longer, it'll hurt worse than you could ever imagine. The longer we let this go on, the greater the pain."

"You'll kill me," Kelly said, hands trembling. "That isn't a dramatic threat. I won't commit suicide or anything like that, but if you leave me now, it's going to kill me. *That's* how much I love you."

Nathaniel clenched his jaw and looked away, tears welling up in his eyes. "You have to trust me. This is for the best."

"There's something you're not telling me," Kelly said. "What is it? Do you have HIV? Some sort of terminal disease?"

Nathaniel shook his head wearily. "No."

"Something else. This has to do with your past. If you're going to dump my ass, you can at least tell me. Please!"

"It won't make a difference," Nathaniel said. "People aren't meant to be together like this. I know society pushes the idea, but it's false. We're happier on our own. We're stronger. You especially. Leaving me won't kill you. You never needed me to begin with."

"*I'm* not leaving *you*!" Kelly said. "And don't tell me what I need or how I feel. I wasn't happier before I met you. I was okay, but since that first day we spent together, when we ran around Austin trying to figure out how to plan something spontaneous—" His voice cracked. "You don't get to tell me how I feel."

"Fine," Nathaniel said, setting his jaw. "Then I'm doing this for me. I can't handle going through this again."

"Through *what*?" Kelly shouted. He felt like crying from exasperation alone. He didn't understand what was happening.

"People change," Nathaniel said. "It can't be helped. We love each other now, but you're just starting out and you don't realize how much heartbreak is around the corner. And I admit it. I'm scared of losing you or hurting you or a million other scenarios that keep me up at night. I'm a coward or maybe I'm just crazy. All I know is that I can't handle this anymore."

"You can," Kelly said. "You're so fucking strong. I *know* you can handle this!"

"You can't tell me what I feel either," Nathaniel said softly. "And you're wrong. I'm not strong. I can't do this anymore. I can't, and I won't."

Kelly argued with him. He wouldn't take no for an answer, wouldn't let things end this way. The night wore on. The food congealed in pots and pans, midnight came and went, and Kelly kept talking until his throat was raw and his eyes were sore from crying. But it didn't matter. Nathaniel really was strong. So strong that regardless of how hard Kelly tried to break him down, to climb that wall and reach him, he couldn't. Eventually Nathaniel stopped responding. He just crossed his arms over his chest and looked away. Kelly kept fighting, but when your opponent can't be budged and won't even strike back...

He stood up from the table, hunger gnawing at his stomach, his head aching, but these discomforts were nothing compared to the pain in his chest. Kelly felt like his heart had been cut open, the love flooding out as if to extinguish the hellish flames that threatened to burn them both to ash. He never knew he could feel so much, that it could pour from him, causing anguish in the process but never diminishing, never running out. Infinite. And so damn painful. Nathaniel was right. This hurt. More than Kelly had ever feared, and the fucked up thing was that the person he normally ran to for comfort, for protection, was sitting right in front of him. Untouchable. Unwilling. For once those hazel eyes weren't shining. The strong brow had lost its pride. Instead Nathaniel looked drained, and Kelly was forced to wonder if he too had been cut, only to find his feelings weren't infinite. Maybe his love had trickled to a stop and dried out, leaving him looking so pale and shaken. Kelly tried once more. A final plea. One that would sting too, just to see if maybe there wasn't something left inside of Nathaniel after all.

"This is going to hurt," Kelly said. "Way more than it does right now, way more than you imagined, because I know how much I love you, and I've felt how much you love me. Your worst nightmare comes true, starting *right now*, unless you risk the future with me."

When Nathaniel still didn't respond, Kelly forced himself to calm down. With a shuddering breath, he willed his pulse to steady. It didn't, but his hands stopped trembling. Kelly used them, bending over to stroke Zero's fur. Then he walked to the kitchen counter, grabbed his phone, and headed for the apartment door. He waited in front of it, one last thread of hope fraying before it snapped completely. Then he turned his back, opened the door, and walked outside. As he went, he felt he was leaving a piece of himself behind, but this time, there would be no artificial substitutes. What Kelly had lost tonight couldn't be replaced.

"I want him back."

"I know you do," Allison said. She sat not across from him but beside him on the couch, her legs angled toward him, her hand on top of his. She gave a little squeeze. "I'm sorry."

Kelly looked over at her hopefully. "You know what to do, right? You understand people."

"Yes," she said, almost reluctantly. "But I can't help someone who isn't willing to be helped. I don't know any more about what Nathaniel is going through than you do."

"You could talk to him."

"If he's open to the idea, I would be happy to. Feel free to give him my number."

Kelly looked down at the carpet. "I've been over there twice since that night."

"How did that go?"

"He wouldn't answer the door. I know he was there because his car was in the parking lot. He's shut me out completely, but maybe if I text him your number... Or better yet, you could call or stop by. Sometimes it's easier to talk to a stranger. If you could get through to him, then I thought maybe—"

Allison patted his hand and stood. She moved back to her usual spot, and Kelly could tell she meant business.

"Okay," he said. "I can't expect you to fix all my problems. I'm sorry. But please, tell me what to do."

Allison considered him. "I want you to listen," she said. "I want you to hear what I have to say, and this time I want you to think about it. Don't dismiss and don't argue. Understood?"

He nodded.

"You need to walk away," she said. "Put as much distance between yourself and Nathaniel as possible. Give yourself the space needed to build up your strength and keep your heart open along the way, because it's only a matter of time before you meet some beautiful boy who is willing to love you back."

"I don't want that other boy," Kelly said, shaking his head.

"You haven't met him yet," Allison said. "And I thought you promised to at least think about what I'm saying. What's the alternative? Even if you coax Nathaniel back into a relationship, it's only a matter of time before one of you ends up hurt again. That's perfectly normal, but for whatever reason, he can't cope. We can't change who he is, and we can't control the outside world, so you need to move on."

Kelly perked up. "You're saying that I should act like I've moved on. That way he won't feel so pressured."

Allison cocked her head. "Legally, I can't slap you. But I can call your mother and ask her to do it for me."

Kelly slumped into the couch. "I don't want to move on."

"You do," Allison said, "because right now isn't a happy place to be. You might wish you could turn back the clock and be with him again, but you don't want to remain stuck in this rut forever, do you?"

"No," he admitted.

"You've been through a lot," Allison said. "Think about how far you've come, how much you've survived."

Jared, William, the accident, the whole mess with Jason, a modeling career, and Nathaniel… All of it seemed to happen so quickly, without much time to breathe in between.

"Maybe it's time to focus on yourself," Allison said. "Just for a little while. Find your bearings, learn to be free again. Everything else can wait. Trust me."

He looked at her, feeling apprehensive about the suggestion.

And also a little intrigued. Kelly had once envied William for doing the same, for leaving behind everything he loved. Now Kelly wished they had stayed in touch. How had life worked out for him? Did William regret his decision? Probably not, or he would have come slinking back to Austin. Instead he was out there living a new adventure every day.

And yet, how could William not regret leaving Jason behind, even just occasionally? Having someone who loved you so completely and then consciously choosing to separate yourself from them… Just the thought of saying goodbye to Nathaniel, turning his back to all the memories they made together and all the potential Kelly still felt they had, was enough to make his throat painfully tight. But what choice did he have? To show up at Nathaniel's apartment night after night, eyes burning with tears as he pounded on a door that wouldn't open? Kelly was going to hurt anyway. He could do so while sitting in the same bedroom where he'd longed for Jared, where he regretted all that happened with William, and where he now agonized over Nathaniel. Or he could leave, venture out into the world and see what else it had to offer.

"Perhaps a short break from modeling," Allison was saying, "A little time off at home or a weekend road trip to the Gulf of Mexico."

"Farther," Kelly said.

"Sorry?"

Kelly swallowed against the emotion rising in him. He thought about it carefully and nodded. "I'm going way farther than the borders of Texas. The world is a big place. Why not lose myself in it while I'm trying to find myself? Is that crazy?"

Allison considered him a moment and smiled. "It's worked for other people I know."

In romantic movies, people often stand in front of an airport gate, waiting to board their flight, just as Kelly was doing now. Elsewhere, their estranged lover would rush through traffic to the airport. Once there they would practically jump over crowds to reach the gate in time to deliver an all-important message or last minute declaration of love. A shame then, that such things didn't happen anymore, if they ever had.

Kelly had parted with his family just before the security

check. Worry had never left his parents' faces. Royal had cried. Few things were more heartbreaking than a sixteen-year-old boy struggling with his tears. Bonnie wasn't so passive with her emotions, pleading with him to reconsider and coming up with a million different schemes to keep him from leaving. But Kelly was determined, and after a round of hugs and kisses, he had left them there. He had glanced back as the security personnel puzzled over his leg. His family hadn't budged. They were probably still standing there now, just in case he changed his mind.

"Ladies and gentlemen, we will begin boarding flight 245 with service to—"

Kelly stepped forward. Technically he was still disabled, and on days like today, he took advantage of that. He wanted to be on the plane as soon as possible. He supposed he could wait around, just in case Nathaniel tried to emulate one of those old movies. If so, he was probably writhing on the ground right now, surrounded by TSA agents as they shot him with their Tasers.

If he even knew about Kelly leaving. He probably did. Kelly had told Marcello, who hoped he would continue to model on occasion. Kelly hadn't completely shot down the idea but already knew he never would. Mostly because Marcello would inevitably send Nathaniel on an assignment, intending they patch things up. That would be sweet but misguided, since it wasn't their relationship that needed repairing. Nathaniel did. And maybe Kelly did too. He handed his ticket to the flight attendant manning the gate and lifted up a pant leg to show why he was boarding early. When he reached the jet bridge, he did glance back once, just in case Nathaniel was lurching his way toward him, TSA agents clinging to his legs. But of course he wasn't there.

As soon as he was seated on the plane and buckled in, Kelly closed his eyes and kept them that way until the flight landed again. Once at the airport, he splurged on a taxi, the last money he would spend so carelessly. He instructed the driver to take him downtown, asking him to stop when Kelly saw enough crowds and life. While the driver fumbled his luggage out of the trunk, Kelly stepped onto the sidewalk, allowing people to swarm around him. Nobody knew who he was here. Nobody cared. Somehow that felt right, because he would be relying only on himself from now on. After paying the driver and watching the taxi speed away, Kelly looked skyward. He thought of all the people he loved and all they had provided him. He imagined each of their faces, ending with Nathaniel's.

"Goodbye," Kelly whispered.

Then he picked up his belongings and disappeared into the crowd.

Epilogue
New York, 2013

Kelly picked up the electronic image of a woman's face and leaned it against a pasta jar left by the previous tenant. When it started to slip, he grabbed two cans of peaches and used them to pin it in place. While he was doing all of this, the woman's eyes moved around the room, her voice commenting on everything she saw.

"Oh, look at those cabinets!" his mother was saying. "Aren't they retro! And how fun it is to see them! Isn't this the most wonderful way to communicate?"

Kelly peered at the tablet's screen and tried to shake the feeling that his mother's head was sitting on the kitchen counter. Or that he owned a magical painting from Hogwarts. His parents had mailed the tablet to him as a surprise present, its true purpose soon revealed when they started video conferencing with alarming frequency. At least his mother understood that she needed to stay on camera. Last time his father had called, Kelly had spent most of the conversation staring at a distant sofa.

"Kelly, can you hear me?"

"Loud and clear," he said. "Just a little lag, that's all."

"How are things in the Big Apple? Is my baby a famous artist yet?"

"Not quite," Kelly said, glancing down the counter where a stack of photos gathered dust. "The thing about this city is that I'm one of a million other guys who think they know how to take a photo."

"Then why don't you head back to Florida?" his mother asked. "You liked it there so much. And you weren't so far."

"Because it's filled with tourists taking photos."

"Why did you leave Montana again? You always sent such beautiful pictures of the landscape."

"Because mountains don't buy photos from struggling artists, and there wasn't much else there. And before you mention Seattle or Minneapolis or any of the other places I've been, I think it's time to admit that location isn't the problem. My photos simply aren't good enough."

Laisha pursed her lips and shook her head, as if he was being silly. "I love your photos."

"Because you love me. That doesn't mean my photos are any good."

"You know they are."

"Maybe, but I think they would need to be exceptional. Everyone is taking photos today. Every single phone has a camera, and people carry them around everywhere. I still love photography as an art form, but it's become too commonplace to make a living from."

"You just need to put together a book," his mother said. "Something nice and big for the coffee table. That's what sells."

Kelly managed a cheerful tone for her. "Great idea. I'll look into it."

"So," she said, smiling broadly at him. "I have a birthday coming up next week."

Kelly already felt guilty about it. He would barely be able to make rent this month. He didn't have enough money to send her a worthwhile present, and he definitely couldn't afford what she really wanted.

"Is my baby coming to see me?" she asked, eyes shining.

At times like these, Kelly missed an old-fashioned telephone, because seeing his mother's hopeful expression wasn't easy. Maybe if he squeezed his food budget, he could manage a bus ticket. "Of course," he said. "You know I'll be there."

Laisha read him like a book. "Is money tight, honey? We can send you a plane ticket."

"Money is fine," he lied. The pasta jar the tablet was propped against had been empty since he moved in. Then again, he'd managed to stretch his modeling savings for three years, which was an achievement in itself. Only recently was he beginning to run dry. "I'm not letting you give me a present on your birthday."

"Okay," she said, still not satisfied. "Have you sold anything from your big exhibition?"

"No," he admitted. "And it's just a record store that allowed me to hang a few things on the wall. Considering how many people listen to vinyl these days, it's quite possible no one has seen them yet."

"Maybe this will help." His mother leaned over, treating him to a close-up of her cleavage as she rustled through papers on the kitchen table. Kelly poked at the screen, searching for an option to disable the video feed. "Your father cut this out of the paper last month, but I'm sure it's still good. Here it is!" She leaned back, returning to focus and holding a scrap of newspaper that she read from. "*The Eric Conroy Foundation supports artistic voices struggling to be heard, exhibiting new talent at our gallery in downtown Austin or awarding grants and scholarships to budding individuals. For more information, please visit*—then it has the website address right here. What do you think?"

Kelly smirked. "I don't really see myself as a 'budding individual.'"

"No, but maybe they'd like to exhibit some of your photos. You're a local artist who travels the world. I'm sure they'll be thrilled."

Kelly shrugged. "Maybe I'll check it out while I'm there."

"So you're coming?" she asked.

"Yes," Kelly said. "I'll figure it all out and let you know my times tomorrow."

"You sure you don't need money?"

"I'm sure."

The view on the screen went crazy for a moment, zooming around the kitchen. When it settled, it was pointed at his father's man-boobs. Cleavage. Again. "Kelly," he said. "I have bad news. Your Aunt Myrtle passed away. I'm so sorry. The good news is that she left you five hundred dollars."

Kelly shook his head. "I don't have an Aunt Myrtle."

"You don't anymore," his father said with a chuckle.

"Really? Your sister just died and you're joking about it? Or is it mom's sister you're laughing over, which seems even colder."

"Uh… She was more of a family friend who we pretended was an aunt."

"Nice try," Kelly said. "Tell my little brother I love him. Now if you'll excuse me, I have more important things to do than talk to two crazy old people."

"We love you!" his parents said simultaneously.

"I love you too."

Kelly tapped the icon to hang up. Then he turned around to face the cramped kitchen. He had some beans to count. Half he would eat, the rest would go toward bus fare.

The Eric Conroy Gallery was just on the edge of the Second Street District in downtown Austin. After parking, Kelly had to wander up and down side streets to find the location, almost missing it behind the overgrown trees. As he crossed the street and saw the art displayed in the window, his gut filled with dread. Once he had approached galleries with interest, curious about what other photographers were doing, or checking out the art on display despite not understanding the medium. Then of course the owner would approach him, eager to make a sale, and be disappointed when learning he was yet another artist hoping to put bread on the table.

At least today he had an appointment. Mr. Wyman had sounded nice enough on the phone. A little gruff, maybe, but he didn't sigh in irritation like the last few gallery owners, or hang up the phone after uttering those two dreaded words: *Not interested.*

Kelly adjusted the portfolio folder under his arm and opened the front door. The gallery consisted of at least three rooms. In addition to the main space he stood in now, two wings branched off, one to each side. A desk sat farther back in the room, currently unoccupied. Kelly approached it slowly while glancing around. Only paintings hung on the wall. There wasn't a photo in sight. Had he told Mr. Wyman which medium he worked in? He sure hoped so, or all this might be a waste of time. He passed a sculpture of an old man, arms so long the knuckles touched the floor, and tried to take this as a positive sign that the Eric Conroy Gallery was open to many forms of art.

Kelly set his portfolio on the desk, noticing the door to a back room just as someone came through it. The guy was handsome. Dark skin, darker hair, and eyes like ice. The man stopped in his tracks, half a sandwich hanging out of his mouth, and stared back. They knew each other, didn't they? Kelly had travelled endlessly and met a lot of people over the last few years. His mind raced through a catalog of faces and places, trying to find a match. Maybe he wasn't looking far enough back. Maybe this was from before he left Austin.

Oh.

Tim, Jason Grant's imaginary boyfriend. This was... awkward? Or perhaps it was a good opportunity. Kelly couldn't decide if it hurt his chances or not, so he put on his best poker face and pretended they were strangers. Tim seemed to adopt a similar strategy, or maybe he didn't remember Kelly at all. Either way, he walked to the desk and set the remaining sandwich on a piece of junk mail.

"Can I help you?" he asked.

"I have an appointment with a Mr. Wyman."

"Kelly," Tim said, but not as a question. His expression betrayed him momentarily, as he either made the connection or chastised himself for not having done so sooner. He extended a hand. "I'm Tim."

"Nice to meet you," Kelly said as they shook.

They stared at each other another moment. Then Tim gestured with his head.

"That your portfolio?"

"Yes indeed."

"Great. Pull up a chair and let's take a look."

Before Kelly sat, he opened the large folder and took out a few stacks. "They're organized by theme," he explained. "Landscapes, architecture, portraits, and abstract. I don't do a lot of that last category, and you might be wondering why architecture isn't grouped with landscapes, which to me refers more to nature, even though I put the animal photos in with portraits. Of course sometimes people are in the landscapes, complicating matters. I tried to go by percentages of what makes up each composition."

Tim glanced up at him. "Don't forget to breathe. You might as well kick back and get comfortable. Art speaks for itself."

Kelly sat and tried to appear casual, even though his muscles were tense. Every photo Tim flipped through made Kelly want to launch into another barrage of explanations. But Tim was right. If his photos were good enough, they would tell their own story.

"I like this one," Tim said, holding up an image of a gritty old farmer standing next to his tractor, one hand resting on the bonnet like it was his faithful steed. "Ohio?"

"Kansas," Kelly said. "Same as that one."

To capture the next image, Kelly had climbed halfway up a utility pole. The only things in-frame were waves and waves of wheat, ready to be harvested.

Tim grunted and continued flipping through the photos, occasionally setting one aside. Kelly hoped that was a good sign. He seemed more interested in architecture than landscapes, singling out more of those photos, especially a series Kelly had taken of abandoned buildings and homes in Detroit that were slowly deteriorating. Then came efforts of a more personal nature.

That smoky photo of Jared, or the one of William staring off into the distance that always made his heart melt. A transsexual couple he had befriended in New York, each heading in opposite directions in regard to their genders. A photo of Royal on the beach in Florida, eyebrows raised over his sunglasses, a group of girls farther down the sand mirrored in the lenses. That had been a good catch. Tim flipped through more familiar faces, pausing when he got to one of Kelly. It was the only self-portrait he had included, one he hoped was humble since in it he was about to trip over a dog, a look of sheer joy on his face as he ran for the first time in years. Not that his artificial leg could be seen, because Nathaniel was in the foreground, blocking it from view. His limbs were slightly blurred, arms and legs in almost the exact same position as Kelly's, as if they were in synch. Kelly's imminent fall suggested otherwise. In more than one way.

Tim stared long and hard at this photo. Then he set it down. "You a runner?"

"Yes," Kelly said. He allowed himself a mischievous smile. "Confused?"

Tim considered him. "You remember me."

Kelly nodded. "Of course. Last time we met, I didn't have this swanky peg leg." He stood and walked around the desk, lifting up one leg of his slacks until he got to the knee.

"You can run on that thing?" Tim asked with interest.

"That and anything else I want. They upgraded me to an X3 recently. Now I'm waterproof. Showers, swimming pools, random assaults by water balloons—whatever happens, I'm good."

"Maybe we can go for a jog together sometime," Tim said. "I'd love to see you in action."

"Sure," Kelly said. "Just try to keep up." He returned to his seat and rolled down his pant leg. "I actually have your boss to thank for this. I used to model for Marcello years ago, and he's been paying for any expenses ever since. Believe me when I say prosthetic limbs aren't cheap. Not when they're this state-of-the-art."

"Big guy, big heart," Tim said, "although he isn't my boss. Marcello is my..." He appeared puzzled. "The thought is kind of disturbing, but I guess you could say Marcello is my best friend. Speaking of which, I didn't know you were close to this guy." He tapped on the photo. "That's Nathaniel, right?"

"Yeah," Kelly said, his voice a little hoarse. "Listen, it's cool that we both know the same people, and as much as I really want this gig, I don't want it for the wrong reasons. Judge my photos by their own merits, if they have any at all."

"They definitely do," Tim said. "You have some themes going here that will really resonate with the public. I'd like to single out a few, and assuming this is just a sample, maybe bulk up some of those themes for the exhibition. I'd also recommend a small selection that tells your story in images. Sort of a visual biography. We can work together on that and—"

"Wait," Kelly said, trying not to grin. "Is this all hypothetical? Or are we really going to do this?"

"Oh, it's going to happen!" Tim said. "The world needs to see what real photography looks like again. Enough with the selfies! The only question is when. Your contact information has you living in New York. Is that current?"

Kelly nodded. "I'm down here visiting my family."

"How long?"

"Just a week, but I could always come back later in the year, if need be."

Tim cleared his desk enough to check a large planner. "Or, if you can extend your stay by another week, yours could replace an exhibition that was canceled because the artist burned all his paintings in protest."

"What was he protesting against?"

"Success, I guess, because you can't sell a pile of ashes. We'd have to start advertising and get invitations sent out right away. Sound good?"

Kelly chuckled madly. "Let's do it!"

"Cool," Tim said. "Now comes the boring part."

First they went over a basic contract. The gallery was non-profit, so if by some miracle Kelly sold anything, he would keep all the profits. He had to agree not to hold the gallery liable for anything that went wrong, but aside from that, it was all straightforward. Then he assembled a list of people he wanted to invite. Kelly doubted anyone he knew would travel across the country to join him, so he starting scrolling through his cell phone for old friends who still lived in the area.

"Should I invite Jason?" Kelly asked.

Tim grimaced. "Lately, anything that reminds him of William

makes him start moping around. A month ago we were watching TV together when a Coast Guard recruitment commercial came on. Jason got up, went to the kitchen, and came back with a bottle of rum and a bad attitude."

"Really? So they're no longer…"

Tim shook his head. "I don't think so. And I planned on using some of your photos of William. I suppose we could leave them out."

"That's okay," Kelly said. "I'll catch up with him some other time."

"Marcello will want to be there," Tim said, jotting down his name. "And I'm assuming you'll want Nathaniel there as well."

Kelly opened his mouth to correct him, but not a sound came out. Tim's attention was on the list, his messy handwriting already spelling out the most precious name from his past. One Kelly still found on his lips occasionally, and even though he managed to avoid speaking it, the name was forever scribbled across his heart.

Not all of Kelly's modeling jobs had been memorable, but there was one he was unlikely to ever forget. He'd been flown to Belgium, where a high-end client wanted to advertise a new line of winter scarves. What better way to do draw attention to such an item of clothing than make sure it was all the model wore? Kelly had been stripped bare, given a ridiculously long scarf, and had been asked to stride back and forth through knee-deep snow. Luckily the snow was fake, as was the winter backdrop, but he was still uncomfortable. Creative use of tape ensured the scarf just happened to be covering his business. Most of the time. When it came unstuck under the hot studio lights, the photographers would pause until this could be corrected. But Kelly had still checked every single image to make sure his integrity hadn't been compromised.

As exposed as he'd felt back then, that was nothing compared to how he felt now. His exhibition was in full swing, every wall covered in his photos. Strangers were pouring in from the street, grabbing free drinks and scrutinizing his art. They had no reason to be kind, or to hold back in their opinions. Part of Kelly felt like hiding, but the rest had him patrolling the room, ready to defend himself if need be. So far everything seemed to be going well. Occasionally he took breaks from his nervous marching to greet old friends.

"Allison Cross plus one."

Kelly spun around, beaming at her and offering a hand. "It's been a long time!" he said.

Allison smiled back. "In my occupation, that's a good thing. I'd be a lot more worried if you were still on my couch every other week."

"I'm sure it's only a matter of time before I return," Kelly joked. He turned his attention to her companion, a short and slender guy with brownish-blond hair. "And you must be Mr. Allison."

The man opened his mouth to protest, but Allison got there first. "This is Ben, my gay husband. He fills in when my real husband is busy. He has his own opening tonight."

"Artist?" Kelly asked.

"Theater. He doesn't perform, but occasionally he writes. And this one here," she put an arm around Ben and squeezed, "usually sings in his plays, but he insisted on a break because he's sad about his man-baby moving out of the house."

"Man-baby?" Kelly asked.

Again Ben opened his mouth, but Allison was quicker. "The kid is twenty-three years old, but Ben here acts like he's dropping his child off at kindergarten for the first time. Ain't that right?"

Ben waited, making sure he wasn't going to be interrupted again. Then he replied. "Your gay husband wants a gay divorce."

"Denied," Allison said, raising her eyebrows and glancing around the room. "We're going to check out your pretty photos now, Kelly. I don't know how long you're planning to be in Austin, but you're always welcome on my couch. And by that I mean the one in my home. Come hang out sometime."

"I will," Kelly said. "Thanks."

He watched her lead Ben away. Then he turned and ran headlong into someone else. Luckily he was one of the most cushioned people anyone could bump into.

"Do try to control yourself," Marcello said. "I know it's been a dreadfully long time since we've seen each other, but dry humping hardly seems appropriate."

"If you hadn't been creeping up behind me..." Kelly said.

Marcello smiled. "I did consider wrapping you up in a net,

but only so I could drag you away for some location shooting. Why must you break my heart and refuse all my job offers?"

Kelly gestured to the nearest wall. "I feel more comfortable behind the lens these days."

"The art world is a richer place for it," Marcello said, "but my clients are made poorer by your absence. I don't just mean that metaphorically. I'm not sure you understand how lucrative your campaigns were."

"If this doesn't work out, maybe I'll come crawling back to you."

"I doubt that very much," Marcello said. "From what I understand, there have already been three sales."

"Really?" Then Kelly rolled his eyes because he saw his mother smiling at him from across the room. "I'm guessing my parents bought all three."

"Two," Marcello said. "I purchased one to give as a gift. Regardless, sales are sales, and I have a feeling success will continue to hound you. Speaking of which. I have something to help you along. A present."

"I really don't need anything," Kelly said, looking away.

"Oh? Not even a Canon EOS 1-D?"

"No. Thank you." Kelly did a double take. "Wait, what? Those cameras are crazy expensive!"

"Indeed. I merely wanted to examine the latest model and had one of my assistants place an order. The silly fool ordered two. Returning the superfluous camera would be a hassle. Clearly I can only trust myself with such matters, and my time is much too precious. I thought you might be interested instead."

Kelly took a deep breath. "I couldn't."

"You might as well. I'll write it off as a business expense."

"But you've given me so much already. Speaking of which, thank you for the X3. The first day I got it, I spent nearly an hour in the shower, just standing there."

Marcello's expression remained neutral. "X3? Is that some sort of fancy new vibrator?"

Kelly snorted. "No. It's the newest prosthetic leg. You flew me back to Germany earlier this year to have it fitted."

"Ah," Marcello said. "I'm afraid you misunderstand. While you were still in my employ, I made the necessary calls to get you into their field testing program. Aside from the limo drive to the airport that day, I never paid a dime to support this enterprise."

"Nice try. I was worried about the bill and asked the technician about it. The field test program isn't free. Not for me, but she said the bill had been taken care of."

"I'm sure it was. Just not by me."

Kelly's grin faded. "Then who paid for it?"

Marcello examined his fingernails. "I was sworn to secrecy long ago. Life is more fun with a bit of mystery thrown in, isn't it? Anyway, do come by my office tonight and at least look at the camera. I'd value your opinion. There are other issues I'd like to discuss as well. I'll be working late. In fact, I'll make sure a car is waiting for you when the gallery closes, yes? Wonderful!"

Marcello patted him on the arm and waddled away. Kelly spun around, searching the guests. He spotted his father pointing enthusiastically at one of the framed photos, chatting with a visitor who had wandered in. Kelly supposed his parents could have paid for his leg, but he didn't see why they would keep it a secret. And they would have had Royal accompany him on his most recent trip to Germany. His mother had worried about Kelly going alone.

In his gut, he already knew. Kelly walked from the main room to one of the wings, as if sensing him there. Sure enough, at the far wall with his back turned, a broad-shouldered figure in a tuxedo studied a photo. Kelly didn't need him to turn around, since his body remained completely familiar. The direction his short hair moved in before swirling at the crown. The shape of his ears and the lobes Kelly used to playfully nibble. Even the two freckles on his neck, toward the right-hand side and just below his hairline. More than once Kelly had stared at all these things as they lay in bed together. Those tiny details and more came rushing back from the past and caused his heart to pound. They say time heals all wounds, but not when time itself is the cause of them. Kelly felt pained that so many years had passed—so many empty days they could have filled with each other.

Nathaniel moved away from the photo, walking toward the main hall but using the far entrance. Kelly watched him go, and could swear he turned to look just before disappearing from sight. His curiosity getting the better of him, Kelly hurried to the main room. He went to the center, looking in every direction, but saw no sign of Nathaniel. The other wing then?

"Excuse me? I'm told you're the artist here."

Kelly glanced over at an older man. He had a camera around his neck, and as it turned out, he was from a local paper. He wanted to take some photos, which Kelly agreed to, and then he wanted to talk shop. The journalist was nice enough, but Kelly remained distracted during their conversation. He kept glancing around, when he saw another familiar face.

William. Kelly wasn't completely shocked by this, since they had recently talked on the phone. His heart didn't suffer palpitations either, not like when he'd seen Nathaniel. Sure, memories came rushing back, and as they walked toward each other, some distant part of him felt like they should kiss before holding each other tight. But they wouldn't. He noticed Jason and Emma then. Their presence was unexpected, but he didn't mind.

"Surprise!" he said, waving and doing a little skip.

William stepped forward and hugged him, the sensation oddly comfortable.

"You're walking," he murmured into Kelly's ear.

"I am," Kelly responded, throat feeling tight. "No harm done. It's like it never happened."

William pulled back, tears in his eyes. Kelly understood how this must feel to him. Like redemption. He was more than happy to grant it. He swallowed against his own rising emotions and looked at Emma and Jason, who remained puzzled.

"Prosthetic leg," he said. "It's amazing what they can do these days. When Marcello found out I was looking into them, he insisted on flying me to Germany, where they have the very best prosthetics in the world. All paid for by the company."

Or so he had always believed. But what else could he say? That the estranged love of his life had been secretly supporting him all this time? He didn't even know if it was true. Maybe Marcello was—

"I love that man," William said. "I love you!"

Kelly rolled his eyes. "Someone fetch William a drink. He gets so emo!"

"Guilty as charged," William said, "and drinking only makes me more emotional, so we'd better stay sober. Unless you want to see a grown man cry."

"Tempting," Kelly said, looking him over. Military service had been good to William. The muscles beneath his navy-blue suit jacket appeared more toned than ever, and his hair was buzzed and bright from exposure to the sun. He'd even managed to get a light tan! None of this filled Kelly with yearning though, which was probably for the best, because Jason was clearly still enamored with William.

"I didn't expect to see you two here," Kelly said, making sure his tones were friendly. "Thanks for coming."

Jason nodded. "It's good to see you again. Sorry for not staying in touch."

"It's fine," Kelly said. "Modeling kept me busy. Then I got tired of the scene and ran away from home. What about you?"

"Me? Oh, I've been…" Jason grasped for words before his shoulders sagged. "Honestly, I'm right where you left me."

Emma rolled her eyes and nudged him. "You never did know how to sell yourself. Jason has been volunteering at the local animal shelter and keeps coming up with fundraising ideas, enough so that the shelter has been able to expand. He also trains new volunteers."

"That's really cool," Kelly said, "and much more worthwhile than what I've been doing. Trust me."

"I don't know about that," Jason said. "People seem to be enjoying your art."

Kelly smiled. "They feel sorry for me. But if you'd like to look around, I'd be interested in your opinion."

"Yeah," Jason said. "Of course."

"I'll catch up with you guys," William said.

Kelly hesitated. As interesting as reconnecting with his ex-boyfriend would be, his search for Nathaniel had been interrupted. Then again, maybe he could do both at once. "Walk with me?" Kelly offered.

"Gladly."

Together they strolled over to the nearest wall of photos. He introduced every piece, and as William carefully considered each photo, Kelly casually turned to search the room. Still no Nathaniel. After ten minutes of this, Kelly turned back around to find William checking him out instead.

"You look good," he said.

Kelly didn't hide his surprise. "If you hadn't shown up with Jason tonight, I'd think you were flirting with me."

"Don't worry," William said. "I wouldn't be so cruel as to subject you to dating me again."

"Oh, it wasn't all that bad," Kelly said. "I've had worse."

"Really?" William asked. "Just how many prosthetic limbs do you have?"

"Ha! Just one, and when you put it that way, you do sound absolutely villainous. But you're not. You've always been a good person."

William appeared vulnerable. "I'm trying to be. I really am."

"You already are," Kelly said. "I'm disappointed. I thought the Coast Guard would leave you more confident."

"That was the plan." William sighed. "And yeah, most of the time I feel like I've gotten my life on track. Funny how temptation can sneak up on you though."

Kelly raised an eyebrow. "Spill it."

"I came back to Austin hoping to sweep Jason off his feet, only to discover that someone else got there first. He's with another guy, and I want to wedge my way between them, but we both know that can lead to disaster."

Kelly tried to hide his amusement and failed. "I can't decide if this is karma or not, but I'm pretty sure you deserve it."

William grinned. "You're such a bastard."

"I know. But you'll be fine. From what I can gather, Jason is still madly in love with you. Give it a few weeks and I'm sure things will shake out in your favor."

"I hope you're right."

They moved to the next photo, but only because it seemed the natural thing to do. "Ever regret leaving town all those years ago?" Kelly asked.

William thought about it and shook his head. "No. I became the person I was meant to be. I wasn't a good boyfriend to you, and I wouldn't have been to Jason, had I stuck around. All the time on my own has made me feel complete, you know? I've let myself be selfish enough that if I get another shot with Jason, I'll be ready to give all of myself to him. What about you? Do you regret leaving?"

Kelly glanced back toward the main room, just in time to see Nathaniel slipping out the front door. So much for meeting him again. He continued to stare at the door, hoping to see him reappear. When he didn't, Kelly took a deep breath. "I can't say I feel complete… But no, I don't regret it. Leaving was the right thing to do."

* * * * *

The lights of the gallery were shut off one by one. Kelly stood outside on the sidewalk, watching Tim as he locked the front door. When he was finished, he walked over with his hands in the pockets of his slacks. The hour was late enough that traffic had all but disappeared, the clicking of Tim's dress shoes loud on the sidewalk.

"Five sales," he said. "That's very successful for an opening night. Especially at those prices."

Kelly nodded, trying to muster some sense of satisfaction, but somehow the night felt like a failure. Holding his first real exhibition, seeing all those old friends, having his family there for one of his proudest moments—even the sales, which showed appreciation for his art—and yet part of him felt emptier than before.

"Cheer up," Tim said, patting him on the shoulder. "There's always a weird sort of melancholy at the end of such things. You'll get through it."

"Yeah, you're right." Once he was back in New York, all of this would be a distant dream.

"You need a ride?"

"No." Kelly nodded across the street at a waiting sedan. A man leaned against the door, smoking a cigarette. "I'm meeting Marcello. He's giving me a really expensive camera, which means he wants something."

Tim nodded knowingly. "I'd warn you against doing whatever he wants, but honestly, you won't know what that is until it's too late."

Kelly chuckled. "Too true. Thanks for this. The exhibition and all the work you put into it."

"My pleasure." Tim took the keys out of his pocket, tossed them in the air and caught them again. "Take care of yourself, Kelly Phillips."

"You too."

He watched Tim climb into a silver car and drive away. Then Kelly looked across the street and sighed. He was tired. Too tired for a mental sparring match with Marcello. If only that camera wasn't so unbelievably amazing. He supposed the fruit a serpent once offered to Eve must have been the shiniest, most juiciest apple imaginable. Sometimes a person couldn't help but take a bite.

Kelly strolled across the street. The driver perked up and opened the door for him. After he slipped inside the car and got comfortable, Kelly closed his eyes and listened to the rumble of the motor and the gentle hum of tires on the street. When these sounds ceased, he opened his eyes again just as the driver opened the door.

He stepped outside the car. The studio hadn't changed at all, its drab exterior still belying the artificial glamour created within. A figure stood in the open doorway with a similar vibe as his driver. Sure enough, Kelly's driver approached this stranger and offered him a cigarette. By the time Kelly strolled up, they were talking sports.

"Sorry," Kelly interrupted. "But are you still going to be here when I come back downstairs?"

"Of course," his driver said. "I'm supposed to stay here all night, if need be."

"Oh. Thanks." Kelly felt a little uneasy as he walked down the hallway, the fluorescent lights flickering as they always did. The elevator doors opened just as he approached. He could imagine Marcello sitting at his desk, watching the security monitor and chuckling at how easily he lured flies into his web. Kelly entered the elevator and turned around, refusing to act surprised or impressed when on its own, it took him to the top floor. In fact, he made sure his expression was positively bored when the doors opened again and he strolled into Marcello's office.

"Don't let them close!" a voice shouted.

Kelly's eyes went wide as a figure leapt over one of the lounge couches and charged at him. He stepped aside just in time for Nathaniel to slam into the metal elevator doors, which had already shut. Then he jabbed at the button to open them again, snarling in frustration when they didn't. Kelly took this opportunity to examine him. Stubble still covered his clenching jaw, the rolled-up sleeves of his dress shirt revealed arms Kelly had once clung to for support, and the strong brow still softened somewhat when turning to him.

"Nice to see you too," Kelly said. "What's next? Are you going to try jumping out a window just to avoid me?"

Nathaniel took a deep breath and huffed. "I'm not avoiding you. I just don't like being trapped. I called a technician over an hour ago."

"Marcello has someone waiting at the door. He probably sent the technician away already. So where is he? Hiding behind his desk, or can he control all of this from home?"

"From his phone," Nathaniel said, leaning his back against the elevator doors and sighing. "I don't want to know what he's playing at."

"He probably thought this was the only way he could get us to talk." Kelly crossed his arms over his chest. "I saw you at the gallery. Why did you run off?"

"I had an awkward conversation," Nathaniel said.

"That's it? That's why you didn't even say hello?"

"You wouldn't understand."

"What else is new?"

Nathaniel's jaw clenched a few more times. Then he pushed away from the elevator and plopped down on one of the couches, burying his face in his palms. Kelly watched him a moment, then went and sat across from him. On the table between them were two presents. One had been opened already, scraps of torn wrapping paper obscuring it from view. The other was a box. The camera, no doubt. An unopened bottle of wine sat near it, condensation dripping down its surface. Next to it, two empty glasses waited. The lights in the office were low, and the air smelled of scented candles, even though they had already been extinguished. Marcello's intent was more than obvious to them both, which made it hurt that Nathaniel seemed so distraught by the prospect. Was nothing left between them?

"I know about the prosthetics," Kelly said softly. "You've been paying for them all this time."

Nathaniel's hands dropped into his lap, his eyes searching. "Marcello told you?"

"I figured it out. I'd offer to pay you back, but I don't have any money. Maybe someday I can—"

"No," Nathaniel said firmly. "I want to do this. For you. Please let me."

Kelly studied him. "Why? I know you promised I would never have to worry about it, but I don't hold you to that anymore. It made sense when you loved me, but not now."

Nathaniel's expression was pained. "That's not fair. Don't make me say it."

"Why not?" Kelly said. "Is that the cure? Does staying silent keep the feelings at bay?"

Nathaniel shook his head. "No."

"And did it ever stop hurting? All these years we've been apart, can you honestly say you avoided what you fear most? Because my heart has been aching since that night. No matter how far I go and how many other people I welcome into my life, there's always a part of me that yearns for you. I've learned to live without you, Nathaniel, and I can keep on doing so. But I don't want to, and the pain is never going to go away. I'm guessing the same is true for you."

"Yeah," Nathaniel said, his voice hoarse. "I love you, Kelly. I'm a piece of shit and I ruined everything, but I love you so much that I think it might be worth the pain."

"It doesn't have to hurt," Kelly said, his chest heaving. "Not all the time. I swear."

Nathaniel's eyes were desperate with hope. Or fear or just pure emotion. Kelly didn't know, and that troubled him. He loved the man so much that sometimes he awoke in the middle of the night, the dreams of them being together again so beautiful that they drove him to tears. But there remained so much he didn't know about Nathaniel, and that made him question everything. Nathaniel stood, as if to come to him, but Kelly shook his head.

"We need to talk," he said.

Nathaniel hesitated and sat back down. "There's someone else?"

"There's only you." Kelly's laugh was ironic. "You made it so I could run again, and believe me, I've been running long and hard. Whenever I look back, I see you're not there and I feel like I got away. But the truth is, you're inside me so deep that there's no escape. All this time I've been running, all I've been doing is carrying you with me. So no, there is no one else. I don't think there ever will be. But I'm finally ready to get to know the man I love. All of him."

"So what do I do?" Nathaniel asked.

"Talk to me. Tell me everything."

Kelly tried to soothe his racing heart as he took a seat and leaned back. This was going to be a long night, but he had learned long ago that dark times are best weathered with those you love. And when the dawn of a new day greeted them, he prayed that the skies would be clear, the rest of their days spent together basking in the light.

The story continues in...
Something Like Thunder

This isn't a coming out story. Nor is it the tale of a lonely heart seeking companionship. This is about how I learned to fight.

My name is Nathaniel Courtney and I'm a survivor. I didn't let the cruelty of others wear me down, and I've weathered the more subtle hardships of the heart. Love is a Trojan horse, slipping past your guard and leaving you ransacked and vulnerable. I emerged from that war not unscathed but as a new man. The only mistake I ever made was letting the right guy get away. Now I've got one more chance. This is the final battle, because if I fail now... *I won't.* You'll see. Just listen to my story, Kelly Phillips, and when I'm done, please don't walk away. Take this weary soldier into your arms so we can find peace together.

Something Like Thunder is the sixth book in the ongoing Something Like... series, shedding light on past events while leading the reader toward an exciting new future.

Experience the story from the very beginning—

—in the *Something Like...* series, each book written from a different character's perspective, the plots intertwining at key points while also venturing off in new directions. The quest for love takes many different forms. Which is your favorite?

Current books in the series:

#1: *Something Like Summer*
#2: *Something Like Winter*
#3: *Something Like Autumn*
#4: *Something Like Spring*
#5: *Something Like Lightning*
#6: *Something Like Thunder*

Also by Jay Bell:
The Cat in the Cradle

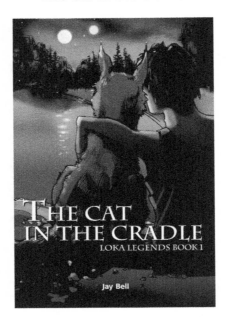

To set out into the world, to be surrounded by the unknown and become a stranger. Only then would he be free to reinvent himself. Or fall in love.

Dylan wanted one last adventure before the burden of adulthood was thrust upon him. That, and to confront the man he hadn't spoken to since their intimate night together. Stealing a boat with his faithful companion Kio, their journey is cut short when they witness a brutal murder. A killer is loose in the Five Lands and attacking the most powerful families. Dylan—a potential target—seeks sanctuary from an unpredictable bodyguard named Tyjinn. Together they decide to turn the tables by hunting the killer down. Along the way, everything Dylan thought he knew about himself will be challenged, but if he survives, he stands to win the love he never dreamed possible.

The Cat in the Cradle is the first book in the Loka Legends series and features twenty-five original illustrations created by Andreas Bell, the author's husband.

Made in the USA
Las Vegas, NV
12 March 2023

68970887R00218